Also by Frank Delaney

Ireland
Simple Courage

Tipperary

Tipperary

A Novel

Frank Delaney

RANDOM HOUSE

NEW YORK

Copyright © 2007 by Frank Delaney, L.L.C.

Published in the United States by Random House,
an imprint of The Random House Publishing Group,
a division of Random House, Inc., New York.

RANDOM HOUSE and colophon are registered
trademarks of Random House, Inc.

LIBRARY OF CONGRESS CATALOGING-IN-PUBLICATION DATA

Delaney, Frank
Tipperary: a novel / Frank Delaney.
p. cm.
ISBN 978-1-4000-6523-3
1. Land tenure—Fiction.   2. Landowners—Fiction.   3. Ireland—Fiction.   I. Title.
PR6054.E396T56 2007   823'.914—dc22   2007013186

Printed in the United States of America on acid-free paper

www.atrandom.com

2 4 6 8 9 7 5 3 1

FIRST EDITION

Book design by Dana Leigh Blanchette

For my brother Michael

AUTHOR'S NOTE

Colonization is one of the world's oldest stories—history, as the saying goes, is geography. Thus, the freedom struggles of countries trying to overthrow their invaders have given us some of our most dramatic legends and our most enduring myths.

The drama is universal. A volcanic core of indigenous people rages secretly against occupation, waiting to erupt. Around them resides a quiet majority, coping with domination. On top of both sits a foreign ruling class, imposed upon and exploiting those below. From afar, the controlling power rules severely—until the inevitable revolution comes.

This is a tale that gets told over and over, in differing ways. Some who joined the conflict fascinate their children with heroic memories. Others simply live out the occupied time, observing but not participating. And when it's over, the formal historians move in to research and interpret; some of them even believe sincerely in objectivity.

This book tells the story of a passionate romance within an epic struggle for nationhood, and the narrators who tell it embody these varying perspectives: A thoughtful wanderer considers his country's upheavals alongside his heart's obsession; the fierce activist records his tale for his nation's archive; and a modern commentator tries to remain objective, until he discovers, deep in his researches, that in Ireland everything is personal, especially the past.

Tipperary

1

Be careful about me. Be careful about my country and my people and how we tell our history. We Irish prefer embroideries to plain cloth. If we are challenged about this tendency, we will deny it and say grimly: "We have much to remember."

"But," you may argue, "isn't memory at least unreliable? And often a downright liar?"

Maybe. To us Irish, though, memory is a canvas—stretched, primed, and ready for painting on. We love the "story" part of the word "history," and we love it trimmed out with color and drama, ribbons and bows. Listen to our tunes, observe a Celtic scroll: we always decorate our essence. This is not a matter of behavior; it is our national character.

As a consequence of this ornamenting, we are accused of revising the past. People say that we reinvent the truth, especially when it comes to the history of our famous oppression by England, the victimhood that has become our great good fortune.

And do we? Do we embellish that seven hundred years since the Norman barons sailed to our southeast shores? Do we magnify those men in silver armor, though they stood only five feet six inches tall? Do we make epic those little local wars, often fought across rivers no more than some few feet wide? Do we render monumental the tiny revolutions fought on cabbage patches by no more than dozens of men with pitchforks and slings?

Perhaps we do. And why should we not? After all, what is history but one man's cloak cut from the beautiful cloth of Time?

Customarily, history is written by the victors; in Ireland the vanquished wrote it too and wrote it more powerfully. That is why I say, "Be careful about my country and how we tell our history." And in this account of my life as I have so far lived it, you will also have to make up your own mind about whether I too indulge in such invention, in particular about myself.

All who write history have reasons for doing so, and there is nothing so dangerous as a history written for a reason of the heart. The deeper the reason, the more unreliable the history; that is why I say, "Be careful about me."

Those paragraphs, written in a looping brown script, sat undisturbed for seventy-five years in a large wooden chest. They lay beneath a pile of clothing: a lady's green gown; a heavier and more ornate green brocade coat, with cream silk finishings; some brown leather gauntlets; a small velvet sack containing tresses of brown hair; and a pair of lady's buttoned boots.

The longtime owner of this trunk, an uncaring man with a runny nose, knew nothing about it or where it came from. It had been sitting for some years in a corner of the shed attached to his hardware premises and, ungifted by curiosity, he had never opened it. To this day he can't recall anything other than that he "bought it from a pair of tinkers," whose tribe had been buying and selling antique furniture and junk all over Ireland in the early 1990s. The travelers, when traced and asked, said that they "couldn't remember it," that they often bought and sold a vanload of "stuff" (or, as they pronounce it, "shtuff") in that town.

Now the chest rests in an attic of a county library in the south of Ireland. The man who donated it bought it from the hardware shop; he recognized it from a description he had been given by a family friend who had often talked about it and who had searched for it.

As a piece of furniture or an antique, it has little interest. Made of oak, with sharp, squared corners, it has a simple brass lock and two ordinary, serviceable handles; and when the lid is raised, the timbers still yield a faint, musty smell, that familiar incense of the past—probably from the fabric of the clothing. However, the antique objects, together with the written contents, assembled with other papers and letters, will soon form an exhibit in the museum section of the library.

It is expected to arouse strong interest—on account of the main document and the story it tells. In a great personal drama, the two principal characters played out their lives against a backdrop of Ireland's most crucial historical period.

The narrator with the sloping handwriting was a man named Charles O'Brien, part wanderer, part journalist, many parts lover. After he wrote those opening "Be careful" sentences, he loaded his document so copiously with details of his world that it has been entirely possible to trace him and his story, and the lives of those he knew or encountered, and the forces and mysteries that became part of his life.

His document, apart from the slightly crumpled top and bottom pages, has remained in excellent condition. Although time and the weight of the clothing in the oak chest compressed the pages, Mr. O'Brien had been careful (and wealthy enough) to use high-quality writing paper, and he wrote with expensive ink, which did not fade; when even the innermost pages were gingerly pulled apart, they lost none of their legibility.

The handwriting helps—his big-handed script had no affectations; every word he wrote is rewardingly legible. As is his style, and in this, Mr. O'Brien was also a man of his time. Other than a breaking down of sentence length and an occasional formality, few major permanent changes have occurred in English writing fashions since the middle of the nineteenth century. The writers of the period, such as Robert Louis Stevenson (who lived from 1850 to 1894), could have been writing today, so fresh seems their general idiom.

Directly after his opening apologia, Mr. O'Brien tells the first of his many tales, a vivid account of an incident from his childhood.

I commence writing this volume (whose genesis and purpose I will presently explain) with a memory that haunts me, and that blazes with the fire at the core of Ireland's history during my early lifetime—the struggle over land.

This report may seem to come from the storehouse of distant recollection, but it has the higher value of immediacy because, at my father's request, I began writing it directly we reached home on the day in question. Save for adjusting boyish errors and excesses, and maturing the style into adult expression, I have not tampered with the account since I wrote it, in June 1869.

I had just reached my ninth birthday. My father and I had been visiting Mr. and Mrs. Treece, near neighbors and well-known to my parents. They owned a good-sized farm, which had been given to the Treece family for helping Oliver Cromwell on his fiery rampage through Ireland in the 1650's.

Mrs. Treece seemed to like me. I remember her as lovely, and I know from my parents' comments that she was considered a great beauty—tall, full-figured, and with a slight snort when she laughed. (My father often made her laugh; my father was a benign and humorous man.) Mr. Treece frightened me; I never found his jokes amusing, and he had that disconcerting trait of making an outrageous assertion without regard to its truth.

"All men who are fair-haired as boys tend to go mad in later life," he said to me that day. I may have doubted him—but I wished for many days thereafter that I had my brother Euclid's coal-black, rod-straight hair, instead of my own Viking curls.

As we departed their doorstep, Mr. Treece suddenly said to my father, "Bernard, I think I'll ride alongside of you—I have a bit of business happening out the road and I might need you to witness it."

We waited in his cobblestoned yard while he saddled up a great mare, close to eighteen hands high. Down the avenue, out through the gates, he rode along beside us, chatting down to my father; Barney, lunging between the shafts of our yellow pony-trap, wanted to race Mr. Treece's horse.

The dampness of the morning had now cleared, with the clouds in those formations that I find unique to Tipperary—big white fleeces drifting across a powdery blue sky. A mile or so along the road to Cashel, Mr. Treece said, "We're down here" and spurred his horse. My father hesitated as though he might not follow; he actually halted the pony. Then he changed his mind and we swung into a lane behind Mr. Treece and his horse's rump.

Around a bend, under some trees, the lane ended and we rode on to a wide place of open grass bordered by the woods. My father said, "Oh damn-and-blast" and pulled up Barney so hard that I was pitched forward on the leather seats; and my father, still talking to himself, said, "Huh. I was afraid this was what the bugger meant."

Straight ahead, a knot of people milled around a long, low house with a thatched roof and whitewashed walls, the kind of dwelling very common in our countryside. Two or three apple trees stood near a small wall that confined a little garden in front of the red door. Outside the house, men in uniform, some on foot and some on horseback, swirled in a commotion. My father breathed, "They've brought in the soldiers. Boys-oh-dear!"

Other men, big-boned laborers, backed up two huge, head-plunging horses with flowing manes until their large, high-sided farm cart met the low garden wall. The men began to unload the cart. First came some heavy wooden poles, which others began to set up in a great, high tripod; next, they hauled from the cart a rattling, clinking length of heavy chain, which they attached to the tripod's neck. Finally, three of the men jumped on the cart and began to push and haul. In a moment or two, a huge wooden beam slid from the cart onto the little wall. It then eased down into the garden, where a workman leaned against it, to keep it in balance against the wall.

At that, a woman of about my mother's age in a drab frock burst from the doorway, screaming. At full speed she attacked the workman near the beam with her fists. She hauled him, she kicked him, she pulled his hair—and she wrestled him to the ground beside the big wooden column. Other men grabbed the huge beam and prevented it from falling over. Two boys, one about sixteen and one close in age to myself, now ran out and joined in to help the woman, whom I presumed to be their mother.

Mr. Treece rode forward. My father muttered to himself, "Oh, typical, typical. The whip'll be next, I suppose." And, indeed, Mr. Treece had been carrying a long whip in his hand as he rode along beside us. (I remember that I thought: Why does he need it? My father never carries as much as a riding-crop—he does it all, he says, with his knees, "as a horseman should.")

The boys retreated a pace or two, and the policemen in their dark tunics and the soldiers in their red tried to haul the woman off the man whom she was beating. When Mr. Treece shouted, they stood back to make room for him. Mr. Treece rode in and, leaning across the little wall, began to lash the woman and the two boys with his whip. He cut the woman about the face and head, he lashed the boys' faces and their bare legs and their heads. When his whiplash left a stripe-mark on the wooden beam, even the uniformed men recoiled.

"And you want me to witness this, George Treece?" said my father to himself. "And you want me to witness this?"

Now Mr. Treece rode his horse into the pretty little cottage garden, and when he reached the kicking, screaming woman, he not only rained blows on her, he tried to pick his horse's legs across the man and ride the hooves upon the woman.

She screeched, and he lashed her again with the whip many times. When she tried to grab the lash, she missed and fell; then she scrambled to her feet and ran into the house, her two boys after her. Mr. Treece called "Get up" to the man on the ground and pulled his horse back. The man arose and seemed rueful but none too injured; he stepped out of the garden and over to where the two big drays swished their tails.

By this time I had been transfixed and could not tear my eyes away—from a scene the likes of which I had never imagined, much less encountered. My father laid his hand on my head and said, "Home?" I did not look at him and he said, in a change-of-mind tone, "No. Maybe you're the one who should be the witness," and we stayed; indeed, he even edged a little closer and swung the pony-trap around for a better view.

Now I saw another player in the drama, a man of about my father's age or older. He stood some twenty yards back from the proceedings, leaning against a tree, seemingly detained there by one of the policemen. When I had a better view, I saw that this man used a wooden crutch; sometime, somewhere, he had lost a leg. He was shaking his head, as if unable to come to grips with Life at that moment.

As I watched him, he began to shout, and the policeman tried to quiet him. Mr. Treece turned around on his horse, saw the man, spurred the animal over to him, and fetched the shouter a lash down across the head and face with the whip, and then another lash. The man would have reached to grab the whip but his uniformed custodian prevented him, and in any case Mr. Treece, generally excited and red-faced, rode back to the front of the house.

"Set it up," he shouted at the knot of men. "What's keeping you back? Set it up!"

The men bustled to assemble the apparatus. They hung the chain down between the poles of the tripod where it ended in a hook. Next, they manhandled the great column along the ground to a point where they could hook the chain into a ring on the wooden beam. When they had made the connection and reeled in some lengths of chain, the post swung clear of the ground like a long rectangular pendulum. They dragged and shoved until the tripod stood right against the wall of the house, near one of the small windows.

Sweating with exertion, the working gang hauled the swinging wooden beam—which seemed at least three feet thick—back from the tripod. For a moment they held it there, out at an angle. Then Mr. Treece shouted, "Let her go," and they released the ram. It swung forward and battered into the window of the house and the wall beside.

My father muttered, "Oh, great Lord!"

Glass crashed and tinkled; the outside of the building fell apart in a blurt of whitewash and brown mortar; I was surprised and alarmed at how much of the house burst under that one swinging stroke. As the men steadied the ram, something flew from the doorway and they reeled back, yelling. Mr. Treece's horse bucked as if stung.

Mr. Treece shouted. "The bitch! What is that?"

A policeman shouted, "Boiling porridge, sir"—someone in the house had hurled the contents of an oatmeal pot through the doorway.

"Draw your guns," shouted Mr. Treece, and with only a short hesitation, all the military and all the police drew their guns with a rattle and held them ready, aimed at the cottage door. A silence fell. Portions of the wall continued to crumble. I looked at the man beneath the tree; he had begun to weep. His tears and his gasping, dismayed face seemed very different from the sadness of my father when my grandmother had died, or when he watched Mother sing his "beautiful Bellini."

"Angle her and go again," Mr. Treece shouted. Beneath a hedge of pointed guns the men rearranged the tripod's angle to edge it farther along the wall. Once more they held back the thick battering ram and released it. This time, its impact went straight through the wall. The hole gaped so wide that we could see the woman inside the house, her face lined with blood from the whip's lashes, which she tried to wipe away with a sleeve.

Mr. Treece shouted, "Get the bitch out of there!"

Nobody moved.

"Then shoot her!"

Under the tree, the one-legged man and his guard began to argue—and suddenly, to my surprise, the uniformed man stood back and the one-legged man crutched himself as awkwardly as a huge frog across the open space of grass toward the house.

The men in the gang saw him and stopped, allowing the battering-ram to swing gently against the house wall, where it made a hefty indentation and then came to rest after a few small bounces. Mr. Treece turned around to see what had grasped his men's attention; he reined back his big horse and waited.

The one-legged man, who had black-gray hair and wore a shabby gray shirt without a collar, stopped for a moment beneath Mr. Treece's horse. He looked up at the rider; Mr. Treece looked away. The man stepped into the doorway and beckoned; then he turned and led his wife and two sons into the sunshine. As they walked behind him, away from the door, the man called out to his family, "Take nothing. Not a thing."

But they had taken something; my father muttered, "Oh, Lord, there's an infant"—and I looked and saw the swaddled packet in its mother's arms.

Still inside the little garden, where Mr. Treece's horse had trampled some of the pretty flower-beds, and where the team of the battering-ram had ruined everything else, the man paused and held up a hand. Behind him, the bloodied members of his family halted.

He turned to them and said, in a loud voice, "Take a good look at this man on the horse. You already know who he is—he's our landlord, George Treece. He's evicting us. Evicting the wife and three children of a man who put on the King's uniform and fought for England. He's evicting us because he wants the land for grazing, because he thinks sheep and cattle more valuable than people. He's evicting people whose family has lived in these fields for more than fifteen hundred years. Look at his face and never forget him—because if you don't meet him again, you'll meet his seed and breed."

He didn't shout these words; he spoke them more as an actor intending to reach an audience, or like a man with an orator's gifts. At that moment it seemed to me that the entire world stood still.

Mr. Treece never spoke; his horse flinched a little, and snorted; the men with the battering-ram stood with their hands at their sides; and the men in uniform quietly lowered their guns and began to put them away. More than a few seemed uncomfortable.

Near the house stood a dense wood, into which this maimed ex-soldier led his wife, their babe-in-arms, and their two sons. Like characters in a magic tragedy they disappeared into the darkness of the trees; the last I saw of them was the blood on the legs of one of the boys. My father exhaled, "Boys-oh-dear."

Mr. Treece wheeled his horse and rode out of the little cottage garden.

"You know what to do," he shouted and stood his horse off some distance.

The men with the battering-ram and its tripod moved slowly enough.

"They've no stomach for it," said my father. In all of this, he never addressed his remarks to me directly; rather, he suspended them in the air for me to inspect.

Slowly the work-gang began to move, aided now and then by a uniformed man, usually if he saw something about to go awry, such as a pole of the tripod about to slip or a slab of thatched roof about to fall down on top of them all. Nobody spoke to anybody. I heard grunts, I saw effort, men wiped sweat from their faces, and the dust from the thatch darkened them head to toe. Their labors concentrated on the front wall, with its two windows and its door, and when they had leveled it to the ground, the little house, with its table and few chairs and tall dresser with some plates on it, looked like something built for a theater in the open air.

At that moment, the men looked to Mr. Treece for direction, as though they might scavenge something for themselves.

"Put the furniture on the cart—we'll throw it into the lake. Level everything else," he roared. "Smash all. If they didn't think enough of it to take it with them, it's worthless. Like they were."

At home, when we heard china break, our housekeeper, Cally, would call from the kitchen her famous apology to Mother (and my father, with a grin, would silently mouth the words): "Wet hands, ma'am." Now, though, the crashing of this crockery sounded different—multiple, deliberate, and awful. For some reason that I could not divine, this affected my father most of all; he wiped a hand across his face, murmuring again, "And he wanted me to witness this."

A fire had been burning on the hearth; the men trampled it out with their boots until only a wisp of smoke rose from the earth, a blue dying breath. Father and I stared at the scene, and we sat in dull silence thereafter for what seemed like an hour.

By the time he turned Barney's head for home, my father had become pale and morose, not at all like him. He was a merry sort of man with apple-red cheeks; he was thirty-two that week and had much enjoyed being teased by Mother about getting old. Now I worried, and tried to speak to him. I moved from my side of the pony-trap and sat on his seat and leaned my head against his heavy sleeve. He thought that I sought comfort from him and reached his arm about my shoulders—but I wanted to make him feel less sad. At the last possible moment, we looked back.

All the walls had come down; they had toppled the chimney. Hauling the cart, the great horses were being led back and forth, back and forth, across the debris, trampling the remains of that modest homestead into the ground. The men had now taken up shovels and were turning the earth in all directions, and by noon the next day, I reckoned, we would scarce have known that people had ever dwelt there. The history of that home had come to an end—and we did not even know the family's name.

But then Father gripped my arm.

"Look! The edge of the wood."

In the county Tipperary we have marvelous forests, deep and absorbing, with hazelnuts and crab-apples, ash and sycamore, cool, spreading oaks and wide, rewarding beeches. Under these branches, in the shadowy tree-line beside this destroyed household, local people had begun to materialize, like ghosts out of the darkness. They never quite stepped into the sunlight but I somehow knew that they had been there all along, watching. Men and women, both young and ancient, boys and girls, both small and growing, all dressed in the uniform shabbiness of the people who lived in the cottages, all gaunt with the same undernourishment—they stood shoulder to shoulder among the green ferns and the red bracken, a long, thin, single line of witnesses, gazing calmly but intently at the eviction.

A hundred or more, white-faced and grave, and unmoved of expression, they never made their presence felt; they spoke not at all. So shadowy did they appear that they might have come from Hades or any other place where Shades dwell.

We watched them for no more than two or three minutes—and then they stepped softly back into the trees, where, as though dissolving, they vanished into the shadows. I almost felt that I had been dreaming.

So moved were Father and I at the sight of these specters that we started with surprise when Mr. Treece shouted. He beckoned to my father—who abruptly turned his head away and flicked Barney homeward with the long carriage whip.

"Don't you talk to me, George Treece," he muttered and never said another word until we reached home.

Mother came to the door when we stepped down from the trap. Pen in one hand, spectacles in the other, she had been doing what she called her "work," the farm ledgers.

"Where were you? You were a long time." She looked at my father, saw his moroseness. "Oh." She stopped. "What happened—?"

"George Treece," said Father, sighing and grim.

Mother knew how Father loathed evictions; he had never put anybody off his own land. And she evidently knew Mr. Treece's reputation in such matters.

"Again?" she said, disturbed.

"Again," said my father.

"Who this time?"

"You know them by sight," he said to her. "That man who lost his leg—I can never remember his name." He sighed.

"But didn't they have a baby last month?"—and she frowned at me. "Go wash and change, Charles."

And then at dinner, a somber, quiet, and somewhat puzzled dinner, when even Euclid, who was only four, had the sense not to say a word, Father said to me, "Please write down what you saw. It will last longer if you do it. These things will need to be known one day."

None of that Treece family can be found in Tipperary today. Their property dissolved early in the twentieth century, when, under new legislation, the British government set a price for any landlord who wished to sell. In many cases, their native Irish neighbors—their former tenants—became the new purchasers, and saw it as no more than the recovery of their ancestral rights. By then, anyway, many of the landlords had been trying in vain to collect their Irish rents. A Treece hadn't lived in the county for years—the name gave off too foul an odor for safety.

The man with the whip died as he lived. A report in *The Limerick Reporter & Tipperary Vindicator* in April 1880 tells that "Mr. George Treece, late of Ballintemple, Tipperary, died at his home in Ontario, Canada, following a fall from his horse, in a violent incident now being investigated by the authorities. He had migrated to Canada in 1872"—that is, three years after the eviction witnessed by the young Charles O'Brien; no further details were given.

Within days after that eviction, Ireland's ballad tradition, a powerful underground, cleared its throat and began to mock:

> To hell with the Treeces, that rack-renting crowd;
> Their finest apparel's the brown winding-shroud;
> From your cats they'd steal fur, from your sheep steal the fleece;
> The world's better off when it buries a Treece.

Mr. O'Brien makes a slight error when he says that the Treeces had been rewarded "for helping Oliver Cromwell on his fiery rampage through Ireland in the 1650's." So they had, but the reward consisted of being granted a bigger acreage in Tipperary than the estate they already farmed in the poorer county of Clare, some sixty miles to the west.

Originally the Treece family had come over from Yorkshire. They formed part of the Munster Plantation in the late 1500s, which sought to replace the native Irish in the country's southernmost province with loyal English subjects. Many went back to England and Scotland when the tides of history began to drown them.

But others of those colonists stayed on. They were called "planters," because they had been planted in the land from which the native Irish had been uprooted. Now they rode the waves of change, and having caused much of the past's turbulence, they had to survive in the ever more violent future.

Of the nameless tenant's house torn down in that eviction, not the slightest vestige remains, not even a mark on the ground. Its location—or, rather, the outlined locus of a tenancy—can still be traced on nineteenth-century land maps. An old fence post still stands that might have marked the tenant boundary, but the ground has long been pasture, probably since the day George Treece leveled the place.

The woods, though, have survived, and increased. After the 1921 treaty between Ireland and England, the new Irish Forestry Commission took over that terrain northeast of the town of Tipperary, close to the village of Dundrum. It maintained the fine growths planted by English governors, and even though some modern house building has encroached on the roads up from the sawmill, the countryside still offers a deep sense of peace. And there are still tall ferns and bracken at the edge of the trees.

As for the people who, in Charles O'Brien's words, "lived in the cottages, all gaunt with the same undernourishment"—they must have traveled some distance that day. Many no doubt came from the village of Dundrum, where the Treeces were particularly hated. It also seems likely that some walked out from the town of Tipperary itself—word of a threatened eviction spread like wildfire in those days.

The fact that they brought no weapons suggests that (a) they had heard in advance that a militia would attend; typically, such evictions could be accompanied by stone throwing and, in larger or more desperate cases, riots. Or, and equally possible, (b) they were generally too disempowered and hungry to offer any significant resistance.

Charles O'Brien's choice to begin his manuscript with such an incident begins to explain why he called his document a "History." He prefers not to call it an "autobiography" or "memoir" because he sought to perceive the dramatic personal events of his own life in tandem with the political upheavals of the era.

As already stated, I have recounted that eviction scene because it has recurrently haunted me; also, because I found it emblematic of the political and social agitations in the Ireland into which I was born. Now I add another reason. The Treece eviction, with its compelling elements of passion, violence, and land, has come to form the opening chapter in what amounts to a History of My Own Life—a task that I undertook for a most specific and personal purpose, which I will here explain.

In the year 1900, when I was forty, I had not yet married (to my mother's oft-stated concern). Then I met an exceptional person. As you shall soon know the whole tale, let me abridge it here by saying that I found myself hurled into a passion deeper than any of which I had read or ever imagined; it was Abélard to Héloïse, Dante for Beatrice, Arthur and Guinevere at Camelot. It elevated my spirit and yet pitched me into an awful confusion, one in which I lost direction for a time long enough to make me think I might never recover it. My wooing began in passion, was defined by violence, and ended up circumscribed by land; and all these elements molded my soul as surely and as fiercely as George Treece and his whip shaped the life of that unfortunate little family.

Of the passion, I shall write more and at greater length—indeed it is, in the main part, the purpose of this History. As to the violence, with the irony that has run through my life as a vein runs down my arm, it began days after I had met this marvelous young woman who, without her knowledge, became the core of my life. I recall reflecting that it was as though the great new beauty in my heart required balancing by the force of the world.

The first attack came after I had spent an afternoon in the city of Limerick, seeking the help of a dear friend. She had listened carefully to my lyrical descriptions of my new love, and then counseled me wisely on how to win the girl. I had left her house and was walking along a street when I saw two men, one fat, one thin, and a shabby woman lounging by a shop entrance. They did not catch my eye in any significant way; they were disheveled and, I thought, of a low type.

Of a sudden, after I had passed them, I received a blow on the side of my head. Never before, not as a child or a boy, had I felt as much as a mild cuff on the ear or any personal assault—and now physical violence arrived with ferocity. A stinging noise sang like a bee in my brain—and more blows landed. Pain seared my mouth as a back tooth was knocked loose; a boot on the shins made me shout with pain. For reasons that I did not yet understand, I thought of Saul on the road to Damascus. My shin received a severe gash, a hobnailed boot struck my hip. More blows on the side of the head followed, more kicks on the shins and hips; I was bewildered and close to tears; I would have wept, I think, had it not become so urgent to fight back.

I began to defend myself—and straightaway hurt my knuckles when my fist struck the fat man of the attackers, not on his face but on a bone of his shoulder, because I aimed the punch incompetently.

"Get him on the ground," the woman shouted. "On the ground!"

Next, both men clambered upon me and their accomplice, with her thin pointy nose, ran forward and began to hit my face and head with her little fists. This annoyed me beyond measure, especially as I, a gentleman, could not fight against a woman.

I began to spin around in a circle, very swiftly, to avoid the harridan's slaps and to dislodge the two villains who were swinging upon me. The fat one fell off quickly and squealed in pain like an infant, and that improved my morale. Although the other person clung tighter, I soon dislodged him too, and I must have shrugged them both off with some force because they lay on the ground in a moaning disorder. The woman came rushing at me, waving her mean and dirty little hands, shouting, "Now look at you! You're after doing them damage!"

This seemed illogical (even for Ireland), so I said, "But, madam, they attacked me."

"You're a scut, that's what you are—you're a rank scut."

Then, as a gentleman opened his door to clear this commotion from the front of his house, the small woman ran away. The two men, moaning and groaning, rose from the mud of the street and took themselves off too. I retrieved my hat, which showed no damage, bowed slightly to the inquisitive house-owner, who went back indoors, and continued on my way.

Who were they? I do not know. At first I assumed that footpads, robbers, had come upon me—but they had made no attempt to take money or valuables (and I was wearing an excellent watch). Next I presumed mistaken identity—that some family or neighborhood fracas had spilt over into the wider streets of the city, and I had somehow been mistaken for a member of the dispute. My questions progressed; perhaps somebody had hired them to attack me, because the assailants and their female companion did not have the appearance of people whom I—a gentleman, and of good family—knew or would have sought for company? But who might have hired them? I believed myself generally popular— even though I admit one or two antagonisms in life, as any man may acquire; but I had no gambling creditors, jealous husbands, or the usual such adversaries.

Now came what I think of as my Damascene moment! To be assailed

physically is to be reduced temporarily to a form of helplessness not unlike childhood. I felt unprotected and in danger. At the same time, here
was I endeavoring to win the heart—and the life's companionship—of
an unusual and important young woman whom I had recently met, and
yet I felt as weak as water. My next thought was: If a pair of ruffians may
so dislodge my general resolve, what right can I have in my romantic am-
bitions? "Faint heart never won fair lady"; truly, "only the brave deserve
the fair."

Generally, in those days, I ambled through the world; I was a reasonable and wandering fellow, I went about my vocation trying to heal the
sick, and I took little thought beyond the morrow. But now! In a blaze of
mental and emotional power, I resolved to become the master and commander of my life. Under a streetlamp, I stood and regained my composure, and felt the vow forming in my heart—the vow to alter myself and
become remarkable.

My method became the material that you now see here: *My Life as a
History of Which I Am Author.* I did not set out to be vainglorious. It is
rather that I hoped by setting my events and remembrances down on
paper, I might come to understand, as a first step, how to make myself
outstanding. Writing the History of my life would, I believed, help me
come to terms with my fortunes, and lead me through the rapids of this
new and dominating passion to which I must fit myself.

As I reflected, a mist lifted and a calm floated down upon me. I
thought: If I can make myself into a good man, a fine man, then it follows as the night the day that I shall be loved as I wish to be, by the person whose love I seek. (My father said many times, "Give her up, she's a
losing bet." I could not.)

But how would I sustain the effort? I have a fear of boredom and
therefore, in this charting of my life, I soon knew that I must write about
matters other than myself. To avoid impatience with the little details of
my own days, I would need a device. Happily, I had one at hand.

I could see from the politics of Ireland that I stood on the lid of a boiling pot—all politics stem from anger at something or other. And since
my own life had now been set ablaze with unfulfilled passion, the fever in
my country, it seemed, echoed the fever in my heart. In short, I would

write a History of my country in my lifetime and it would also be a History of my life.

How different it could be, I thought. I have had the good fortune to see Ireland at first hand, often in most intimate circumstances, because I commenced my adult life as a Traveling Healer. Up and down Ireland I visited the ailing in their homes. Castle or cottage, I cured them—or tried to. With drinks and poultices made from the herbs of the countryside, plucked from the hedgerows and sometimes mixed with secret mineral powders, I was often able to make people better in their health; I brought about recovery. As a consequence they loved me, they welcomed me back into their houses, they celebrated me—and they gave me their confidences.

Next I acquired another means of intimate access to my country's people. Although I am neither trained historian nor scholar, I have always gathered people's tales and I have always enjoyed meeting figures of interest and significance. Thus, while healing the sick, I also worked as a Traveling Correspondent. I was retained permanently by no one periodical; rather, I gathered impressions—of peoples, places, occurrences—and put them together and submitted them.

Many of my accounts and essays appeared in distinguished journals and newspapers, notably the *Vindicator,* and I was much fulfilled by that. Consequently, I was granted access to anybody whom I chose to meet; I am still astonished by the zeal with which people want to see their names in printed pages. Thus my twin professions of healer and scribe opened many doors. I felt confident that the narrations I derived from such a life would stand one day as a modest achievement, a small personal History of Ireland during my lifetime—a life of love and pain and loss and trouble and delight and knowledge.

A portrait in oils of the woman with whom Charles O'Brien fell in love hangs in Trinity College, Dublin. It was painted by Sir William Orpen, a distinguished Anglo-Irish artist of the Edwardians. Orpen saw a very beautiful thirty-year-old woman of determined character. Her heavy and shiny fair hair has been cut to neck length. Orpen painted her mouth in a straight line, and her brown eyes looked directly at him.

He seated her in a chair covered with gold velvet, and she is wearing a plain, rich, cream dress, like the wife of a Roman senator; there's some beading at the boat-shaped neck. Her hands clutch the arms of the chair; she wears many rings; her shoes are simple, strong, and black.

The little brass plaque on the gilt frame beneath the canvas reads, "April Somerville, London 1912"—and that is why the painting proved so hard to trace. Mr. O'Brien met her as "April Burke," in Paris, in 1900, when she was eighteen.

She had an unusual personality. When he met her, he saw initially a young woman who detonated charges within him. That ignition evidently happened at first sight, a fact remarkable in itself but not all that unusual in the often powerfully volatile psyche of the adventurous and energetic nineteenth-century man.

What he could not have seen at that moment—but would soon begin to observe and report—was the tail of the comet. Behind this young woman trailed a legend of intrigue; it included the sulfurous whiff of blackmail, heart-cutting tragedy, plus an old scandal at whose core lay a mystery. And she also brought danger and actual harm to those who loved her.

Throughout his "History," however, Mr. O'Brien never casts her in that light. Always and ever she is his great love, and while those around him gasped at her behavior, he never judged her anything but wonderful.

Charles O'Brien lived in a culture of narrative. The Irish people of his era, with, as yet, scant literature to hand, told the world in stories. Naturally, therefore, he begins at the beginning—of his own existence, with his first memories. As he embarks upon his journey to "improve" himself, his "History" also supplies a portrait of life in a well-to-do Irish rural family of the mid-nineteenth century.

The names of my parents are as follows: Bernard Michael O'Brien, from the county Tipperary, and the former Amelia Charlotte Goldsmith, from the county Roscommon; he a Catholic, she what they mistakenly call "Protestant." The term should technically refer only to the Reformed churches who protested Rome as Luther did. In Ireland, it applies to every person not a Catholic, and therefore my mother, an Irish Anglican or Irish Episcopalian, a member of the Church of Ireland, is counted Protestant.

My parents thus entered what is said to be "a mixed marriage." Father came from the ancient Irish native roots that went into this ground once the Great Ice Age melted, ten thousand years ago; and Mother sprang from the English "strangers" who have long ruled this island. Our branch of the O'Brien tribe or clan managed to hold on to their land down the oppressed and confiscating centuries. Mother's antecedents, of the same stripe as those oppressors and confiscators, came into Ireland around 1590 and were given many, many acres in reward for their military support in the great English attempt to eradicate the Irish people. She therefore qualifies as "Anglo-Irish."

Let me define the nomenclature once and for all. The Anglo-Irish comprise that peculiar breed of people of English ancestry who settled in Ireland on land that was taken by force from the native Irish. By virtue of having been planted in their new acres militarily, they became economically superior to the natives—a superiority they also assumed to be social; and they spoke a different language (the Queen's English). Soon they had so thoroughly merged with their new land as to be neither English nor Irish. Many of them—in fact, most—fell passionately in love with the country that they were given; they became infected with its imagination, and they made significant contributions to it. Many others behaved like ignorant, bullying savages.

Whether I am Irish or Anglo-Irish I do not know; I fit the hat to the moment, and as a consequence both peoples greet me as their own. With the grandees in their limestone mansions and their vividly painted walls and their great furnishings and *objets d'art* I have an easy familiarity. But with the native-born folk in the cottages and small farms and their wonderful spirit, their music, their passion, their stories in their dense, ringing accents—with them I am alive to the quick.

To keep this adroit balance going, to broaden the tightrope a little under my feet, I—almost militantly—do not practice any religion, although I was tutored as a Catholic and can spout the liturgy with the best of priests.

My family lived in a house on a wooded hill in County Tipperary. I was born there, on the twenty-first day of June 1860, not far from Cashel, which is a landlocked and fertile town, a fortress of Ireland's faith in medieval times. At my conception some wonderful spiritual exchange must have happened between my father and my mother, because my chief asset is, I believe, a notable zest, an exuberant, rich energy for all the excellent things that Life can bring.

I love wines, I play a smooth hand at cards, and such horses as I have wagered upon have almost won a number of races. Travel delights me, the opportunity to look upon other faces in other circumstances. I enjoy good company with many tales told, and I have been given to understand that my gifts as a raconteur stand up well.

Excitement has come to me often, and its glories make me impatient with those who have not understood it, who have often used words such as "reckless" and "feckless" when they speak of me to others. (This being Ireland, I hear such remarks not long after they are uttered—even if they were spoken at the opposite end of the country.)

Some parental characteristics have landed upon me. My father too had hair the color of hay; now his head resembles an egg; and my mother has grave, gray eyes that lit up when she and my father engaged in one of their jostling talks.

"Amelia, your eyes rob me of my arguments," he would say, and he'd touch her cheeks with those huge hands of his, which I have inherited. (Many ladies have spoken to me of my own gray eyes, and I have my mother's laugh-crinkles.)

Neither parent had the blessing of excellent teeth; nor have I. My father long thought about acquiring false teeth, of the kind sported by his friend the Bishop of Cloyne, who drank much port—but that gentleman had to learn to smile with his lips closed. I have a pair of feet that seem to go out of true too easily; my toes look like small hammers and cannot be as prehensile as I would wish. And I am a creature built for pleasure, I think, in the general arena between my upper and lower extremities.

As to my appearance, people in general often remarked my wild mop of yellow-blond hair, and my height of six feet three inches, and my wide shoulders. Not that I am perfect; I have a small birthmark on my right hip, which, I have been told, looks like a dragonfly. Mother has assured me that it manifested itself at my arrival into the world and she interpreted it as a sign of good luck, of which the dragonfly has always been an omen.

My father talked all the time, as though he feared silence and what it might bring in on its quiet wings. He talked for the sake of talking, for the sound of words. In his head he carried much knowledge, and when he required to know something that he did not already know, he invented it. Very early in my life I heard him call out the Seven Wonders of the World—and I heard them many times more.

"Let us always be alphabetical where we can," he would begin. "It preserves order." And off he would go: "The Lighthouse of Alexandria. The Temple of Artemis. The Hanging Gardens of Babylon. The Pyramids of Giza. The Tomb of Halicarnassus. The Statue of Zeus. The Colossus of Rhodes." As many times as I heard it I would puzzle at his system of alphabetization—and then he would launch into his next list, "The Seven Wonders of Tipperary": "The Rock of Cashel. The Devil's Bit. The Weir at Golden. Tipperary Castle. The Shores of Lough Derg. The Glen of Aherlow. Kitty Cahill's legs."

By Father's side I saw these local marvels—all but one; the legs depended from a lady whom I never met, and whose character my mother disparaged. Memories of our other county "wonders" have constantly delighted my mind, and one of them, Tipperary Castle, came to dominate my existence. I am most pleased, however, by the fact that I learned of them through my father; their flavors and moods count among the many gifts he gave me.

Here is a small tale of my father: As a young man he delighted in practical jokes until he found them too cruel; however, the memory of a certain escapade still tickles him. In the village nearby lived a solitary and very cranky little gentleman, who barked at one and all. He had an Achilles' heel, though, and the local boys, including Father, soon discovered this vulnerability. The little gentleman, when wages had been paid on a Saturday, tackled his pony to its cart, set off to the next village, and in the hostelry there imbibed until midnight. Then, drunk to insensibility almost, he came out, mounted the cart, said "Hup" to the pony, who then trotted him home, and the little gentleman fell asleep on the cart.

One summer night, the local boys waited until the pony drew to a halt outside the little gentleman's door—which, in common with all our houses, was never locked. They gently took the sleeping man from the cart and carried him indoors. Next they untackled the pony and led it into the house. Now they loosed the cotter pins in the axles and removed the cart's wheels. They reassembled the cart inside the house, tackled the pony to it again, placed the little gentleman—still snoring—back on the cart, and tiptoed away, closing the door behind them.

In the morning, of course, the little gentleman awoke and found himself inside his own house, on a cart that could not possibly have fitted through his door—or so all logic told him!

I have heard of that jape being practiced elsewhere in Ireland, but my father swore that he was the sole inventor.

Mother was and remains a lady, by birth and by nature. She placed great value upon social grace (which my father, she said, possessed naturally). From her I learned never to keep my hands in my pockets in the presence of a lady. Mother also taught me that "a gentleman should contribute something of his own to every conversation."

She spoke candidly about things that fascinated me. My birth, she said, was headlong and energetic; the midwife exclaimed, "Look! He can't wait to get into the world." I was born at half past eleven on a Thursday, and it being in Ireland and therefore half an hour west and behind Greenwich Mean Time, the true moment of my birth might be accurately categorized as noon on Midsummer's Day.

"No more fortunate day," Mother claimed, and my father said that it was lucky I came out at all; I might "just as easily have decided to stay in there, a grand comfortable place like that."

Mother described my birth as "a delight" and was always ready to tell me how she had counted my fingers and my toes. "And I went to count your teeth," said my father. "Like I'd do to a foal. But you didn't have any"—and he laughed. She did not employ a nurse to feed me and did not, as my father had recommended, drink any liquor during my time at her breast. He said that was a pity, because he wished me "to get used to the taste—save a lot of time later on." In that month, among our neighbors, I was the only one of five newborn infants to survive, a proportion slightly greater than was usual.

However, neither parent had told me the full truth of my birth, which I discovered only many years later. My mother had had severe illness and frailty all through her confinement and, more dangerous still, my birth came a margin early. On that midsummer morning, a frightful thunderstorm broke out as my father set out to fetch doctor and midwife. He needed the carriage for their transport, and as he crossed the river bridge a mile from our home, lightning, attracted by the water, struck one of the horse's harness-pieces. The animal reared in fright and swung so violently that he dashed the wheel of the carriage against the pediment of the bridge and broke the red spokes. (Once, I was comforted and pleased to learn that very similar circumstances had attended the birth in Italy of Michelangelo.)

My father untackled the stamping, frightened horse, calmed it, mounted it, and rode on to fetch the midwife, a woman almost too heavy for walking. I understand that she clung to my father on the back of the horse so closely that he said afterward he had not been so intimate with a midwife since the day he was born.

Once I had come into the world—and both parents have said this of me—I showed no signs of ever wanting to leave it. My infancy grew more and more robust and I proved inquisitive and mellow, no trouble to my parents or their helpers. As a small child I developed a personality so clearly defined that I was soon known by name to the adults of the locality. Our workers (my father prohibited the use of the word "servant") became my companions, and I was set, it seemed, for a regular life as my father's successor on the farm. But the world's circle did not turn that way.

Life in Mr. O'Brien's surrounding environment was desperately poor. Existence for most Irish people was at that time brutish and unjust. But nothing else has greatly changed in the young Charles O'Brien's neighborhood. All the "wonders" of his father's Tipperary recital still exist (except, of course, the renowned limbs of the vaunted Miss Cahill).

The Rock of Cashel sits like a Disney creation high on a limestone crag over a wide and handsome plain, watched over by the gap-toothed Devil's Bit Mountain. Near Golden, four miles west, the river Suir (pronounced "Shure") still flows over a shallow and placid weir. The shores of Lough Derg, in the northwest of the county, give Tipperary its border along the river Shannon. And the Glen of Aherlow, it is said, contains more sunlight and shadow than any other valley in Ireland.

As to the remaining "wonder," the magnificent Tipperary Castle—Mr. O'Brien has no doubts as to its place in his narrative; when he remarked that it "came to dominate my existence," he understated.

Even though he begins his recital of himself with the memory of the violent Treece eviction, it makes sense to take as a truer starting point his view of himself at the age of forty. After all, that was when he met his motivation for writing, April Burke. Therefore his physical description probably shows us what she saw: a "wild mop of yellow-blond hair, and my height of six feet three inches, and my wide shoulders"—and his tone suggests a man looking in a mirror in the prime of his life.

To touch his "History" is to bring him closer than that. His papers convey a feeling far above the inanimate; they stack so pleasantly in the hand. He chose almost the texture of a linen weave, slightly heavier than the commercial writing foolscap of the day. The pages have colored gently with age.

He used a light sepia ink, close to a coffee color, and a medium-broad nib. Unlike most manuscripts of the day, his shows none of the tiny spatters at, say, the beginnings of sentences or paragraphs. Then there is the numbering of the pages—in the top right-hand corner he placed neat figures, each succeeded by a firm dot or full point. The entire script runs so smoothly, so uninterruptedly, that it proves impossible to say where he left off one day's work and began the next.

This orderliness of penmanship contradicts the "feckless" opinions of him that he himself openly reports. In later pages we infer, and encounter directly, a man seen by others as somewhat wayward and unsteady. Yet the management of his manuscript shows a figure in charge of what he was doing. There are perhaps no more than twenty small corrections in a handwritten document of several hundred pages.

As to content, although he seems conscious of the need for faithful chronology, he does not conform to the disciplines of academic historical narrative. He shuttles back and forth all the time, plucking an anecdote from his childhood here, a chance encounter with a great person there, a public incident somewhere else. Yet he always keeps hold of the thread of his history. He's like a man from a myth, drawing himself along a golden rope—not to immortality, but to the moment he eagerly wants to reach.

No matter how great the person he meets, or how absorbing the event he reports, he gives the impression of wishing never to stray far from his pursuit of April Burke. And he interrupts his narrative time and time again to cry out his passion for her. Sometimes his outburst occurs unexpectedly, and he becomes almost lost in a strenuous hymn of love.

I know that I am a Romantic—I am more influenced by my imaginings and more driven by my passions than anyone of my acquaintance. In this, I also feel myself to be deeply elemental. The mountains enchant me and I think of each peak as I would of a person; the clouds cast shadows on them as moods traverse a human face. I love rain and often tilt my face to feel its full cool sheet and I thank it. How often have I lain on the ground merely to gaze at the traveling clouds and thought of myself pillowed upon them, like some sultan of the universe.

When I first saw her whom I have made the love of my life, I instantly wanted to share such things. I wanted to point out to her the small but infinite wonders that fill me with pleasure: the webbed filaments of a chrysalis tucked into the angle of a leaf; the brown impertinence of a sparrow pecking crumbs; the austerity of a hilltop tree leafless against a winter sky; white gravel in the bed of a clear stream.

I owe the awareness of these mysteries to my wonderful parents, who ever availed of an opportunity to show me how the hidden world works.

One afternoon, I remember, when I was very young, my mother spent many minutes coaxing a ladybird to open the wings beneath its black-spotted red back. Another time, she showed me the paper hulk of a wasps' nest long after the summer—and the stingers—had left.

"Nobody loves a wasp," she said, "except another wasp," and she told me how a wasp will give its own life for its comrade. In general, never did we observe an unexpected insect without her inquiry being excited.

Let me now describe the instant when I first saw my beloved. I shall recount all the circumstances later, but for now I must tell how she looked; how she filled the space in the air of the room all around her; how she seemed to me both human and divine; and my own physical reaction, so strong that I feared it must become noticeable to others present.

She was standing on a chair, arranging a picture's hanging, when she first looked into my eyes. She is, as it happens, notably tall anyway—when she stepped down from the chair I then believed she stood five feet ten inches, and she has confirmed this.

"Force of presence!" cried my mind at once; but she did not consume the air, as some very strong people do. She occupied her space like a slim perpendicular column of some classical style.

Her being was composed of warmth and energy; she had a capability, an aura of efficiency; she gave off a feeling of knowing what to do, not just in the instant, but in life generally—and she possessed great beauty.

I stood and stared; my manners must have abandoned me. She had the courtesy to ignore my staring and she turned away—and of course she had the good breeding not to address me until we had been introduced, which did not occur for some days. As to my reaction—I began to sweat; the back of my neck grew damp and my skin began to prickle. My eyebrows shot up almost beyond retrieval, and my mouth felt dry.

Believe me, I have trawled for comparisons of that moment—and herein lies the value of writing a History of myself that is also a History of my country. I have had the privilege of looking back at each and every great event that I have witnessed, and accordingly I have been able to trace those that seemed remarkable and important, and I have been able to measure how they influenced and even altered my life. Through them all, November 1900 in Paris shines unchallenged.

In today's terms, Mr. O'Brien's reaction may seem excessive. Not in Queen Victoria's reign, when the idea of romantic love, descended from the times of the troubadours, had well and truly taken root. In an era where prudishness and repression were equated with prudence and responsibility, all that was left to a man by way of expressing love was the report of his own passions.

The poets had led the way; "Byronic" had long been a shorthand term for passionate emotion. Charles O'Brien, in common with so many other men of the day who fell suddenly in love, had solid precedent for seeing himself as a dashing and romantic figure. Windswept and interesting, moody and wild with love pangs, he was prepared to surrender all for love.

But he was a little older than the typical Byronic figure with the brooding lips and flowing white shirt. This was a man who had already lived well more than half the male lifespan of the day. He had claimed no prospects that he could offer a girl. And he seemed to depend upon his paternal family and home far more than the typical man of his time.

My first complete memory—that is to say of a cohesively remembered moment with its own Beginning, Middle, and End—comes from my life at the age of almost four. I have other fragments from times before then, the commonplace memories that I expect are found in all small children: my father lifting me high while I looked down at his laughing, exerted face; a curtain fluttering at an open window; a butterfly finding its way into the drawing-room and mistakenly alighting on a flower in the furniture's fabric; the taste of sugar upon buttered bread, which Cally gave as a treat; the tightness of a shirt-collar, worn to be gracious when Grandmother Goldsmith or Aunt Hutchinson came visiting; the quiet hum of deep, approving conversation as my parents pored over my mother's ledgers. (Father was an excellent and successful farmer.)

That very first memory, though, brought my introduction to fear and its thrill, and it took place in the safest of surroundings. Our domestic bathing arrangements never varied; Cally or Mrs. Ryan took responsibility for my hygiene until the age of ten—when my father, with whispered asides to my mother, consigned it to me alone. He supervised me, and in due course taught me to shave: "Keep the razor wet!" One evening, early in 1864, Mother came rushing to the kitchen, where I was often to be found among the women (I was quite their pet), and she cried, "Bathing! We must bathe Charles now!" Her urgency puzzled all until she explained in whispers—and then Cally became urgent and raced me to the bathroom, half-carrying me. Mrs. Ryan, who was as stout as a hippopotamus, huffed along after us.

Hot water was brought upstairs, and I was washed as never before. So distressing did I find this that Mrs. Ryan and Cally conspired to tell me.

Mrs. Ryan: "A girl's after dying in Limerick. You have to be scrubbed and scrubbed."

"Why?"

Cally: "She died of an awful thing."

"What?"

Mrs. Ryan: "An awful thing altogether."

"What's an awful thing?"

They looked at each other and agreed with their eyes.

Mrs. Ryan: "She was a leper."

I thought they meant that the girl had somehow jumped off some great height and died.

"Why do I have to be scrubbed because she leapt?"

The women began to laugh; Mrs. Ryan had her hands in the tub washing my feet, and her great forearms all but heaved the water everywhere. When they subsided, the women grew serious again.

Cally: "She had the leprosy."

Mrs. Ryan: "She caught it off a sailor's clothes that she was washing."

Cally: "An African sailor, he was—he had it. A black fella."

"What's leprosy?"

Cally: "Your nose falls off."

Mrs. Ryan: "And your hands with it."

Cally: "They have to give you a bell to tell everyone you're coming and they're to get out of the way—so's they don't catch it."

"How can you ring the bell if your hands have fallen off?"

Mrs. Ryan: "Well, you can."

"Is it a big bell?"

Mrs. Ryan: "No, no, a small little bell and you've to shout and warn them."

"What do they shout?"

Mrs. Ryan: "I s'pose they say, 'I have the leprosy, I'm a leper.' "

Cally: "No, they say, 'Unclean, that's what I am, unclean.' "

Such a gift to a small boy! That night, to Mother's horror and Father's delight, I took the serving bell from the dining-room table and went about the house calling out, "Unclean! Unclean!" But it was true; a young servant-girl had contracted leprosy in Limerick and died.

Another memory: three years later, early in 1867, our house became a place of secrets and furtiveness. At night I would wake suddenly at the sound of hooves or a cart or carriage rattling and jingling. Once or twice, I went halfway downstairs and watched as big men with long beards came through the front door, hauled off their greatcoats, and greeted my father. I heard much talk of "ships" and "landing" and "rising"—which I took to be the motion of the ship on the crests of the sea.

Beyond my imaginings, I achieved no knowledge of what lay behind or beneath these visits, and my questions at breakfast next day accomplished nothing other than deflection and a caution from my mother: "Charles, we don't like people knowing our business." Even if I didn't understand the words, she conveyed an unmistakable force of meaning.

Years later, I discovered the reason for this nocturnal activity, which lasted many months. The Fenians, an international assembly of zealous republicans dedicated to the independence of Ireland from England, had planned—and, indeed, carried through—an insurrection or uprising, hence "rising." Much of it had been focused in our province of Munster and, in due course, with Tipperary as a crucial member, the other five Munster counties, Cork, Kerry, Clare, Limerick, and Waterford, intended to flame with rebellion, which would then spread to the rest of the country.

Unfortunately, as has so often been the case in Ireland, two constant facts of Irish life prevented the rebels from gaining wide ground: the weather and loose tongues. On the night of the rising an unprecedented snowstorm hit the country. In addition, everybody around us—the local priests, the local newspaper editor, the local washerwomen and shopkeepers, the police and the army—knew all the plans in advance. Wagging tongues saw to it that little blood would be shed for Ireland that night.

"All cloak and no dagger," said my father when speaking of it to me years later. "Too many saddles, too few horses."

I asked him what he meant.

"They were generally useless as rebels," he said. "Great company, though. Great to argue with over a drink."

Yet History has credited them with "the Rebellion of 1867," even though handfuls of men here and there, with old muskets and some pitchforks, were merely rounded up by police, the more threatening ones lodged in the cells for a few days and the rest sent home. *The Cork Examiner* newspaper carried reports of numerous arrests, but the Fenians had, as yet, been mainly drilling and marching, and had not fired a shot. Such was the level of Irish uprising in the middle of the nineteenth century.

Then, when I was ten years old, the countryside resounded excitedly to a significant political development. Mr. Gladstone, the Prime Minister, saw his government pass a Land Act for Ireland that permitted tenant farmers some new rights. They now had to be compensated for any improvements to their farms, and eviction could occur only for nonpayment of rents. However, since the landlord could raise the rent at a whim, the protection, when scrutinized, seemed infirm. My father's pronouncement seemed to echo the country's response: "Well, it'll give us something to talk about for a long while."

To confirm: *The Limerick Reporter & Tipperary Vindicator* dated 29 January 1864 printed that "Mary Hurly, aged 23 years, a victim of leprosy, died in the County Infirmary Limerick, on Sunday last. This disease, it appears, she contracted by washing the clothes of some foreign sailors."

Charles O'Brien was born into a theater of national events. Not since the heaving of the earth's plates beneath the North Atlantic Ocean finally split the island off from England and Europe has Ireland had a more dramatic, compressed passage of history than the period of Mr. O'Brien's lifetime.

Such a claim, in such a vivid land, requires justifying. True, she was a sophisticated country socially and politically—and even economically—around the time of Christ. A system of "kingships" governed the country. Chieftaincies in local structures observed and paid taxes to overlords in the south, the east, the north, and the west. These provincial kings of Munster, Leinster, Ulster, and Connacht (or Connaught, in the anglicized version) paid homage and tribute to the high king at Tara.

True, too, that the stability of this structure resisted all invaders, and over time the country developed a social and artistic culture that continues to this day. Then, beginning in 1167, came the Norman barons, owing allegiance to the king of England. Soon, the long British shadow began to darken the country.

All of these movements took place over many centuries—but the most significant convulsions, the most conclusive politics, happened inside sixty years. They had begun in Ireland before Charles O'Brien was born. Events abroad had stirred the Irish and set an example. The Americans in 1776 had thrown out the English, and the French of 1789 had overthrown the upper classes.

The Irish sought to combine these influences. In 1801 the country had lost all sovereignty. An Act of Union bound it with vicious indissolubility to England. For two centuries before that, we had been steadily losing all human rights. We lost education, the right to our Catholic faith, and above all the ownership of our own land.

When the tide began to turn, it became a wave. The first crest was a law forced through the English Parliament in 1829—Catholic Emancipation. It restored freedom of religion to the massively larger Catholic population of Ireland. From it, everything else began to follow. Up rose the political agitators fighting to recover native acres from the English landlords. Revolution became a certainty.

In all of this, Charles O'Brien's family was unusual. They had somehow contrived to hold on to their lands down the centuries (and had expanded by buying adjoining fields and woods). As a consequence, they occupied one of the safest possible positions; they became witness to all that went on, yet party to none of it. And they did so through astute social politics, through vigilance during every successive political shift, and through care for each successive generation.

Just before the time of my birth, the teaching of children became a matter for everybody, not just the ruling classes of the Ascendancy. By law, village "national" schools opened all over Ireland. At last, after many generations of enforced ignorance, our Irish people were allowed once more to have learning. Reading was no longer banned; Catholics were no longer flogged, deported, jailed, or executed for owning books; their teachers were no longer outlaws, to be shot on sight. As the new schools opened, many of the illiterate parents almost carried their children in their arms to the school doors, so intent were they on bettering their families' future. Some refused to engage with this system; old suspicions died hard—and in any case the Irish language, spoken by the majority of the people, was banned in the schools.

My parents, for their own reasons, wished to have no part of this, and I believe that it caused some difficulties between them; such national matters often did. Mother desired that I should have the more formal and classical education of the English—perhaps go to a school in England, and thence to Oxford or Cambridge University. My father wished me never to be away from home as a child. He told my mother that he would suffer "unendurable lonesomeness" were I to be boarded away at school.

But Mother could not countenance one of her children mixing so intimately with so many Catholics every day. So they settled their differences by choosing four tutors for me, two from each parent. (They would later do the same for my brother.)

Rarely in life can a boy have been exposed so closely to four such different people. One of these tutors I never saw sober, though he was marvelously entertaining, and from him I learned what he called "Greek mythology, Latin scandal, and Catholic nonsense." His name was Buckley; he had everyone call him that—no "Sir" or "Mister" or Christian name. Many years after he died (he fell under a military cart in Paris), I learned that he had been a priest unfrocked for persistent adventures "incompatible with the calling" (as they say), and that he had also elicited money from many women.

Buckley had wonderful sayings: "A bird never flew on one wing"—meaning that one drink would not suffice; "A woman with a hard heart is more dangerous than a runaway bull" (he seemed to have known some, because they came calling, grim-eyed and intent, to our house and my parents always concealed him); "Never trust a woman that wants you to guarantee tomorrow"—meaning that Buckley did not like ties of any kind.

My other three tutors offered more orthodoxy. Buckley had been Father's choice, as had the meek John Halloran. Mr. Halloran specialized in mathematics and drawing. His chief teaching later enabled me to calculate complicated odds for the placing of bets on horses and roulette (and I have sometimes won). He also left me with the ability to draw swift and reasonable likenesses of people's faces.

Mr. Halloran taught me French and Italian, and he excelled in what he called "General Subjects"—he would discourse for an hour or two on the business of Luck; or he would speculate about whether foretelling the future had any validity. In the course of such lessons, he dragged in extraneous facts from all sorts of sources.

"The smallest dwarf in history stood one foot four and weighed five pounds. Her feet measured two and one-quarter inches, and she was called the Fairy Queen." And: "You can never fold a piece of cloth or a piece of paper double more than seven times." And: "If you tie both ends of a cord and make a circle, you can then turn that circle into any other perfect geometric shape." I never met a man with so much superfluous knowledge, except perhaps my own father.

Of women, however, Mr. Halloran (unlike Buckley) taught me nothing at all. He blushed when he encountered a female of any species, and when I once asked him had he ever been married, he murmured a throbbing and passionate "Oh, my Heavens, no!" As he did when Buckley called out to him each morning, "Did those bowels of yours move yet?"

The balance between the tutorial sexes was provided by Mother's choices, Miss Taylor and Mrs. Curry, who came from Dublin and London. Miss Taylor wept easily at the great tales she herself told, and Mrs. Curry walked like a turkey. Both schooled me excellently. Where Buckley regaled me with the indulgences of ancient Rome and Greece, and showed me engravings of naked statues, the women tutors held me to the memorizing of whole texts, be they history, geography, English literature, or French.

Although I liked neither woman, I excelled at their lessons. (Also, I much enjoyed the rough teasing they had to endure from Buckley. Judging from the ladies' faces, he whispered amazing questions and raw commentaries to them.) Each lady set out to make of me a man who would be suited to the company of women. In common with Mother (who probably instructed her to do so), Miss Taylor taught me what she called "appropriate demureness." This had to do with standing in a special fashion, my upper body leaning slightly forward to cast my lower body into shadow and thereby eliminate what she called mysteriously "the wrong impression."

At some point in this recurrent lesson she would emphasize once again the importance of "never having anything exaggerated in the male appearance." And she counseled me against ever having my trousers made from any fabric of light gray.

Mrs. Curry's husband had died by misadventure in India. As a consequence and out of respect for her dead spouse, she would not eat any meat other than pork, ham, or bacon. (I believe that a wild pig attacked Mr. Curry and that she was filled with vague revenge.) She taught me how to kiss a lady's hand and began by kissing mine; she had rather dry lips and she disconcertingly licked them a little before swooping down on my young paw. Once fixed there, the kiss became almost a suction—which then she invited me to emulate. She specified the length of time that the kiss should linger: "Think of romantic interest, not cannibalism"; and "The teeth must never touch the lady's flesh."

Also, she said, I should create "a compartment" in my mind which contained the knowledge of this kissing technique and "it should never, ever, not on any account, be used for anything other than the kissing of hands." Buckley said, "That's multiple ways not true."

Mrs. Curry always became quite excited during this instruction, and Buckley assured me—mystifying to me then—that she had "let her mind wander."

All in all, they taught me well, if eccentrically. I have been imprinted with some of their habits. Where Buckley said an expectant "Well, now" when he walked into a room, Mr. Halloran rubbed his hands; I do both. I have Miss Taylor's swiftly raised eyebrow, Mrs. Curry's nervous belch. And although they differed widely in their teaching methods, they all exercised one delightful practice for which I am most grateful of all—they conducted tuitions in the open air. When the weather permitted, which, in truth, happened on more days than not, "Teaching becomes walking," to use Miss Taylor's rendition.

Such an education tells a great deal about the young Charles O'Brien's family. Modern Ireland has been called "classless," and it's true that, in terms of social hierarchy, today's divisions are defined by meritocracy. However, before the creation of the two states of Ireland in the treaty of 1921, a marked social division already existed between the native Irish and their Anglo-Irish landlords.

Mr. O'Brien's earlier definition of the Anglo-Irish has an accurate—if unnuanced—ring to it: "that peculiar breed of people of English ancestry who settled in Ireland on land that was taken by force from the native Irish." But he neglects to say (although he implies it) that he was educated in the Anglo-Irish tradition of tutors and governesses—in other words, in the tradition of the European aristocracy.

The subtlety of his not saying so—or even being conscious of it—derives from his Catholic father's example. While enjoying the life of an

English or Anglo-Irish landlord, Bernard O'Brien also wished to keep on the best possible terms with his native Irish forebears and neighbors.

And he knew how to do so; that was part of the vigilance. He had married a Protestant girl, and thereby appeased the ruling classes while not becoming one of them. And, by mixing easily and amiably with his Catholic neighbors at all levels—he seems to have employed only Catholics—he obstructed any resentment of his Anglo-Irish style of life.

The house in which Charles O'Brien was born and raised may easily be viewed today—a strong mansion on a hill. O'Briens no longer live there; an American family now owns the estate. The woods and its botanical curiosities still exist, as does the walled garden; and the fields that Charles O'Brien and his father so loved show a long history of excellent farm maintenance.

My family's home, Ardobreen, is painted a strong pink; it still stands, on a crest overlooking the road that travels between Tipperary and Cashel. The pigeons *roo-coo-coo* on slender white columns that support a portico over the front door; deep bow windows curve on either side of the entrance. Great lawns roll away from our terrace, down to a dense, downhill wood, over whose treetops we had views to the Galtee Mountains. Through this wood run paths that were cut by our great predecessor, Captain Ferguson, an eccentric officer who had inherited part of this land and who liked to walk naked about the fields at night-time (and sometimes by day).

I say "great" predecessor because Captain Ferguson made the wood his especial project. He purchased semi-mature, and sometimes mature, trees from all sorts of quarters, including abroad, but mainly from the estates of his friends on the southwest coast of Ireland. Around Glengarriff and Bantry, many subtropical species flourish in the warmth of the Gulf Stream's North Atlantic Drift. As a result of the good captain's researches and plantings, our wood still boasts many exotic and unusual growths. For example, at each of its four corners stands a great palm, whose fronds, glimpsed through a boy's window, might as well be waving in the South Seas.

My instructors deemed the wood and the grounds a source of education, and I spent many hours walking the glades and the fields, being taught my lessons and reciting them aloud. Each of the four tutors interrupted the curriculum of the moment to point out this plant, investigate that tree, marvel at the other shrub.

As a consequence, I formed an early and deep attachment to our "O'Brien Territory," as I might call it. I came to believe that I understood the smell of the earth, that I grasped the deep satisfaction a man might feel when his plowman turned a deep furrow, or reaped the plumpness of a harvest—and the tragedy of people who are denied the continued humble delight in their own land. That is why I found the great battering-ram of that eviction I witnessed so deeply upsetting. Much more than the whipping of their bodies and faces, I felt a pain in my soul for those people losing their land.

After all, even though I was not yet ten years old when Mr. Treece was wielding his whip, my own life was filling up daily with riches from the experiences of our own farm. I had seen my father breaking open an ear of wheat, feeling and sniffing it to determine which hour—not which morning, afternoon, or day, but which hour—would prove most perfect for harvesting.

The expression on his face as he walked his own fields conveyed as deep a sense of fulfillment as a man could have in life. He bent down to scrutinize it if he saw an unusual blade of grass; I now do the same. He surveyed the pulsing of a frog if he saw one; I always do likewise. He delighted when the mushrooms began to appear, and he would take a hard stalk of long cloverweed, thread it through the mushroom stems, and hand the collection to me like a perpendicular shish kebab. I have brought many such gifts to houses that I have been visiting, and in some cases I have deployed this excellent *fungus vulgaris* toward my cures.

Sometimes I even had the mystical pleasure of encountering the netherworld. We had on our farm, at the top of the farthest hill, a fort— a "fairy fort," to give it the full local name. It consisted of a circular rampart, bushy with trees and briars. Nobody went in there; the cattle, it was said, disliked grazing it.

But Artie Ryan Bull went into the fort and he died. He was called

"Ryan Bull" to distinguish him from myriad Ryans in our area; we had Ryan Brick (he lived in a brick house), Ryan Handsome, Ryan Pug, Ryan Ears—and Artie earned the subriquet "Bull" because he derived part of his income from owning a bull that serviced his and his neighbors' cows. Also, he had a short, thick stature; nothing separated his neck from his jaw.

Artie hunted rabbits over everyone's land; he had a black-and-white mongrel terrier by the name of Ollie. ("Named after Oliver Cromwell," said Artie, "another vicious little bastard.") With Ollie and a ferret whom he called Catherine (people suspected that he named the creature after his mother-in-law), Artie went into our fairy fort one day—and next morning my father's foreman, Billy Stokes, found him lying dead on the edge of the rampart.

"Sir," Billy said to us all in our hallway, "he was only purple. Not mauve, ma'am—purple. He musta seen something terrible to kill him of a fright like that."

As Mother said that evening, the fact that Artie drank a bottle of whiskey every two nights, and weighed as heavily as his own bull, might also have made some difference. Nevertheless, the legend of the fairy fort in Irish life had another cubit or two added to its stature—and an extra room opened up in my young imagination.

A "blind tasting" of Charles O'Brien's nationality, a guess at his racial background from his writings could produce only one answer: Irish. It's manifested in his desire to express himself colorfully. In his willingness to see life as a drama, he likes to place himself at the center of his own stage. These flamboyances, and the fluid lyricism of how he addresses his world, do not readily hallmark other nationalities. Like all the Irish, he has a story to tell and he knows it.

This national tendency toward vivid self-expression is much derived from Irish history. From the late 1600s, when the subjugation of the people began to intensify, new dark ages shrouded native Irish expression. The Irish "cause" had been routed, resurrected, exploited by monarchs and others with axes to grind against England—and then resurrected in many halfhearted rebellions, and routed again. As the original Irish landowners lost more and more of their territory to the English, a new class emerged: the dispossessed.   •

Those leading families who were thrown off their own land, expelled from their own houses, ripped from their ancestral moorings—they either left the country voluntarily or were deported as slaves to the Caribbean and the Americas. Or they stayed in Ireland, where they traveled the roads, hunkering down to some kind of appalling and meager existence. Many chieftains ended up living in mud hovels. Some folk memories claim that they were the progenitors of today's travelers, or "tinkers."

Thus, Charles O'Brien was relatively unusual for his time. The "outsider" status so shrewdly pursued by his father and forefathers kept him out of the mainstream, where danger flowed. His education at the hands of his four maverick tutors turned out a boy who had been exposed to many influences.

He had learned to read—not merely in the sense of being literate and knowing his ABC's, but with discrimination. And he had learned to write, not just headlines with Victorian sentiments in a boyish hand— "Competition Is the Life of Trade"—but also the language of an idea and how to structure an anecdote. He had knowledge of the classics and the Romance languages. And he knew something of art in varied forms.

Therefore, whatever his misfortunes on the streets at the hands of assailants, or the view taken by the woman who was his heart's desire, this was no unlettered oaf. This was a man who, when sent out in the world, had a refinement and sensibility that would have graced any society drawing room.

One further characteristic marks him with Irish distinction: his response to land. From childhood it held something mystical for him. To be sure, not every Irishman responds to an acre of earth with a poetic longing. Most who own land have been too busy wresting their livings from it. But their passion for their earth often transcends all other feeling. Charles O'Brien understood that and, following his father's example, saw the land, the clay, the dirt, the mud as a matter of the spirit.

Daily, and in intimate terms, my father taught me how Ireland is formed—how, for example, the people in the North save money more effectively than the people in the South, and are, in his opinion, more trustworthy. He told me my first tales, many of which came from the world around us, gathered from the many people to whom he spoke; and he liked to speak to everybody. And he had a great number of stories, some acquired down the years and some assumed by him to have been in his head since long before he was born. Many concerned land and the ownership of land, which was the question burning through the entire country all throughout his boyhood, too.

Thus, as other boys grew up with tales of pirates and trolls and ogres and wizards, I was raised on landlords and tenants and oppression and dispossession. Here is a story of a man who went to serve writs of eviction on some farmers over near Kilshane, about six miles from our home; I wrote it down from Father as he spoke it, several years ago.

"They call such men 'process servers,' and they make their money in a despicable way—they serve writs; other men make the bullets and they fire them. There was a man called Nolan—and, yes, indeed, some of them were natural Irishmen who chose to serve the landlord's writ on their fellow-countrymen. I wouldn't give a sour apple to a man like that and you wouldn't give a sour apple to anybody.

"This man, Nolan, left Limerick by the morning train and had someone meet him with a horse along the railway line somewhere near Bansha. He was carrying notices of eviction from two landlords, a man called Gibson, a bad pill that man, and a landlord called Birkin—two Englishmen, as you can tell from their names. All in all, the foolish Nolan was carrying in his leather bag nine white Court Orders.

"He rode his horse into Kilshane, up along the high road into the woods, and from what I heard of the story—a man living there told it to me—Nolan served the first writ and set out for the next house on his list.

"These small places—you'd think they had tom-toms or some kind of jungle communication, because as he rode on, he looked over his shoulder, and following behind him, on this narrow little road, came a bunch of about twenty men. And they looked grim. And then he looked ahead of him and saw twenty more, grimmer fellows.

"There was no escape. They caught Nolan's horse by the bridle, held the animal, and took down the rider. By the way, I heard that they took away the horse and painted it a different color until the search for it was over, and then they sold it for a good price at Mallow fair.

"These men began to kick the foolish Mr. Nolan, and hit him and punch him and pull his hair. He gave no fight back at them—too many against him, I suppose. They took his leather satchel, read out loud the writs and the civil bills. And then they tore them into flitters, and the scraps of paper, they blew away across the hedges like a little blizzard.

"Now the next thing was—several of the men in this affray began to blow hunting horns. Half a mile away, when this sound was heard, the chapel bell started to ring. These were signals, everybody knew them, and folk hurried from the north, the south, the east and west of Kilshane—which isn't a big place at all—to where the hunting horns were blaring.

"By now this bailiff was well beaten, but he still had his wits about him—which was what they wanted. There's a river flows down at the bottom of the hill, a little river, a tributary of the Suir, and they took Nolan down to this river. The men stripped his clothes off him and hauled him into the stream. Two of them went in with him and ducked him well and then took him out again and stood him on the bank.

"They pointed to him and they jeered him and they mocked him and then the men stood aside of him, and the women came through the crowd. One woman held up his right hand, one held up his left, and two more dragged his legs apart and he was held there, upright and naked, like a man being crucified without a cross. Then the prettiest few women in the crowd broke off branches of furze bushes—furze has more spikes than a rose, ask any man who has ever fallen off his horse into a furze bush. Prickly all over.

"These young women began to tease Nolan, naked and spread-eagled as he was, with the furze bushes. Up and down his body and in and out, anywhere they could get a few needles of furze to poke and sting—he must have gone mad.

"Then they brought forward a bucket of tar. It wasn't roasting hot, for that would have killed him. But it was warm enough to spread, and so they covered his body with this tar, and then they stuck white goose feathers all over him and they tied him to a tree. The constables from Limerick came out to rescue him, in response to a telegram they had received. They asked everybody, they quizzed all over the place, and of course nobody knew anything or had seen anything and there was nothing for it but to search the countryside.

"With no help and no direction, they found Nolan the bailiff as naked as the day he was born, feathers sticking everywhere out of him, tied to a tree out in the middle of the fields and shivering. It took two days of him being rubbed all over with butter to get all the tar off—a nurse in Limerick did the job. They say she did a great job too, every nook and cranny of the man. What a job to be given."

And my father winced.

Such violence had long been taking place in Ireland, not only in our province of Munster but also in our county of Tipperary, where the land is so rich. The bailiff Nolan had been one of the fortunate ones. In my grandfather's time, the Whiteboys, a notoriously violent secret society, believed that the landlords should be driven out by much more savage force. They roamed the fields at night, wearing white smocks that made them sinister in the darkness—and to me therefore somewhat thrilling.

When I asked my father about them, to my surprise he spoke vehement condemnation. Yet I knew that he agreed with their aims; he too loathed the absentees—those owners who never appeared on their land but controlled the lives of all who lived as their tenants. It was the Whiteboys' methods that my father so gravely disliked, because they attacked the landlords' cattle and horses. They "hocked" them—they cut the tendons in the animals' legs, rendering them crippled and ready for death.

"How any Irishman can leave a field with a horse moaning in such awful pain," my father said. "He's no kind of Irishman, he's a barbarian."

I grew up, therefore, in territories of conflict—in a beautiful land of old castles, woods, and rivers, where sinister figures had but recently roamed the land at night, garbed in white, dealing out heinous violence, and where murder was often committed in the name of land. In childhood, my parents shielded us from reports of such occurrences, although we knew that at crossroads, in villages and in towns, people held turbulent gatherings to debate their rights to their own fields, and mainly to discuss the ousting of the landlords.

Once or twice, coming home at night from a neighborly visit, we encountered knots of such people holding such meetings. Much shouting seemed to be taking place, and the air felt disturbed. We ran into no immediate difficulties—when they saw my father, they waved us through with a laugh and a light cheer—but we knew that others had been turned back or not allowed to pass or, often, had been forced from their carriages and obliged to walk home. Next morning the carriage might be found in a disheveled state many miles away, and the horses nowhere to be seen.

Charles O'Brien knew that he came of a kindly and relaxed parenting. Those two people loved each other, loved their two children, and loved their existence in a simple and intelligent way. They gave their sons as good an education as their joint political agreement would permit.

Each tutor they hired opened a different window on the world. Nobody in that household feared eccentricity or shrank from individuality. A high sense of justice prevailed. And their patriotism seems to have stemmed from love of their land and their people, rather than from some acquired ideology or the pressures of history.

This is a man who should not have felt a need to "improve" himself. While under his father's roof, he had confidence and a happy inquiring sensibility, which he took with ease into his adult life. Did his uncertainty, his lack of faith in himself, simply arrive with one bound when he fell in love with the eighteen-year-old April Burke?

It can't have done. If the boy had grown unaltered into the man, he might have had something of the charm, the dignity and composure, that he saw at home in both his parents. Therefore, she might have been less brutal in the rejection that he mentions so early in his text.

Nor would he have issued such a self-negating warning about himself: "Be careful about me." Admittedly, he includes it in the lee of the general, totally accurate, and justifiable warning about our emotional system of history. The Irish have always turned defeat into moral and emotional triumph. But his text begins to suggest that, somewhere along the line, after his loved and imaginative boyhood, and his lively and enjoyed adolescence, Charles O'Brien changed—into an anxious, self-doubting adult.

His journey from childhood is charted in glimpses. For instance, as the prelude to a major chapter, he tells—almost as an aside, and again out of chronological order—an illuminating story of an encounter with his father over a giant. After that, his tale spreads across Ireland as his life begins to find its first direction.

Father's discourses seemed unceasing but never intrusive; he knew how I loved to hear him talk, even when he was giving me difficult advice about my life and how to conduct matters. But is it not essential to trust a man who has encouraged one's every thrilling discovery? And who then has cushioned one's disappointment when, say, a hero turned out to be human, or a miracle's blinding light turned out to be the deft mirror of chicanery?

For example: When I was nine years old, I read in one of Father's many periodicals of America's great and amazing Cardiff Giant. In the state of New York, some laborers digging a well on a farm discovered the almost-preserved remains of a man ten feet tall. I ran, shouting, through the house on that rainy Sunday morning and found my father.

"You see! You see! The old stories are right—there were giants in days gone by, there were! And if there were ancient giants in America, then there could easily have been giants here, couldn't there?"

Father took the paper from my hands and read it gravely, muttering, "Boys-oh-dear, boys-oh-dear." Then he and I shared some days of wonderful conversation about giants, and whether giants' graves lay beneath any curiously shaped hill that we knew, and might we even have had giants among our own ancestors? To which my father said, "Well, they told me my father had an uncle who was six feet six, and maybe he was a bit of a giant."

However, sometime later, Father came to my room at bedtime and said, "I have grave news for you—but it doesn't have to change any of our beliefs."

He read to me, from another newspaper, that the Giant of Cardiff was a hoax. Some gentleman had "created" the giant out of gypsum in order to fake support for an argument about whether giants had ever existed. My father sat down on the chair by my bed and said, "Well, I suppose you and I will just have to puzzle this out until we know what our hearts have to say about it."

I now understand that, over the course of the next few days, he let me down lightly—but he also turned the Giant into a teaching. "A thing doesn't have to be true," he said, "for a person to get joy out of it. What it has to be is not evil or malicious."

Deriving from that exchange, it did not take me long to understand that Father and I shared a willingness to believe in the impossible, especially if it offered any assistance to someone's life. Ten years later, when I was nineteen years old, Father demonstrated this by going on—for him—an entirely improbable journey and one that altered my life and my soul.

He announced at breakfast one morning that he was "taking Charles and Euclid on a little holiday." Mother scarcely raised an eyebrow. Cally, Mother said, would help us pack the bags, and we now had a girl to help in the kitchen, a thin girl who ran like the wind everywhere. Her name was Nora Buckley, and I soon asked whether Nora might be a relation to my beloved tutor. Mother shook her head and said, "You can't throw a stone in Cork or Kerry without hitting a Buckley."

When she first came to the house, Euclid whispered to me, "Easy to remember her name—look at her teeth." Nora Buckley had prominent front teeth, a little splayed. She said, "Yes" (with a spray) to every word spoken to her, and she blinked a great deal, but she intended to please every person; we soon loved her fondly.

Mother asked, "Where will you stay?"

"We'll cross the Shannon at Killaloe. And then I suppose we'll try and get as far up as we can toward Gort. We could stay with the MacNamaras, and then the boys would like to see Galway city."

"The City of the Tribes," said Euclid, who knew all these names and nicknames. "Where Mayor Lynch hung his son."

"Hanged," said Mother, "is the correct word. And then?"

"Ah, maybe Connemara or so," said my father, and I knew that he was being evasive.

Mother began to laugh; Father began to blush.

"That's why it's called 'lynching,' I think," said Euclid. "Because of Mayor Lynch."

"And I suppose," said Mother, laughing harder, "there's every chance you'll go somewhat north after that."

Father, now blushing heavily, laughed too. "A bit, maybe."

Mother said, "I wasn't aware that we needed a miracle."

Euclid fastened on this like a cat on a bird.

"Knock! Knock! Are we? Are we going to Knock, to the shrine?"

Father looked ever more sheepish.

"If you are," said Mother, "and I've been wondering how long you'd hold out, take Nora with you. Her aunt lives there—she'll know every-one."

As a simple preface, let me explain that Father—and all of us—had been pursuing in his newspapers the apparitional events in Knock, County Mayo, where the Blessed Virgin Mary and other divine figures had flared in bright white light on a church wall.

Traveling a long journey with my father had an epic and intrepid feel. No pony-trap this time—we took what he called "the long car," a brougham with seats along each side. Our valises and our food sat in the well. An Indian summer had delayed the fall of the leaves, and we left the house in a blaze of gold; Mother waved smiling and laughing from the portico.

Even then, young as I was, I liked to stand back, as it were, and view every situation in which I found myself. That morning, this is what I saw; Polly, our great, gray mare, with her white plume of a tail waving as she lunged forward; and how the harness shone and rattled. My father, his muttonchop whiskers crisper than ever, and his large body teeming with life, called now and then to Polly, "Hup, there, hup, girl."

Beside him on the brown leather bench, hoping to stay firm and well, sat Euclid, a plaid rug of red, brown, and green about his knees, even though that September sun would have ripened a green tomato in a day. He looked everywhere about him, taking in all the world with those great eyes and yet unable to ingest enough; he scarcely ceased jigging with excitement. Behind Euclid, on the side-seat, sat I, facing outward and pleased beyond measure to be traveling thus with two of the three people I loved most in the world. Across the car, at my back, sat the nervous and swift Nora Buckley; she was under strict directions from Cally and Mrs. Ryan never to take her eyes off Euclid except when he was "at the necessary"—and above all to make sure that he reached bed safely every night.

We had left in the early morning and made wonderful progress through the villages of Cappawhite and Cappamore, where, to judge from the sleepy windows, no person had yet arisen. Not far from Newport, Father halted at a quiet turn in the road and announced that he had drunk "too much tea." He gave us what he called "voyagers' rules": he, Euclid, and I would climb into one field to relieve ourselves, Nora to the field on the other side of the road. Afterward we all stood in the roadway and stretched, bending this way and that.

Euclid had declared that as the crow flies our house lay thirty-four miles from Killaloe, and my father said he would try his best to "do as the crow does." In his younger days, he said, he had "hunted all over this barony" and soon, to the alarm of Nora Buckley but to the delight of Euclid and me, he decided, as he announced, to "go across country." He steered Polly off the road and we swung down a cart track into someone's farm.

Thus began the first truly exhilarating journey of my life across the Irish countryside—and that is how I began to form my taste for such travels, sitting beside my father in the pony-trap or, as now, behind him on the long car, swaying and rocking to the clop of a horse. That day, we traveled down rutted tracks, splashed across streams bright as tin, up hills almost too steep, and over grassy headland plateaus. Here and there, as we drove past, a farmer or his wife waved from a doorway, or an inquisitive child came out to look, and a dog to bark. My father knew all the sweetest ways, and we never felt imperiled by the roughness of the ground over which he took us.

Birds flapped up from the long grass with a sudden clatter of wings. A deer, rare in those parts, cleared a low fence ahead of us and bounced away haughtily. We saw a fox, who walked astutely along a ridge and inspected us from a distance, its tail held out behind it like a bushy spar. Rabbits sat and twitched their noses, not at all bothered by this curious conveyance with the small, intensely frail, pale-faced boy wrapped in a rug in the front seat, who was counting the rabbits but looking for hares.

I heard him ask Father, "And shall we see eagles?" and Father replied, as I expected he might, "If you want to, Euclid. If you want to."

One field remains in my mind like an encouraging dream. Father consulted his compass frequently and sometimes, directly after a reading, we found ourselves on or off a roadway. Now we trotted along a graveled avenue, at the end of which Father steered Polly into a wood with a broad pathway running through it. No branches overhung and we never slackened pace. We cleared the trees, climbed a hill, and ran along the top. Father drew Polly to a halt and said, "Now look back."

Below us, a long slope stretched away down the fields; two ribbons of roads from different directions intersected the patchwork of green; and in the distance shone a third and brighter ribbon—the river Shannon.

"This is a good place to eat," Father said, and we opened the boxes that Cally and Mrs. Ryan had supplied and packed under Mother's supervision. Eggs had been crushed and mixed with chopped ham and onion; we had chicken with onion; Father chose roast beef and some slices of onion. Nora Buckley, perilously with such teeth, elected to eat a soda-bread sandwich of onion and chopped egg; neither Euclid nor I dared look at each other as she ate. When she finished, she said to Euclid, "Somebody in your house must be famous for onions."

We drank mugs of milk poured from a tall, shining dairy-can, and we looked at the countryside for a long time. I would have sat there an hour and more had Father asked.

"The battles fought over that land down there," he said. "Troy didn't give as much trouble."

He pointed out the Silvermines—he called them "mountains," although Euclid said that they seemed like hills to him, "because by geographical agreement a mountain needs to be over a thousand feet high."

Far away, across the fields, a tiny man herded thirty or more tiny cows up a patch of hill field and into another patch of pasture. We could hear his dog's distant excitement; and we sat for a little while longer in the glorious sunshine of the autumn, looking at the green and tawny and gold and brown patchwork quilt of fields.

The Shannon, when we crossed it at Killaloe, thrilled us as much as the Tiber might, or the Mississippi. We liked its width, and its refusal to be hurried. Soon the stone walls of the west appeared and the sun went down, leaving the sky red as a blushing face.

That night in the little town of Gort, as I reflected on our traveling across the country, and as I could hear Father's laughter downstairs, where he took a drink with our hosts, I would have said that it had been one of the most beautiful, serene days of my life. I have had many more since, but that day on which I first crossed the Shannon into the West of Ireland remains for me one of my most memorable.

Next day we bowled into Galway city, all bridges and cobblestones. I chiefly recall watching a basket-maker in the square outside our hotel, and being transfixed by the speed of his hands as he wove the hard strands into firm patterns. The hotel introduced me, I feel, to a taste for such comforts that still directs part of my life. For me, to this day, the most restful moments come when I luxuriate in a great hotel, receiving my meals with deferential service and sleeping between starched linens.

We stayed there for two days, and during our first breakfast, Father counseled Euclid, Nora, and myself to tell nobody of our destination. In the many conversations that we overheard in the hotel, the name of Knock recurred frequently. All remarks had the same tone: "Do you believe it?" and "I suppose it is possible" and "Don't you know what they have up there now? Miracles! They have a miracle nearly every hour."

All of this threw Euclid and Nora Buckley into states of fantastic longing, with Euclid whispering to me at every turn, "Do you think we'll see an apparition?" Nora worried, "If such holy folks appeared—well, when they're gone, what's to stop the Devil comin'?" (She, of course, pronounced it "Divil.")

My father, I know, also felt excitement, but his anticipation derived from the opportunity to meet those local people who had actually seen the Virgin Mary on the gable wall of the church in the rain. Yet he did not wish people to think him religious, and that is why he asked us not to divulge our destination. He justified his journey by saying, "You know, people should always make a pilgrimage to a phenomenon."

After Galway, we spent two days out in Connemara, lingering by the lakes of Corrib, Mask, and Carra. My father had fished the mayfly there, and he told us of those brilliant early summer days when, for one week, men would come "from all over the world." He continued, "Now if you fellows were here that week, you'd make a fortune catching that mayfly in glass bottles and selling it to the anglers for their bait."

The light over the lakes seemed to change every half minute, and we saw rainbow after rainbow.

This paragraph comes from a County Mayo guidebook:

> In August 1879, more than a dozen local people in the hamlet of Knock, in the county of Mayo, reported an apparition that is still venerated today. This was never rich land. Oliver Cromwell chose not to bring his marauders over here because one of his generals had reported that the country west of the Shannon contained "not enough water to drown a man, wood enough to hang one, nor earth enough to bury him." The apparition, however, brought fame and fortune, as such mystical occurrences do. Hundreds of similar appearances by the Virgin Mary have been recorded, most prominently, Fátima, Garabandal, Guadalupe, Lourdes, and Medjugorje in Croatia.

In all those cases, and in Knock, too, the life of the surrounding countryside changed for the better. Lourdes, originally a village near a cave in the Pyrenees, gained a huge infrastructure. With a basilica and an airport, it attracts pilgrims from all over the world daily, to be dipped naked in the miraculous waters.

At Fátima, visitors rip the skin off their legs as they traverse a huge plaza on their knees, praying as they inch the hundreds of yards from the bus parks to the steps of the basilica.

Knock, when the apparition was reported, suffered the official Church skepticism with which all such reports are typically greeted. But the local people and their clergy prevailed. For them, whether they said so or not, this became a further liberation, an extension of Catholic Emancipation. It took some time for validation to arrive; today, Knock has its own devotional infrastructure, including an international airport. It was crowned by a Papal visit in its centenary year of 1979, and receives close to two million pilgrims annually.

We spent a night in a Claremorris boarding-house, where the landlady, who had fat earlobes, joked, "I s'pose people like yourselves are never going to Knock?"

Father replied jovially, "No need to knock, we're indoors already." To us he murmured when she'd gone back to the kitchen, "Never give a nosy person room for a comeback. Humor is the great escape."

The landlady poked her head out of the kitchen and said to Nora, "Aren't you a Buckley girl from near Knock? I'd know you anywhere," and Nora whispered to us, "My mother has very big teeth too."

Father whispered gallantly, "You haven't big teeth, Nora, you have small jaws."

Next afternoon we drove to the church where the people had seen all the apparitions.

"We'd better count them up," said Father on the way. "Now, who exactly made an appearance?"

Euclid, naturally, had devoured every detail.

"This is what the newspapers said. The Virgin Mary, Saint Joseph, Saint John the Evangelist, and the Lamb of God were seen by a total of fifteen people altogether, and they said that the Virgin Mary was wearing a white robe and a gold crown, and that her husband, Saint Joseph, was wearing a white robe and that he was very old."

Father said, as though thinking aloud, "I wonder what time of his life

Saint Joseph was at when he agreed to make this appearance? Or maybe there's no aging in the next life? But if there isn't, why does he look old at all, why can't he look like he was when he was, say, thirty? Or my age? The forties are a good time for a man to look handsome."

Euclid said, "And Saint John was wearing long robes too—"

Father interrupted. "Did they say what color?"

Euclid said, "I think green."

Father said, "Ah, yes. Green for Ireland. I wonder do they change colors according to the country they appear in. Maybe the red, white, and blue for England. Or I s'pose England doesn't get divine apparitions; they're not deserving enough."

Euclid said, "There were angels hovering around the lamb."

Father said thoughtfully, "And not around the Virgin Mary or Saint Joseph or Saint John? Boys-oh-dear. Well, that's a strange decision the angels took. Maybe they knew they'd irritate the people? Or maybe they knew the lamb mightn't care too much, might like the companionship?"

This grave conversation continued until Nora, from her perch on the long side-seat, said, "Sir, there's Auntie Mary's house."

We all disembarked and Nora went to the door of the cottage. A gray cat looked at us, stuck its tail up in the air straight as smoke from a calm day's chimney, but then disdained us. Next a lady of about Mother's age—that is, in her early forties—came out to greet us. She wore a saintly face, carried rosary beads, and responded to Nora's introductions.

"Sir, you're very welcome to Knock, but when you get up the road, you'll find it packed. There's people here from everywhere in the world."

My father said, "Is there any harm in asking you what you saw? Or are you sick and tired of being asked?"

Nora's Auntie Mary said, "Sir, how could you get sick and tired of something like that and it so wonderful and now with all the miracles?"

Father said, "And a very bright light, I hear?"

"Oh sir, it was the light of Heaven, we know that now, and the Blessed Virgin herself the brightest light of all."

Father said, "I suppose she'd have to be, wouldn't she? If she wasn't given a bright light what hope would there be for any of us?" He spoke so warmly to Auntie Mary, so charmingly.

"She was two feet off the ground, sir, and her eyes lifted to Heaven in prayer for us all."

"Did she say who she was praying for?" Father's questions had a profound effect on Euclid, who angled himself so that he could look up and see both faces.

"No, sir, she didn't say a thing. But you could tell from the look on her face that she was praying for all of us, and sure she'd have known we were after having another famine here, with the potatoes failed again."

"I heard that," said Father, as somberly as a heart breaking. "I heard that indeed. I'm sorry for your trouble."

"Oh, sir, we're out of it now—there's so much money coming in, sure, can't we buy potatoes. We've all these people coming here, thousands and thousands. Didn't I hear there's people coming here from Portugal?"

"Portugal?! Well, well." But Father seemed intent on getting back to the apparition. "So the Blessed Virgin was in a white robe and a gold crown, they tell me, and you saw her and she was two feet above the ground. What of the two gentlemen? Were they—were they hovering too?"

In all my time, I have never encountered a man who speaks so kindly to others as my father does. Nora's Auntie Mary warmed to him.

"Sir, they did, they hovered a bit, about two feet up, I'd say. Yes, about two feet, that'd be it."

I saw Euclid hold out his hand to try and measure two feet above the ground.

"Did they say anything? Or did they look at you?"

"Sir, not one of them said a single word. And how could they look at us and their eyes raised in prayer to Heaven above? Although Paddy Hill, he's taller than the rest of us, he was able to see into our Blessed Lady's eyes, right in—and he could see the very cores of her eyes."

Father said, "The lamb, was that now a young lamb, I mean newborn, or was it maybe a few weeks old? We've lambs at home."

"Sir, the fleece was like snow, pure white, and the little mouth soft as velvet, and it had a meekness to it that'd make you proud. As to its age, I'm no good at guessing the age of a lamb, sir. I'd say—well, very young."

"Did anyone notice how many angels?"

"Oh, sir, they came and they went, fluttering their little wings."

Father said, in a grave tone, "I see. I see. Well—I s'pose that's what angels do, isn't it?"

"It is, sir, didn't we always know that? Especially the smaller angels."

"Oh, indeed, indeed." Father sounded ever more grave. "I mean to say, if it was a large angel and anyone got a clout of one of his wings— I mean, a swan can break a man's arm with a wing." He prepared to go. "Well—it's very important, we can tell that for a fact. Very important. And yourself? Did you feel in the better of it?"

"I did, sir, I felt better than I felt my whole life and I always felt good, mind you, I was never one for complaining. And now I've no need to complain at all."

My father's hand romped in his coat and drew out his wallet. "And I hope people are generous to you? For your time? And for giving so hearty an account of your great experience?" he asked.

"People are very good, sir. God is very good."

"Ah, He is," said my father, handing over some money, which the lady took and folded into her hand but never inspected.

"Sir, He sends me blessings every day."

She directed us to the church: "You can't miss it anyway, but you'll have to walk the last bit, there's no horse'd go through a crowd like that."

Euclid had never seen a crowd of people and seemed apprehensive. I said to him, "But we have had many people in our house and on the terrace."

Euclid said, "But they were our guests and we knew how they should behave."

In Ireland, in my time, I have seen a great love of prayer. I myself do not pray, but many good people do, and I respect them for that. The sincerity of prayer that I have seen by people's sick-beds, and the faith that I have heard people express, and the fervor with which they speak their pleadings—all such prayer, I have concluded, comes to resemble a kind of love, a passion for the God who looks over them, and who will bring them hope and salvation.

Many things move me to my soul and one of them is the sight of a venerable priest, all alone in the world, kneeling in his church and taking the opportunity for a quiet prayer in the day, when the church is empty. As I sometimes desire sanctuary from my busy life as a healer, I have seen this sight many times. I have also seen an old gentleman or lady come in to pay their respects to their faith, and sit or kneel there quietly, their lips moving tenderly. And I have been moved to my heart's root, and at times have wondered whether my own life might be richer for the inclusion of such faith.

That day at Knock, however, when we first saw the throng of people, I felt none of the peace that such glimpses of quiet piety granted me; indeed, I felt at first fear, and then pity.

We left the house of Nora Buckley's Aunt Mary and Father steered Polly along the road to the village. As we rounded a bend we saw before us as many people as I had ever seen. They stood pressed against each other, moving forward. A general silence prevailed, not a common occurrence in an Irish throng, but this silence had a rustle to it, as of leaves blown along the ground. The crowd edged forward, and as we drew nearer I could hear that the "rustle" came from the shuffle of the feet and the murmured chorus of breathed prayers.

An excitable man waving his arms directed us to a field which contained many conveyances—where another man (clearly the twin of the excitable one) made my father aware that a "donation" in respect of "guarding your side-car, sir," would be looked upon with approval.

Father again handed over money. He remarked to us that "God has indeed been good to Knock" and we joined the rear of the crowd. Father and I kept Euclid firmly between us as we pressed forward; from behind Nora Buckley grabbed my coat and said that she was afraid.

"Nora, stay close to us," said Father, "and you'll be all right."

"Is this apparition thing dangerous, sir?" she asked.

"It could be, it could be—but not to us, Nora," and I saw that Father smiled.

We now shuffled forward for many minutes and, ahead, I soon perceived the church. By the roadside, men stewarded the press of people forward at a steady pace, saying to us, "Keep going now" but in a gentle and unhurried way. They knew (as did we) the crowd's purpose: to pass the holy place and also hope to see a new apparition.

Soon, we came level with the wall of the church, and Father, using the bulk of his body with great firmness, eased us out of the crowd.

"I want to have a good look," he said.

A man came forward and said, less than gently, "You can't stop here," but when Father shook the man's hand "carefully" the man subsided. So we stood and looked—and I also inspected the faces of our little party.

Father scrutinized each part of that church wall as though in its rough surface lay some message, some secret. His eyes traveled from the eaves to the earth—and then he repeated the exercise. Euclid did likewise, and when he found nothing in its blank face he looked above him, seeking to discover, it seemed, whence the apparitions had descended. Again he looked at the wall and once more at the sky, and his expression, though guarded within the sight of so many people shuffling by, had enough in it to tell me that he ranged among excitement, fear, and doubt.

Nora Buckley, when she looked at the wall, whispered to me, "Is there prayers we should be saying? Will that only bring them back? They'd frighten me."

For my part, I could see a flat surface upon which a vision might with great facility be discerned, I could see above my head the great clouds rolling by, bearing inland on winds from the west—but I felt neither rapture nor mystery. Perhaps, I thought, all this has too recently occurred for the church to have yet a powerful odor of sanctity; and so I turned to look discreetly at the people.

The breadth of that moving stream was about six to eight persons abreast on the narrow roadway, and there seemed no end to the tail of this long, gentle, shuffling animal; more and more people pressed forward—and this was not a Sunday.

All of Shakespeare's Seven Ages of Man were represented. I saw infants held aloft to receive such blessing as the apparition had left in the air; children of school age with shining faces looked wonderingly from the lee of their parents. Men and women of marrying age, alone or in the company of their families, ill-dressed or comfortable, paused, stared, and bowed their heads in prayer. Two soldiers in red coats, one with a beard, walked respectfully within the crowd and for once did not receive taunts or strained gibes.

I was surprised to see so many people of comfortable means there, and my father, I noticed, nodded to a corpulent gentleman, whom he later named to me as a prominent judge, and then said, "Now what was he doing there? Seeking forgiveness, I suppose."

Some pilgrims—for that is what I must call them—seemed exotic, dressed in what they must have considered their best attire, as though they had come in a bright garb intended to decorate such powers as they might find here. And I saw men who must be scholars, farmers, clerks, travelers in commerce, cattlemen, merchants, priests. Most of all, I saw old people; they made up the great bulk of this crowd, and their lips moved unceasingly.

At the foot of the wall crouched a line of strong men, close-knit in their grouping; they waited there to fend off those who would try and capture a relic from the fabric of the church. However, they or the authorities competent for this place relented in one wise, the most poignant sight of all; they had created a separate arena where people who evidently seemed in dire need of divine aid could congregate closest to the church.

I saw that day sights and shapes that I had neither encountered nor imagined; men and women, boys and girls with deformities and physical detractions that I could not have contemplated, much less have lived with. Their faces raised in hope, they and their accompanying relations—parents, sisters, spouses—prayed with a fervor of desperation.

Near our house there dwelt a family where a boy of my age shuffled and made foolish noises. I had seen him but once or twice and, truth to tell, felt in fear of him—and ashamed of myself for that fear. Now I saw more and worse than that: mouths drooling, eyes rolling, figures without arms or legs carried there in giant baskets. I had the thought that, if we were truly to witness miracles, did that mean that we would suddenly see an arm sprout, then a leg, then another arm, then another leg?

This irreverence, I knew, defended me; but as I stood there I saw that Euclid had begun to weep and, though no longer a baby, he turned and buried his face in the skirts of Father's coat.

And I? I made a vow that day—a vow that I must help people, even though I did not have the knowledge as to what fashion and by what means.

For nearly three years I contemplated that day's visions at Knock. We traveled a straighter road home, and we spoke little of our experiences. I kissed Nora Buckley one night beneath the trees in our upper field, a kiss full of teeth and softness. She held me kindly, her arms about my neck, saying, "We shouldn't be doing this" and "Oh, you're very nice." Soon after, she left our house for work in England, and she died the next year in a mill accident; we sat about the table distraught when we heard the news. Euclid and I mourned her together and Euclid told me that he had always felt safe with her, and that on the days when he felt at his weakest, she gave him strength and made him laugh.

I now began to travel. My parents gave me letters of introduction and I rode here and there out across our lovely country, each journey a little longer than the one before, and I admired and relished what I saw, and I felt soothed every day by the trees and the rivers and the hills and the woods. And all the while I thought of the afflictions I had seen at that unforgettable shrine and wondered whether I might help to alleviate them.

Charles O'Brien was nineteen years old when he felt moved by what he saw at Knock. In a more traditional or conventional Irish household he might have been shaped at that moment for the Catholic priesthood. Yet his future had, it seemed, already been outlined. He, as elder son, would inherit and continue.

Surprisingly, this did not happen; Knock, apparently, handed him a spur that prodded him forward into a life very different from the one anticipated for him. To the natural forces that had already been shaping him, he now added a wish to help his fellow man.

To begin with, he had been born with the poetic advantage of living in a beautiful land. And he wished to remain permanently aware of it. The O'Briens lived in the South Riding of County Tipperary, "riding" being an old Norse term for a "thirding," or a third of a land tract. It runs from Hollyford and Holycross down to the county's capital, Clonmel, birthplace of Laurence Sterne (and, therefore, Tristram Shandy), and home for a time of another English novelist, Anthony Trollope, whose sons were born there.

Beyond Clonmel, the South Riding reaches down to places with lovely names—Kilsheelan, Carrick-on-Suir, Ardfinnan, Knocklofty. The people who live in those lower reaches, flanked by the counties of Cork and Waterford, will tell you that Tipperary grows lovelier the farther south you go. Not much more than sixty miles stem to stern, this is inner space, luscious country, full of limestone beneath the soil, excellent for the bones of racehorses, with a rougher charm than the horse farms of New England and Kentucky or the stud farms of England. At least one racing stable ranks among the most successful in the world.

Although he doesn't mention it, Charles O'Brien must have been put on a horse in early childhood. In the days when all gentlemen saw riding as their primary mode of transport, his father would have taken particular care to introduce his son to it. In time, Charles refers to his mare, Della, as though to a family member, and she gave him a service that lasted for almost thirty years, a good span even by today's well-vetted standards.

On horseback, everything looks different. No truck, juggernaut, or car offers anything like the same vantage or intimacy. The countryside looks richer, sweeter, nearer—and the South Riding through which Charles O'Brien traveled has changed little. From his saddle today he would see the same freshness of green in the fields, the same mottled gray-white of limestone in the ruined abbeys and castles, the same enchanting dimness in the woodlands and copses, the same brown-and-silver sheen of a river glimpsed from the roadway.

Many of the horsemen of his time avoided the thoroughfares and rode their own routes. On the western journey to Tipperary, the shapes of old Norman castles, gaunt and alone against the sky, must have given him a sense of romance. As he rode east, the gentle sweep of the river and the stone arches of the river bridge in Golden brought him harmony, and an encouragement toward pleasant reflection. This was a universe in a small place.

Above all, if, during his first mile east or west of his home, he looked south, he saw through the trees the turrets and ramparts of the great mansion that would one day become one of his life's two great preoccupations.

Furthermore, he knew from his own locality that the Irish countryside abounds with history, a serious factor in his life. Barons and despots led armies across here. Wild men abducted beautiful women here. Poets wrote famous songs here. Conspirators plotted revolution here.

And in the ordinary commerce of the time, romantic yet practical figures crossed this stage—such as the wine salesman from Woodford Bourne, in Cork, who rode across this countryside to the well-to-do houses (such as the O'Briens'); or the undertaker's clerk, who rode down through the woods behind the house to measure old Mrs. O'Brien, Charles's grandmother, for her coffin. And the ghosts of two famous hunting hounds ran the crests of the hills in winter twilights.

Judging from his powers of observation, Charles O'Brien must have known all these haunting things, and his sense of story glowed brighter and brighter. Therefore, when the time came to choose a life for himself, he did not elect to stay in one place. He found a means of combining his three loves, of looking at the countryside, learning about his land and its people, and contributing to their lives—while observing them.

When I gained the age of twenty-one, Father deemed my four-handed education not merely complete but the equal of any university. Buckley, he knew, would have no ongoing part in my life; Mr. Halloran had shown, in his timid way, some impatience with my mathematical endeavors. Mrs. Curry's influence with Oxford, and Miss Taylor's with Trinity College, Dublin, took no root in my father, who said that too much further education might weaken me. He had expected that I must follow him into the management of the farm. If he felt disappointment that I did not do so, he concealed it from me; Father's good manners inspire all who know him.

At one time after this decision became plain, it had crossed the fam-

ily table that I might try for being a doctor. Mother praised my humanity and Euclid thought that I should enjoy very much "meeting the people," as he put it, "and cutting them open." I believe that the idea of
medicine had originated with my father—but then he changed his mind
and said that being a doctor carried with it a difficult and, in his view,
inessential burden of respectability, and a man should not think of such
things until he had sown some wild oats.

"But if healing the sick seems like a necessary power to you," he said,
"you might think of belonging to an older tradition than doctoring. And
it'll get you out and about."

He sent me with a letter of introduction to a man some miles away,
near Bansha, a man named Egan. I remembered this man well, and with
good reason. At the age of six, I became covered in ringworm, an infection picked up from our cattle. Large circles of sore and itchy red scales
covered my body from my ankles to my neck, and we saw doctors in
Limerick, Cork, and Dublin, as well as our own beloved Dr. O'Malley.
None of them, for all their goodwill and sympathy, could help me; their
ointments and oils failed to make a cure.

Down in the kitchen, Cally, the housekeeper, and Mrs. Ryan's daughter, Biddy, who plucked our fowl for the table, directed us to Mr. Egan.

Biddy, from among the feathers: "He's a quack all right, ma'am, but
he's kind of, like, a better class of a quack."

Cally, hands a-floured with baking: "Isn't he back from Colorado, isn't
he, working on the railways with them Red Indians and them sort of
people?"

Biddy: "And he brought the snake-oil home with him, ma'am, and
anybody'd tell you that snake-oil is the best thing of all. I heard the Pope
uses it if he has anything at him, like, you know, boils and things."

Oh, I wanted to see snake-oil. Did it have iridescent colors? Was it
compounded from different venoms?

I remembered Mr. Egan as an exceptionally kind and warm-hearted
little man, with a huge wife. ("He has a mountain to climb," said my father on the way home. My mother laughed and laughed; I was only six.)
My parents and I had been shown into a small bedroom at the rear of the
cottage, where portraits of racing greyhounds had been pinned up

around the walls. Mr. Egan looked at such ringworm on me as he could view without my undressing, and said to my parents, "We'll only try it out on what we can see."

He produced the bottle, which, to my disappointment, contained a muddy green liquid streaked with yellow and orange until he shook it, when it became an opaque mud color; I had expected glittering scales and diamond patterns. When I took off my shoes and stockings and rolled up the legs of my knickerbockers, Mr. Egan, using a large goose feather, began to paint my sores. The liquid hurt like fury, stung me to tears.

My perturbed father asked, "What is that stuff? Is that—?"

"Snake-oil, sir."

"And what kind of a snake?"

"They call it a king rattlesnake."

"Ah, no wonder it stings," said my father. To console me he said, "Now you'll never be killed by a king rattlesnake; you'll have the antidote already inside you."

"That's so," said Mr. Egan, and we all agreed afterward that he seemed an especially sound man. We agreed it doubly when, next morning, the ringworm began to disappear from my skin. The raw red badges seemed almost to fade even as we looked at them, and we were jubilant. Mother then painted the other affected parts of my body, and by the weekend each ringworm circle had receded to a mild glow; Father kept the rest of the bottle for the cattle.

"I'm going to put money on a horse for that man," he said. He often did this—but he never told them beforehand; as he said, "I don't want them following the race and then being disappointed."

Recently, I asked Mother, whose memory remains excellent, whether she had ever heard anyone thank Father for the winnings from such a gift. She looked at me, reflected for a moment, and then crumpled with laughter.

Given that little oasis of personal history with ringworm, I felt more than pleased when my father suggested that I learn healing from Mr. Egan—who, when I went to see him, remembered my parents and me, and therefore listened attentively to the notion of my becoming his apprentice. His wife, larger than ever, seemed especially interested in the venture. But it seemed to present a difficulty to them, and I understood the problem: the slow business of teaching someone else all that Mr. Egan knew; the presence of another person by his side all day, every day; the confidences that he must exercise, yet keep. And he put these points to me very clearly. However, I am pleased to say that my father had given me liberty to make an offer of payment for serving my time. I was proud to have overcome Mr. Egan's objections by increasing the amount a few times, whereupon the good healer caved in—and most graciously.

His first lesson drew on knowledge that I already possessed—recognition of wild plants. Mr. Egan sent me out to collect foxglove, *Digitalis purpurea.* I knew it well and I knew where to find it—in hedgerows facing southwest and sometimes a little overhung by the shrubs surrounding it. When I returned, Mr. Egan expressed his pleasure.

"And you didn't get it still green?" he said. "Well, very good."

He then showed me his preparation, which he gave to people with weak hearts. I have undertaken to keep his secrets, and therefore I cannot pass on to the world his excellent remedy for all manner of heart ailment.

"When I started using this first," he told me, "we had a little accident. Well, she was an old lady anyway, and there was a sense in which she had a blessed release. But it taught me never to mix too strong a mixture. And you know, don't you, that you should never eat the foxglove itself? Down you'll go like a stone if you do, straight down dead. Well, experience is the best teacher."

Urtica provided my next quest—the common nettle; I never learned the other half of its botanical name. But through Mr. Egan I did learn of its efficacy in bringing about sleep if mixed in a soup; and of rubbing it on the skin to cure wasp and bee stings. Mr. Egan asked if I knew where to find nettles, and I said that they grow in many places. However, he directed me to the most abundant source of all.

"Outside any house," he said, "find the plot of ground where people empty theirselves and that's where the nettle grows." And, as I told him, I already knew how to pluck a nettle—reach straight for it, grasp the leaf directly, and it will not sting.

One day, we sat outside Mr. Egan's door in the sunshine, mixing his powders and allocating them into his little boxes. ("My boxes," he would exclaim when we traveled, "did I forget my boxes again?"—but he never did.) At noon, a most exotic gentleman arrived. Mr. Egan jumped up to meet him and they had a vigorous and delighted exchange. The man wore a wide scarlet cloth bound tightly about his head, and his mustaches looped like the horns of a foreign ram.

Mr. Egan introduced me. "Mr. O'Brien, come here till you meet my friend and colleague Mr. Juniper Singh."

The man smelt of coconut, and he had a delightful smile. I learned that he supplied Mr. Egan with powdered juniper, whose efficacy contributed much to Mr. Egan's repute; it often proved satisfactory in the release from "the stone." Many Irish people build stones in their kidneys; Mr. Egan takes the opinion that it comes of drinking too much milk.

Juniper Singh agreed: "Yes, very definitely, very very definitely. Much too much milk. And we must not forget—much too much cream."

I shall refer again and again to my seven years with Mr. Egan—they proved enchanting. At the end of it my father said, "Hippocrates is up against it now" and then added, "And so, by the way, is King Croesus."

At which I smiled ruefully, and thanked him mightily, told him that I would prove a credit to him. He said that I already was, that he had been hearing details from all around the countryside as to what a kind healer I was turning out to be, and that several people believed that they owed to me some great improvements in their lives. It was true that I had visited many homes—always, of course, with Mr. Egan. We saw myriad patients with myriad illnesses; some we cured utterly and some less so.

Especially satisfying to me were those cures, as with my ringworm, where everything else had failed. A man in North Cork approached our booth at a cattle fair one day and asked whether we could help cure his throat ailment. He opened his mouth; Mr. Egan looked in, recoiled a little, and then said to me, "Mr. O'Brien, I'd much appreciate your opinion."

I looked in too, and this poor fellow's throat was shining-red raw—how he spoke I do not know. Mr. Egan looked at me inquiringly, and we both pondered for a little time.

"Do you swallow much?" I asked the gentleman. "I mean—outside of when you are eating or drinking?"

Later, Mr. Egan confided that he thought me brilliant for thinking of such a question.

"I have a nervous disposition," said the man. "I swallow a lot even when my mouth is dry, and it's a bit of a habit with me now."

"You mean—when something threatens you or makes you feel uncertain, you swallow."

"And swallow again," said the man. "My wife is a bit on the harsh side."

"Therefore," I deduced, "if you have nothing to swallow, you merely rub the sides of your throat against each other."

So I devised a small piece of iron for him, to keep in his cheek until he recovered from the habit. In other words, I replaced his fears with a greater fear—that of swallowing the iron, which, I told him, he should never be able to pass through his system, and that it would therefore live in him and rust in his body's waters and cause severe illness.

Then we gave him a sage-and-chamomile powder, told him to make it as if making tea, and to gargle with it. Mr. Egan lastly sold him a lavender-and-eucalyptus oil, which the sufferer must rub into the skin of the throat. He went on his way a pleased man and, as the word spread around the fair, we spent the rest of that day overwhelmed with people seeking our skills.

On the easy pathway to his "career" decision—love of the countryside, the wish to discover his nation, the desire to heal—Mr. O'Brien omitted one colorful detail. In his youth he would have seen interesting travelers arrive at his home. Nineteenth-century rural Ireland abounded with itinerants of all kinds. Every country fair, parish, town, and village had a traveling somebody-or-other—herbalist, singer, peddler, storyteller, troupe of actors. Many of these, such as Juniper Singh, had an exotic whiff.

Peddlers, often with their goods on a brightly colored tray or in a gaudy tin box, sold hairpins, bootlaces, cotton thread on reels, cards of elastic, needles, and pins, decks of playing cards. Juniper Singh (whom it has proven impossible to trace) was almost certainly an Indian peddler who got to Ireland via London and Liverpool, and whose exotic appearance formed part of his commercial style. Other itinerants, dressed like Gypsies, told fortunes. "Cross my palm with silver," they said, and, naturally, the more silver coins, the rosier the future.

The healers sold magical oils—hair restorers, "vigor potions" for men, elixirs of love and life. More seriously, they brought cures, which would be discussed long after they had departed. Some claimed to specialize, such as in settling rheumatism or, in Mr. Egan's case, curing ringworm, which was widespread in the rural communities.

Renown went according to efficacy, and fame was available. Certainly the arrival of a healer with a reputation brought an audience. To this day, certain healers—admittedly of the more mystical kind—will pack the halls in some Irish counties. A seventh son of a seventh son is still thought to possess extraordinary powers.

Charles O'Brien made no such quasi-divine claims. He served his time to a man who at least had tried to understand how herbs worked in various treatments. Formal medicine had not been available to the dispossessed Irish peasantry. Therefore, their reliance upon nature and its blessings continued, in part, far into the twentieth century.

His brevity at that moment in his text arose from his great passion. At a point when he might have been expected to write expansively of his healing works and his interest in curing people, he proved impatient to get down on paper what he saw as the main event of his life. Whether from a desire to share it with his putative readers or from a need to objectify it by writing it down and then viewing it, he fairly races to it.

In effect, he withholds the experiences and observations of several years of traveling around Ireland (and major information about his own place in history) in order to begin describing what he considered the crucial moment of his existence.

It is time to introduce the first accounts of the enduring passion at my Life's core. This madness, this obsession, began (as I have earlier stated)

in 1900, on a November afternoon in Paris, and it endures to this day, more than twenty years later.

When my seven-year apprenticeship with Mr. Egan matured and when I—or, rather, my father—had purchased from him my rights to use his many secrets, Mr. Egan and I parted company in a most amicable way and I set out on my own. I was in my twenty-eighth year.

My mentor and teacher had kindly allotted to me many of his patients, some of them ill indeed, and I began my journeys here, there, and everywhere to see them. Mr. Egan and I had undertaken to avoid conflicting our interests at fairs and suchlike—we reached an arrangement whereby I would practice in the North and West in the winter, the South and East in the summer; in his travels, Mr. Egan would reverse this. We joked that we might meet in Athlone, the very center of the country, at the equinoxes of mid-March and mid-September.

My visits seemed to fall out, turn and turn about, in the homes of the native Irish and the Anglo-Irish. They continued in this fashion for a decade—a decade of enjoyable travel and mostly rewarding attention to the ill and the frail. People recommended me to their friends and relations, and often I found myself being handed around in a circle of appreciative connection.

One such circle, when my fame, such as it is, had spread, led me to attend—with great success—Lady Mollie Carew in her summer home at Bantry. (For obvious reasons of taste and discretion, there will be many occasions when I do not reveal the nature of what I was required to address.)

Lady Mollie was a well-traveled woman and a *gourmande;* my herbs and powders allowed her to continue her enjoyment of food on the epic scale that had become her way. During August 1900, I spent a most enjoyable few days with her; we sat on her lawns and watched sea-mist roll up from the Atlantic Ocean on evenings of great balm; she seemed most contented, and we knew great fondness for each other.

In November 1900, then, I received a letter from her, sent to my parents' home in Tipperary. (Fortunately, I had been in Kilkenny and intended to call and see my family, from whom I had been away that year for several months.) She had written to ask urgently whether I could, with my "great powers," discreetly help her "dear friend." If I would journey to Paris, she would provide for me "to meet this great person and I only pray that you shall arrive in time."

For Lady Mollie I would undertake any obligement, and I know that she would be the first to agree that many mutual appreciations have passed between us—but she spurred me further with the name of her friend, which caused me intense excitement. I left home immediately and traveled in a welter of anticipation. By nightfall I was headed to the coast, thence to England, thence by train to Dover, and thence (with a short delay occasioned by fog in the English Channel) to Calais—and at last Paris, where, one morning at eleven o'clock, I presented Lady Mollie's letter of introduction and met my patient.

I was the fifth person in the room that noontide—and one of us became immortal. The visiting doctor, from Her Majesty's Embassy, went home to take luncheon with his wife. Another English gentleman, his face turned away from the rest of us, wept freely—in anticipation, I suspected, of the mourning to come. A nursing attendant came and went, sour as a sloe. And I? I had come to heal the man who grew immortal.

My letter of introduction was taken in hand by the English gentleman, a Mr. Turner, who dried his tears and exclaimed, "Ah, Lady Mollie Carew's healer"—at which point the doctor, I observed, graciously excused himself. I was led forward to the bedside, but could only see my patient from behind—the bed had been turned about in the apartment and faced the window for the sunlight.

Many rooms of infirmity give off an odor—of medicine, of physical failing; in this bedchamber, I caught the scent of lavender.

"He's here," said Mr. Turner to the person in the bed, and stepped aside for me to be greeted, and to greet.

I saw a man in considerable pain, and then I heard a man of unforgettable voice.

"Sir, I have been awaiting your kind skills," said Mr. Oscar Wilde to me—Oscar Fingal O'Flahertie Wills Wilde.

I felt shy, but not intimidated—a man of such perfect manners knows how to put one at ease. He bade me sit beside him and began a pleasant interrogation; he asked me a multitude of questions about my journeys, the people I had met, the cures that I had effected, my family. When I told him that my mother came from the same stock as his great playwriting predecessor Oliver Goldsmith, his eyes lit up.

"Dear Noll," he said. "I was told that he looked like an ape. His appearance was so grotesque that children threw stones at him in the street. I take it that your mother fared better?"

I assured him of her beauty.

Could it be that this remarkable man was to be my patient? His name aroused such passion—of opprobrium and support. He had written one of the most delightful plays in the world, *The Importance of Being Earnest,* which I myself had seen four times. On the heels of this and other great successes, he had then been tormented in three court trials.

I had long known what he looked like—who could have not? His jowled face, his velvet suits, the tapered alabaster hand holding out a flower to the world—these had been every caricaturist's delight.

I said, "Sir, I hope that I may have the honor to do you kindness; please let me take your hand."

A patient's touch writes a message to me; a hand says more than a face; a grip will tell more than a frown. Mr. Wilde had an excellent hand, though a trifle cold; more significantly, he did not confine himself to a passing handshake—he took my hand and held it, and I felt the urgency of his appeal.

His face had become mottled and purple; he had not shaved for many days; his great eyes looked at me like carriage-lamps, with the appeal of a creature seeking help in a desperate way.

"I am in terrible pain," he said, "and I have no money. I cannot tell which of these cuts goes deeper."

"Where does your physical ache hurt?" I asked.

He gestured. On the side of his head farthest from me and therefore until that moment out of my sight, his ear wore a heavy dressing.

"They say that I am deeply infected," he said. "And—" He hesitated; I waited. "I miss my children. I have two boys, you know. They are not allowed to see their papa. They are not allowed to remember him. Do you have a son?"

I shook my head. "Sir, I am a bachelor. Not through wishing to be, but I have not yet found a true love."

"A bachelor is a man with no children to speak of," said Mr. Wilde, and we laughed.

That moment of first inquiry with a patient has a powerful importance. It enables the healer to ask questions that nobody else can broach; it permits the necessary familiarity—intimacy, even—that allows a confidence essential in healing to pass from one to the other and back again.

"Sir, perhaps you will be good enough—if it doesn't tire you too much—to tell me the history of this ailment."

"You know, I do not think that I have ever before seen a man with actually yellow hair," he said. "I assumed it belonged only in mythology."

With that, Mr. Wilde and I began our treatment.

He told me that he had fallen on a stone floor, and that in the fall he had cracked his head. Next morning, he had felt a "whirling" in his ear, and next night it had begun to ache unendurably. I asked what treatments he had so far received, and he said that the only potion he had valued possessed opium, "for dulling all my senses, including pain."

We then talked of his food and drink; he said that his enjoyments had lately shrunk, and that he might accommodate truffles, but "the season and the economies" currently ran against him. Wine still agreed with him—he liked a light southern white wine.

"And to my astonishment," he said, "I find that I like German wines. Do you?"

"Some," I said. "A hock here and there."

"Oh, I like that," he said. "A hock here and there."

I began to take notes.

At four o'clock I returned. With permission from the hotel kitchen, I mixed some herbs in a pot, added a powder of my own devising, which contained alum and potassium (I am not permitted to disclose other ingredients), and set it to cool upon a window-sill. My treatment would commence with an application of this mixture to Mr. Wilde's ear. If I could begin to dry the suppuration, which the dressings scarcely absorbed, then I could address the underlying ailment. I believed that he had suffered an internal perforation in his fall and, due to his unfortunate notoriety, he had been attended to carelessly or not at all.

By the time my mixture had cooled, Mr. Wilde had awakened. The nursing gentleman, Monsieur Hainnen (of whom, regrettably, more later), began to change the dressing, and this afforded me the opportunity of applying my treatment. With great care, I poured the lotion into Mr. Wilde's ear, asking him what, if anything, he felt. Other than a cooling sensation, he told me, he felt nothing. I allowed the lotion to rest a moment or two; he still felt nothing, and I directed M. Hainnen to apply a new dressing.

Mr. Wilde turned to me in a mood of great beseeching.

"I feel no better," he said in a disappointed voice. "And I have such high hopes of you."

"It seems to me," I said, "that in the interest of not adding to your discomfort, I may have under-strengthened the medicine. In the morning, if you feel that no efficacy has taken place, I shall think again. This may take some time."

He took my hand again.

"Cyril and Vyvyan," he said. "Those are my boys. Do you have brothers and sisters?"

"I have a brother named Euclid," I said.

"Oh, splendid!" cried Mr. Oscar Wilde. "Euclid O'Brien! Splendid."

He was the shooting star of his day, and he streaked across the sky from Ireland to England. His father, Sir William Wilde, a Dublin ear, nose, and throat surgeon, after fathering numerous bastards had married an unusual woman, Jane Francesca Elgee, who became a political activist writing under the name Speranza. Oscar was born in the small conduit street of Westland Row in October 1854, the second legitimate child of his father.

Brilliant in school, he shone ever brighter at university, and soon became a student legend. Once, a professor asked him to recite, from the Gospels in Greek, an account of the crucifixion of Christ. Oscar rattled it off—and kept going. The professor repeatedly attempted to interrupt: "Thank you, Mr. Wilde, you have amply demonstrated your knowledge of the text." But Oscar pleaded, "Oh, do let me go on—I want to see how it all ends."

He was too aesthetic for the hearty athletes in Oxford, who came to his rooms to "rag" him; but at six feet three he threw them down the stairs. And later he coshed with a beer mug American miners in a frontier town who'd assumed that the man in the velvet suit reciting verse from the stage of the saloon was a sissy.

Oscar's brilliance flamed through nineteenth-century London. Those who saw him in action at dinner remarked upon the gold of his language, the silver of his tongue. He became a big man in every sense; his appearance matched his performance. He dressed with a dandy's power. A heavy and sensuous face, with a purse of the lips, was overlooked by dense eyelashes, which prodded a later poet to write of his "bees-wing'd eyes."

Energetic as perpetual motion, he turned out poems, plays, articles, and stories of great charm and insight. He could sketch a heart or a garden in a phrase. Devoted to his wife, Constance, and their two small sons, commanded and inspired by his dominating mother, he stood out in the landscape like a pillar of brilliant glass—which shattered.

Oscar had an underlife, in which—perhaps, innocently enough to begin with, and for sheer delight in beauty—he vociferously expressed romantic love for the young Lord Alfred Douglas. "Bosie" was as seductive as silk. He led Oscar down the darker alleyways of London, where rent boys lurked and orgies burned like secret fires in the night.

Bosie's father was the tempestuous Marquis of Queensberry (famous for drafting the safety rules in professional boxing). One day, scandalized by the talk of his son's antics, he left a card in a gentlemen's club, calling Oscar a "somdomite." Perhaps as much for the misspelling as anything else, Oscar sued for libel, then withdrew the case—too late.

He was criminally indicted under the laws of indecency that governed all homosexuality at the time. The jury disagreed, but he was prosecuted yet again and received a merciless two-year sentence in jail. On the railway platforms, as he was transported in chains from London to Reading Gaol, the public spat in the face of this gilded man, whose soul had previously set the world alight.

When Lady Carew summoned Charles O'Brien, Oscar and his friends had already tried many avenues of medicine. Penicillin would have cured him, but it still hid in the future. The ailment proved insusceptible to any medical treatment, and thus Mr. O'Brien was clutched at as, veritably, the last hope.

His description of that first encounter may have been discreet as to the true appearance of Oscar Wilde. All other eyewitness accounts tell of a once-gorgeous man now bloated, jaundiced, a ruin; Oscar was forty-six.

Incidentally, the doctor in question was Dr. Maurice a'Court Tucker, an English doctor in Paris sent, as Mr. O'Brien discovered, to Wilde's bedside by the British ambassador to France.

It will not, I hope, compress my account unacceptably if I tell that, over the next week, I attended Mr. Wilde every day, twice a day—once in the morning to assess the effects of the previous treatment, and again later on to apply a new measure.

On the second Tuesday of our acquaintance, matters disintegrated suddenly and regrettably. As usual, I called upon him in the morning, and now I found him truly desperate. In the previous days, he had become more and more distressed in himself and, wincing with anxiety, he had begun to implore me for different treatments, better results. In the kitchen of the hotel I mixed my strongest potion yet.

Came the afternoon. The morning had already had its difficulties; nobody had told Dr. Tucker that this healer from Ireland had called on Mr. Wilde *every* day. Although I had seen the doctor on my first visit, I had not yet been introduced to him. He always arrived after I had gone. To be plain, educated physicians do not like herbal artists such as myself—to them I am a quack, a charlatan—and this was the first occasion on which Dr. Tucker and I attended our patient at the same time.

I became vaguely aware that today he had brought with him from the British Embassy a young woman; I believe that I heard him murmur to someone, "Mr. Wilde's new companion."

As I approached the bed, Mr. Wilde was being assisted by the nurse, M. Hainnen. This unpleasant and self-important man with pale gray skin had a stiff way of standing that made him look like a dead tree. He now helped the ailing giant into his braided, wine-colored velvet smoking jacket, which looked incongruous over the nightshirt that billowed underneath it. I said that I needed to apply my treatment, and M. Hainnen waved me away. But Mr. Wilde heard me and called out, "In a moment, Mr. O'Brien. We shall do it when I am in my chair."

I stepped back as Dr. Tucker and Mr. Turner then assisted Monsieur Hainnen; and they all half-carried Mr. Wilde to the large chair that gave him a view over the roofs of Paris.

As Hainnen stood aside, having removed Mr. Wilde's dressing, I stepped forward with my flask, ready to pour. I asked the nurse, fairly cheerily, "How's the patient?" and he looked at me coldly; he had bitterly opposed my ministrations of the past days.

"Maladroit! Imbécile!" And having hissed his insults (too cowardly to speak them aloud, lest Mr. Wilde come to my defense), he huffed past me like a train leaving the station. As he did he jolted into me and knocked the flask from my hand to the floor. It did not break—but it did spill the potion I had mixed, which then began to spread across the carpet in a wide smear. Indeed, the nurse had proved the maladroit one.

Hainnen now rushed forward, as did Dr. Tucker, as did Mr. Turner, who skidded a little on the spilt mixture, which, because it had a sulfur base, began to burn a smoking hole in the carpet. Mr. Turner staggered against the wall and put out a hand to save himself, thereby dragging out of true a picture hanging there. All persons, except Mr. Wilde and myself, became alarmed. I retrieved the flask from the floor, but he waved me away.

"I am too ill today, Mr. O'Brien. Come back tomorrow."

Mr. Wilde then gestured to the askew picture; and the young person of whom I had been but dimly aware darted forward. She stepped quickly onto a low chair—and that is how I first gazed upon the woman who became my beloved. Swiftly and with assurance, she adjusted the picture, looked straight into my eyes—I was no more than two few feet from her face—stepped from the chair, and returned to Dr. Tucker's side.

Mr. Wilde assessed the corrected picture, nodded his approval, settled, began to a breathe a little easier—and Dr. Tucker stepped forward.

"Mr. Wilde, you will recall that I offered you some excellent company. May I present her?"

The girl stepped forward, to be in Mr. Wilde's full view. When I saw her face and her entire being I began to feel a strange force around my heart and my eyes. As from a great distance, I heard Mr. Wilde say to Dr. Tucker, "How kind of you to bring me not only beauty but young beauty."

My heart began to thump, my eyes began to blur, and my breath began to catch, as though a hundredweight pressed upon my chest. Mr. Wilde waved a hand to distribute everybody around him. Dr. Tucker introduced a hassock and obliged the girl to sit on it—at Mr. Wilde's feet, so to speak.

"What is your name, child?"

"April Burke."

"Child, one must always ask a lady her age—it thrills her to be given an opportunity to lie."

"I fear that I am no more than eighteen, Mr. Wilde."

"Ahhh!" He sighed like a bellows organ. "Only the young fear being young."

"May I make you comfortable in some way?" she asked. "Shall I read to you?"

Mr. Wilde reached forward, took her hand between his, and reflected.

"Burke?" He played with the word. "Irish, yes? A Norman? A de Burgo was among the first Normans to land in Ireland." He paused, thought for a moment. "You know—I knew of a Burke, an actress. She was as tall as you, though not so blond nor so composed. And her name, her name—" He paused, as if in wonder. "Do you know, child? I believe that her name was also April Burke. Yes! She was"—he spoke it slowly—"Mrs.—Terence—Burke. Yes. But I do recall that her name was April. Oh, my Lord! She vanished, you know—she disappeared. Yes. April Burke. I met her. She was beautiful. As are you, child."

The girl leaned forward to claim his attention. "I believe, Mr. Wilde, that my grandmother was an actress who disappeared."

That afternoon Oscar Wilde gave his last performance. Delivered in private, it changed two people's worlds forever, and the echoes have been resounding across my life for the decades since.

In 1900, Queen Victoria was still on the throne. The British Empire had redrawn the map of the world. And the name Oscar Wilde remained a synonym for disgrace. Other than the two agonized masterpieces inspired by prison, *De Profundis* and *The Ballad of Reading Gaol,* Wilde scarcely wrote again.

After his release, he became a lumbering, pained wanderer. He turned up in towns and villages across Europe, approaching people for free meals in return for telling them what he called "the extraordinary story of my life." And he never condemned the man who brought him down, Lord Alfred Douglas, the dreadful Bosie, disliked by all who knew him—except, fatally, Oscar.

When Constance Wilde discovered that, after prison, Oscar had once again had a meeting with Bosie, she divorced him. She changed their children's surname to Holland—and she died, of spinal cancer, in 1898, a few months after Oscar was released.

Oscar fell like Lucifer tumbled out of Paradise. This was a man who had changed the meaning of the word "style." He believed that creativity applies all across life. If one is artistic, he insisted, one should not be afraid to let the world see it—in dress, actions, household, presence. That was "style." Now he lay in a room whose decor he famously disliked, desperately seeking any kind of help to stop his body from closing down, and having a last fillip of glory from nothing more than the memory of an actress he had once fleetingly met, and theatrical gossip he had once heard.

Oscar *gave* all the time—he gave in talk, in story, in money, in suffering. His impact on the theater and its practitioners was enormous, and continues. The world still flocks to *Lady Windermere's Fan,* to *An Ideal Husband,* and above all to *The Importance of Being Earnest.* Any English-speaking school that attempts drama has been bound to consider him in its repertoire. Many of his plays have had more than one production for the screen.

Those who knew him said that Wilde seemed incapable of being dull (which was, of course, his greatest fear). Before he died, distraught and reduced as he was, he could still have a profound effect on those around him. Charles O'Brien saw that, and said as much: Oscar's "last performance," he observes, "changed two people's worlds forever." To this day, Oscar Fingal O'Flahertie Wills Wilde affects all who consider him. Largely redeemed by history, and liberated in the huge advances of moral tolerance, he became even more influential after his death.

The great man became animated; he sat higher in his chair. Dr. Tucker smiled in approval at his young *protégée;* this was exactly what he had hoped she would do—cheer up the patient by listening to him, encourage him, attend him with her eyes and ears.

"Now I remember! Yes, April Burke, she had dark eyes like Constance. Constance was my wife. Dark eyes like you. Yes, oh, I recall it all now."

April Burke said, "Please tell me about her."

I felt myself tremble; a sweat began cooling my hot neck. Her face seemed to be alight. Without yet knowing that I had done so, I had determined that this was the woman who would make me safe, who would make me aspire to—and reach—greatness.

Taking his hands back from the young woman's, Mr. Wilde spread them in an Italian gesture and began.

"When I met her, she had come down from Belfast, part of a troupe that played the cities and big towns for most of the year. I was barely twenty-one; I had been visiting my mother in Dublin and had gone to Jammet's Restaurant with two friends to eat snails. She came in—no, she entered; yes, "entered" is the word. She had the true gift of drama, which is knowing how to gain immediate and universal attention.

"Of the people with her, I recognized a fellow called Fallon, who introduced me to your grandmother and said, 'This is Mrs. Burke. She is greater than Sarah Bernhardt.' And, my dear child, she was enchanting.

We spoke only for a moment, and yet for days I continued to think about her; and even though I do not wish to dwell upon this, she had something of Miss Bernhardt's background, or so it was said."

Now more comfortable, he warmed up his story. It appears that he had continued to make inquiries about the beautiful actress for many years—and needed to, because her story had such strangeness in it.

April Burke the First (as Mr. Wilde now called her) had been born in County Limerick, along the river Shannon's banks in a place called Parteen. In those days, and indeed even in 1900, actresses often ranked no higher than courtesans. It seems that, with very considerable bravery, April Burke the First took her beauty to the stage, where she sang and danced in all manner of companies. Here, I shall try to replicate the richness of Mr. Wilde's narration as he told the grandmother's story to the unknowing but glowing granddaughter.

She had an elegance of movement; her walk was a glide. And being a gifted actress, she had the same elegance in her hands too, and her arms. She gestured much when she spoke, and her gestures added the commas and brackets to her physical conversation. I remember her eyes—so much like your eyes, child, that deep softness of brown velvet. She had a long nose, not so retroussé as yours, not so tip-tilted, and with not the same curve at the end of the nostrils. Her lips had some but not all of your voluptuousness. And she had your smile, a wonderful, curving slice of joy. Nothing pleases a man so much as a woman's smile, particularly if she wants something from him.

Next day, I wrote to this Mrs. Burke at the theater in which she was appearing. I had to leave for London, but my mail was being sent onward to me. For days, then weeks, I waited for the favor of a reply, but none came—an unthinkable matter in those days of good manners. My life naturally took me over, and even though I never forgot that luminescent encounter, I did not pursue her as actively as I wished I had done.

Some years later, I wrote a play in which she would have been perfectly suited—like you, child, she had the willowy height, the abundant hair, the force of presence. I made inquiries about this beautiful Mrs. Burke and found that, even though nobody could offer any proof of anything surrounding her, a tale had begun to grow up—a tale of passion and sorrow and lives interrupted and Life turned violently around.

It appears that her husband, Terence Burke, owned a large estate in Tipperary, a county with which, as with so many others, I am unfamiliar. Mr. Burke had fallen in love with his actress in a frightful village hall, where she performed extracts from Shakespeare. Smitten to his heart, Mr. Burke pursued her, taking his carriage across the country to see her every performance.

After many such journeys, over many months, she finally agreed to marry him—I am given to understand that the winning note was sounded when he promised to build a theater in his house for her. And he did—he built a fully equipped theater seating one hundred people. When the last nail had been hammered into place, Terence Burke made this beautiful woman his wife. Part of the marriage bargain was that she should return to the stage for some time.

But another part of her bargain with Mr. Burke said that after a number of years she would retire and have children. And she did retire, and I believe that a son was born—in the great house.

Now the story's thread begins to fray. As I have heard it, when Mrs. Burke concluded her confinement and when doctor and midwife pronounced her fit and well, her husband came to see her, to receive and admire his son and heir. She is said to have handed him the child in the confinement room, showed him also the nursery that had been prepared, and slipped quietly out of the room, never to return.

But I have also heard that before her husband came to see his son, Mrs. Burke had received, in conditions of great secrecy, another visitor. This person, a handsome lady, quite exotic, had bribed the midwife to permit her entry to the confinement room through the servants' quarters. And I have heard that, after exhibiting signs of great distress at this stranger's arrival, Mrs. Burke, the beautiful actress, crept away with this creature that night.

Mr. Burke, understandably distraught, arranged for a great hunt to be mounted. He called upon all his rich friends and they assembled militias of searchers, but the beautiful fugitive was never found. She had quite simply vanished.

Soon after, the unfortunate man, having lost his wife in the worst way of all—by which I mean, to circumstances that remained inexplicable—died of natural causes. He was found—I could not have written it better myself—on the stage of his own theater in his own castle; he had suffered an apoplexy. The child disappeared, and I have no knowledge of the estate's resolution; I heard that lawyers closed the house up after his death, and that it lies disused. I expect it has fallen into the hands of the probate courts. Which must be a shame—I recall hearing that the house may have been one of the most beautiful in Europe, and therefore in the world.

And that, child, is the story, as I know it, of the beautiful Mrs. Terence Burke. Indeed, I recalled the plight of her child when I was writing the character of Jack Worthing in *The Importance of Being Earnest*—Jack, you remember, was found in a handbag.

During this narrative the room had fallen still. Outside the window, the hooves of Paris clopped by; I could see a gaunt tree on which a few leaves continued to cling. My mind ricocheted between the young woman before me and the house whose enchanted turrets I had seen across the fields since my first awareness—a place that indeed lay disused and disputed. I longed to burst forward and tell how Tipperary Castle had been in my eyes since birth—but Mr. Wilde had grown tired. He sagged in his chair, and his hands dropped from the many operatic gestures which he had employed to tell the tale. His brain had not yet dulled, and he had one last—and, for me, consuming—thought to offer.

"Do you find it curious, child, that so much of you resembles the leading lady in this drama?"

Her eyes had never left Mr. Wilde's face. Of all the people there she had been the one most affected by what was narrated, and so had given Mr. Wilde the audience every man craves: a beautiful, attentive, and appreciative listener. She extracted herself from her reverie.

"Mr. Wilde, I am the only child of—" She paused, and her hands became a knot. "A man named Terence Burke. That is my father's name."

"How old is your father?"

"I do not know."

"How much do you know of his antecedents?"

"Very little."

"Does not your mother know? I find women much more inquisitive about breeding."

"She died when I was very young."

"Then, dear child, might it not be the case that you are the sole heir to a great Irish estate? A mixed blessing, perhaps?"

Like the novels of the nineteenth century, Victorian Ireland abounded with spectacular tales of crazy inheritance. They were crazed by the law and its labyrinthine complications; crazed by the disputes of politics; crazed by estates left aslant and unused when their bachelor owners failed to return from a war or two; crazed by medieval practices such as "entail"—a law under which women had no right to inherit.

Tipperary Castle, as Oscar Wilde sensed, had all the potential for intrigue. He was a dramatist by profession, and therefore needed no proof that the girl sitting before him was the granddaughter of the vanished actress.

But who, if anyone, had inherited the place? Did those who reared or represented the infant Terence Burke ever attempt to recover the inheritance? Even if they knew of it, who would have taken on such a task, given the news in Ireland? Assassinations, cudgelings, fires, boycotts—every possible means had been tried to intimidate the English landlords.

And for those who chose not to live among such risks, it grew even worse. When absentees failed, year after year, to return for any length of residency, their hold on their properties became less and less secure. Soon their great houses stood hollow and all but abandoned. The law was supposed to help, as were the authorities. But when a neighbor allowed his goats or cattle to slip through unkept fences in order to graze bigger fields, no amount of law helped.

Estates fell down. Local merrymakers broke into the empty big houses. They danced in the hollow-sounding ballrooms. They disported themselves upon the furniture. They poked fun at the marble and bronze statues. They defaced the paintings that still hung on the walls. Therefore it could not be surprising if nobody had spoken up for the infant Terence Burke when he reached an age at which he could inherit.

Mr. O'Brien admits that he didn't intervene during Oscar Wilde's tale. He had enough on his plate. Perhaps he was still embarrassed over the spilled medicine. Also, he was being smitten by April Burke. And he surely knew or sensed that his distinguished patient was near to death and that he had failed to help him. Without question, however, the O'Brien family must have known a great deal about Tipperary Castle and must have spent years speculating upon its future; they were the estate's closest neighbors.

On Saturday morning, the first of December, I was sitting in the Café Beauregard, near the Pont-Saint-Michel, when the word came in that Mr. Wilde had died. This gave me the opportunity that I had so far been denied; I had gone back to the Hôtel d'Alsace, had not dared to go in, and had lurked about in the hope that I might meet April Burke again, but I never saw her.

When I announced in the café that I had known Mr. Wilde, and indeed had been one of the *médecins* attending him, I became the center of attention. Through this celebrity I gained much free coffee and cognac; more crucially, I gathered the details that, following a Requiem Mass in Saint-Germain-des-Prés, my beloved patient would be buried in the cemetery at Bagneux.

I attended both. The Mass was said by a fellow-Irishman, a priest from Dublin, a Father Dunne, but I saw no sign in the church of April Burke. Nor did I see Dr. Tucker. Four carriages followed the hearse; since the first appeared overcrowded, I assessed the second. It seemed to have been allocated to the clergy, which consisted of the priest and an altar-boy. This left plenty of room for me, and my tragic expression easily got me on board.

I rode to Bagneux in a silence that Father Dunne must have taken for grief; and the priest, though he looked at me sharply, asked no question.

Far from grief, however, I was obsessed with the prospect that I might meet April again, and consumed with anxiety as to what I must do should she not be there.

She was there! Much credit falls to her and Dr. Tucker that they did not take part in the unseemly wrestlings by the graveside. Several gentlemen attempted to gain the frontmost position at the prayers over the coffin—one dandy almost fell into the grave—and some time elapsed before order could be restored.

I watched April and her conduct. Standing a little way back from the main press of people, she wore a long black coat and had some white lace at her throat; her hat, small and shapely, served to heighten her beauty, especially as its veil did not quite cover her face. She behaved demurely, with downcast eyes and hands appropriately clasped.

When the funeral ended, the mourners dispersed loosely and moved along the narrow rows of graves to the gates. I walked too, watching for a chance to speak to Miss Burke.

The carriage in which she and Dr. Tucker had come to the funeral stood a little distance away from the others. Someone claimed Dr. Tucker's attention for a moment and April strode on. This gave me an opportunity; I walked briskly after her. When I drew level, she glanced at me and started.

"Oh, I thought you were Dr. Tucker."

I said, "My pathway never formalized my medical skills. But you and I have been in the same sick-room."

She stopped. "Have we?" She lifted her veil to look at me.

"Mr. Wilde was my patient—I am grieving for him."

April then jumped back from me by two or three feet.

"But you're O'Brien? The quack?"

"Yes. No."

The fact that she had stepped back enabled me to take a fully close view of her face. Tall and glorious, she seemed to me perfect—an improvement on Mr. Wilde's laudatory description of her grandmother the vanished actress.

"I have great skills as an herbalist."

"I do not wish to associate with you."

"Mr. Wilde liked me."

"You must excuse me——"

"I have never seen a creature as beautiful as you," I began, in a speech that I had prepared. "I have seen butterflies, I have seen kingfishers, I have seen hummingbirds——"

"Please go away from me," she said.

"May I see you one day? May I walk with you in the Champs-Élysées?"

"No. Please—I must go."

She had more maturity and firmness than I could have expected—a great deal more composure than I'd had at eighteen.

Walking after her, I declaimed, "My name is Charles O'Brien. I am a rounded Irishman in that, by virtue of my birth, I am welcome among the aristocracy and the peasantry, and I know not which I prefer. I delight in the Ascendancy's taste, and I thrill to the common people's wit. Surely I can be of use to you in your retrieval of your ancestral home—a place which I have known since I was born? My family, madam—we *live* beside it."

She said, without turning around, "Shall I have truck with a fortune-hunter? No. And sir, your clothing—it is, it is—unclean."

"I have been in mourning for Mr. Wilde and neglected to take care of my linen."

"I must go."

"I heard Mr. Wilde's story of your grandmother." My foot caught the edge of a grave, and I almost fell.

"What makes you think I will try to recover that estate?"

"All beautiful women need property—they must have something other than themselves to decorate."

"Sir, now you try to ape poor Mr. Wilde. You dismay me."

She reached her carriage and climbed in; I stood by, not knowing what to do. Behind me I heard the patter of footsteps, and then Dr. Tucker walked past me, looking at me sidelong all the while but never raising his hat to me. When he too had clambered into the carriage, the coachman immediately drove away.

I was still in possession of considerable funds from a card game that I had lately entered in Pigalle, so I prevailed upon the carriage with Father Dunne and the altar-boy to go back into Paris by means of the same route. From time to time I glanced ahead out of the window and eventually, at the corner of the Rue Seminole, I saw Dr. Tucker's carriage turn and stop. The two occupants emerged and climbed the steps to one of the distinguished houses, where Dr. Tucker used a key—I had found where she lived!

That night at dinner, I pondered the events of the day and consequently drank too much wine. I had genuinely liked Mr. Wilde, and I also knew that this young woman had captivated me—in the fullest sense of that word, she had taken me captive. My room on the Rue du Bac looked out on the street, and after dinner I sat at my window.

As the wine wore off I began to weep—at the puzzle of the thing, at the insult. I have never borne malice to another human, I have never willfully attempted to do anything but be helpful and considerate—and tell the truth. But I had somehow, it seems, gathered an offensive reputation in her eyes, and I knew not why.

When I had wiped away my tears and recovered from my loneliness, I found courage. I told myself that I would pursue April Burke diligently until she acquired the sense and understanding to soften toward me. And that night I wrote the tale to Lady Mollie, who understands and admires passion, and who would surely counsel me.

The Wilde funeral became notorious. As Mr. O'Brien describes, men wrestled for prominence in the cemetery at Bagneux. This was a less than prestigious burial—but better than it might have been. Oscar Wilde had committed an offense under French law by registering in a false name at the Hôtel d'Alsace. In fear of taunts and abuse he had been wandering Europe as "Sebastian Melmoth."

He died of encephalitic meningitis (although some insist that he had syphilis). And he died as he had lived—beyond his means (as he said), much loved, and in conflict. He told a journalist friend that he and the wallpaper were "fighting a duel to the death. One or the other of us has to go."

Oscar's rooms in the Hôtel d'Alsace had become a combination of debtors' prison and shrine; he owed money everywhere. But, as ever, he also attracted unsought acts of kindness. The hotel's proprietor, Jean Dupoirier, without Oscar's knowledge, and aware that the writer was dying, gave substantial credit. In today's terms the bill ran into thousands, and Dupoirier personally ordered extra luxuries, and such medicines and liniments as Dr. Tucker wished to see be employed. Dupoirier's kitchen, as with so many small hotels in Paris, was not equipped for anything more substantial than breakfast, so the hotelier also paid for the meals that were brought in every day from nearby restaurants—they were ordered regardless of costs, and for all Oscar's friends too.

And had it not been for the interventions of his friends, Oscar's body might have been taken to the public morgue. Instead of being laid out in beauty, he might have been given a pauper's grave. As it was, he received a "sixth-class burial" in the Cimetière de Bagneux, which is actually in Montrouge, a southern suburb of Paris.

Nine years later, the body was removed to the celebrity graveyard of Père-Lachaise, where the grave became and remains a place of pilgrimage. The marble stone is stained with red and pink marks; it is a tradition to wear lipstick when kissing the grave. His epitaph consists of four lines from his own poem *The Ballad of Reading Gaol:*

> And alien tears will fill for him
> Pity's long-broken urn,
> For his mourners will be outcast men
> And outcasts always mourn.

In Ireland, rumors flew that "Wilde the pervert" had repented of everything on his deathbed—and converted to Catholicism. Father Cuthbert Dunne, who officiated at the funeral, had certainly been called. It is also true that Oscar had long professed more than a passing interest in Catholicism; he loved liturgy, rubric, and the theater of religion.

Sadly, Death had traveled fast, and at the end, Charles O'Brien no longer had access to Wilde's sickroom. If he had been present, all the conflicted reports about Oscar's death, his last words and whether he took the rites of the Catholic Church, could have been cleared up. However, Mr. O'Brien might not have been the most reliable of reporters, given his sudden infatuation and the bluntness of its object's rejection.

Courage: that is the word by which I guide myself, the star by which I steer. Next morning, I rose early and walked briskly across Paris to inspect the Rue Seminole. A cul-de-sac, it offered certain difficulties in terms of patrolling without being observed; I could get out only by the way I came in. Nor could I linger and watch Dr. Tucker's house; I should immediately be seen, as very few people came and went in that street— the rich stay indoors for long hours.

My vigil never flagged. Dr. Tucker's life, I reflected, must be governed by exceptional order; other than grocers, butchers, and other deliverers, nobody came to his door. Eventually, I was justified when, at three o'clock in the afternoon, the door opened and out, alone, strode April Burke. I concealed myself by walking slowly on the opposite side of the street, in the same direction, head averted and eyes down, until she had passed by, in a long stride.

Soon, she had more than a hundred yards' start on me. This proved to be a good fact in that she did not look behind, a bad fact in that I had no easy chance to intercept her. I possess long legs, but my goodness how she raced! Presently, I began to understand her destination: she was bound for Her Majesty's Ambassadorial building on the Faubourg Saint-Honoré. In due course, she entered the magnificent place and I remained outside.

Estimating that she might be in there for some time, I sought a café. Not that I dallied long; I could not see the building, so I hurried my coffee and cognac. On the way back, I passed a stall selling pretty little manikins and I bought one, as a whimsical gift.

By the time April reappeared, I had planned what to do. Head down,

I would stride busily along the street and overtake her; I knew that this would require me to walk extremely fast, but I reasoned that this would merely convey an air of added industry.

Fortune favored me; April walked toward me, and I was able to create a great impression of surprise.

"My goodness!" I cried as I halted almost alongside.

She stopped and within half a second recalled me.

"Oh, Jehovah!" she said, in a tone of great irritation. I raised my hat.

"How wonderful to see you again," I said. "I haven't yet left Paris."

"Really? Do you say? Are you still here?" She began to step away from me.

Sarcasm ill becomes most people; it is best to pretend that it has not appeared.

"And how are you? So fortunate to have met you—in fact, I have just taken delivery of a gift I have purchased for you; that is why I happen to be in this neighborhood."

"Gift?" She frowned in suspicion.

I handed her the doll, which she unwrapped.

"It is a doll."

She looked at it. "You have not 'just taken delivery'—you bought this for a few centimes from that old crook at the corner of the Rue Napoléon."

She threw the doll into the street.

"Please," I said as she turned and strode away. "Are there no circumstances in which I may be of service to you?"

"None."

I followed. "Is there no care that I can give you?"

"None."

"Are you not too harsh upon me?"

"No."

"I am sad," I said, and the note in my voice caught her.

"Are you to follow me like a puppy dog everywhere I go?"

"If I am to gain your kind attention I will go anywhere," I said.

"Then go back to Ireland; go back to your bogs."

"But how will that gain your attention?"

She looked at me, those strong brown eyes beneath that abundant hair.

"I cannot stop you from walking in the streets. But I can stop you from following me around. If I have to."

"May I see you tomorrow?" Perhaps the note of entreaty in my voice softened her, because when she spoke her voice had a resigned tone.

"Doubtless you will. So—may I now walk home? Alone?"

I took off my hat like a musketeer and bowed deep and low. April, still looking warily at me, walked on—and stepped fruitily into a dog mess.

"Ohhh!" She held up her foot with the soiled shoe. "Look! You did this."

"No, I believe it was a dog."

"Ohhh!"

April Burke had a friend in Ireland, Mrs. Katherine Moore, whose brother had been an old friend of April Burke's father. Mrs. Moore had become something of a confidante to the motherless girl, who wrote many revealing letters to her, including one sent from Paris late in December 1900.

> *My dear Kitty,*
> *Please forgive the brevity of my last letter; I was sad when I wrote it,*
> *and I remain so. I know now that my sadness was caused by more*
> *than the loss of dear Mr. Wilde, whom I scarcely had met, but who*
> *had reached directly to my heart in a brief time.*
>
> *You asked me for a complete description of Mr. Wilde in his end*
> *of days. I find that I may be too much moved to tell you competently.*
> *He wept much. Was this pain? Yes, but also pain in his heart,*
> *I think. He grieved for his sons.*
>
> *His rooms grew very still in his last week. I bathed his hands*
> *often, and this seemed to calm him. He surged in his bed and was*
> *most restless and spoke not much sense. Twice on his second-to-last*
> *day, he called me to him. Each time, he said the same words. "Be*

sure to keep beauty preserved." I am sure that I do not know what he meant by this. He had been most flattering to me, but I think he meant a greater matter than mere compliment.

When I last saw him, hours before his passing, he perspired much. I felt so inadequate to his needs; I bathed his face with cool towels and he felt it not. All his friends had gathered, and I never saw men so moved, so sad, so quiet, and I wish never to observe such sorrow again.

Your friend, Mr. Ross—indeed, as you say, a dear and gentle man—held Mr. Wilde's hand and said over and over, "Oscar, we love you, we love you very much." Mr. Wilde had spoken quietly to Mr. Ross too, regarding the late Mrs. Wilde and their sons. Both men wept.

Now, dearest Kitty, I have a request of you. I was accosted in Paris by a strange man—a big Irish fellow, with, I confess, a light in his eyes and a deep voice. His name is Charles O'Brien—do you know him? He may live near you, for all I know. Even though he seems to have well-trained manners, I am given an impression that he may be quite dangerous. He attended Mr. Wilde as a healer and much havoc ensued. Certainly he is unsteady and keeps himself not very clean.

I should be most grateful for any knowledge of this fellow, as I fear that he may become a difficulty to me and I know not yet how I should address it. In Paris he followed me so assiduously that Dr. Tucker, who was most put out by him, had to send for the authorities. O'Brien came to Mr. Wilde's room, I believe, through a friend of Mr. Ross, a Lady Carew; do you know her?

My work at the Ministry will begin on Monday, the 7th of January; and Papa is to cease working for Mr. Whitbread at the end of the year, and so will spend all his days at home. I am pleased that he shall have some rest; and I am pleased on the double that I shall have more of his company.

We have a new maid, from Ireland. She is young and inexperienced, but she may prove quick to train, and she speaks interestingly. Now that I am quitting Paris, and that my duties

*should prove more regular, I shall be able to write again when
I have settled back in London.*

*Your affectionate friend,
April.*

A note may be required here as to Charles O'Brien's view of himself. Perhaps as a matter of personal style, he seems never to acknowledge how his efforts or presence may be seen. Not only did the treatments of Oscar Wilde fail to work, but even on his own account he was mixing herbal potions that contained the possibility of serious burns. If he did so much damage to the carpet, what might he have done to the man he had come to heal?

As to his reception by Miss Burke—first of all, he more or less sprang upon her, and she was a girl who might never have spoken unchaperoned to a man who was not a relation or close family friend.

Secondly, judging from her correspondence—a kinder tone than she showed to Mr. O'Brien—his appearance obviously gave her cause for concern. This is puzzling, given Mr. O'Brien's cultivated background. She saw in front of her (or thought she saw) a fearsome stereotype, with embellishments. A wild Irishman with a mop of yellow hair who had almost burned a hole in the head of Oscar Wilde was now apparently pursuing her. Not only did he want to get his hands on her heart, he was also chasing her possible inheritance—of which she had just recently heard so vividly.

From my Journal:

MONDAY, DECEMBER THE 17TH 1900.

Such a cold night, yet the stars have magnificence. I sit on the deck of a steamer awaiting clearance to leave the port of Rotterdam. In a moment we shall be under way again and I shall reach home for Christmas. How I wish I could have remained in Paris, but I had little choice. I am very mournful. Now I hope that the company of my parents, and Euclid's wit and affection, and the animals in the yard, and the clouds in Tipperary will mend me, will heal this racking cough and this sad heart, and will give me time to reconsider my approaches to my future.

I shall leave it for my Journal to reflect my melancholia of the moment; and I shall content myself here with the repeated expression of surprise that Miss Burke took so furiously against me. What occasioned her contempt? Do I carry a mark upon my forehead? Has somebody spoken against me? It is a mystery that a young woman should take so against a man she has never before known.

When I reached home, I decided to tell the whole story, and I can truly say that I have never captured my family's earnest attention so completely as on that first night at dinner. They listened, with no more than an occasional interjection, and they listened with attitudes of great sympathy. When I had finished, Euclid, red with anger, asked the first question.

"Do you think she is dangerous? Might she carry a stiletto?"

Mother said, "This is a young woman who has not yet learned to care for herself, has only been trained to care for others."

Said my father, "Was Wilde as tall as people said?"

"Indeed," I said. "As tall as you and me."

"Goodness," said both my parents. Then began the advice.

"Go and find her," said Mother.

Euclid: "I shall make maps of London and Paris for you."

My father said, "Go and look at the estate."

He confirmed that in general Mr. Wilde's story of Tipperary Castle's fate had been what he understood, too, that there had been, as he said, "some old story; my father knew it. The lawyers go up there every few years and look at the place. And we rent conacre from them, when we need extra fields."

When turbulent, I try to step back and view myself. To this end, I soon found myself walking in our wood, in mid-winter, though in mild weather, and in turmoil. Captain Ferguson's plantings had allowed for the seasons, and many orchidaceous blooms gleamed like colorful lamps among the bare trees.

That morning, I saw a sad man no longer young, wrapped in an oatmeal-colored tweed ulster, and wearing tan boots and gloves. Hatless, his thick yellow hair flew back from his forehead in all directions, and as he walked he clapped his hands together and talked aloud to himself: "Learn from what has happened!"

My mother and brother had said that I must go and find April—but I knew not where or how. And my own father—whose advice on life ultimately seemed best fitted to my nature—spoke only of the estate. I found that Father had the best proposal; if I could not as yet associate with the object of my desire, perhaps a visit to the inanimate would inspire me. I strode from the wood and saddled Della.

Charles O'Brien makes it difficult to judge him. At the age of forty he seems not to have made any permanent relationship or experienced significant romantic liaisons. Judging from the tone of his utterances regarding April Burke, if there had been a notable love affair, or even a passing romance, he would almost certainly have mentioned it—unless he was practicing discretion.

Does this mean that he had known no strong feelings for any woman until he reached the age of forty? Or ever felt a desire to settle down? His connection with his parental home seems never to have dimmed. It remained his major port of call—as witnessed by the fact that after the cruelty of Paris he made straight for home and took solace there. Nor did he keep many secrets from his parents. He confided his feelings to the entire family and listened to their advice.

Overall, though, a picture is forming. In 1898, Auguste Rodin unveiled his controversial statue of Balzac. It showed the novelist as a figure of some giantism. Wrapped in his robe, he stands huddled against the world, eyes deep-set, head held proud, his mane of hair a plaything of the breeze. Rodin gave Balzac more than a hint of Beethoven. The statue has bulk, and a ferocity of withdrawal, a denial of the world; this is a big man, somewhat preoccupied and defiant.

Charles O'Brien may have had none of Balzac's rage against the world, nor his frantic industry. Nor did he have Balzac's—or Beethoven's—desperation to write as much as he could as often as he could. He does, however, have a touch of the same "square peg" syndrome—but he has no great sense of it, no anguish at his own misfittingness.

And he does have the same hint of inner torture—which then escalated sharply under Miss Burke's brusque contempt. Also, in those early pages of his text, he defines a major chasm between how people perceive him and how he thinks they see him.

Who, therefore, was the real Charles O'Brien, and in which direction would he develop? Was he an undeveloped man with character blemishes or an amiable figure like his father? We are about to discover the key that will unlock him.

From years of local knowledge, imbibed unknowingly, I had the impression that Tipperary Castle touched deeply all who saw it. Not many knew of its existence, but those who had heard of it, who had traveled there in search of its legend and then found it, sighed with surprise and pleasure. It exceeded, I understood, what they had expected from the hearsay.

Many local people already knew the house's effect and visited it regularly; a number of them went there often, along their own paths through the wood or by the lake shore, simply to gaze.

Strangers discovered the place in the old formal way that was once open to all. First they struggled through an overgrown gate serene with lions on the pillars, then walked half a mile of a graveled avenue that had once been planted either side with great beauties of trees and flowering shrubs. Then, around a long, gentle corner, the house appeared—at the top of a slope, with green fields leading up to its forecourts. My mood, as I rode, varied between somber and gay. Would I be further cast down that I could not bring this estate into my life? Or would its sight fire me, inspire me, and in some mysterious fashion teach me the way forward?

I succeeded in opening part of the old gate sufficiently wide to lead Della through, and then I remounted. The avenue was quiet, save for a rustle here and there as a small animal slipped away from the intruding hooves. Then I rounded the corner—and gasped.

It commanded total attention, a full halt to take in its splendor. Who had ever seen such a building, such grandeur, such romantic mystery, except in the pages of a child's story-book? From a distance the house looked steady and intact, and the towers had such authority; the walls so strong, the terraces so wide, so generous, the little bridge so sound and firm. I had been here once before as a boy of twelve or so; but this view far excelled that memory.

The construction of the house had been famously sturdy; therefore ruin had entered with caution and it advanced only slowly. Shales of glinting slate held many blue-black expanses of the roof together, and the square eastern tower stood completely intact, with its battlements like rows of teeth.

A great front door stood askew within its frame, leaning as though it had a hand on its hip. It seemed barred in some way from inside. I remembered Father telling us that the timber had been so massive it took six men, using ramps and wedges, to hold the door in place while the carpenters hung it on hinges that were almost six feet deep; they secured it with nails seven inches long that they had fashioned at the site.

My father had told me not to expect too much from the place—he'd said he feared that damage must have been accumulating. From what I now saw, his fears were not justified. In the empty times after the owner's fate, local men had tried to plunder the house by entering through the door—but they had merely forced it partly off one hinge and then had to walk away, irked at the door's victory. They'd never tried again, preferring to talk about their defeat in terms of the door's heroic stature; it had, after all, been built and hung by their grandfathers. Lawyers (as I would learn) had then come by and established iron bars to secure the door further.

The stonework showed no wear and tear. In the construction, the blocks of limestone had been hewed in delicacy or roughness according to their places in the house. Where the finish needed to be robust, on corners and buttresses, the stone had been cut like tweed; on the decorated cornices it looked smooth as silk.

Many of the windows had received elegant and pointed arches; not so crude as Gothic, they gave the impression of having been built for ladies looking out of their boudoirs to see what gentleman might come riding hard across the fields to carry them away. On several walls, window-slits had been inserted—a whimsy on the owner's part, since bows and arrows no longer played a part in defense of a castle when these walls were being built.

And that, I surmised, had been the point of the creators: to make a house like a legendary palace, but with all the warmth of a home. This success of temperament must have made even the house's enemies— hostile tenants, would-be owners—gaze with wonder when they stood in the overgrown avenue. At the end of the march of one hundred beeches, amid gnarled cherry trees and sprawling, uncontrolled espaliers, the layers of stone rose one above another like a child's wooden blocks.

I could imagine walking those grass terraces, giving the Orders of the Day to my steward. My wife, April, could stand in the great—now restored—doorway, welcoming family and friends. A girl—our daughter, Amelia—might stand at her window and let her hair down, like Rapunzel. Our son, Bernard Euclid Terence Oscar, could roam the ramparts and spy through the archery slits, preparing to repel invaders. And, as an entire family, we could walk down to the lake after breakfast on summer mornings and stand on the little stone bridge, talking to the swans.

When I looked at the mountains in the distance, the Galtees, and the peak Galteemore, they were blue as the sky on this winter day; and with the terraced fields and gray sunken stone fences leading down to the lake, and the slopes on the far side climbing up into the beech and ash woods, no other estate in Ireland could have granted as much to the beholder. Here was peace indeed—here was beauty and light. This place, I told myself, is where I belong; I knew not why, but I felt it to be as true as the beating of my heart.

One last observation called me; my father had mentioned that Mr. Terence Burke had locked the theater when his wife vanished. Its fortifications had proven so strong that nobody had been known to breach it, not even the most disrespectful of the local men. I found the doors through which the audience should have entered, and I located the more discreet access marked "Actors"; all felt as though they had been secured from the inside with bolted cords of wood.

I walked back to the ramparts. The unfortunate Terence Burke (how I felt for him!) had taken the structure erected by his ancestors and increased it in wonders until it became as marvelous as a poem. If love and passion can be measured in stonework, the woman who married here had been loved with one of the greatest passions ever felt in a human heart. How matters run in families!

Down the faded avenue, I looked back from my saddle. The house seemed different—and I know how often the face of a beautiful woman changes. I called out, "Halloo! Halloo!"—and the house gave me back my own voice, a sure sign of emptiness. Firmly I vowed that I would make it echo to laughter, and words of love and joy. I received such force of optimism from this idea that I galloped Della all the way home.

The Anglo-Irish houses often excelled the châteaux of the Loire, the palazzi of the Italians, the country seats of the English and Scots. Their occupants lived up to the style. Few societies had as much eccentricity as the Anglo-Irish or lived so incomparably fast a life. They rode to hounds, they played tennis, they staged theatricals, they built inventions—such as the huge telescope at Birr Castle. On their terraces strutted peacocks; along the eaves squatted fantail pigeons; in their fields rose the brilliant tails of pheasants.

Some tastes were much stronger. Sir Henry Bellingham of Castlebellingham, in County Louth, employed a man to do nothing else but rake over the gravel after anyone had walked on it. Lord Dunsany in County Meath so liked order and respect that, out riding one day, he directed his steward to shoot a tenant who had forgotten to raise his cap to his lordship. (The steward refused.)

Many Great Houses had ballrooms and, amid house parties with hunting, shooting, or fishing, they held seasonal balls. Attended by friends from all over Ireland and from farther afield, numbers of a hundred and more were not uncommon in a house's dozens of bedrooms.

Intrigues and scandals broke out everywhere. More than one man saw his wife disappear from the dance "to take the air" and never return, departed with a younger or more eccentric or more dashing blade. One night two English gentlemen, staying a summer in a West Cork mansion, exchanged wives—permanently.

The women often possessed heart-stopping beauty; the men undertook hair-raising escapades. All spent money resoundingly. Lady Ormonde in Kilkenny would never dream of coming down to dinner without a full diamond tiara. The men splashed out on yachts, cars, and card games, on "slow horses and fast women."

As their end drew nearer, their dances grew wilder. And when the money from their tenancies began to dry up, whether through law or attrition, bankruptcy rolled through the Anglo-Irish houses like a poison gas. Few of their enterprises earned enough to support such lavish style. Soon the servants departed, the beds went unmade, and the bankers came to collect on myriad mortgages.

As the banks sold off the land, usually breaking up the estates, the local people at last got their hands on what they felt was rightly theirs. With memory so bitter, no native Irish family ever moved into any Great House. After the inevitable auction of possessions, often not even attended by the long-gone and faraway owners, the new owners let the hated edifice stand in ruins.

Their farm animals sheltered in the marbled halls on summer days. Or, from time to time, they stripped the house of its best stone to build new houses for themselves, or for their cattle, pigs, horses.

That is, if the house remained standing. As rebellion intensified, many Irish estates came to grief when the local republican guerrillas torched them—sometimes with the landlord and his family still inside. Thus, in magnificent Irish architecture, was the baby thrown out with the bathwater—and few young inheritors of the time would have dared put a toe into such a cauldron.

Tipperary Castle, as yet, fell into none of these categories—and it was the prize. By all accounts, it not only matched but surpassed the other houses in Ireland: Bessborough, Castletown, Lyons at Celbridge, Rockingham, Strokestown. To accompany and reflect their facades, columns, terraces, and towers, their creators had made beautiful landscapes, so that the eye found beauty everywhere. Terence Burke had chosen the gardens of Versailles as his models, and Charles O'Brien had now fallen for it all as surely and heavily as for its possible chatelaine.

2

After I visited Tipperary Castle, the clamor in my head grew louder; and the often burdensome affliction of love weighed heavier. I thought of Miss Burke every moment; I envisaged a life together, of goodness, peace, and kindness to others. To gather my feelings into some order, I set myself to listen to a different clamor, namely the public refrain that I had been most loudly hearing in my life—land and its agitations.

In 1850, ten years before I was born, my grandfather's close friend Mr. Charles Gavan Duffy, for whom I am named, founded the Irish Tenant League. I never met Mr. Duffy, because, to my grandfather's sadness, he migrated to Australia when I was very young, but I am told that he was a great lawyer and an impatient politician.

He founded the Tenant League because over ninety percent of all Ireland's land was then in English hands. And since tenants were neither prosperous nor secure, Mr. Duffy set out aims that he called the Three F's: Fixity of Tenure, Fair Rent, and Free Sale. He hoped that this effort would give an Irish tenant farmer the minimum protection of a lease—at that time, anybody could be summarily evicted.

Likewise, as I have noted, rents could be—and were—raised on the landlord's whim. And if by chance an Irishman owned his land, Mr. Duffy's movement sought to allow him to sell it on the open market and not succumb to a forced sale at a price stipulated by his nearest landlord.

The O'Briens, although we lived outside such matters, have always been a very hospitable and convivial family, and thus we heard everything. All political news, rumors, family scandals, allegations, all births, legitimate or merry, all betrothals, marriages, murders, and deaths—all reached our paneled rooms. We heard the laughter of the people and, my parents being what they are, we also dried many tears. So, although from the banks we watched the rivers of blood flow through Ireland, we played no part in the eventual Land War, as it came to be called. Its forerunners of murder and debate merely took their place among the other great topics of discussion that ranged up and down our long shiny dining-table.

How, therefore, may I characterize this important period, this gripping movement for land reform? Naturally, I remember it chiefly through conversations; for the moment, permit me to try and understand its spirit.

From my father, as I have said, came the feel for land. But he took it beyond the personal experience; when he first began to teach me the story of my own country, he made land the central character of the drama. Logically, then, I should always have been prepared to interrogate the Irish passion for land.

We are no more than a tiny North Atlantic island of thirty thousand square miles, and with no mountain high enough to stand near a Himalaya; our tallest peak, in County Kerry, stands a racing length above three thousand feet. Nor does every square yard of our country yield riches; our coasts are rocky and, to the west, harsh upon the Atlantic facade; not until the earth has settled many miles inland do we reach our renowned fertility. Yet, all over, whether in fat or bony fields, the Irish savagery of feeling, of earth hunger, exceeds all human ferocities. It is an emotion, and it comes of long history.

Here is an account of my visit to a native Irishman who believed that his fields had rightly belonged to him and his family since the dawn of time, and who, as with our family, somehow contrived to continue owning his ancestral farm. My father directed me to him; I had often heard him say of this man, "Ah, he likes his land." He lived outside a village called Oola in the county Limerick, a man by name of Martin Lenihan.

Mr. Lenihan farmed not much, but he farmed it well; forty acres of good land, with a little marshland, some woods of hazel and beech trees; and he had water by way of a small river. I was no more than twenty when I visited him, bearing my father's good wishes; he had finished securing a new roof of straw thatch and, as I walked down the hill, his long house gleamed golden in the sun.

We sat outside, by his front door. He had one son, who played nearby, a sickly child of four or so who gave him concern; the local talk said that his wife must have no more children.

"May I ask you a strange question?" I said to him.

"Like a policeman?" he asked, and he laughed.

"My father often says of you that you love your land."

Martin Lenihan leaned back a bit in his chair.

"Indeed I do. I do indeed."

"May I ask you, sir—what does that mean, that you love your land?"

Martin Lenihan said nothing for a moment, and then he began to speak in his slow, comfortable way (whipping up a deal of spittle as he did so). Mr. Lenihan spoke so slowly that it was a pleasure to record his words—but in any case I had by then learned a version of Mr. Pitman's shorthand.

Well. You know. Land is an odd sort of a thing—because it drags you in. I never seen the sea, I seen pictures of it, always moving, restless. It catches men up. Well, land is the same, a kind of sea that will only take you down into it in the end, when they lay you six feet under. But that's not what you're asking me, I'll bet. (Here Martin Lenihan laughed, a kind of gurgle.)

If you work with land, you get to know it. I know every field I have here, I know how the clay, the earth in that field will feel if I bend down and pick it up in my hand and crumble it. I know where there's a corner of a field that's a bit wet, and I know where there's a crest of a field that has a bit of chalk in it—well, not chalk like school chalk, but a bit more limestone than usual.

(Martin Lenihan's hands lay quietly on his knees; tufts of jet-black hair made the knuckles look like little pet creatures.)

And my fields have names, like a dog has, or a horse. There's a field called Jimmy, because my great-great-grandfather Jimmy Lenihan, won it playing cards. There's a field called Cicero—for what reason I don't know. We have a field called Harry Lyons because a man called Harry Lyons was born inside it—his mother was caught out there in a shower of rain and didn't get home in time for the midwife. The field down by where the river comes in is called Soda, because my grandmother baked the best soda-bread she ever made, she said, from wheat grown in that field one summer.

What else? Oh, I've a field called Jennifer—I named it that myself because I like the sound of the word.

I'll tell you now when I first noticed land—I noticed it on my hands and knees and I was only about eight years old. We had turnips planted down there in the Road Field—that's a long stretch that runs nearly the width of the farm. It was raining and cold and my job was to thin the young turnip shoots so as to leave the plants to grow fully—they shouldn't be near each other or they'd all grow too small.

And I began to see how the color of the clay under my hands wasn't one color at all but several colors. Well, I thought, this is like a bit of magic. And I began to think, What else is like this? What else in the world is anything like this? And I couldn't think of anything.

And to this day I don't know of anything like the earth, especially when you dig into it. (By now Martin Lenihan had begun to sit a little straighter in his chair, and his face had grown a little redder as his subject excited him.)

So when I went home I sat down to eat my dinner and I said to my father, "Do you like looking at the clay in the fields?"

My father was the kind of man you could ask any question and he wouldn't think it ridiculous. He stopped chewing and he said to me, "Is that what you're finding—that you like looking at it?" And I said it was. My father chewed on and he didn't say anything more until he had finished chewing.

Then he said, "I like looking at the clay in my fields. Here's when I like looking at it. When I've turned it open from the grass and seen its fresh bright brownness. When I dig into it and see its lumps and powders break on the blade of my digging. Or I bend down to pull out a root of weed and I get the dirt under my fingers. If I kneel down on one knee to look at it, I might see if it's too wet for a grain crop, or will it take potatoes this year. And I'll pick it up and hold it under my nose and smell something—and I don't know what it is that I'm smelling.

"Except that it was a smell that was in that same ground when there were kings here ruling the province of Munster and the county of Limerick. And that smell was in that same ground when Saint Patrick walked here. And when Vikings with beards, Danes and such people, came in here looking for what they could rob from us.

"And the Norman princes who came in here seven hundred years ago—they got that smell, and so did the English that their Virgin Queen sent in, and all the English after. And that's the smell that drives men mad. Especially if you get it and can't have it. The smell of the land. The smell of our own land."

That was my father's speech that day and my mother stopped in the middle of the kitchen floor, still holding a bowl, to listen to him say it. The dog stopped barking when he made that speech.

Martin Lenihan rose from his chair and began to pace his yard; this quiet, undemonstrative man had come almost aglow when talking about his father and his land.

I asked, "Did you yourself—have you become aware of that smell of the land?"

Martin Lenihan spoke again.

My father said that you can only get this smell if you understand land, if you understand all the little roots and stones and worms and other works that are part of any piece of ground that you open up under your feet. He told me to watch out for the way the clay, the earth, allows little creatures to travel in it as we travel our fields. And then he pointed out to me the greater wonder that lay ahead—that when we planted things in this substance they grew and became large enough to eat and to keep us alive. "No wonder," said he—"no wonder men go mad for land." And I recalled how I had seen him kneel down and part the grasses of a field with his bare hands.

We're not a boastful family. And we don't say a lot. But we held on to our fields. My family has been on this farm since before Saint Patrick, and I'd kill or die before I'd let another have it. If I didn't have the land, what would I have?

(Here Martin Lenihan described a large fat circle in the air with his finger.)

Nought. The duck's egg. Zero. That's what I'd have.

So spoke Mr. Martin Lenihan from Oola in County Limerick. I have known many men like Mr. Lenihan, and in his words he told me the essence of this country's ancient story.

But the people, the incomers, such as my mother's family, the Goldsmiths, and the Treeces, to whom land had been given as royal reward— what of them? Many had farmed their lands for, by now, several hundred years. Shall we believe in our hearts that Mr. Lenihan possesses the greater rights? Yet the Protestants have lived here for long enough to feel Irish, to belong to the fabric of the country's earth. For how long, for how many generations or centuries, may the Hand of History reach down to control?

After unearthing the ancient roots of Mr. Martin Lenihan, I set off to examine the newer tradition of Irish land—the recent, yet rigid foundations of Mr. Henry Catherwood. He is a giant man of Ulster whose family has not had the same long-lived residence on the island of Ireland as Mr. Lenihan's; the Catherwoods took occupation of their fields in 1692. Mr. Catherwood stood at least six feet six in his stockings; he had feet like canal boats, and at least eighteen buttons secured the fly of his trousers. We sat to talk in the parlor of his stone farmhouse, with its slate roof, its lace curtains, and large portrait of Queen Victoria.

Look. I possess large hands (said Henry Catherwood). So did my mother—"Large hands can make a large fortune," she said. As they did on this farm and always can. Provided a man has no fear of hard work. Not of hard work am I in fear. Nor of anything else that I have yet encountered.

My mother's father bequeathed her this place. We're some three statute miles southwest of Newtownstewart, a mile west of the road to Drumquin. Not a large farm at all to begin with. In my great-grandfather's time they had a few cows and some cattle for slaughter and some pigs; they ate a beef and two pigs every year and chickens and such. 'Twas the same when I was a boy.

Now, my mother had a wee fright of dogs, so I had no dog. I had a cat, Walter, who came into the fields with me. That cat knew that my true home, the home of my spirit, lay in those fields. Every clement day from the age I was six I roamed these fields.

At the same time my mother had a servant, Annie Heaphy; now, she was a Roman Catholic. When we hired her we couldn't get a good Protestant girl—they were all gone to the cities; they weren't born to be servants, and the Roman Catholics were. I paid dearly for the lack of good Protestant help. With my mother out of earshot Annie Heaphy often taunted me.

"Hi-boy, I tell you there's a day coming when youse folk will be offa this land. This wasn't your land, you were given it by the dirty oul' King of England. And it was never his to give. So cling to it while you can, wee Henry. Cling to it while you can."

Now, I was too young to understand what Annie Heaphy meant. So I did what she said. I clung to the land. Meaning, I went out into the fields and I looked at every hill and hollow in our fields and I acquainted myself with every one. I say "acquainted"—I mean intimately, like. If I found a ridge in the ground made by an old plow or a finger of God, I traced it with my boots. If water gathered after heavy rain and made a small lake, I drank from it. In the summertime, I followed the reapers as they ran the rabbits out of the barley. I relished it all, the way you'd enjoy eating meat. I saw shelves and furrows of all shapes and sizes and every one of them was like a face, every one had something to recall it by—eyebrows or jaws or cheekbones or shoulders.

Above all, I lay on the ground to try and put my arms around it and find out its mysteries. That summer was a particularly fortunate one in terms of warm weather. It was so hot we had swarms of bees flying by nearly every day—they were all looking for a house with cool, deep eaves. Every field on the farm, every place I could lie down, I pressed my face to the earth, me a Protestant boy who is not permitted to believe in such foolish things as magic or . . . or . . . poetry. That was for the Roman Catholics, and damn little's the money they made out of it. (He cackled.) And you see, and here's the merry hell of it—I thought I was obeying Annie Heaphy's orders to "cling to the land." (Henry Catherwood's cackle deepened into a chesty wheeze of laughter.)

I found a lark's nest in the grass. And, good boy that I was, I never troubled her eggs; I walked far around them. It was that kind of a summer anyway—we had apple windfalls, a baby rabbit that got lost and was made into a pet, a house down the road that had a new infant.

We're hardy people, Protestants. We mostly know what we're doing, because we don't waste time or thought on unnecessary matters. There's nothing much to be gained from trucking with, say, music—outside of a good strong hymn, maybe. The Roman Catholics, they stay up half the night listening to some old tramp of a fellow with a fiddle, and then they're not fit for work the next day. Not that they do any work.

So, one day, I went back to the house and I got out of the barn a loy— that's a big kind of a shovel or spade for digging. And I went back to my little notch in the ground and I used the loy to pare back the grass and open up the clay beneath. Bit by bit I did it—it was hard work, a loy's a heavy implement—but I soon opened up a wide enough swatch and I was like a man in a laboratory. I looked at that ground, I sniffed it, I rolled on it, and I had to wash my face in the pond before I went back up to the house, because I was after putting my face down into the clay over and over again. (Mr. Henry Catherwood was now very excited.)

Look at me! (Henry Catherwood flung open his arms like a man about to embrace a long-lost friend.) Do I look like a man—I'm what, nearly seventy-seven and not yet shrunken—do I look like a man who'd say a thing like that, that the world has a skin?

My friend, with your curly hair and your big smile—I'm telling you that the world has a—a—(Henry Catherwood struggled to find the word)—a complexion. That's it—a complexion. And that complexion is the brown of clay, the lovely tan and gold and dark and brown and amber and nearly black. I mean our own skin, it's nothing like the earth, oh, no! Not at all! Your man in Africa or the swarthy Moroccan or the people in

India—they're the boys, if it were to be determined by likeness alone, they're the meek who must inherit the earth.

But because I looked at and touched the skin of the world—I became a farmer. And I expanded this farm to a farm of four hundred acres. In these parts that's a lot of skin.

Now you know, young O'Brien, this island has a lot of land agitation going on here. People are looking for what they're calling "Land Reform"—you know that, don't you? Well, I tell everyone—the land doesn't need any reforming, the land is fine. It's the people that needs the reforming. And I can tell you—I'll reform them, so I will, if they try and take any of my land away from me. King William gave my family this land, because the people who were on it were too dirty and too lazy to work it well. And it's our land now and there's an end of it.

In those two cameos, of Mr. Lenihan and Mr. Catherwood, Charles O'Brien encapsulated Irish life in the last reaches of the nineteenth century. Although he managed to extract unusual candor from each man, it wouldn't be difficult to find such attitudes in today's Ireland, even if said more reticently. More importantly, Mr. O'Brien reached down into belief. And thus he tapped into the core of the Irish land culture.

It lies at the root of almost every serious conflict the island has ever known; history is geography. Mr. O'Brien, in setting out the size of the country, implied—accurately—that the scarcity of land connects directly to the hunger for it.

The sheer visibility of everybody on such a small island, the capacity to see a neighbor's prosperity across a hedge, a fence, or a stone wall, and the envy of land and its potential—all of this exacerbated the desire.

Under the old systems of kingships, most of the people had an opportunity at least to wring a living from the earth. Ancient Ireland was a network of small farms. When the planters came in, and farms were confiscated and merged into huge estates, the land hunger only went underground. It never disappeared.

In Mr. O'Brien's childhood—indeed, in the precise decade before he was born—it broke the surface again, and he lived, therefore, in a time when it became patriotic to want land. Nobody had any illusions; this earth formed the key to all economies.

As may be judged from the separateness between Mr. Lenihan and Mr. Catherwood, the question of Irish land reform posed seemingly insurmountable problems. I must now relate my distressing part in the life of the man to whom people turned for his understanding of all the argument's facets; my account will take some time.

Early in my healer's apprenticeship, Mr. Egan began to encourage me toward the necessity of vacation. He believed that healers endure considerable demands on their spirit and that they must rest. I observed that he did not spare himself any time off and I said so, but he nonetheless insisted that I free myself of his constant attention (in his words) and find means of relaxing.

"A nice long distance away," he used to say pleasantly. "Mind you go home first and talk to your mother about clothes for traveling in. Rest easy about hurrying back."

As I have always enjoyed traveling and meeting people, I took him at his word. This practice I have continued since I became my own master, and so, in the summer of 1889, not long out of my apprenticeship, I betook myself off to London, where two of my old tutors, Buckley and Mr. Halloran, had long before gone to live. It was June, a few days short of my birthday, and I felt hopeful that both gentlemen might be able to share the day with me.

London in general proved delightful; and I navigated the city easily. I found Buckley, though with some difficulty. When I called at his address, as he had furnished it to our family, an elderly lady closed the door in my face; I supposed her fearful of a strange young man with, to her, a foreign accent. Nearby, a tavern-keeper directed me to Buckley's new residence.

The house spoke of grandeur, with great windows set in walls painted an excellent cream color. A bell jangled to my touch, but no servant appeared, and no sound issued from within. I pulled the bell again.

"Shhhhh!" came an indignant whispered bellow from behind a garden wall. "Do you want to wake the whole house?"

It was past three on a bright afternoon. Then a garden door opened, and I knew my man and he knew me. We exchanged a most vigorous handshake.

"Come in here, come in," he whispered and led me to the garden. He wore a straw boater with a green hatband, an elaborate shirt, and a waistcoat of yellow, which he tapped.

"I look like a goldfinch, don't I?" He stopped and raised an eyebrow.

"*Carduelis,*" I said.

"Great out," said Buckley.

"*Elegans,*" I said. "For once you might like the second word."

"I do. I do." He wheezed. "And what do you think of the britches?"

"*Elegantissimus.*" He wore trousers of broad green and yellow stripes, surmounted by a white cummerbund.

"Show the flag," said he, still whispering. "The boss loves it," and he indicated a window upstairs.

Buckley led me to a garden table on which tea service had been set out. He gestured.

"D'you want a cup?" he said. "I always make it for the boss."

We sat. "I miss you. I'm healing now," I told him. "I travel the country."

"D'you know, didn't I hear that? A woman from Kilmacthomas, a Marge Callanan, said she met you. I've sore eyes myself."

"Use your spittle," I said. "But you look wonderful."

We gazed at each other and smiled for the sheer joy of being together.

"Tell me, any news of Mrs. Curry? I often think of her. But she had a bit of the rose-bush about her—enticing to look at and spiky to the touch."

"How do you come to be here, Buckley?"

"Well, Charles, 'tis a long story but for telling somewhere else. Tell me, did that Miss Taylor ever catch any man? Your mother used to despair of her—the bit of a mustache, I s'pose." Then Buckley looked past my shoulder and rose to his feet with more respect than I knew he possessed. "Hah, the boss."

I turned—and I have remembered the moment ever since. Striding toward us came a man I had dreamed about, whom my parents had dreamed about, and he walked in Euclid's dreams too, a man whose name had been spoken in our household many times a day for a decade, a man whose name, stature, and spirit I'd heard being called down in every corner of Ireland that I had so far visited. It behoved me to stand, it behoved me almost to kneel—but I could scarcely move for being awestruck.

Yet I somehow rose as Buckley scampered across the lawns to meet the man he called "the boss." That Buckley should ever exhibit a sliver of deference speaks in itself volumes for the gentleman approaching. They had a swift and urgent exchange; I was looked at, and the gentleman seemed to be receiving reassurance from Buckley—who then beckoned me.

"Sir, this is Charles O'Brien, from Tipperary. Charles, you know who this is."

"Well, your name is a good one," said Charles Stewart Parnell—Father's hero, Mother's hero, Ireland's hero. "I'm well disposed to the name Charles."

"Sir, it's an excellent name for you to have." I confess that I did not know what I was speaking.

"I'm pleased that you approve," he said, and sat down.

He seemed altogether more stern than I had thought. Yes, I had heard my father talk of his fiery speeches, his fearless challenges in the Parliament; and yes, I knew that he had defied the might of the Crown, who'd imprisoned him for his political beliefs and then had to release him, so greatly did the people love him. This man, though, seemed quite consumed with his own authority.

He gestured to me, and I sat down.

"For all your appearance, you do not look like the son of a tenant farmer. Which O'Briens are you?"

"Sir, my father is Bernard O'Brien."

"Married to a Goldsmith?"

"Yes, sir."

"Hmm, near Cashel, yes? Your father has what? A hundred and fifty acres? And no tenants?"

"No tenants."

"And a Catholic?"

"Yes, sir."

Mr. Parnell rapped the table.

"You see! That's what we're driving for, that's what we want! The O'Briens—they survived all plantations or they refused to be planted? Which was it?"

Buckley intervened. "Sir, if you met Mr. Bernard O'Brien—nothing would drive that man off his farm."

Did Mr. Parnell's demeanor soften because of my father's—to him politically ideal—status? Perhaps—but how can I judge? At that moment, another ameliorating factor materialized, in the form of a lady who drifted toward us across the grass as though on air. I stood again.

"We have a guest?" she said. "Good!"

"My dear," said Mr. Parnell, "this is Charles O'Brien."

"How do you do, madam?"

Mother had impressed upon me to bow slightly when introduced to a married woman, and as I took her hand I observed with pleasure the lady's many rings.

We all conversed easily, Buckley, the Parnells, and I. Mr. Parnell talked of Avondale, his family's home in County Wicklow. I had not been to Rathdrum, I said—the nearby town—though I had heard that it was very pretty.

"No, not at all," he said, "Rathdrum cannot be recommended, but my family estate is several hundred acres and we have perfect tenant relationships. If the other landlords would but listen to me, we should get a good way toward resolving many of our difficulties."

His lady said little in all our discourse. She laughed once or twice—I think that she found Buckley amusing—and as she sat a good distance from me, I was able to have a clear view of her. The word "gracious" sprang to mind, though I found her not as gracious perhaps as Mother, by whom I set all standards.

I asked permission to sketch the couple; after some whispered exchanges, it was agreed. I made a rough sketch of them side by side—I knew that I should improve it later.

The sun shone and the tea flowed. We talked of many things, but principally we listened to Mr. Parnell, and I could have listened to him all evening and all night and all next day. Still, I wondered that he had gained such great fame for his filibustering ability in Parliament; he seemed to me a halting speaker, and of a reticent inclination. Yet it must be reported that nobody had such capacity to stay so closely on the point of the argument. Land, land, land was his topic—and soon the shadows changed the light in the garden and the temperature of the air.

When darkness began to gather, it seemed polite to take my leave. To my pleasure, Mr. Parnell accompanied me to the gate. That is how I shall remember him: slight, the beard deeper in texture than I had thought, the eyes wide apart, the face a little round perhaps—and the voice hypnotizing.

We shook hands.

"The best meetings are often in private, Charles O'Brien."

"Sir, this has been the greatest privilege of my life."

"You seem a discreet young man."

"Sir, I like to cultivate distinctiveness."

He seemed about to ask something of me, but he changed his mind and stepped back from the gate; the night's shadows took Charles Stewart Parnell, and I never saw him again.

In the history of Ireland, few people ever achieved the heroic and poignant stature of Charles Stewart Parnell. Under the political system of the Victorian British Isles, Ireland held elections for the English Parliament. The candidates often came from the more educated—that is to say, the upper—classes. Their voters sent them to the Parliament at Westminster with strong and clear mandates to press for land reform.

For the House of Lords, operations were constructed in a mirror of what had always taken place in England. An Irish peerage was created, of Irish landlords, taken exclusively from the Anglo-Irish. (One of Oscar Wilde's more famous lines was "You should study the peerage, Gerald. . . . It is the best thing in fiction the English have ever done.")

Thus, among the Irish politicians and peers who sat and spoke at the Parliament in London, an interesting and typically Irish anomaly arose. Some of the voices calling loudest for land reform came from landowners of the Anglo-Irish ruling class.

Parnell was a perfect example. He was elected to the British Parliament in 1875, one of many Anglo-Irish landowners who wanted to change the relationship between Ireland and England, between tenant and landlord.

Close behind that ideal came thoughts of Irish self-rule. The Act of Union, passed in 1800, had cemented the political relationship between Ireland and England so brutally that it rankled more and more.

Over and over, the country's orators pointed to the success of the Americans in 1776 and the French in 1789. One populace threw out the English, and the other threw out the upper classes; in Ireland the targets were, heavenly possibility, as one. With land agitation achieving results, the talk of "Home Rule," as self-government was called, buzzed louder.

Parnell became key to this. After all, he was the one who had famously said, "No man has the right to set the boundary to the march of a nation."

Throughout his public life he pursued a policy of obstructionism. Resorting to all-night filibusters, he attacked existing legislation, and then joined the major Irish land reform movements. Hundreds of thousands of people turned out to hear him speak at rallies all over the country.

His stature began to worry the London authorities. They tried to silence him; for his encouragement of—and active part in—violations of the existing land laws, he was jailed.

He had the political astuteness to use the moment as a way of turning up the heat; from prison he told Irish tenants to stop paying their rents. The government made a deal; if Parnell would stop advocating such resistance—which had begun to cause violence—they would release him.

The militants, though, had momentum. Even though Parnell kept his side of the bargain, the killing began to spread. By an unfortunate coincidence it culminated in a major assassination. In 1882, in the Phoenix Park, near Dublin, the Irish Invincibles, an armed secret society, killed

Lord Frederick Charles Cavendish and Thomas Burke, respectively chief secretary and undersecretary for Ireland.

Parnell denounced the killers—but he couldn't stop them. The Irish Party, which he led, had habitually voted with the government, keeping it in power. When the government extended tough Irish anti-terrorist laws in response to the assassinations, Parnell and his colleagues voted against them and, in 1885, brought down the government. This gave Parnell a power like no other member of Parliament, and he and the government knew it.

Then came scandal.

That night in London, I visited my cousin in Farringdon. Edward Goldsmith worked as a barrister at the Inns of Court and knew many people. We dined in a chophouse near his rooms, amid a great crowd. Though he is senior to me by several years, he and I have always liked each other; the fact that he near-worships my father would have made us friends in any case. Edward had long professed an admiration for the letters I wrote to him, and he had suggested many times that I work for newspapers. Now he raised it again.

"I know so many people here who would find such an erudite correspondent in Ireland rather appealing. Good Lord, look at the news from Ireland; look at the need for us all to be informed as to what is occurring there daily."

"This afternoon," I said, "I took tea with the leading actor in the drama."

"You mean whom?" Edward put down his chop, which he had held by the lug of the bone.

"And his wife."

"Whose wife?"

"Mr. Parnell's."

"Parnell doesn't have a wife."

"He does. She's named Katharine. I met her today." And I showed him the sketch, now much improved.

Somebody called his name; and Edward—still startled at my information—looked across the room. He waved and leaned forward to me.

"Now, here's a man who will take an interest in you."

A lean, pale individual came and stood by us; his black eyebrows met.

"Billy, this is my cousin from Ireland, Charles O'Brien—a writer-in-waiting, if ever there was one."

"Billy" looked at me down a long length of nose.

"What have you written?"

"Only my Journal," I said.

"He's just met Parnell." Edward beamed. "Show Billy the portrait."

Billy, had he been sitting down, would have jumped up. He snatched the drawing from my hand.

"Write about this. It will make a nifty page. When do you go back to Ireland?"

"Saturday."

"Come to my office tomorrow and I will pay you well."

It has to be said that my account of meeting Parnell caused a sensation. It appeared—with the excellently printed portrait—in *The Chronicle* (where Billy worked as a senior editor) on the Thursday. Edward had arranged for us to dine again at the same chophouse; and I, flush with guineas from my writing (and a separate fee for the sketch), anticipated the pleasure of returning his hospitality. I had not, however, prepared for the merriment and celebration directed at me when I arrived.

It seemed as though hordes of people thronged the old place. As I entered, I saw Edward straightaway, and he roared, "Here's the chap! Here's my cousin! Welcome, Charles O'Brien!" A great cheer rose, and Billy stepped forward.

"Thank you, old man. Wonderful day for us."

Apparently, my article had become the talk of London. I knew that I had been bold; for example, I had written, "May I beg to differ from those detractors who call Mr. Parnell 'arrogant' and 'conceited' and 'pig-headed' and 'contemptuous' and 'boring' and 'politically unskilled.' I spent four hours in his company this Monday past and found him a delight. His demeanor may be called all the more pleasant, since he had but minutes earlier risen from an afternoon sleep with his charming wife,

Katharine, and many men who have just awakened require time to adjust their temperament to the world at large. Not so Mr. Parnell—and I may add that his husbandly attentions exhibited the utmost tenderness of affection. And of course I saw them reciprocated."

(As I'd written these sentences in Billy's office, he'd praised me over and over, and I'd pronounced myself gratified that this new way of writing about great figures had found a home.)

How we ate and drank that night! Many arms wrapped themselves about my shoulders, many hands thrust ale and spirits at me, and I might have eaten ten—or fifty—dinners for all the food I was offered. I said to Edward, "If this be journalism, I'm game for it."

Next day, I called to see my other old tutor in the area, Mr. Halloran. He worked in great offices within an eye's blink of Westminster and Parliament. Once, I should have been intimidated by such a powerful building, with its crests and escutcheons and marble and panels. Now, a new man, I sat in the hallway as a lackey took my card to Mr. Halloran's office.

Soon a lady approached me, dignified and quiet. "Mr. O'Brien?"

I rose, expecting to accompany her.

"I have a letter from Mr. Halloran"—and she handed it to me. With pleasure, I recognized the tight, formed hand—but the pleasure ended.

"I am too distressed today at what you have done," said the note, with no address, no familiar greeting, "and so we may not meet."

That was all.

"Oh, dear," I said to the bearer, "I wish him better. Will you tell him that from me?"

She nodded and departed, and I reflected how easily distress used to visit Mr. Halloran when he lived under our roof.

I caught the boat train. My crossing took all night, and I slept on deck, in a chair, knowing I should never have such air again for some time. I awoke after some hours with a feeling of great unease. "At what you have done"—what had Mr. Halloran meant? Thinking on, I began to ask myself if I had somehow been duped by the London crowd. Their jubilation seemed excessive: Why should they have so relished my account of Mr. Parnell if they professed him their foe? Was there something in all this of which I had no knowledge—some nuance that I did not understand?

When we docked at Kingstown, I longed for hot tea and great slices of bread with bacon. As I left the gangplank and began to walk the short quayside to the street, a man ran after me from the ship; I had seen him speaking with the purser and they had been looking at me, but I knew not why and thought nothing of it.

"Are you O'Brien?" he asked—very rough, I thought.

"Yes. Charles O'Brien."

"You bastard! You yellow-haired, treacherous bastard!" he accused, and he reached to hit me. I easily controlled him, since he stood no more than five feet eight or so, but he began to shout in a most unpleasant manner.

"This is him! This is him! This is the bastard who wrote about Parnell!"

Others began to collect, and I must say that I ran—and swiftly enough to outpace them all. Not until I met Mr. Egan again next day did I discover the reasons for this unpleasantness. Mr. Parnell had no wife, and his lady, "Katharine," bore the name of her husband, another Member of Parliament—one Captain Willie O'Shea, who had now begun divorce proceedings. All commentary suggested that this scandal would bring about Mr. Parnell's political downfall.

As it did. The Catholics of Ireland could not accept leadership from a man who consorted illicitly with another man's wife. Parnell lost his Irish Party, his place in the world, his repute. He and Kitty O'Shea became the major scandal figures of the day and the decade—even though the world of politics had long known of their relationship. She had been Parnell's mistress for years, and had borne him daughters.

Captain O'Shea got his divorce, Parnell married Kitty, and they went away to live quietly on the south coast of England. Less than two years later, he died of pneumonia, the "lost leader," whose spirit, they say, was broken in his fall from grace.

⊠

In October 1891, I became part of the largest crowd that I have ever seen or expect to see. Today, Ireland buried Charles Stewart Parnell, under dark skies. Although the funeral was timed for the light of day, the people in the cortege continued to walk to Glasnevin Cemetery all night long. Yesterday, I went to the grave-digging, where I stayed, my hat pulled low over my face. Many came to me and asked my business there and I said, "A family mourner," and they departed, satisfied with my answer. I told no lie; my purpose transcended that of all save Mr. Parnell's family.

For a number of years I had attempted to reach Mr. Parnell or—as she became—Mrs. Parnell. All efforts had been rebuffed; notwithstanding my lingering for hours on the porch of his house in Brighton or under the portico of lovely Avondale in the county Wicklow, Mr. Parnell's reserve did not melt. I believed that he accused me of "heavy irony" in the article that I wrote. Now I hoped that my presence at the funeral might cause his wife to unbend in forgiveness.

We rarely see our hopes fulfilled—but I did today. Repelling all entreaties to move aside, I remained as if a stone on that spot. They carried the coffin to the graveside; and I approached the figure in black.

"Mrs. Parnell," I said. "I am Charles O'Brien, the man who—"

"Oh, I know full well who you are. I remember our tea." She did not raise her black veil.

"I never meant anything but well. Think of how respectfully my account was couched."

Mrs. Parnell laid her hand upon my arm. "I told my husband so. Many times."

"But they say that the rejection of the people broke his heart. And I fear that I brought it about." I was near to tears.

"Mr. O'Brien, our love had long been known. Nobody else had the respect to write about it with tenderness—and they had not the courage to write about it disrespectfully. Nor could they allege my adultery without being subject to a lawsuit. But they were able and pleased to print your piece because it was so beautifully couched—and they knew that we would feel unable to sue for libel."

I stepped back, struck, as it were, by a light dawning.

"Oh. I never knew."

"I thought not. You are forgiven—there is nothing harsh in me toward you. I merely wish you the fortune of a good woman to guide you—as my husband believed I guided him."

So overcome did I feel that I could not stay there for Mr. Parnell's burial.

By the time Parnell died, at the too young age of forty-five, the Irish farmers had achieved their Three F's: Fixity of Tenure, Fair Rent, and Free Sale. And even though he had not been the author of the legislation, there seems no doubt that his great agitations helped to bring it about; and he also came within votes of having generated self-government.

So, every sixth of October I wear in my buttonhole an ivy leaf, Mr. Parnell's symbol, and I mourn our uncrowned king, this landowning gentleman of the Anglo-Irish aristocracy.

My heart ached that night, sore again from the damage that I had done to Mr. Parnell, and hurting even more deeply from the kindness of Mrs. Parnell. I found lodgings in the home of an old friend near Glasnevin Cemetery, Tom Childs, a man of kindness and decency. His peaceful house (assailed only by his occasional rants against his "hound" of a brother, Sammy) gave me a bed for the night and, mercifully, nothing to drink. I lay awake for many hours, hearing the footsteps of the mourners returning from Mr. Parnell's funeral. At about five o'clock in the morning, I drifted to sleep.

Next day, I set out upon the best cure that I know for grief and remorse: a journey; Ireland's hedges and streams are filled with balm for the spirit, and I was back at my healing trade. My first assignment required me to cure corns—and I all but wept once more as I advised and then put the measure into practice: bind tightly the toe with an ivy leaf.

Parnell's funeral went on for days. People from all over Ireland insisted on being able to get to the graveside long after the burial. Estimates of the crowd run to over a million people. By then the full story of Kitty O'Shea had become a tragic Irish romance, eventually visited by Hollywood, and television drama. It still engrosses historians and biographers.

The entire matter was a morass of hypocrisy. Long before it became public, Captain O'Shea had tacitly sanctioned the relationship. He had even been sponsored into politics by Parnell, who went against the members of his Irish Party to secure his cuckold a seat in Parliament. But when it looked as though Parnell's strength was becoming unstoppable, his political opponents decided to try to harness this open secret. Plotters close to the establishment paid O'Shea to issue divorce papers. Ireland, with its newfound Catholic zeal, would never vote for a Parnellite again.

The impact of the "uncrowned king's" fall reverberated in Ireland for almost a century; only recently have the last wearers of the ivy leaf died out. And nowhere in the Parnell canon of history or biography does the name of Charles O'Brien appear.

In my zeal to examine the arrival of April Burke in my life, I have insufficiently reported in my History, I feel, many of the experiences I saw with Mr. Egan. We rode together through the country, as close as Don Quixote and Sancho Panza, as Robin Hood and Little John. I can see us now, as we came down the hill into a place that expected us. He had a small roan mare, Teresa, and I had Della, the bigger horse for the bigger man. We carried packs behind our saddles, with all our boxes of powders, our bottles of potions, our salves and ointments, and our clothes. He had a flat black hat, I wore a wider brim—he told me that I looked like a musketeer; I told him that he looked like a preacher.

We traveled well together. Since he made a great deal of money, and my father had provided me with an income, our food and accommodations proved more than satisfactory. We never quarreled, never disagreed; now and again he fell quiet in himself, reflective, contemplating a recent patient, thinking out an improvement to a cure; and he complimented me many times for not intruding upon such moments. Usually we talked easily or had pleasant mutual silences.

Remarkable were the impressions that we captured of life in Ireland, in city, town, village, and parish. We met huntsmen and hawkers, ladies and louts; we met plowmen and poachers, girls and grocers. Mr. Egan always addressed me as "Mr. O'Brien"; we were, he said, "professional gentlemen, and we must behave as such" and, after every discussion of a patient, he had the habit of saying, "But, Mr. O'Brien, all people are equal until we discover that they're not."

I do not need to search my memory for the more unusual events that we saw together; they seem to have occurred at the numerous fairs where we most successfully plied ourselves. We saw cattle fairs and horse fairs, where men made many bargains or none at all, but always there was the joy of livestock. And, with a notable absence of joy, we saw hiring fairs.

My first hiring fair was witnessed on the bridge at Golden, right by the old Norman castle, a few miles from my own home. I had heard of such events many times and had often wondered why my father never frequented them, even when he found himself a number of men short at a harvest or in the lambing times. Soon, I understood.

I had been with Mr. Egan a little over two years and, after some days of mixing his herb mixtures at his home, we had come up from his house near Bansha to visit a woman in Mantle Hill who had damaged a leg in a fall in her yard and had been unable to recover its use. Our way, we found, was blocked when we came to the river and, indeed, the entire winding street of the village thronged with people.

On one side of the thoroughfare (if I may call it that; this is not a large village) little rude platforms had been arranged; onto these stepped a variety of men. Many had red faces, all had loud voices, and they shouted their names and their places of origin: "John-Joe Kelly from Limerick itself" or "James Prendergast all the way from Clare." Having secured an audience, each of these shouters then made way for a succession of diffident people, who stepped onto the podium and waited until told by their barker to step down again. These were the men and women, boys and girls who offered themselves for hire.

Some attracted no interest. If a man seemed unusually strong, a voice called, "Why aren't you working already?" Or someone would step from the crowd and begin a physical inspection—he would check the poor fellow's hands, feel his legs, open his mouth, look at his teeth.

"They don't want to hire someone who's sickening for something," said Mr. Egan, beside me.

"This is humiliating," I said.

"Wait a minute and you'll see worse," said Mr. Egan.

The candidates stepped on, stepped off again. Once or twice, a boy of fourteen or fifteen attracted attention; I observed two such, and both had abundant hair. The farmers who showed an interest poked and prodded. One man hired one boy; the other lad drifted loose.

Then came the women and the girls. Fewer in number, some quite lovely, they stood there, eyes downcast, evidently poor, as their barker shouted their experience: "Worked for a farmer's wife over near Charleville" or "Was eight years with a lady called MacMahon in Clare until the lady died."

Once or twice, men fortified with drink stepped up and began an inspection. No man actually put his hands lasciviously on any woman (some constables lingered near), but they leered to the onlookers, and curved shapes in the air with their hands, and turned the poor creatures this way and that.

My heart wept for these hopeful people. When an interested call came from a member of the public, the person on the podium looked eagerly toward that voice. How willingly they displayed themselves, even if the inquirer was merely having sport with them. And how dreadfully sank their smiles, men and women, boys and girls, when asked to step down, and they realized that another day had passed and they had no work to feed themselves or those at home.

I have heard that the fair in Golden differed from most hiring fairs in that the barkers charged an "introduction" fee to anyone hiring from their booth. At other such events, the people for hire merely came into the streets and stood there, hoping for someone to offer them the desperately needed employment. In either case, I wished the hiring fair abolished. But it ranked as nothing beside what was to come that same week; and I still rage and wince at the memory of that occasion.

In Golden, we had received word of a "good fair" to be held next day in the town of Mallow, in the north of the county Cork, some forty miles away. We arrived at about ten o'clock in the morning and our intelligence looked well-founded; this fair indeed promised well. Large crowds had already gathered; stalls of food smoked to the sky; music jingled here and there.

Within moments of setting up our tent, we had patients—in fact, fifteen people lined up, and we began the day busily. I handed Mr. Egan every bowl and bottle he requisitioned; and I took money from every person with whom he consulted. One woman complained that the ointment he brushed on her skin had a sting to it; I dabbed her arms gently with cold water. A gentleman from Fermoy said his bunions had come back; I showed him how to burn them off with a candle taper.

All through this, I had a question in my mind: What was this occasion? Why so many people on a day that had no seasonal or religious or holiday significance? Finally I had a chance to ask, and a couple said to me—indignantly, as though I should have known—"Shanahan!"

For months, a search had been going on for a dreadful villain who had taken the lives of his wife and her mother and father. Today he would hang. He had been a surly and disliked fellow, with bad reports from all who had known him, ever since childhood.

The hanging was scheduled for noon. I asked Mr. Egan, "Do you wish to see this?"

"We have to stay. Afterward is when people will want us—their stomachs will be bad." Then he asked, "Did you ever see anybody swing?"

"No."

"No eating beforehand," he said.

At five minutes before noon a party of soldiers and Royal Irish constables escorted a cart through the crowd to the end of the Main Street. No drum rolled, no horn blew. The high sides of the cart had been covered with burlap to conceal anything inside; the escort—of more than a hundred men—seemed to me especially large, considering that this had been such an unpopular fugitive and thus an unlikely subject for a rescue attempt.

This corner of Mallow was a well-known place of execution; a high wooden structure existed there permanently, ready to take the post and beam of the scaffold. In a matter of moments the gibbet of wood was raised. Over the beam they threw a rope with a noose.

We were close by—because our stall had been set up there for the densest throng. The police and soldiers formed a ring around the gallows and then faced the crowd. Brusquely they pushed us back and back, until a wide circle had been cleared.

When the flap on the cart was raised, it was impossible to see from any quarter, because so many police and soldiers stood around it. Soon, a man in foul clothing, the unfortunate Shanahan, was stood up, carried—he refused to walk—and then propelled up on the high platform, directly beneath the noose.

The people buzzed when they saw him, and some jeered. Shanahan, looking nowhere, and to my eyes appearing more numbed than sullen, was manhandled to a point directly beneath the rope. He was small and fidgety, prematurely bald, about thirty-five years old, with bandy legs and dark eyes.

A plump man with a beak of a nose drew the noose over Shanahan's head and arranged it round his neck, then chucked it tight, making Shanahan wince. By now a priest had climbed the platform, but Shanahan turned his head away, like a man who had already decided where he was going. The priest stepped down.

I heard a noise like a wooden gunshot—and a wild cry. The lever had been pulled and the narrow platform dropped—and there, some yards from my face, in the gap beneath the trapdoor, hung Shanahan, in eternity. The shriek from him had startled me.

He did not die. He hung there, twisting a little, his wrists secured behind him, his feet in his tied ankles moving up and down like those of a dancer at practice, his face turning this way and that as though he was trying to get his head out of the noose. Twice he looked into my eyes; twice I looked away. Of course there would be no escape, and after a few minutes Shanahan began to expire, his face turning blue, his lips foaming.

Some cheers rose up, perhaps from the neighbors and families of the victims. Not many people joined in; all, like me, remained where they stood. For my part, revulsion overcame me. I had no feelings about

Shanahan; I had not even known his name when I woke up that morning—but even at my twenty-three years of age, my entire spirit convulsed at the pleased deliberateness of the execution, and the waste of a life.

People in general, I am convinced, know everything, even before they know that they know. At that point, by all the usual practices, that crowd should have turned away. Instead, everybody stayed fixed—they sensed another drama.

The militia in front of the scaffold redoubled their attitude of sternness; the soldiers drew bayonets and the police aimed guns, and we were pushed back farther. A puzzled hum rose from the crowd—and then it grew to a shout, as a figure recognizable to us all was taken from the cart and manhandled up to the scaffold.

Over the previous months, a long trial had been taking place in Cork, of a young land agitation leader, David O'Connor, accused of murder. All opinion called the accusation false; witnesses palpably committed perjury; the judge refused to hear respectable contradictory evidence; and the prisoner had been silenced when he tried to speak on his own behalf. At one stage in the trial, the judge had threatened to take the case back from the jury (all landowners, but some of them showing uncertainty) and himself pronounce verdict and sentence. So prejudiced had the trial appeared that delegates had been sent to London to request the attendance of observers at the appeal.

Now no appeal would take place. The authorities had smuggled young O'Connor, a doctor educated in Spain, past the vigil at Cork Jail and would hang him here at Mallow.

I looked at Mr. Egan. "Will they riot?"

He shook his head. Most people sank to their knees in prayer—and I, to my shame, turned away. I could not allow myself to see young Dr. O'Connor die—and I was unable to eat again for two days.

Those who have told me eyewitness stories of the Great Irish Famine of the 1840s talk of the quiet in the countryside, the absence of birds, the unbearably sad muting of the neglected animals. Such tales have been especially poignant when coming from musicians, who are bidden to fill places with enjoyable sounds. That afternoon in Mallow, all the fiddles and all the pipes ceased their playing. I have never heard such silence as I heard in that crowded, stricken place, and I never wish to hear it again.

Capital punishment ceased in Ireland more than forty years ago, its abolition a by-product of the Catholic Church's opposition. Today, membership in the European Union precludes it. In English-occupied Ireland it happened everywhere, often at a whim.

Contaminated juries, perjured evidence, selected and selective witnesses—many of the trials had more rigging than a sailing ship. Justice was not so much blind as blindsided.

And the hangings caused a vicious circle. A landlord was killed. Local men were hanged in reprisal after sham trials. Another landowner got murdered—Irish roulette.

Out of the multitude of commonplace miscarriages of justice rose a rebel spirit. Fair-minded people everywhere might have murmured horror when a Protestant and his family were slaughtered or burned out of their home. But a wrongly executed Catholic raised an outcry. Every unjust trial, every hanging judge, created a new hero-martyr. The ballads and laments found a new power base.

In fact, they became a weaponry. And they helped to create the new voice of the majority. The purer literary impulses of the educated Anglo-Irish, such as Oscar Wilde, George Bernard Shaw, and William Butler Yeats, had already been resounding. Their unique tone brought the English language to bear on the Irish imagination. Now the Catholic martyrdom in miscarriages of justice created a different Irish sound.

In the fusion of the two traditions, the cool and educated Anglo-Irish styles and the raw, often ironic, mourning ferocity of the ballad tradition, was born a new Irish voice.

My fortune has been to live through such comprehensive times. As I witnessed the great will to recover the country's land for the Irish, I also observed another and separate movement of restoration: the recovery of the native soul.

By the turn of the century, many Catholic writers and poets had begun writing about the glories of ancient Ireland. They had not previously been allowed to write, they had not been allowed to read, they could be—and were—deported for owning books. I was present to observe how the Celtic world came to the fore once again, with many passionate declamations in verse and prose, with vivid translations from the Irish language into English.

Great men were rising in all this. Some were already established in repute; some had yet to make their names but would go on to garner fame and respect. I met them, and in their company, I would recite a tale I had heard, as I believed that I should attempt to contribute. And I am pleased to say that I was often gratified by their evident acceptance of my performance—though it was always followed with a longer effort of their own, or else a lofty and steel-edged repudiation of my tale.

Some of these literary figures planted themselves in my memory, not from works they had yet written but from force of presence. One day, the sixteenth of June 1904, I was sitting in a Dublin public house after a lunch of Gorgonzola cheese with a glass of Burgundy. It was late in the afternoon and I was writing in my Journal when I caught the attention of a young man in his early twenties. He was wearing light shoes, of a kind people usually reserve for playing lawn tennis, and he wore a yachtsman's cap. With a jaunty and confident air he slouched over to me.

"What are you writing?" he asked me.

"I try to keep a Journal," I said, "though I fail to address it every day."

"No man's life is interesting enough for every day to be recorded," he said. "Except mine."

"Do you have an exceptional life?" I asked him.

"Exceptional. It gives me deep satisfaction. Today, for instance, I shall meet with a young woman who, of her own free will, shall yield up to me the mysteries of her existence."

He told me that his name was James A. Joyce and that he came of an ancient Irish family whose ancestral lands could still be found in south

Galway. When I told him my name, he pronounced with great delight that I must be one of the "royal O'Briens of Munster."

Mr. Joyce said, "Therefore, I suppose you have a pound on you that I might borrow? By way of gratitude," he added, "I will allow you to read me what you have been writing in your Journal."

I said, "I cannot; I have been transcribing a legend I recently heard about a deer, but it is unfinished."

"You are speaking to a man who believes that in Ireland the artist is the proud stag torn down by the vile hounds of the populace. And that metaphor, if metaphor it be, is certainly worth a pound."

I gave him the requested money. Mr. Joyce waved the banknote like a small banner, promised to pay it back, and said, "This may be the unit of currency that launches a great literary career."

"What do you intend to write?"

"I have it all planned out," he said. "After some pithy observations of my fellow-citizens here in Dublin, I shall write a memoiristic but brilliant satire on the human soul. Then I shall write a large novel, modeled on the wanderings of Odysseus, but it will be all about a man brought low in life by a woman. Inspired, of course, by Mr. Parnell."

To which I replied, "When you write, if you write, be sure to make it complicated. It will retain people's attention. I knew Mr. and Mrs. Parnell—they saw little that was simple in their lives."

Mr. James Joyce rose from the bench beside me, clapped a hand to his forehead, and cried, "My God! It is I who should be paying you for that incisive advice. 'Make it complicated.' I shall remember it all my life"— and he departed the public house with a gracious nod to the barman and the cry "Any word on the Gold Cup?"—for it was Ascot week and all of Ireland placed wagers on the horses that were running on that great racecourse.

"It'll be tonight before we hear," said the barman.

Mr. Joyce departed—and sprang back through the door a moment later.

"You must go and tell Mr. Yeats your story—he lives up on Rutland Square. He'd love to hear it; he welcomes all mythologies."

That afternoon, I did as young Mr. Joyce suggested; I called, unbidden, on the renowned poet Mr. Yeats. Ofttimes I had seen him, vague and flowing, in the streets of Dublin, wearing a voluminous black cloak and a floppy bow-tie and his great scarab ring.

I was curious to meet him. People said many things—that he was arrogant; that he made poems out of works in other languages and did not acknowledge them; that he loved widely, though often with ladies who did not live in Ireland. When I came to his house, I found him on the doorstep; he was emptying tea leaves from a large brown teapot into the street drain.

I introduced myself, and Mr. Yeats asked, "Why have you come to see me?" and I told him about meeting a young man named James Joyce.

"He's so sarcastic. You can't take seriously a word that he says. He's always sending people to call on me even though he knows how busy I am; I think he does it to stop me writing. Did he try to borrow money off you? Don't give him a penny," said Mr. Yeats. "Come in anyway."

At first he proved short with me, but then he behaved very graciously when I told him some of the story I was writing about Finn MacCool and the deer. I said that I had heard it on my travels and he leaned forward with great attention, his spectacles winking in the afternoon sun.

Mr. Yeats then began to ask me questions about myself (he was five years younger than me), and I told him something of my life. He pronounced himself enchanted with the notion of my wandering hither and yon, healing people, and at the same time gathering stories and setting them down, and writing reports upon the world.

"Oh, your life is a kind of poem in itself," he said in his deep, booming voice.

I was much complimented and said so.

"And you look like a poet," he said. "A man does not have to write poetry to have a poet's soul."

I pressed him on this point and he said, "Warmth of spirit. Love of humanity. These are poet's gifts. You have them abundantly."

I felt my heart opening up, and in a fit of confidence I related the story of my great unrequited love. At the conclusion I said that I had written many letters and none had been answered, that I thought of this lady night and day and that my courage had now abated.

Mr. Yeats took off his spectacles, wiped them on his floppy bow-tie, replaced them, and began exhorting me.

"I remake myself many times—to ensure that I am the bravest who will deserve the fairest. Feather yourself," he said, waving a hand at me to indicate me head to toe. "Wear bright plumage. Present a wonderful façade to her. Women enjoy a dandy."

It had been three years, six months, one day, and twenty-two hours since I had last seen Miss Burke, on the street in Paris as she dismissed me. I have already recounted how I brokenheartedly returned to Ireland via Holland. Mother, seeing my distress, had advised me to write to Dr. a'Court Tucker's house. I wrote many letters, all civil, some apologetic, none without the utmost courtesy, but I never received a reply.

When I told this to Mr. Yeats, he said, "I like few men but I am comfortable with you. Therefore, why not seek her father? Can there be many men in London who go by the name of Terence Burke?"

I told him that I already knew the gentleman's address, and had indeed sent letters there too.

My only visit to England had thrust me into the fracas over Mr. Parnell—but when I returned to my family and narrated Mr. Yeats's advice, they supported his idea. Mother supervised all my clothing, and, days later, as I left for the train that would take me to Kingstown and the steamer to England, my father gave me a generous financial support.

"New clothes. Shiny boots. Best foot forward," he said. "Make her father see what a fine man you are."

Consequently, I enjoyed the good accommodation of Mr. Brown's hotel in London, and after a day of resting and walking and visiting a gentleman's outfitters, making sure that I was not prone to accusations of dishevelment, I set forth to the house of Mr. Terence Burke. It was my forty-fourth birthday, the twenty-first of June, and I hoped that this would be of good omen.

A girl with red hair and many sun-freckles opened the door at 29 Alexander Street, Westminster, and I recognized—and said so—that her accent came from Cork. She called herself Mary, and after our little conversation about the pleasantness of her native county, she went to fetch Mr. Burke; not being a trained servant, she forgot to ask my name.

Presently, the gentleman appeared, a tall, thin man, with spectacles pushed up on his forehead. I could at once see his daughter's resemblance to him; and although he seemed to have the slow movements of those who suffer chronic ill-health, he had a vigorous personality.

"Goodness," he said, "what a gentleman I see here, mmm? Who are you, sir, and how do you do?"

He impressed me as delightful.

"Sir, I fear that I am Charles O'Brien. Himself. In the flesh, as it were."

"Charles O'Brien?" It became plain that he did not know the name, for he said next, "And—why do you 'fear' that you are Charles O'Brien, mmm? Is it such a terrible thing to be Charles O'Brien?"

On some days I believe a dullness slows my intellect; on others I have a certain sharpness—which now I found.

"Oh, sir," I said. "To fear that one is oneself is such a great terror that one needs no other fears—and so are burdens lifted."

Mr. Burke laughed. "And a wit. Come in, Charles O'Brien."

He led me into his inner rooms, through a most pleasant house, full of comfort and warmth. I felt some surprise; perhaps my sharp encounters with his daughter had led me to expect a colder home.

We sat and Mr. Burke offered me tea, which I declined, and a drink, which I also declined (I needed my wits about me). He settled in his chair.

"Now, Mr. Charles O'Brien, I have the pleasure of a visit from a fine man on a fine summer afternoon; what may I return to him?"

I said, "Sir, this concerns your daughter."

He laughed. "Do you know April?"

I said, "Yes, sir. I do. I was with Mr. Wilde in Paris."

"Ohhhhh," he said, changing to a grave mood. "What a great loss he is to us all! April was most upset and still mourns him. Which is not usual in a young person."

"Sir," I blurted, "I fell in love with your daughter in Paris and I wish to press my case forward with her and with you."

He laughed again. "Well, you can try to be lucky! Have you seen how direct she can be?"

I winced. "Has she told you of me?"

"No. April tells me nothing of her suitors—except that she has none and entertains none."

"Sir." Fear seized me, in case I had already established false pretenses. "I must tell you the whole story. Your daughter has already rejected me."

He waved a hand. "Pish! A thing of nothing, as Shakespeare said. It's what a girl feels she must do to a suitor. But tell me anyway."

About myself, I have many doubts, but I do not doubt that I tell a good tale. For the next twenty minutes, Mr. Terence Burke sat transfixed as I told him of my life as a healer, of Lady Mollie Carew, of my journey to Paris, of my failure to help Mr. Wilde. Then I told him of April's arrival with Dr. Tucker, and of the great tale that Mr. Wilde told, of my pursuit of April, of her blunt rejection and my subsequent despondency.

When telling a story, it is important to observe the face of the listener. From the many aspects that passed across Mr. Terence Burke's face I was reminded of clouds passing over a mountain on a sunny day: first there is light, then there is shadow, then there is light again. Soon, I knew that he had not previously heard anything of this tale, not even the part concerning his own birth.

As I finished, he gazed into the fireplace, now filled with pine cones as a summer decoration. He said nothing; then he looked at me and made a gesture with his hand that said "Stay" and he rose and left the room. I heard his footsteps on the stairs; I heard him cross a floor over my head, retrace his steps, and return down the staircase.

He stood by my chair and handed me a small rectangle of stiff paper.

"I am one, mmm, of the few gentlemen in England," he said, "with a very small birthright—this is it; this drawing."

Naturally I recognized it at once—a perspective of Tipperary Castle from the side on which stands the theater.

"How have you come by this?"

He said, "I was told that my mother died in my childbirth and that she died in the West Indies, that she came of a Northumbrian family who lived in this castle"—he tapped the rectangle of paper—"but that the ancestral home has been long ruined."

"Who told you this?"

He said, "The people whom I have always called 'family'—my guardian, as I understood her to be." He sat down. "Here we have a mystery."

"Does your daughter know of this?"

"I must say that I do not know. She expresses no affection for Ireland and the Irish. None at all."

Raised in Somerset, he had been given to understand that his father, a soldier, had died in the South Seas a month before his infant son was due to be born. Then his mother, overcome with grief, fell dangerously ill in the last month of her confinement and died. He was saved, and his aunt adopted him. Of the story he told me, only two facts had a ring of truth: his father had indeed been named Terence Burke; and his mother had indeed been an actress—"But a most respectable actress," he hastened to say.

I had not, as yet, asked the question that burned me: Where was April? Was she still in Paris? Or had she, as I feared in my general anxiety, gone farther afield? At least I had ascertained that she had no suitor and no consort and, I gathered—or made bold to assume—no intention of having such.

"How are we to get to the bottom of all this?" he said. He stood; he sat; he stood again; he sat again; he rose and paced; he sat again—all in silence, his knuckles to his mouth.

When I saw a moment of composure, I asked, "Where is your daughter these times, sir? Is she still with Dr. Tucker?"

"Oh, no," he said. "She works here in London now—she has been given an excellent post in the government, in the Ministry that deals with France; she's one of the few ladies at work there. But she lives here; she will be home this evening." He sat. "Now, Charles O'Brien—what is to be done?"

I said, "Sir, this may be your estate. It has, I believe, four thousand acres of prime Tipperary land. It lies in the Golden Vale, one of the richest seams of earth in the west of Europe. It is your birthright, and you must prove your title and assert your claim."

"But how can I do that?"

"In truth, sir, I do not know. But my father will know—he knows many lawyers. And I will assist in every way that may be useful."

"A true gentleman," he said quietly. "A true gentleman."

The clock on Terence Burke's mantel told me that it was past four. He saw me glance at it and said, "My daughter comes home at twenty-five minutes before seven every evening."

"Sir, if I may—let us have you tell your daughter of my visit. I shall return tomorrow and you shall report to me."

I learned that his daughter took luncheon at home on most days; we arranged that I should arrive next day before she did, and we parted most warmly. My efforts had exhausted me, I had much to think about, and so I hailed a cab to my hotel. I dined alone with no liquor, retired early, and slept not at all, because my mind raced across the words of the day. How should we establish that Mr. Burke had been lied to about his origins—which was my first suspicion? Then I supposed: What if he had not been told lies? What if the house and estate belonged to another family? My father had told me when I returned from Paris that, yes, the family name of Tipperary Castle had, to his memory, been Burke, and this seemed to confirm the story that Mr. Wilde had told.

Yet my hopes of capturing April Burke—and I believed that the regaining of her ancestral home must aid me in this—still rested principally on a tale told by a playwright, therefore a maker of fictions. As these uncertainties made me unable to sleep, I rose and sat by the window, ceaselessly shuffling a deck of cards.

Next morning, I walked along Bond Street, took coffee at Mr. Fortnum's, and purchased some candied peel for my mother, some crystal ginger for Father, some "furnace-hot" peppermint for Euclid, and a bottle of Tuscan wine for my noonday host, which would be delivered with my compliments in advance of my arrival.

Mr. Burke greeted me with a long face.

"I fear I have to disappoint you."

Already I knew, and indeed had half-expected what he would say.

"My daughter will not join us. She has declined on account of—" He halted and held out his hands. "I do not know. But your excellent wine has come."

I said, "Let us employ our time usefully over lunch to see how we may further your birthright claim."

We had a most agreeable luncheon. Although my heart continued to beat fast at what had evidently amounted to another rejection, I continued to enjoy Mr. Burke's company. We straightaway got to the business at hand—namely, how to establish who he was, and whence came his family. I asked of him that he tell me all he knew about his childhood and growing up, and who might still be living in Somerset with knowledge of his past.

Our plan came together smoothly. As he, being retired from his place of business, had time on his hands, and as I had come over from Ireland to spend as many days on this matter as would be necessary, we would journey to Somerset the very next day.

Then I said, "Sir, are you acquainted with Mr. George Bernard Shaw, the renowned critic of the drama?"

He said, "I have never met him, although I know who he is."

I said, "Mr. Shaw is known to love actresses, and I feel that this inquiry will intrigue him. The span of time is not long—he may know someone who can shed light on the life of your dear mother."

I had heard that Mr. Shaw was among the easiest men in London to find, and we did not experience much difficulty. The critic and playwright was known to hold forth in a Covent Garden dining-hall before he went to the theater or the opera. We saw him straightaway and walked to his table.

His beard wagged as he spoke and he breathed the most oppressive breath; he was much given to the eating of fruits, vegetables, and nuts. But Mr. Shaw had the cleverest eyes, and the quickest, merriest smile.

Sadly, he helped not at all. He greeted us very cordially, and pressed upon us some pamphlet that he had been writing about the Solomon Islanders and his desire to bring them an education. Not renowned as a listener, he nevertheless gave us his attention as Mr. Burke bade me tell the story. I saw Mr. Shaw begin to remember my name, and when I had finished he chuckled and said to me, "Ah, yes, I have you now—you're Mr. Parnell's old friend."

I said that indeed I had known Mr. Parnell, and Mr. Shaw said no more on the subject. He told us then that he had not known an actress by the name of April Burke and had never heard of her; "Or Mrs. Terence Burke, or Mrs. Alphonsus Burke, or Mrs. Edmund Burke, or Mrs. Aloysius Alhambra Burke."

When we left Mr. Shaw's company we were no wiser than before, but we had enjoyed meeting him and we laughed much at his various passions and schemes.

"He talks a great deal," said Mr. Terence Burke, who dined with me at my hotel.

Shaw was four years older than Charles O'Brien. He had known a great deal less privilege, but had accomplished much more. With a fearlessness that Mr. O'Brien had not found in himself, Shaw struck out for unpopular causes. He also supported the works—and made the names—of emerging playwrights. And he was one of the champions of Oscar Wilde, by whom he was much impressed.

His presence in London typified a kind of long-standing phenomenon. The Irish in England have achieved roles that were never reciprocated. Richard Brinsley Sheridan, Edmund Burke, Oliver Goldsmith, Shaw, Yeats, and Wilde—no Englishmen got comparable status in Ireland.

For obvious reasons. Whereas the sound of an English accent in an Irish ear long spoke of brutal colonization, the presence of a cultivated Irishman in London salved the conscience to some degree, as if to say, "Look, we've been educating these savages." Or, if entertaining, supported a stereotype: "Oh, such charming rogues."

Shaw, more than any of his fellow countrymen, understood these mind-sets. He came from poor Protestant Dublin stock, therefore from an unfamiliar, disconcerting mold—he could not be pigeonholed. And he was self-educated, self-made, relentlessly clever, and prepared to take on anything.

If he found himself in the wrong upon a question, he publicly allowed himself to think his way to a different point of view—and then announced that he had changed his mind. When he did so, he changed many other minds.

He knew how to attack with humor; he ridiculed England's stereotypical thinking just as satirically as Jonathan Swift had done a century and more earlier. And Shaw did so just as viciously, if in a little more nuanced way: "An Englishman thinks he is moral when he is only uncomfortable," he wrote.

By the time Mr. O'Brien and Mr. Burke met him, he had created a formidable presence as a columnist and pamphleteer. A music and drama critic too, whose playwriting career had just begun to flourish, he was also an activist whose principal desire was to make the general mass of the English population more political.

Shaw's great ego opened many doors. Although Charles O'Brien, through Mr. Burke's presence, was guaranteed a safe passage about London as an obviously civilized Irishman, Shaw could have introduced him to a whole new swath of people.

And Mr. O'Brien would have been a hit. His "mixed" background would have confounded all sides. Shaw knew that Mr. O'Brien's class status wasn't traceable by accent. "It is impossible for an Englishman to open his mouth, without making some other Englishman despise him," he once uttered.

If, through Shaw, Charles had met the Anglo-Irish landlords or the British establishment in their London drawing rooms, he could have exchanged news about upper-class friends in common, such as Lady Mollie Carew. And if Shaw had taken him to meet his socialist fellow travelers, Mr. O'Brien could have spoken to them at length about his travels through Ireland. They would have been more than interested in his assessments of the country's mood in the middle of the "Irish Question."

Regrettably, however, Shaw did not take Mr. O'Brien on a tour of inquiry among the era's actresses. Shaw knew them all, and had many famous dalliances and friendships—always assumed to be platonic—with leading ladies of the day, such as Mrs. Patrick Campbell. Had he known

April Burke, he would almost certainly have fallen for the woman described by Oscar Wilde.

The farmhouses in England's West Country seemed appealing and secure. Across undulating land, we glimpsed distant church spires, on a day of great sunshine and a clear blue sky. After a train luncheon of less than moderately good food (it stuck to the roof of the mouth), we alighted at the town of Yeovil.

His childhood home, Mr. Burke told me, lay between Yeovil and Bath, near the village of Doulting. A hackney car took us there, and we found an excellent inn where we guaranteed rooms for the night. I longed to ask him whether he had told his daughter of our excursion, but I decided to wait until dinner and a glass of Madeira.

The Brook House lay in a small valley, where the summer seemed more intense than anywhere else. A long building, it had a stone doorway to the street, and a lengthy blank facade with two windows—sparse appointments in such a building.

"The house's greater life faces the garden," Mr. Burke told me.

We opened the latch on a green wooden door under the arches of branches, and there, some ninety feet long, stretched a beautiful terrace of paving-stones. As we entered, the garden came in view to our right—sloping lawns filled with yellow and white blossoming trees, and deep, wide beds of flowers in their glorious summer colors.

"I have not been here since I was twenty," Mr. Burke said, but when we knocked at the door, he immediately recognized the old lady who answered. She knew him too, and professed herself delighted—but with my experience of calling upon people in their homes, I thought her wary. We did not enter; she led us to a bower with garden seats and an air of peace and pleasantness, and she rang a bell that hung from a branch. A gentleman appeared, a truculent man; "Harris!" cried Mr. Burke.

"Oh? Hullo," said the worthy, and never uttered another word. He brought us lemonade and sat with Miss Gambon, for that was her name. And she, as I soon found, had been the person who raised Mr. Burke!

After much talk of neighbors and memories, of childhood escapades and great feats of the weather, Mr. Burke, in his charming way, declared, "Now, Mater, we are here on a mission. Tell me, do you know anything of a Great House in Ireland? Of which you gave me a drawing when I was very young?"—and he pulled it from the leather attaché case he had carried with him. I had set myself to watch rather than speak, and I know that Miss Gambon recoiled and looked at him with some malice. She concealed it cleverly—but she knew that I saw it. Then she answered:

"I don't know. Somewhere in the past, I feel, we did have an Irish relation."

Mr. Burke pressed on: "I have never visited my mother's grave." Had I not had such a good impression of him, I might have believed that he was taunting her.

"Oh, but do you not recall? She was buried at sea, on her return from Spain."

"What?" he said. "Was I born at sea?"

She had the air of someone grasping at a straw of hope—and she had been bewildered by this thunderbolt into her life from such a clear blue sky.

"Oh, yes, at sea, yes."

"But is not my birth registered here at Bristol?"

"That is where the law required," she said. "It had to do with the place in which the infant would reside. And—" Here she stuttered a little. "Also. The ship—it had sailed out of Bristol port." (I was mindful of Mother's remark that "a lie needs two legs.")

Mr. Burke believed her, but I did not. I studied her—and she saw that I studied her. Although she wore excellent fabrics, she had nothing of Mr. Burke's looks; indeed, she seemed coarse to have reared such an elegant man, and I came to the conclusion that nothing in this story might be what it seemed. I also concluded that we should not get at much truth in this garden at this moment.

In a short time, she terminated the encounter, saying, "You must forgive me. I tire easily these days; I never leave the house anymore."

Mr. Burke and I took our leave of her. In the lane outside the house, he said that he wanted to show me his "haunts," and we walked up to a hill from which we could look out over a wide swath of the countryside.

"The locals told me that on a clear day I should glimpse the sea from here," he said, "but on a clear day, we always seem to have a haze that obscures our chance. I find that to resemble Life itself."

And as he laughed, I wondered whether he had begun to ask himself questions about the obfuscations that might have been his lot.

That night, in the inn they call the Pilgrim, the landlord required that each of us sign the Visitors' Book and gave us a workman's supper of beef, potatoes, and ale. Mr. Burke and I discussed the day's proceedings. He saw nothing untoward in the speech or attitude of Miss Gambon, expressing only surprise that he had not been told he had been born at sea.

"By Jove!" he said, over and over, and then, in a typically forgiving remark, "Perhaps she thought it would have been too much for a small chap to bear. Especially with his mama being buried at sea—although I confess that I should have been very intrigued at such a notion."

I learned that what I had seen of the house represented no more than a third of the establishment, that behind the very large trees at the end of the terrace the main building spread longer and wider.

"How came your aunt by such a fine place?" I asked.

This innocent man replied that it had been in her husband's family "for centuries"—that, as he understood matters, the Gambons had been yeoman farmers, meaning that they had not been tenants; they had supported themselves throughout history, with their own livestock and their own produce.

By now, Mr. Burke gave the appearance of fatigue, and I knew that the day must have been exhausting for him. I did not try him further in family matters or the question of his beautiful daughter's affections. Instead I sent him to bed early, with a warning that the hackney was to come at nine o'clock, so that we might get back to Yeovil in time for the London train.

Next morning I rose at six o'clock, prepared myself for the day, and set out on a walk to the places we had visited the day before. They were but a mile distant and it had dawned a beautiful morning. As I strode down the lane to Mr. Burke's childhood home, I saw that a good hansom cab had drawn up outside—an unusual sight, I surmised, in that countryside. Concealing myself behind a tree, I watched, and soon I saw Miss Gambon appear, dressed for town. She carried a small case, such as people use for documents; this was a person bound on business. Harris, the surly manservant, helped her to ascend, and then he climbed to the box beside the driver, and the cab went up the lane and took the road for Bristol. I thought it unusual that a lady so old should take a journey so elaborate so early in the day.

In this pretty corner of England's West Country, Charles O'Brien was thrust into confusion. He had believed that his beloved's father had been taken from Tipperary Castle as an infant. According to the story Mr. O'Brien heard Oscar Wilde tell in Paris, the mother had previously vanished mysteriously, in the company of a strange woman who showed up unannounced.

The grief-stricken father, Terence Burke the First, so to speak, had searched high and low for her but never found her; she had vanished. Oscar Wilde had met her when she was at the height of her dazzling career.

Now Charles was confronted with an entirely different tale—of a child born at sea, and of a secretive old woman who obviously told lies ("I never leave the house anymore").

Victorian literature and theater abound in such intrigue over inheritance. Even now, disputes over land ownership and testatory challenges break out in Irish courts all the time: "Where there's a will," they say, "there's a lawsuit."

Essentially, Mr. O'Brien found himself in the center of such a plot. Even though he never says so, how could he not have speculated many times as to why Terence Burke—and especially Terence Burke's spirited daughter—never bothered to pursue such a potentially huge inheritance in Ireland? Whether they admit to it, many of the English have long had a romantic love affair with Ireland. To them it was always a land of castles and charm, of horses and great drinking feats, of misty hills and dreams.

It's possible that the Burkes, father and daughter, suspended the romance because they feared the circumstances, and then simply did not let on to Charles O'Brien. To claim an Irish estate at a time of such turbulence over land might have struck the gentle Mr. Burke as, to say the least, risky. Nor would his daughter, who cared for him deeply, have wanted her father to feel stress of any kind—especially if it had been generated by somebody she had already dismissed as an insanitary and unreliable ass.

My journey back to London in Mr. Burke's company had the pleasantness of friends accustomed to traveling with each other. When we had seated ourselves in the train, he thanked me for this excursion into his past.

"I have been greatly moved by it," he said. "My daughter shall know how this has added to my life."

Upon this he fell silent, and we both contemplated the passing countryside.

The orderly hedgerows and green leafy richness, though not as wild and inspiring as those in my beloved native land, soothed my eye and encouraged my reflection. How could I reconcile the two opposing stories of Mr. Terence Burke's origins? Where and how had he been born? In a safe confinement bed within that beautiful house in Tipperary or tossed in a schooner's bunks upon the notorious Bay of Biscay? Who was his mother, and what had become of her? Had she gone on to achieve fame through her beauty and acting brilliance or does she lie "full fathom five" in a watery grave off the rocky coasts of Europe? Was my judgment of the old woman accurate? I found her furtive and uneasy. How would all of this affect the possible advancement of my affections with my heart's desire? I dreaded that she might blame me for having stirred up an intrigue within her steady life.

Thus did my thoughts grow morbid. As to the general oddity of the thing, I felt not at all dismayed. Such tales seem ordinary to me; I had long heard stories of family mystery within my parents' home, and on my travels it seemed the very fodder upon which people feasted—a mainstay of table conversation.

For example, I recollected that in the town of Roscommon, they celebrate a notorious woman, by name Lady Betty. According to the legend, when she was a young wife, her husband died, leaving her with an infant son. They eked out a dreadful existence until the boy reached the age of fourteen, when he emigrated, promising to send his mother money from the New World. She never heard from him again, and she continued in disappointment and havoc, dwelling in an abandoned hovel with rags for her bed.

One winter night, as the story goes, a handsome and wealthy young stranger called and asked for a roof under which to stay out of the rain and cold. While he slept, Lady Betty killed him for his money. In his pockets, she discovered papers that informed her she had murdered her own son—who had come back rich and successful to salvage his mother.

Lady Betty screamed her sorrow up and down the streets of the town, and she was sentenced to hang. But the hangman took ill; and, as several hangings had been arranged for that day, Lady Betty volunteered to become the executioner in exchange for her own reprieve. So effective did she prove that she gained a salary from the King and apartments in the jail.

Across such lowering topics did my thoughts flow as we steamed through the pretty English countryside on that sunny day. The prospect of meeting Mr. Burke's beautiful daughter, the permanent resident of all my thoughts for almost four years now, did not cheer me as it should have done. I knew of a certainty that she must greatly disapprove of her father being taken through such a tiring experience without her foreknowledge.

When we reached Mr. Burke's home in Westminster, nobody was there; the maid, Mary from Cork, had her afternoon of liberty, and we sat, pleased to rid ourselves of our weariness. Mr. Burke provided a bottle of Madeira and we set to it, and thereby did I forgo my pledge to myself that I would not imbibe strong drink in this important adventure. But one glass always requires a supporter, notoriously so with delicious Madeira.

Cried Mr. Burke, "A bird never flew on one wing."

"But sir, my old tutor, my dear Buckley—he used to say those very words."

"A good tutor, an excellent tutor!"

Soon, Mr. Burke went to fetch the next bottle of the sweet beauty. He survived a little mishap (I heard the noise of furniture being accosted) and returned triumphant. Between us, we managed to extract a difficult and recalcitrant cork; we filled each other's glasses to the brim and drank yet another toast to "New Friends"—and, I added, "To Great Estates."

Mr. Burke sat back in his chair in a manner of great comfort and said, "I should like to sing to you."

I applauded.

He said, "I shall sing 'Greensleeves.' Do you know that it was written by King Henry the Eighth?"

I marveled, and he began.

" 'Alas, my love, you do me wrong—' " There he halted abruptly, saying, "I have forgot the tune." His eyes were droopy.

I said, "Sir, would you like to sleep awhile?"

He laughed, saying, "My dear friend"—and my heart soared; I had won his approval.

"Permit me to sing you a lullaby," I said, at which he took my hand in a most touching manner and held it as a child might. I knelt beside his chair, and began to sing; and I have a good voice—of that I am certain, on account of the many compliments that I have received. Indeed, he found my lullaby affecting, for soon Mr. Burke began to snore, and Madeira, I know from my father's life, produces loud snoring.

At that, somebody must have opened the door from the street, because some instinct made me look up. There I saw Miss Burke standing in her own parlor, gazing at me, as I knelt beside her father's chair, holding and stroking his hand and singing a lullaby to him in the Irish language (I had learned it of Cally) while her father snored with his head back and his mouth open. Two empty bottles that had lately contained Madeira stood nearby.

It became an ugly circumstance. Notwithstanding my fine clothing, and the efforts I had made to make myself look a gentleman, she continued to see me as the "lout" (her word) whom she had last encountered on the streets in Paris. I tried to explain, but she would have none of it.

"Your father and I have been to his childhood home," I said. "He has been much enjoying—"

"What?!" She was capable of such explosion as I had not seen in my placid household. "My father is not permitted to travel. And you have led him to drink—and drink can prove fatal to his health!"

"But he has enjoyed—"

She all but shouted. "What?! 'Enjoying'? 'Enjoyed'? Is 'enjoy' the main word in your lexicon, sir?!"

Her father did not cease snoring, even though voices had become raised.

"You lout! You—you scandal! Leave this house now."

In the interest of order and calm I moved very quickly to quit that room and house. On the street outside I continued my hectic pace until I had traveled some distance. Then I paused, and found a bench with a view upon the river, where I reflected upon the latest great misunderstanding.

I admit that I began to shed tears. It all seemed so unfortunate, and my case seemed so futile. Not for one moment had this young woman, who seemed even more beautiful than in Paris, and with a new poise, I thought—not for one moment had she allowed any judgment of me other than the forms she had already settled in her mind.

For a time, all other thoughts departed my mind as I contemplated my own condition. There I sat, at forty-four years of age, a time when other men have maturing and loving children—and some even close to grandchildren—and I had surrendered my life to a dream of love that would never reach fulfillment. I had money in the bank, because I had saved prudently, and because I had a generous father; across the land of Ireland, people knew and liked me, even loved me; I did not frighten children, offend ladies, or cause distress to clergymen; even now, I remained as diligent to my parents as when I had wanted to please them as eagerly as any small child; my knowledge of diverse and useful matters was wide and copious; I was instructed in art and science, in poetry and healing; important people knew my name and found pleasure in my company.

And yet this young woman of twenty-two years could not find it in herself to look at me beyond her own prejudice of me.

Perhaps, I thought, I carry a mark on my forehead. Perhaps some wrinkle of my complexion, like a hidden sign, says to the world, "Here is a man to be kicked. He will not retribute." Perhaps my anointed function in the world chose me to be a butt to some people, in order that they might express unpleasantness safely upon somebody who could be trusted not to damage them in return. If so, that is a useful purpose to them, and I must bear it.

As he always did when distressed, Charles went straight to his parents' house—to unexpected developments.

His mother's letters and journals, not known to her son, and never read by him, became available in 2003. She recorded his arrival, how the family gathered around him to hear what had happened, and to commiserate. Her papers also reveal what happened next. First, she received a letter.

> *Dear Mrs. O'Brien,*
> *I am given to understand by mutual friends that you are the mother of one Charles O'Brien, who lately visited my father in London and took him upon an excursion to the county of Somerset.*
> *It would prove of inestimable value to me should you provide me with a means of reaching your son. I should also feel most grateful were you to provide me with the name of a lawyer in Ireland whom you recommend without qualification.*
>
> *Yours Faithfully and in hope,*
> *April Burke.*

Amelia O'Brien couched her reply in terms meant to smoke out April Burke's intentions and yet offer no clue that she knew anything of the young woman.

Dear Madam,

Forgive my impersonal greeting, but I am unaware from your manner of signature whether to address a married lady or not.

If you will tell me some reason for your needing to reach my son, Charles, I shall be happy to pass on any communication. He leads a busy life, he is much in demand, and at his request all correspondence will pass through his father or myself. May I also ask the names of the "mutual friends" whom you mention?

As to the unqualified recommendation of a lawyer, I fear that my husband, who addresses these matters, refuses to believe that such a creature exists as a lawyer whom he or anybody feels he can "recommend without qualification." He also asks me to state that before giving a name he must "take the cloth to the tailor"— meaning that the nature of the legal business must guide the recommendation.

Yours Faithfully,
Amelia O'Brien.

The letter contains a number of slap-downs—the failure of April Burke to identify her single status (a matter of manners and breeding) and a certain bridling at the younger woman's importuning a total stranger. Nevertheless, within days came an answer.

Dear Mrs. O'Brien,

Thank you for the favor of your prompt reply. Your name was given to me by the Countess of Athlone, with whom I believe you are well acquainted, and she gave me a most warm opinion of you.

As to the body of my letter, I fear that I put the cart before the horse, as the expression goes. Your son has directed me to my possible

ownership in an Irish estate of which he has knowledge, and I
required further details from him. Then, in order to pursue such a
claim, if indeed it should exist, I reasoned that I must need an Irish
solicitor versed in land matters.

My gratitude to you bears repetition.

Yours Faithfully,
April Burke (Miss).

Amelia O'Brien wrote back (in her superb copperplate handwriting) and recommended her husband's legal firm in Limerick—Stokes and Somerville, on Catherine Street. In subsequent exchanges of correspondence back and forth, for six weeks, travel arrangements were made that would bring April Burke to Ireland and have Charles O'Brien show her the house in Tipperary. She arrived at the O'Brien household on the afternoon of Saturday, 1 October 1904, accompanied by Mary, the maid from Cork. Here is Amelia O'Brien's journal entry describing the occasion:

It is late; the night outside is beautiful. We are still warm with the summer. And we have had such times. If a day can be so crammed with new matter as to last a hundred hours, this was such a day. Charles came home last Wednesday. He has grown thin, and I do not like that. I fear that this unrequited love he suffers has now begun to hurt his body as well as his soul.

Bernard took him riding to Kilshane, whose wood Charles so loves. They had a long talk. Bernard reports that Charles seems almost unable to contain his excitement at the prospect of this young woman staying under our roof. Is my son too boyish, too unformed, for a man his age?

She arrived, this Miss Burke, this afternoon. I mean to gather my thoughts here so that I may try to understand her. But I have been much disposed to a strong dislike of her on account of her view of Charles. And her behavior toward him. Also, if she has not the acuteness of mind to perceive my son's innate goodness and innocence, I should not wish him to throw his life away on a hope of her.

I did not like the nearly peremptory tone of her letters to me. And I thought the freedom which she felt to approach me had in it something of the "user."

So it was that I expected to meet a conniving young woman. Careless of the feelings of others. Willing and prepared to make use of those whom she had but lately injured. Not at all a prospect to be cherished.

And I fear to say that I found a conniving and icy young woman. With little heart and no interest at all in my dear son—except, I fear, as to how she may use him in her own interests. In my life I cannot remember a time when I have taken so against another woman. She glanced this way and that, assessing us and not finding us wanting. But rather she conveyed surprise that we did not live in some mud hut like savages on the Equator.

My Bernard has charms beyond most men, and he failed to touch her. She did not smile at his sallies, she did not laugh at his jokes. (I, who have heard them many, many times, can still be prostrated by them.) Perhaps worst of all, she gave no impression that she might find the company of any of us to have value in any wise. This is a dreary and cunning young woman. Of great beauty, I grant, but I should not choose her company were she and I alone in a boat at sea.

Her first impression is of some money in her family system. How that can be I cannot know. Bernard says that she hired her car and driver well, with good horses, from an excellent livery in County Cork. That she has manners goes beyond doubt. But I fear that they may be trained manners, rather than the grace that comes from within. She behaved elegantly toward me, and false-prettily toward Charles—whose face whitened with strong feeling as he greeted her.

Bernard and I had made an understanding that Charles must introduce her to us. All morning he fretted, pacing upon the terrace, asking over and over how long the drive from Cork must take. Of Euclid, Miss Burke made no show. A mistake, I think; can she not know of Charles's fond affections for his brother? He judges people by their expression of regard for Euclid.

My impression of her has not yet been a good one. She presents herself as if in expectation of the world's unquestioning appreciation of her beauty. Forthright and confident in her views. Very sure that her beauty will open all doors.

Charles stumbled and hesitated in her presence. I watched closely. She took less and less regard of him, except what courtesy demanded. I am glad to say that his manners showed him to be a gentleman. I had feared that he might have crumbled. But he behaved so beautifully that I wonder how many men of such manners and gentleness does she meet that she can afford to spurn him?

Bernard and Charles showed her our gardens, our horses and cattle, and our beloved wood. Bernard reports that she talked amiably but showed little interest in the creatures or in the wood's eccentric growths or their history. She came back to the terrace and sat for tea. And she accepted our sensible invitation to stay the night. Charles has undertaken to show her the disputed property over at Tipperary Castle. They will go there tomorrow.

When Miss Burke had repaired upstairs to change for dinner, Charles naturally and with heartbreaking eagerness asked Bernard and me if we liked her. As we had had no opportunity to confer, we retreated a little. In such circumstances, Bernard always believes it best to tell what he calls "the truth of the moment." He said, "She is such a beauty." I said, "I will make up my mind about her when we have had dinner. And I will give you my candid opinion."

Charles then turned to Euclid, who said something I believe to be unfortunate.

"She'll change," Euclid said. "She'll learn to love you."

Oh, dear me! If we had any means left by which we might encourage Charles to extricate himself, we lost them at that moment.

At dinner tonight we were five. I had decided not to invite friends or neighbors until we had seen her further. She has excellent table manners. I would expect no less from a young woman who has worked for our Embassy in Paris. Bernard told a story I have heard many times (about a man who caught a fox, a rambling and funny story). Euclid told about electricity and what he had learned about it. Charles said little but for an occasional remark. The young Miss Burke looked at each speaker in turn as if calculating them in some way, assessing them.

Then came a moment which caused me to understand my son's infatuation. He must have seen something of this side to the girl somewhere. She spoke of her father, not in extravagant terms or in a surfeit of any emotion—but she spoke of him more tenderly than I ever spoke of my father, fine man though he was. Or than I have ever spoken of my adored Bernard and my two sons.

It was not so much the words of her speech. It was the light that she gave to us. Her face changed and lost some of its watchfulness. At least I call it that—I hope that it's not outright cunning, barely concealed. She could not hide her feelings for her father. From Charles's reports, Mr. Burke has much to recommend him.

"I would do anything for Papa" was her concluding remark. And, perhaps in the same mode of kindness, she turned to Charles and said, "That was a great gift you gave him, that journey to his childhood home." But Charles had told me she had cast him down for making the journey. Does this young woman have two faces? And perhaps more?

A worse question is: Have I deprived my darling son in some way? Did I withhold praise and approval from him? So much that he now inhales any approbatory remark as a dog takes a bone? When he had acknowledged her remark with a smile and a murmur, her earlier self returned. We saw again the cold and deliberate young woman whom I disliked at sight.

Tonight I go to bed with a heavy heart. My son loves a girl who will not judge him well. Who will not see that he is a fine and darling man. If he does win her, she will ruin him with her coldness and her calculations. If he does not win her, he will lead a lonely life. What am I to say to him in the morning? Shall I keep my counsel until she has left? And I hope that will occur soon.

In September of that year, 1904, it became known to me that new events would soon unfold and that they would join my life, at least in one form, to that of Miss Burke. For reasons of discretion and privacy I cannot disclose what transpired; suffice it to say that, owing to kind intermediaries, in particular the Countess of A——, some letters passed between my mother and my beloved. On a certain Wednesday, I was in the town of Kilkenny when a railway porter came to me with a letter from my mother (my parents always know where I am to be found in any week), saying that I must return home immediately, that Miss April Burke was "about to present herself."

As I galloped back through the gold light of evening, my mind raced; the "why" and the "how so" and the "wherefore" and the "which" and the "what" echoed like bells—and like bells they offered little beyond their exciting voices. Did she come to threaten me? Mother's letter said she was to visit "as a result of some correspondence"; was this some complaint that she meant to bring? As I always go to the foolish extremes of every thought, I naturally said to myself next, "Perhaps she has found that she loves me, that her father spoke well of me, and that she means to apologize, to say that she misunderstood me."

When I reached home, Mother told me that the letters gave ample direction as to the reasons for this astounding turn of matters, and on condition that I do not disclose them, she showed me. My heart leaped further as I read them—she meant to pursue the ownership of Tipperary Castle! If successful, would she live near us? I kept myself in check; disappointment has too long been such a companion to me that I knew I must not raise my hopes.

On my return from the mixed adventure that I had known in England, I had resumed my works. I healed a child in County Wicklow who suffered from sore eyes (bathing with day-old cold tea); and I spoke to men who planned political revolution and wished all our land matters, now significantly resolved, put behind them, so that a freedom and a self-government of the people and for the people could be determined.

One of these, a Dublin man of a few years more than thirty, by name of Arthur Griffith, told me that he would presently found a new political movement whose name would, he said, "echo in every home and in every heart." I spoke to Mr. Griffith in his newspaper offices in Dublin, and afterward I wrote about him as follows:

> He seems to maintain a balance of fierce and wise, of astute and idealistic. Of his Irish patriotism, he has no doubt; and his greater sarcasm has been reserved, he told me, for those who deem him "British," because Griffith, his ancestral name, is Welsh and not Irish. With his eyes aflame he said, "To paraphrase that diminutive Englishman, the Duke of Wellington—if my forefather was born in a stable, does that make me a horse?" He gave me the name of his new political movement, Sinn Fein, meaning "We Ourselves," and he declared as its aim the restoration of Ireland as a separate condition of statehood under the British monarchy. He would abolish the Act of Union of 1800, and in this way he believed that Time would present Ireland, after years of peaceful self-determination under the Crown, with a pathway towards total self-government.

I received much praise for this contribution, and I must confess that when I heard who was to be a guest under our roof, I contrived to leave a copy of the newspaper in her room, open at that very page.

Came the day she arrived. Of the Five Senses with which we are blessed, I cannot for certain say that one took precedence over another on that exquisite morning; Sight and Hearing flamed into life and remained in full bloom from the moment I opened my eyes (which was at six o'clock, almost before the sun); Smell and Touch followed hard behind; and as to Taste, I should have thought I had been eating raw board, so dry did my mouth feel.

Never did I shave with such precision. (I resist a beard, as I do not wish to be a creature whose fashion is led by the King's style—too many young men affect the royal shape of beard.) Nor have I ever chosen linen and outerwear with such hesitancy, such indecision. Evidently I made some good choices, because when I came down for breakfast Mother said I looked "dashing" and Father said that he hoped this girl had "a pair of eyes in her head." Euclid asked, "Charles, why am I not as handsome as you?"

It is my blessing to have so loving a family.

I was standing on the terrace, looking south to the mountains, when I saw her car arrive. From the stiffness of her posture I could tell that she has had little practice of traveling in sidecars, and I was there to receive her hand when she stepped down—the first time, believe it or not, that I had touched her, and I felt a blade of thrill shiver up along my arm. She greeted me warmly (though eschewing the use of my name—she said neither "Mr. O'Brien" nor "Charles"), and I led her forward to meet my family.

From that point the day seemed to dissolve into a kind of glow, and I am tested to recall its particulars. She sparkled among us like a wonderful stream—she gave us so much of her spirit with warmth and friendliness, and she turned to me with a doe's eyes, and she deferred to me, and she charmed Euclid and flattered him, and my father lost his heart to her and Mother smiled and smiled.

We walked with her through the gardens and the wood, and she liked everything so much and was so attentive to my old tales of my tutors that I could imagine her having been here with me in those past days—and I knew that I could eagerly share all this with her now and forever.

Then we saw the horses with their glossy strength, and the cows with their wrinkled brows, and then we repaired to the terrace for tea. I can bring to mind little of what was said. The sun shone and this young woman, the queen of my soul, sat with me, here, amid my family, at my home, listening and speaking and looking as beautiful as a dream.

Mother invited her to stay with us for at least one night; we all concluded that she must be too fatigued to ride over to Tipperary Castle
that evening, and that perhaps tomorrow morning would prove more
appropriate. When she agreed, Mother accompanied her upstairs, Father had to reach the yard before milking began (some errand or other),
and Euclid went to take his daytime rest, which he needs if he is to enjoy
dinner.

For my part I walked through the wood, and I confess that I talked to
the trees. I felt like singing, but I knew that the peculiar corridors between the growths permitted sound to carry to the house and I feared
that I might disturb that beloved girl who, even now, was resting beneath
the roof under which I was born.

In time, in blurred and happy time, I too went indoors and changed
for dinner, and there passed as pleasing a meal as I have ever known
under that or any other roof. April sparkled again, and she asked many
questions—about land and ownership nearby, about neighbors, about
the safety of circumstances.

Father, bless him, assured her that were she to enter our society, she
would come in as our friend, and therefore would have all the protection
of our society, which, as he put it, "goes from the lowest to the highest
and back down again." When he added, "And the lower you go, the safer
you'll be," she looked alarmed—until we all laughed, and she seemed re-
lieved and joined in the laughter.

She inquired as to other landowning neighbors. Father gave her a verbal tour of our district, and he named many names. Of each one she
asked questions, and she seemed in danger of tiring herself, until I
stepped in, as it were, and advised her that were she to get the legal proceedings under way, I should make it my business to introduce her to all
these people—and my parents began to name the names, such as Lord
and Lady Cashel, Lord and Lady Knockavilla, the Countess of Dundrum, Lord and Lady Fermoy, the Honorable Mrs. Prendergast, and, of
course, Lady Mollie Carew.

"To name but a few," I said, and received a smile of great beauty.

This moment in Charles O'Brien's narrative is very telling socially. It's important to keep bearing in mind that the O'Briens were, in part, Irish Catholics, of longstanding native stock. Their tribe went back to the days of pagan Ireland, before the arrival of Saint Patrick in 432, before the birth of Christ and the beginning of A.D. (or "C.E.," as we must now call it). Therefore, Charles, and his father, and the family belonged among the dispossessed—in theory.

In practice, however, those Irish families who survived wave after ghastly wave of genocidal plantation discovered that they had created, in effect, a different—and very superior—class. On the one hand they bore none of the colonists' taints and stains. On the other hand, no aroma of victimhood clung to them, no self-pity.

These were the true Irish aristocrats, the families who went back more than two thousand years. And perhaps even beyond that. If they said that their ancestors caught the very seeds the birds dropped to fertilize the new loam thrown up by the melting tides of the last ice age, who could contradict them?

Such families had the respect of their Anglo-Irish new neighbors—many of whom wished fervently for such a long pedigree. And they had the respect too, though tinged with envy, of their fellow Irish, who were forced to the roads or the emigrant ships. Thus, they could easily name as neighbors—and indeed claim as friends—that list of lords and ladies, countesses, marquesses, and honorables.

By mentioning such names to April Burke, the O'Briens—both Bernard and Amelia—showed shrewdness and delicacy. In choosing to evoke titled families, they made her comfortable, and paid her a compliment. They naturally expected that she knew how to mix with such people. At the same time, had they sought to advance the romantic suit of their son, they were demonstrating to Miss Burke how they lived.

The general account of April Burke's first day in the O'Brien house and the very different reports of Amelia and her son bring up another curiosity. Nothing seems to have been mentioned of April's grandmother, the allegedly celebrated actress—"April the First," as Oscar Wilde called her.

Given a man as steeped in knowledge of his countryside as Bernard

O'Brien, it would have seemed natural and to be expected had Miss Burke plied him with questions. If she did, we have no reports of it; nor do we have any record or evidence that she asked many questions about Tipperary Castle.

Why not? Did she have something to fear? On the face of things, no. Surely she needed as much information as she could get about her possible inheritance? In fact, it can be fairly well assumed, judging from the next and vital passages from both Charles's and Amelia's records, that Miss Burke, on her first night at Ardobreen, never mentioned the possible origins of her interest.

The matter had proceeded as follows: Charles journeyed to the west of England in June 1904. And Miss Burke wrote to Amelia O'Brien six or seven weeks later. In that period she evidently decided—which she had not done since November 1900—that Tipperary Castle and its estate warranted a look serious enough to make a visit; and to spend a potentially embarrassing time in the family home of a man to whom she had at best been dismissive.

All the impressions of her at this stage suggest a young woman who never did anything spontaneously. Amelia O'Brien discusses her in strong terms—"conniving" and "icy" and, almost expletively from such a woman, "cunning." Depending on only the O'Brien observations, we can therefore assume that April Burke knew what she was doing when she decided to travel to Ireland.

In her terms she was going to darkest Africa. She had grown up with daily reports of murders and other outrages out of Ireland. In London her only contact with the Irish would have been at the servant level, with beggars in the streets, or perhaps with an occasional Irish lord or lady.

It's perfectly feasible that until she met Oscar Wilde she had never encountered a cultivated Irishman. She failed to see past Charles's rather careless facade to the honest and earnest man beneath—who was now about to show her a magnificent possibility. Have two people ever had such different intentions on a Sunday morning outing?

I did not sleep that night. She lay mere yards away from my room, along the west corridor of our house. The moon rose late, and I sat at the window looking out at the garden and the wood. With foreknowledge of the boards that creak, I stepped out and walked to her door. For a long moment I stood there and my mind reared under many lashes; I pressed both hands to my face, seeking composure.

The catch on that lock has some indifference to it, and I knew she would not be certain that she had closed her door. I pushed gently, and the door opened back. From inside I could hear deep breathing and almost a hint of snoring; and from the room in general came a faint and sweet perfume that I shall ever associate with her.

I stepped into the doorway; she had drawn all curtains tightly closed—no moonbeam would gain that room. Along with the perfume I caught the smell of the candle that she had recently doused. From the moonlight of the corridor I could see that the newspaper I had left for her to read (with my disquisition on Mr. Griffith) had a valise sitting upon it. No doubt she intended to read it upon the morning.

Then I caught my breath. Here I stood, a man in a lady's room without her invitation or permission! I retreated immediately, ashamed that I should have advanced so far. As I closed the door tenderly, I knew that she had not stirred, and therefore my little visit had passed unobserved.

April rode well. We gave her Nonie, a nine-year-old mare who had thrown one foal and was therefore inclined to be placid. As I watched the horses being readied in the yard, Father appeared. Mother walked with him and they had deep conversation, both looking at the ground; I doubt not that they discussed this remarkable young woman and her suitability for their son. When they saw me, Mother waved a warm hand, said something to my father, and returned to the house; she fills her life with work. Father came over and asked how prepared were the horses. When he discovered that some minutes remained before both should be watered and saddled, he said, "I want to look at something in the garden."

Ours is a walled garden, of warm red brick; few places that I have known give such secluded peace. There is a ruined abbey chancel in County Longford where the sun on a winter's day may be as hot as summer, so warm are the walls, so secure the shelter. In south Galway, I know of a graveyard where the western wall of an old family vault has a kind of pocket in it, which keeps out all wind, and when the sun beams directly into that spot, it becomes a Mediterranean place. Of Glengariff, nothing need be said other than it grows tropical palms.

Likewise Ardobreen's walled garden, which runs down to the little Multeen River, and that morning the warmth of the Indian summer had accumulated and heated the old red walls.

"I have been trying to grow globe artichokes," said my father, and I followed him to a patch half-covered with panes of glass resting upon some stakes.

He picked a sphere off the matured plant and caressed it; Father breathes slowly through his nose when he is contemplating, as he did now.

"Now, why did I grow these rough old green things?" he mused. "Maybe I just wanted the feel of a baby's head about the place," he said. "Maybe I just wanted to remember what you were like as a little baby. Boys-oh-dear, and how I would have done anything in the world to keep harm from falling on that little head."

He handed me the globe artichoke. "Feel that."

I ran my hands over the leaves and marveled that he had achieved a crop; we get much rain and unsteady temperatures.

"You know, 'tisn't often we grow things we want to protect," he said. "And look at this thing. I grew it to eat it. I suppose someone's always around to eat what you grow. Whether you want to protect them or no."

His voice cracked a little, and I looked and saw that he had tears in his eyes and on his cheeks. It was my instinct to say that he felt too much moved by a vegetable; therefore I said nothing.

"Ride slowly today," he said. "Stay on the level, don't bother jumping any fences; she's not knowledgeable of our Irish ways."

He stayed in the garden and I returned to the yard, where the horses, pleased with each other's company, were now prancing a little. I mounted faithful Della and led Nonie behind me to the terrace, where already April waited with Mother. Euclid had found a gap of sunshine and lay on a chaise, the early beams falling across his face. He waved us off.

Of all the days in the week, Sunday is the most tranquil in that country-side. Their ride can be traced. From the front of the house, they rode to the top of the avenue, which then slopes sharply down. Captain Ferguson's exotic wood stands to the west, open paddocks and pastures to the east. The slope lasts about two hundred yards, and at the bottom a white gate now stretches across the property. Inside the hedge to their right, they would have found a well lined with pewter-colored stone, and brimming with water.

Then they began a gentle climb to the main road—and from here anybody hiding in the trees of the castle could watch them all the way.

As I have stated before, from the lower end of our avenue, we see the peaks of Tipperary Castle and the battlements and the two small square turrets; we see the giant trees, the beeches and oaks, their bushy heads inclining toward the beauty of the house like eager men toward a lady in a salon. At the moment it all came in view April and I were riding alongside; through lack of practice, she had been keeping her eyes on the ground, as do many unaccustomed riders.

"Raise your eyes," I said. "There is your inheritance."

We reined in at the same time and gazed at the great house. She looked and looked but said nothing.

"Is it in any way familiar?" I asked.

She waited before answering, then said, "Only in dreams." I had difficulty making out the words, so softly did she speak. "Nothing prepared me for this," she said, again in a low voice.

We sat for some time and she looked all around; I believed her utterly pleased at what she saw—and I asked her as much.

"Pleased indeed," she said, and repeated it. "Pleased indeed."

"And you have seen but a fraction," I told her, and we nudged our horses forward.

We trotted along the roadway for about half a mile and then I changed our direction; we passed through an open gate, rode to a wide gap in the long hedges of hawthorn, now thick with hanging knots of gleaming red berries, and began the long sloping ascent to the house. Our view of the estate improved with each yard we took. We splashed across a bright stream.

I said, "You are now on the estate itself. This is where the acreage begins."

Ahead of us, birds rose screeching from thickets.

"How far does it stretch?" she asked.

"Almost to the mountains."

I decided that we should climb to the old lawns that sat almost level with the south side of the roof. Nobody had ridden this path for some time, and we forced our way past some brambles and briars. In the distance rose the high walls of the main building; the bright light of the morning made the cut stone seem more tailored than ever.

April looked at everything: the sealed windows and their sleek, pointed architraves; the great door that had resisted so many attacks; the manicured cornices and peaks. We turned our horses up one last, steep path and there we stood, with all to be viewed.

The estate is wider than it is long and stretches mostly south and east.

"Four thousand acres?" She repeated my answer to a question that she had asked. "How shall we find out exactly?"

"The authorities keep a land registry," I said. "The council in Clonmel or Tipperary town—whose spires you can see off there in the distance."

With gestures I showed her the extent of the estate, as I believed it to be—south, southeast, and east of where we sat, until we had turned about in our saddles and faced toward Cashel, where I showed her the medieval buildings on the great Rock five miles distant. Her level eyes observed all; her cool manner took in everything; I saw as yet no excited response.

"And you have not seen the prettiest part," I said.

We rode down from the old lawns to the northern terraces, where grass abounded between and over the wide paving stones. When we had cleared the corner of the building I said, "Now look."

Beneath us lay the lake and the bridge that crossed the little river. So thoughtful had been the placing of the trees and the shrubberies that the estate's shape had remained firm down through the decades of disuse. At this distance, everything seemed normal—the shrubs had blossomed and the trees still carried a great abundance of leaf, now golden and ocher in the fall of the year. All growth seemed to lean toward the house and protect it, and I pointed out to April how the plantings had been so arranged as to give shelter from the northerly and easterly winds. She made no comment. Instead, she eyed some cattle browsing by the water's edge.

"Who owns those creatures?"

"I suppose some neighbors have taken the liberty of using the land. This estate has not been in working ownership since—well, since whatever happened," I reminded her. "Mr. Wilde's story."

"So they graze the land free?"

I said that I supposed they did, yes.

"Hmm." She sounded determined. Then she sat back and viewed the house. "The roof seems sound."

"I believe it will need some work," I said, and I pointed out some damage to an expanse of slates.

"Is it possible that we can get inside?"

April dismounted (without my help), and we walked to the front of the building on the south side. The great door, I knew, had iron bars and daunting locks on the inside. I looked here, I looked there, but no entry could I find.

"We seem blocked," she said.

I took this as a test of my resolve and I stood back and surveyed.

"What are you doing?"

I said, "Mapping the building. Let me judge which rooms sit where."

The most recent addition to the building began down to our left, on the southwestern side, and seemed almost a building unto itself. I knew that this must be the theater, and I remembered that, almost four years earlier, when I had first scrutinized this place, I'd believed that I had found it.

"Down here," I said. "We may be lucky. In a few minutes, begin to call out."

I climbed a tree near the theater's roof and looked down upon a flat surface. In the center two iron arms poked up, as of a ladder. I was able to step from the tree's strong branch onto the flat roof—and I found that it was, indeed, an iron ladder that led down to a doorway recess below the surface to the roof. The ladder seemed strong enough to hold me, and I came down to the door—which had no lock. Inside, further ladders, which I felt but never saw, led me down to a wider place; all was pitch-black.

On a firm floor I reached out a hand and touched velvet; I felt that I must have penetrated the theater itself—and it proved to be a seat, on the edge of an aisle. Yet my eyes picked out no shapes; I still could see nothing, but my hands found a wall and I edged along it until I came to a curtain. This cloaked a doorway—but it yielded not at all. On and on I went, around each wall, until I reached a point where I could hear April hallooing. At another curtain here, the door behind it opened easily, and now I had more than a glimmer of light. It came from a stained-glass panel in the ceiling, and I discovered that I stood in the hallway of the theater. Ahead of me stood the door, which was barred from the inside— but the bars had no locks securing them. When I opened the door the sunlight flooded in.

April came running to my shout and we opened all the other theater doors. Within moments we had a full view of the auditorium, on whose stage her own grandfather—if the legend was accurate—had died of apoplexy.

The world may boast greater theaters, but it has few as lovely. That velvet which I had touched had been made of a turquoise color, trimmed with a gold braid; and the seats in their neat and almost intimate rows— we counted that the auditorium accommodated one hundred—had been made of a gentler hue, almost the blue of a duck's egg, which excellently complemented the curtains and the other trim. Tiepolo himself, I reflected, might have painted the ceiling; it billowed with his soft blues and whites, and I subsequently learned that the painter, an Italian by name of Rampalli, had been commissioned to paint it after the fashion of Tiepolo.

We could not yet see the stage. The curtains, of gold with the same turquoise braided trim, had been drawn closed. Securing the curtains, in the very center, hung an aged object—and closer examination disclosed a long-dead funeral wreath. A card pinned to it said, simply, "Terence Burke *Requiescat in Pace.*"

Upon this discovery I called April over.

"Look. Perhaps some of the legend is true," I said.

She said nothing but stared a long time at the remains of the wreath; and she turned the card with its black borders over and over in her hand. Then she asked, "Do you think it possible to enter the house?"

We tried and tried again. Two passages led from the theater, but each one ended at a door that had been secured from the other side, and no amount of tugging and heaving would take us through. When we finally ceased we returned to the theater and inspected every part of it.

It had been excellently appointed, and the stage and auditorium had been raked to perfect angles. I found the winches that operated the curtains, and now we could see how it was meant to be when a play was being staged. No scenery could we find, not a painted fly, not a sculpted backdrop of "pillars" or "columns," and we made our way backstage.

Here we found three large rooms, marked, "Green Room," "Ladies' Dressing-Room," and "Gentlemen's Dressing-Room," and two smaller rooms. The first of these said, "Principal Actor"—and the second said, "Mrs. Burke." We stood in front of this and I thought of Mr. Wilde and his description; I can still recall the words: "She had a long nose, not so retroussé as yours, not so tip-tilted, and with not the same curve at the end of the nostrils. Her lips had some but not all of your voluptuousness. And she had your smile, a wonderful, curving slice of joy."

"The case," I murmured, "seems incontrovertible."

She simply nodded; not a word did she say. Instead she opened the door of the dressing-room that only her grandmother would ever have used or entered. It was dark but surprisingly free of any musty odor. When I pressed the door to its widest we saw that some candles still sat in their sconces, and I lit them; to my surprise, the wicks took.

This dressing-room had been furnished for an empress. A great looking-glass dominated one wall from the ceiling to the floor, and it had an answer from another large glass over the dressing-table across the room. I doubted that the room had ever been used; no brushes, combs, or other grooming implements stood on the dressing-table, no wig on the wooden block. But in a corner I saw some objects resting on a great chair, and I took hold of them—a lady's heavy green gown; a long and generally decorative green brocade coat with cream lapels and revers; a pair of broad brown-leather gauntlets, small enough for a lady; a small cloth bag which contained brown hair (a wig, I presumed); and a pair of lady's buttoned boots, also brown. Dust flew, and we coughed.

SUNDAY NIGHT, THE 2ND OF OCTOBER.

Charles and Miss Burke returned in time for a late luncheon. I prevailed upon the young lady that she need not change for the table. In the country, I said, we rest easier about such things. Perhaps she has gone back to England thinking us barbarians. I do not care. And I do not care for her. A cool young miss, indeed.

Beforehand, Bernard and I talked for an hour and more about our son's love affair. Bernard confesses that he is distressed. So am I. He says that he sees full well why Charles became infatuated. I said that I do not. Bernard said that if a woman so beautiful once turns her lamp upon a man, he is caught in its beam. I protested that it is such a cold beam. He said, "So is the moon's."

Why do men like being thus fascinated? I have no patience with it. It distracts from the work of Life. It preys upon the spirit of the innocent—like Charles. But what am I to do? I told Bernard that I shall wait and watch—for the moment. But I do not promise to keep silent or distant if I see that she plays with Charles too much like cat with mouse.

She is such an icy one! I might have thought that she would return from such an important adventure with some imprint of excitement upon her face. Instead, she sat to table

as cool as a leaf. Bernard asked her opinion of the house and
estate—which is easily the finest for many miles around.
"Quite pleasing," said Miss B.

Quite pleasing, indeed! Here is my poor son turned inside
out, from heat to harness, over this woman. Here is she with
the likelihood to become one of the wealthiest landowners in
the county by neither strength nor effort. And all she can say
is "Quite pleasing."

I fear that I pressed her.

"We found the theater," she said. Then I learned that
Charles had found it, by dint of enterprise and imagination.
But she joined in the claim. Is that what she is? A claimer? She
shall not claim my son until and unless she can prove to me
that she has a heart worthy of his.

I watched her closely. Her hands are bony and will age
badly. So might she. She eats not at all—a pick here, a morsel
there. So she is not generous even to herself? Nor did she give
much to me, when I asked her questions about her ride over
to Tipperary Castle. Is it not a fine place? How did you like
the land? Did you observe how beautifully the stone is cut?
"Oh, yes," and "It's agreeable," and "I know little about
stone."

At that moment I wished that I had not reared my sons to
behave elegantly toward women.

During the meal a visitor came. We have a long view of the
avenue from the terrace. It is a courtesy in the country to ride
slowly into another's property. This newcomer knew of such
manners and trotted his horse nicely.

Bernard did not know him, nor did I—nor did Charles
nor Euclid, and they know everybody. He came close to the
terrace and dismounted without speaking. He took off his hat
and approached us—thickset, short, and black-haired.

"Forgive the intrusion," he said. The coat he wore might
have been Spanish. "And forgive a business mission on the
Sabbath Day."

"Your courtesy forgives you, sir," said Bernard. He can be irksomely florid at times.

We invited the man to join us. He told us that his name was Dermot Noonan. We shall hear more of him. He came to inquire whether we knew that somebody was trying to claim Tipperary Castle.

That was when I understood the wideness and depth of Miss Burke's nerve. She never moved a particle of her body.

Bernard asked the stranger why he inquired.

"I believe it should belong to the people," said this Mr. Noonan. "It's been vacant a long time. It should revert to its neighbors; it was our land once. All of us from around here."

Euclid's eyes grew round, a sight I always enjoy. And Charles's occasional shrewdness kept him silent too. Mr. Noonan had a hardness to him.

"Where do you come from?" I asked him.

"I was educated at Salamanca, Mrs. O'Brien."

Few people around here have the composure to call me that; "ma'am" or, more commonly, "Missus" is what they call me.

"And why are you here?"

"I am riding to all the local houses to tell of my intention to go to court over that estate"—and he gestured past his shoulder.

He took a drink, asked many questions, and gave few answers. But at least he told us that he was a lawyer. (Bernard said that he should "try and get that cured.") During the time he was among us this Mr. Noonan began to fasten upon Miss Burke. And she upon him. I know that I saw warning signs, threats to my son's heart.

What will come of this? And why did Mr. Noonan stop here? Had he heard of her mission? Their eyes locked together many times. She is just the sort of woman to be enticed by a man such as that.

When we returned to our horses where they grazed, April continued to look around. I waited while she enjoyed the view; in my hands I carried the green dress, the brocade coat, the pretty gauntlets, the cloth bag with the wig, and the buttoned boots. She looked at them and asked, "Do you think they were a stage costume? Or her actual clothes?"

We laid them on the grass and opened them tenderly. No clue could be found, not a note, not a ribbon; no powder marks on the coat's collar, nothing but the faintest—or did I imagine it?—perfume from the hair. The shoes contained nothing; nor did the gloves.

Looking almost merry, April first tried the gauntlets, and they slid onto her hands with only a little effort.

"Excellent leather," she said and slapped the gloves together.

I knelt to help with the boots, but they proved too small. Then I opened out the coat and she put it on. It looked splendid on her, and I told her so.

"Where is there a glass?"

At my suggestion she went to look in the water of the lake at the bottom of the hill while I stayed with the horses. They had become restive since our return; even Della stomped and shook, unusual behavior. I watched as April twisted and turned, trying to create a reflection in the water that would give her an idea of how she looked. She came back up the slope, red of cheek and merry of face, and to my astonishment she took my hand.

"I must thank you. I must thank you for—this." She waved a hand to include the countryside and the house and the coat that fitted her supremely well. "Thank you, thank you again."

These were, in all consideration, the kindest words she had yet spoken to me. I was newly lost. She removed the coat, and I bore it and the other pieces on my saddle in front of me.

Within a moment or two I was obliged to ride close alongside her, take her horse's reins, and chuck in the creature tight, to reduce the skittishness exhibited by both horses.

"Something's troubling them," I said. "I know not what."

I knew within a minute. We heard two loud gunshots, and the bushes nearby hissed and rattled. The horses reared at each shot; I was able to control both pairs of reins.

"Are we being shot at?" she asked, not at all perturbed. "Goodness! What a tale to tell in London."

"Fowlers," I said. "Every Sunday they shoot. There have always been stocks of woodcock and partridge here. From the old days."

Animals, especially horses, always know things; our two mounts settled down after that, and I took this to mean that the fowlers and their guns had left the area. I am conditioned to expect anything in the Irish countryside, but April was not, and yet she took it like a warrior; I do not doubt that were we armed she might have returned fire!

When we returned to Ardobreen and one of Mother's very best lunches—carrot soup, mutton shank, and apple pie, all of our own farm's produce—April seemed composed and at ease. She remained thus all evening.

Her driver came on the Monday morning, and April rode away. She carried my father's letter of introduction to his solicitor in Limerick, old Mr. Henry Somerville. She had decided, upon all our urgings and for obvious reasons, to go there at once and begin the proceedings. Father warned that everything legal "takes four times as long and costs eight times as much." She waved to us as she rode off.

I walked in our wood and fields for a long time, savoring the fact that she had been here in my house, and that she might soon be here always, and that I loved her more than ever.

MONDAY NIGHT, THE 3RD OF OCTOBER 1904.

She has gone! That felt the longest visit of any house-guest that I can recall. Not even Aunt Hutchinson troubled everyone so. No, the water's too hot. Now the water's too cold. Are these your best towels? Doesn't Mrs. O'Brien have her own towels that I could borrow? Cally asked, "Will you let me pizen her, ma'am?" Poison seems an appropriate match.

How I wish, for Charles's sake, that I could have liked her more. Bernard said tonight that he now has digestion pains. Charles has gone out to mope somewhere. Euclid says that when Miss Burke was born, there had been unusual turbulence in the spheres that week. I fear we may receive some more of her turbulence here.

3

Vigor fills the void we call melancholy. For an hour and more after April's departure, I walked slow as a stork about Ardobreen, seeking to converse with Mother or Euclid or my father; I hoped that they might offer me an opinion. Did they believe, having seen us together, that our fortunes belonged side by side? But Mother had engaged with our neighbor Mrs. Thompson (about eggs); Euclid slept late (as ever); and Father, I discovered, had gone over to Golden (in pursuit of some recommended plowman).

My mood sank lower and lower, so I made myself vigorous, prepared my bags, and embarked upon the road once again; healing others restores me. My destination, Bruree, would take until darkness to reach; I would see my patient there in the morning. On the main road, I turned to look at the towers of the castle; they are so staunch and constant. But an unexpected sight intruded—a hundred yards from the road, on a knoll in the field, sat a horseman, looking at me. I waved cordially; he did not move a muscle; I waved again.

The fellow made no response at all. Unperturbed, he sat there on his big roan mare, his gaze as glittering as a hawk's. I puzzled a moment, rode on, and then looked back. Still he stared after me; he had not moved. I stopped, turned Della, and began to ride toward him, to inquire his business, but he spurred his horse and rode away toward the castle. Many fences had fallen down over the years, and it is difficult to say whether he knew—or cared—who owned the land over which he galloped.

I needed to press onward, and though uneasy over the strange rider, I put Della into the merry clopping pace that she could keep up all day. As I rode, I set my thoughts toward my patient. A young wife with no children, she had never been "strong," as she told me at my first visit; "delicate lungs," she said, and complained of sometimes a cough of blood. Mr. Egan had taught me to listen for the words "not strong." He said, "Take it as the consumption, Mr. O'Brien, no more and no less."

If my patient still failed, what must I prescribe on this, my third visit? I had so far tried linseed oil, and sweetened it with honey, but she could not tolerate the taste. When I last saw her, I had advised a routine of garlic with cloves, boiled, strained, and served warm in honey; and I said that she must drink goat's milk three times a day.

Thus preoccupied, I traveled about an hour, and then took a bridle path that led me south of Tipperary town into secluded fields and tall hedges. Suddenly, from behind me, I heard loud hooves. With the path wide enough for wagons, I moved aside to let the horseman pass by. But his pace eased and his hooves quieted—now I could hear the noise of his horse snorting at being slowed, and then the sound of trotting right behind me. Next the horse's head drew alongside, and I recognized the roan mare that I had seen on the knoll near the castle. In a moment, the strange horseman clopped cheek by jowl with me.

"Good morning," I said.

He made no answer and kept looking hard at me; he had red-rimmed eyes.

"Are you traveling my road?" I asked pleasantly.

Still no answer came, and his gaze on mine never faltered. This, I thought, promised to become an odd encounter. I surveyed him; he wore a good enough coat of brown broadcloth, with large pockets and a great belt and buckle. Since he carried no baggage of any description, I presumed him local. He lacked the middle finger of the right hand, but he had outstanding horsemanship; he seemed to meld with the leather of the saddle.

When he did not answer I looked away, but I knew that his eyes continued to watch me. I spurred a little; he kept pace. I slowed down; so did he. He showed no signs of attacking me, and as we had no highwaymen, rapparees, or other thieves at work in our country, I felt that he must want something else.

"May I help you?" I said, trying to remain pleasant.

No answer: close and cold, he continued to look at me, his hard eyes searching mine.

"Will you not speak?" I asked. "Or somehow tell me what you want?"

Not a word did he say, and I returned to looking ahead. In the distance, I could see Cullen's Ford, a place where people linger going to and from the town; trees overhang the river, which is wide, shallow, and cool there. My head had begun to sweat, and I felt ill at ease.

Suddenly, the hard-eyed rider leaned across and with his maimed hand jerked my reins from me. He rode forward a few feet, flogged my horse's face with the leather reins, and then threw them insolently back at me. Della reared; the menacing fellow wheeled, rode at me as though to attack, spat at my face but hit my shoulder—and galloped fiercely back the way we had come.

Della reared again, almost throwing me. With my hands down on her neck, and soothing her with words, I settled her, then turned in my saddle to look back. The insolent stranger rode as fast as any man I had ever seen; within a moment he had vanished around a bend. Disconcerted, bewildered, I resumed my own journey down to the ford. Ahead stood Mrs. Cullen, leaning on her gate, in her ever-present black shawl. I looked forward to meeting her again—some minutes of her good-natured conversation would restore me—but when she saw me, she went into her house and shut the door. The family with whom she had been talking headed south in their cart, leaving the ford deserted.

Shaken a little by the sinister horseman, I stopped, dismounted, wiped the spittle from my coat with some grass, and gave Della her head to drink the sweet waters of the river Ara. (The name Tipperary comes from the ancient Irish words "tobair," meaning a well of water, and "ara," meaning the river—"tobair-ara"; my tutor Buckley told me this, and then said that too few Irish place-names had their origins in what we drink.) When Mrs. Cullen showed no sign of emerging from her shuttered cottage, I remounted. The rest of the journey proved mild and peaceful, and I rode into Bruree on a sharp, clean trot.

A big white moon stood over the town as I looked from the window of my room. In the silence of the night, I reviewed the past few days. For the first time, April had taken my hand, had placed a trust in me, had spoken warmly to me. Was not this excellent? Yet—I felt a discomfort that I could not name. Once again, much of her behavior had too much sting in it; was that it? Or was I discommoded at my family's formality with her? I had expected them to be easier in her company.

I slept restlessly; my thoughts were as knives. Next morning I saw my young patient. She still had a pallor that we must remove, the skin on her hands like linen, but goodness! the improvement in her—I was very pleased. So was she; and she said so again and again. When I first reached their farmhouse, she had elected to remain in bed; however, her husband, with his big, shy, shiny face and curly hair, scarcely concealed his excitement. His wife, he said, had been able to get up and walk about "and even stand at the door on a fine day," as she had been unable to do for fifteen months.

After my bedside visit, I waited in the kitchen while her husband helped her to rise; she came and sat by the fire, her slippers delicate as toy boats. He, so tender to her, so grateful to me, made us powerful tea, and offered some of the apple pie that his mother had made. I do not often eat apple pie so early in the morning, but this represented a celebration. A neighbor came by, an exceedingly tall, thin young man with, of all things in Bruree, a Spanish name. He bade us good morning; he had a most compelling voice, deep as a drum in the same slow, east Limerick accent. When I met him again, more than a decade later in vastly different circumstances, I recognized him at once; that is how distinctive he was. (The apple pie had cloves; he will always remind me of that taste.)

In the warmth of the sunny noon, I said good-bye to my young couple. My patient stood at the door and told me further good news: with the help of some money from an uncle in Chicago, they had begun the business of purchasing their own farm. They would soon, as she put it, "never again be anyone's tenants."

✂

TUESDAY NIGHT, THE 4TH OF OCTOBER.

I am a coward and I dislike myself for it. Yesterday morning I sheltered behind Mrs. Thompson and her new poultry enterprise. Charles prowled at the windows, looking in beseechingly. I know that he wanted me to give an opinion of his Miss Burke. As I cannot tell him what he wishes to hear, what can I say? That she is grasping? Almost contemptuous? Too distant for one so young? So sure of herself with that proud stride and toss of the head? In order to avoid Charles I fear that I detained Mrs. Thompson longer than she wanted.

Charles says that he has returned to his healing. He seems very rewarded by his patients. I know it sears his heart that he cannot heal Euclid. He will not even speak of it. But I know that he asks everywhere for a cure for his brother. People tell him that Euclid will continue to waste away.

Bernard has been of little help in all of this. He left the house early this morning. I saw no wish on his part, either, to converse with Charles. It cuts my heart to see how Charles depends upon his father's every word. And it cracks my heart open to know that Bernard loves Euclid more. That he thinks Charles foolish. I am glad that Bernard knows how to conceal his feelings.

Euclid cannot walk anymore for wasting. Charles cannot think anymore for excess of feeling. My two sons are not playing Life's cards with success. This is my fault. I have not educated them in the more mysterious parts of living, and they seem bound to fail. But I shall do as I have long decided. I shall go on loving them, and hope that my love keeps them alive and safe. I know no other way.

In October 1904, Edward the Seventh had been king for three years and nine months. Although his dominions still daubed much of the world map with Britain's red, the Irish Question boiled on. Little green shoots of rebelliousness had begun to raise their spikes in the top northwest corner of the British Empire.

By then, given the success of the land reforms and their new laws, Bernard and Amelia O'Brien must have known beyond doubt that their property was finally safe. No more "footwork" was needed; no more astute marrying into the establishment.

But—such an irony after all the centuries—their lineage on that land had begun to come apart. And from the inside. The natural inheritor, Charles, had shown no interest in the farm. Nor, it seems, would—or could—his brother. Nowhere in Charles's history or Amelia's journal do we find any suggestion that Euclid is likely to take over from Bernard.

By the time April Burke first visited the O'Briens, Euclid was in his thirties. Yet all we ever see of him is an eccentric, loving, often recumbent figure who has much to say, little to do. Repeatedly, a frailty is hinted at or mentioned; it's never explained, only alluded to in passing. Now, in Amelia's journal, the word "wasting" gives us the first solid clue.

Evidently it was chronic—we first learn of it on the trip to Knock, when Euclid was fourteen and Nora Buckley was delegated to care for him hand and foot. And it surfaces more than once thereafter in Charles's remarks—Euclid sleeping late, etc., although Charles never tells us what was wrong with his brother.

It could have been tuberculosis, which had been long endemic in Ireland. That would explain some of the reticence; the "consumption" had a stigma attached, of poverty and undernourishment. But if Euclid had been suffering from tuberculosis since the Knock visit or before, he would almost certainly have been dead by the time he reached thirty.

More probably he suffered from a form of anemia. With poor or, at best, unscientific diet, no blood tests, and with half a century to go before the arrival of modern pharmacopoeia, anemia went undiagnosed and uncured. In a country so medically undeveloped, Euclid would simply have drifted down the years, getting weaker and paler. "His blood is thin," they'd have said, and they'd have loaded him up with beef and liver.

Given that possibility or something like it, the family would have believed him too fragile for the farm. The O'Briens had a robust existence; they farmed seriously a daily bulk of animals and a full roster of seasonal works. They had a vigorous and involved team of workers, and people came and went all the time; Charles makes the point more than once that his household had a lively knowledge of everything that went on around them.

Any young man who was not in the thick of all that must have had something wrong with him, and therefore the seriousness of the illness could be defined by Euclid's contrast to his environment. He was more than a touch sequestered—we never see him doing anything other than reading or pursuing his "researches."

Everybody would have seen his condition—and had comments to make. Ireland being Ireland, where envy often wears the mask of kindness, they surely said, "That poor, weak boy—sure, isn't he paying the price for the fine life the rest of them have?"

From Amelia we also begin to understand why Charles mentions Euclid's illness so infrequently, and so insubstantially. It made him feel helpless. Although sickness provided his daily trade, he couldn't heal his own brother.

Or himself. In October 1904 Charles was some months beyond forty-four years old and still suffered from immaturity and uneven development. Worse than that, his continued innocence drifted from naive to foolish. Where a more developed person would have started to make connections—an assault on the street, gunfire through the trees, a sinister horseman—he attempted no penetration, or even inquiry. In today's language, did he not think to connect the dots?

This was a man who, at best, lacked alertness and, at worst, avoided looking at any difficulty in his life—although he confessed to self-examining thoughts once he had met Miss Burke. In that encounter and others, he had but a poor idea of how others saw him. With no talk of a future, or directed ambition, he more or less drifted across the landscape. He had no anchor—except this great, unrequited love.

Oddly enough, his passion, and the naive profession of it, may be the easiest thing about him to explain. Nineteenth-century men had many curbs on the ways in which they could express themselves. Despite some unexpectedly swift mail services, communication was generally limited, so a romance had few escape valves.

As a further restraint, all aspirant lovers were weighted down with Victorian respectability. In any wooing they did, men like Charles were obliged to convey purity of heart. It's even remarkable that he was able to speak to April without a chaperone (although that probably had to do with her self-assurance).

So in terms of managing his own life in his early forties, the most positive thing to be said of Charles O'Brien is that in his lowest moments, he proved capable of taking some sort of action, however indirect. As witness his trip to Bruree, where, unable to heal himself, he had healed someone else.

And, of course, he displayed his historical value by the way he describes his visit—with brief but eyewitness clarity. Against the background of the era's great theme—"land, land, land," as he earlier put it—he reported, a moment at a time, people's lives. With small, even delicate touches, he captured their moods, feelings, details—as with the tubercular young wife. In other words, such strength as Charles O'Brien had yet developed lay in his acute powers of observation.

The general knowledge of the day has served an important purpose when setting down my History. In this spirit, I wish to record the number of people living in Ireland during the periods about which I have been writing, because the Census findings in descending generations tell a powerful story of Ireland.

If I look at the population in my father's boyhood, a total of 8,175,000 people lived in Ireland in 1841. After Black '47, the worst year of our great potato famine, that number shrank drastically, and in a Census taken the year after I was born, the Census of 1861, the total population amounted to 5,797,000. Of these, 4,504,000 professed

Catholicism, and the remaining number of 1,293,000 consisted of "Protestants"—which included in the main Anglicans or Episcopalians, as well as Presbyterians, Methodists, and Baptists.

On the year 1881, I can cast no such light; I have been unable to acquire the figures from the authorities in Dublin, who tell me that they "can't find them." My most recent figures, which come from the Census of 1901, show the population of the island at 3,221,000, with a thousand fewer men than women. Therefore, from 1841 to 1901, almost five million people—that is to say, sixty percent of Ireland's inhabitants—left the country, whether through migration or death. It is widely understood that almost all of these came from the native, or Catholic, population.

Given my family's mixture, I was most interested in the polled figures of the religious denominations. In the one instance I have been able to acquire, it seemed that the Catholics outnumbered their landlord Protestants by between three and four to one. But I did not need a Census-taker to tell me that; the Irish people know their country. In some Catholic houses, I even heard them claim that the proportion fell closer to ten percent owning ninety percent.

Nor have I ever needed a Census-taker to tell me that I lived in a land of two peoples—and of such marked contrasts. I rode through the country for many years, on early mornings, high noons, late evenings, and often on dark nights; I rode from province to province, from county to county, from town to town, from village to village; I rode into places a horse had difficulty climbing; I rode down broad streets, gay with awnings. And in my journeyings I met and talked to two peoples, all the time, everywhere, deep in their baronies, boroughs, and parishes, two categories of Irish who resembled each other not at all.

They wore different clothes, ate different foods, and read different books; they danced to different music, answered to different Gods, asked different questions. "Many a time and oft," as the poets and story-tellers say, I reflected upon these divisions on such a small island, and marveled at how wide was the chasm.

When I visited an Anglo-Irish—that is to say, Protestant—residence, I met gentlemen in shiny boots or shoes, in cutaway coats and fine trousers or knee-britches, with rings on their fingers and linen on their backs. They shone in waistcoats or vests made of brocade or silk, often of rich colors. At their throats, they folded elaborate cravats or, sometimes, wide and thought-provoking bow-ties. When going to church on Sunday, they sported hats and greatcoats; some carried walking-sticks. At the hunt, a few affected the red coat of the English—"the pink" as they call it, after Mr. Thomas Pink, the preferred tailor of many Englishmen and, therefore, of many Anglo-Irishmen.

The ladies of the Anglo-Irish wore gowns, and they cultivated airs of fashion. They professed an awareness of London and Paris; some even talked of America and what the "quality" wore there. I took it that the clothes in which I saw them—dressed for receiving visitors on ordinary days or for visiting their friends or for dining—reflected the world abroad.

Therefore, I concluded that London and Paris and the United States of America had a taste for brown and gray, and in summer, yellow and green, with trimmings of lace and other embroidery. Unless faced with a widow—always dressed simply and in black—I encountered bright fabrics and elaborate designs. Most women wore their hair up, except when retiring for the night. All gowns observed the ankle, and only in circumstances of great good fortune did one glimpse a shoe. But in time, I perceived such restraint beginning to ease, particularly among the younger women. When April strode about Paris, she cared not that her ankles showed now and then.

An Irish tenant farmer and his wife, however, dressed very differently. Their appearance generally lacked style; they could not afford fashion; and they scarcely wore any color other than brown for both man and woman, or green, and sometimes an unattractive black. In good wear, on Sundays, they might sport shirts or blouses of white, but in general they confined themselves to drab colors from easily available—and therefore inexpensive—fabrics. Among the Catholics I have seen serge but no silk; they wore tweed but no twill; no barathea, no bombazine, some sleaze, especially among the very poor, and a little cotton and linen.

They had no style; their tailors were often their wives, or a local village man who had little training, no flair, and poor ability. The women's skirts reached to the floor; the men's trouser-legs terminated above the ankle. Both sexes wore boots, and it would be a sign of a certain well-to-do comfort if, to Mass on a Sunday morning, a wife wore shoes rather than boots. Their children, in the main, went barefoot. In the—rare—childless house, a little more quality might be seen in the costume of husband and wife.

As to food: in the great houses of the Anglo-Irish, I have eaten some disgusting meals. I often wondered whether the Catholic cooks of my Anglo-Irish friends spent a deal of time trying to poison their privileged employers. This theory, however, collapses upon scrutiny, because the kitchen staff had so little knowledge of cooking that they would not have known where, or how, or in which dish to apply poison.

Some meals were worse than others. One day in March 1892, having been long expected for luncheon, dinner, and breakfast at L—— House, I arrived at a quarter before noon. The butler (who had bulging eyes, one of them turned to the wall—quite disturbing) led me straight to the dining-room, where sat my old friend Daniel B.

"You are so punctual, Charles. Luncheon will begin presently. Let us pity ourselves in advance."

I sat down, and in due course, his mother, Lady G., and his sister, Miss K., appeared. Both greeted me prettily and Lady G. said, "Only a true friend would stoop to share our food."

Miss K. added, "This is not a house that flatters the palate."

Daniel completed the sentiment: "But excellent for the bowels."

Luncheon was served. At that moment I began to understand the slenderness of the ladies. Judging from the offering before me on the table, they cannot have eaten much on any day of the week. I still do not know what lay in my plate; I can only describe it, and I shall not permit myself to recall it at length.

All seemed gray or black—excellent colors in themselves, but not in meat or potatoes. I thought I was looking at beef until Lady G. said, "Why must we always have mutton?"

To which her daughter replied, "Mama, this is pork."

Lady G. replied, "I lost my sense of taste the day that I came to live here."

Daniel ate his meal heartily and with great speed.

"The only way," he said, "in which I can address such offerings is by eating very fast. I bypass the mouth and aim straight for the throat. At least the stomach is filled by my method."

"Mr. O'Brien, please drink much water," said his sister. "It is necessary." She did not explain why.

A pudding arrived, which required Daniel to stand up and press the knife down with great force in order to cut it. I was quite unable to chisel even a crumb from my portion; for a while I contemplated licking the side, but I gave up when I saw that the dog, named Disraeli, refused Daniel's piece and left the room.

As the maid took away the plates, Lady G. said, "Mr. O'Brien, are you a religious man?"

"Not at all, madam," I said, "but it is my principle to respect those who are."

"Good," she said. "You will note that we did not say a Grace before our meal, because we simply could not bring ourselves to say, 'Oh, God, for what we are about to receive make us truly thankful.' "

Her daughter said, "Here, we say a Grace *after* we have dined."

Daniel: "My father began this practice. He passed away soon afterward."

Miss K.: "He passed away one night after dinner."

Lady G.: "You may have heard it, Mr. O'Brien—Hebrews, thirteen: eight."

All three bowed their heads and intoned, "Jesus Christ, yesterday, and today: and the same forever."

Strangely, the food of the Catholics could prove more generally edible, however spare it might have been. On many occasions I have eaten in the humbler houses of the tenant farmers and the cottagers—the "peasants," a term that they dislike. For economic reasons, they could not provide much variety at table, and it was the more fortunate who ate two meals a day. For breakfast they took porridge, made of oatmeal and cooled with the milk of their domestic cow or, more often, goat. But it was often excellent porridge, salted and with a good consistency. (Porridge must be almost capable of being poured, must hesitate on the thick side of liquid;

and the best method is to mix milk with water equally at twice and a half the quantity to that of the oats.)

No matter how good the oatmeal, however, affluence stayed away from the table. Though all the family partook, they often had to wait their turn for the use of a utensil; the bowl or spoon had to be rotated according to the seniority of the family members. The father went first; the mother usually waited for the last child to have eaten.

If they were well enough off to take luncheon, it typically consisted of no more than a bowl of milk, with perhaps some of the soda-bread the woman of the house had baked, if she was industrious and if the family could afford flour. But in many houses no such meal was afforded, and all, including the youngest children, had to wait until evening. Then the family dined (I hesitate to use the word) on potatoes that had been boiled in hot water.

Of some such families, I have heard of an irony that they practiced—that they called their evening meal "potatoes-and-point." This derived from the fact that the family had, hanging from the kitchen rafters, a flitch of bacon, which would remain there until Christmas dinner. However, until then, all raised their potatoes on their forks and pointed at the bacon, in the pretended belief that the flavor of the bacon would somehow travel through the smoke of the kitchen and invest their potatoes with its tang.

As will be understood, this culinary experience differed severely from that of some of the Great Houses—where, should the cook be a person of capacity, often foreign, it was not unusual to dine on pheasant and salmon, pastries and wine. But mostly, these delicacies were also dreadfully prepared.

When I observe that these two peoples of Ireland "read different books," I am arrested. Books stand at the center of my family's and my country's lore.

Not all of my forebears possessed the gift of "footwork," as described by my father. One antecedent, by name Michael Joseph O'Brien, who lived in the south of the county around the year 1790, had received some education abroad, where some of the great Catholic universities contentedly took in Irish boys who sought education. This Michael Joseph went first to Louvain, where he took a dislike to the Belgians. He fared better in Salamanca. ("The Spanish have wine," said my father, "and the Belgians have only beer.")

Upon his return, my forebear was shrewd enough to conceal all his volumes about his house, because the possession of books was, for a native Irishman, a serious crime in those days. But Michael Joseph O'Brien grew defiant and quoted from his books when arrested. He was flogged and sent to Van Diemen's Land, a poisonous island off Australia, where he prospered and eventually died among his many children.

When education and the owning of books became free of criminality, many Catholic households—even quite poor ones—rushed toward reading. Printing-houses in Dublin began to enjoy a vivid trade. People would read anything; some printers even published in daily book form the proceedings of sensational court trials.

As the century wore on, Mr. Yeats and Lady Gregory began to make clear the value of ancient Ireland's traditional legends and culture, and literature became a symbol of national patriotism. The Catholic Irish flocked to these renditions of their past. In their houses, I have heard them read aloud the mighty tales of Celtic gods and heroes—of the boy-hero Cuchulainn (whom some call "Coo-Hualann" and some "Koo-Kullen"), of the warrior-god Finn MacCool and his hunters. They regale me with the stories that they find in these books; they know that such tales were originally handed down by word of mouth, and now they joyously rediscover them—and pass them on.

I have taken care to acquire some myself; and here is a story that I tell when I am among them. When I first heard it from an old story-teller, I took the precaution of transcribing it while I remembered it well, and since then I have memorized it; I rehearse it often.

As you all well know, Ireland is a country where magic rises out of the ground. There's magic around every corner, in the branches of the trees, in the beards of the bushes. The story I'm going to tell you is about magic that came out of the woods one day in County Louth.

If you go to the village of Dunleer, there's a hill. Nearby there's a great plain of land, and in days gone by there was a wood bordering that plain;

it ran all around the edge of it like the whiskers on an old man's chin. Before our time and before that time again, great warriors and hunters strode this beautiful country, and the greatest of these was a man called Finn MacCool. He was named Finn because the word means "blond" and he had hair the color of straw on snow. And he was named MacCool because he was the son of a man called Cool.

Finn always hunted with a band of companions. He was a young man and young men like each other's company, and there was no wife at home to tell him that she didn't like his friends. One day they were all on this plain, hunting near Dunleer, and out of the woods steps this beautiful deer. She was young, she was limber, she was lovely, not much older than a faun. The dogs began to bark and the hunters began to run, their spears at the ready.

Off runs the doe, like the wind; she heads up by the edge of the wood, onto the breast of the hill, and across the top of the ridge. They could see her clear against the blue sky, her movement fluid and graceful. She had that effortless flow of all great athletes, who never seem to be hard-pressed.

Finn and his hunters thought they had no hard job in catching her, but to their amazement they never got near her. Not only that, but one by one the young men and their dogs were unable to keep up the pace. Only Finn had the stamina. Finally, he and his two dogs drew ahead of the rest and were soon lost to sight.

As the great man and his two hounds came down a steep hill, they saw the deer ahead of them. She must have slowed down a bit and Finn thought she was tiring—so he urged his two dogs on faster and faster. To his great surprise, the deer lay down on the grass. She lay there quite happily—as though she was waiting for the dogs. When the two hounds came to the deer, they ran at her—but they didn't bite her, or rend her with their teeth. Instead, they stopped and began to lick her, and play with her, and gather round her in a protective manner.

You could have knocked Finn MacCool down with the feather of a Galway goose. He stood there and he watched the three animals, the deer and his two dogs, nuzzling and nosing and caressing, the best of friends.

The deer rose from the grass, and the two dogs, like escorts, began to trot across the fields with her. Finn followed them, and by now the rest of his band had begun to catch up. When their dogs went after the deer, Finn's dogs bared their teeth and barked—they were not going to let anything, man or beast, harm that deer.

Soon, Finn began to understand that his dogs were leading the deer home, and sure enough, when they reached his mansion gates, his dogs turned into the yard and led the deer into a comfortable stable. The dogs ran back and forth, to and from to the barn, and made sure they brought enough hay and straw in their mouths to make for the beautiful doe the most comfortable bed in the palace that night.

As the deer bedded down, Finn and his companions went in to dinner, and their talk for the evening was full of this mysterious deer, with which they had all become enthralled. They drank a lot and they ate a lot, and after the day's exercise out in the open air they soon began to feel sleepy, and off they all went to bed.

At about four o'clock in the morning, the hour when all strange things occur, something wonderful happened to Finn MacCool. A bright light filled his bedchamber, so dazzling that no man could stand a chance of staying asleep. Finn woke up, and standing there in front of his bed he saw the most beautiful young woman that he had ever seen. He reckoned that she was about nineteen years old but with the maturity of a grown woman. Tall, slender, and with long hair that was ornamented with tiny golden balls, she wore a gown of green and gold, and she had a serious face that now broke into a smile as sweet as the sea on a sunny day. The beautiful young woman spoke, and this is what she told him.

She said, "I am the deer whom your hounds pursued today. When I was a girl in my father's house, a Druid visited us, an evil man. He sought to marry me, and when I refused, the Druid cast a spell on me and threatened to turn me into a deer. And so he did, and his hounds chased me out of my father's house. I had to run fast in order to escape, and I ran and I ran until I reached a wood in the west of Ireland.

"There I lived a terrifying life, hunted every day of the week from dawn to dusk by every passing stranger. Many of the hunts, of course, were caused by the Druid and his hounds, and one day last week, to fool him and his huntsmen, I ran to his house, where I hid in his orchard. A young servant-girl saw me, and saw that I did not run away from her. She asked me was I the girl cursed to be a deer. I nodded my head, and she told me that she had overheard her master say that the only man who could break this curse was Finn MacCool inside his own house, which was a place free from all bad magic.

"So I set out, and I ran night and day across Ireland until I found you and your huntsmen today and your two lovely hounds, who are not fools and who know the difference between a real deer and a woman in a deer's form."

Finn MacCool looked harder and longer at this creature, and fell in love with her. The next week he made her his wife; their marriage began in a peace as deep and quiet as the first snow, and every minute of every day he looked at her with love in his eyes and his heart, and he thought himself the most fortunate man in the universe.

But Finn MacCool was a man of duty, and one day duty called. The King of All Ireland sent a man on a fast horse to Finn, telling him that raiders from across the water to the east had landed on the coast. Finn's lovely wife told him that he must, of course, go and do his duty, that his King and his country expected no less. Taking a leave of her as tender and tearful as a child on a first day going to school, Finn set off.

What Finn didn't know was that, for all these months, the Druid had been aware, through his own magical powers, of where the deer-woman had gone. So for several months he had been camped in the woods near Finn's house, waiting for the day when Finn would leave his house and his wife unprotected.

The morning Finn rode off to war, the evil Druid knew that his chance had come. He changed his shape to that of Finn MacCool and he rode to Finn's castle. On the ramparts, looking out across the open plain, her hand shading the sun from her eyes, stood the young wife. When she saw what she thought was her husband suddenly returned, she shouted with joy and came running down to his arms.

At the very last moment, she realized her mistake as the Druid waved his deadly wand and changed back to his own shape. She called out, "Please don't harm me. I am carrying my husband's child." Of course, this only angered the Druid more, and he touched her with his wand and she became a deer once again. She raced from the castle, out across the countryside, pursued by the Druid's hounds.

Finn MacCool came home from the war, and when he heard what had happened he felt a great crack split his heart, right across the middle. He mourned and he wept, and he wept and he mourned. He strode around the castle holding his head in his hands, making great loud moans. Eventually, his companions persuaded him that he should go out and look for his beloved wife, saying that he had found her before and he might find her again.

For seven years they hunted, seven years, seven days, seven hours, and seven minutes. They never found his deer-bride and they never found the evil Druid; and they returned home, heavy-hearted, and never were so many deer spared by huntsmen in Ireland. And they never found out what had happened—nobody did, because Finn's wife, in her deer form, had managed to stay ahead of her pursuers. Then, when her time came, she lay in a cleft deep in a wood on a mountain in Donegal and gave birth to a beautiful baby boy.

But no animal is made for producing a human child, just as no human woman may give birth to an animal, and the wife-deer died in childbirth. The birds in the trees were watching this event, and they sent out their signal songs, and the animals of the forest came to the bed of ferns where the expired deer lay and they saw this dear little baby boy, lying there on the ferns, kicking and smiling.

A male fox and a female badger agreed to adopt the baby, and they carried the infant to the badger's sett, a safe, large, warm nest deep under the ground. And as the baby grew and grew, they made wider and wider the badger's burrow, so that one day the boy would be able to look out, and then climb out, into the wide world outside. And he did—and he learned to speak to all the animals, and they taught him how to find berries and nuts and other foods, and he never, ever killed for food an animal or any living creature with a face.

For a further seven years and seven days Finn MacCool sequestered himself in his castle, mourning the loss of his wife and—because he had already known she was expecting a baby—his child. Nothing captured his attention—no dice game, no hunting, no story, no song. He moped and he wept, and he wept and he moped. Finally it all became too much for his companions, and one day they came into the castle and confronted him where he sat gazing into the fire that was blazing on the great stone hearth.

They said to him, "Finn, you've been mourning now for fourteen years and that is longer than a deer's life span. You cannot become an old man through grief."

Finn, a noble spirit, heard and heeded, and soon he began to hunt again. He went back to all his old haunts and found that time is the great healer, and he became the best huntsman of old, always leading the chase, with his two hounds no more than a few paces ahead of him.

One day, they were hunting on his favorite mountain, the magic mountain of Ben Bulben in Sligo, and as usual Finn was hundreds of yards ahead of his companions. The dogs suddenly stopped, puzzled, and Finn wondered what had arrested them. Up from the long grass a few yards ahead rose this tall, majestic boy. He was about fourteen years old, with long hair of a deep auburn color; he wore a tunic made of leaves.

Finn's companions had by now caught up, and they stood and they gazed at this apparition. And everybody there on that hillside that day knew what they were seeing; they were looking upon the son of Finn MacCool and his magical deer-bride, the lovely fawn who'd been briefly changed back into a woman and who had married Finn MacCool.

Finn laid down his spear, held out his arms, and walked forward. The boy walked to meet Finn and they embraced, and that is how Finn MacCool met his famous son and gave him the name we pronounce "Osheen"—which, as every man, woman, and child in Ireland knows, means "little deer."

Almost never did I find a Protestant Anglo-Irishman telling such a tale. To be sure, one or two, such as Mr. Yeats and Lord Dunsany, have explored the hinterland of Irish lore—but in most Anglo-Irish houses the books (if any) consisted of farming manuals and almanacs, and very few of those. However, where a Great House had turned bookish, splendid collections could be found, and some of the libraries of my parents' friends and acquaintances have been inspiring to my own family. Otherwise, I fear that the literary Anglo-Irish represented a minority—even though they have been educated in the British Empire's best schools.

With music, the divide plunged even more deeply. From time to time, during family events or at Christmas or to observe the Monarch's birthday, the great stuccoed drawing-rooms of the Anglo-Irish echoed to the stately notes of formal dances. The lords and ladies and their friends danced the Lancers or an occasional gavotte or a prim quadrille; the Irish countryside was many years behind London (some say many centuries). Musicians played violins and a piano, and maybe even the viola, and the event was ordered and stately. The arrival of the waltz removed some of the formality; and the works of Gilbert and Sullivan grew popular quickly.

"Down among the Catholics" (as the landlord's phrase often goes), nothing so regular ever took place. Night after night, some house or other glistened with music, and through the candle-lit open door the music carried across the fields. Fiddlers played faster than fury, pipers kept up; and the skin drum, the "bowrawn" (from an Irish word meaning "deaf") kept time, amid cheers and unbridled energy. All ages took part, and I have seen a man heavy as a horse dance a light-footed jig on a dinner plate without cracking it.

Irish traditional music throve on spontaneity and improvisation. A tune would begin with the squeezed notes from, say, a concertina, held small as a handkerchief in a farmer's huge hands. As the musician felt surer of himself, and his music quickened, someone else sat down near him with a fiddle. Then came a banjo man or a girl with a whistle, and soon another fiddler, and in due time each one of these slid into the main tune and decorated it.

Some would depart from the theme entirely and then return to it by paths of genius. By that time they had invented and played another melody, yet stayed within recognizing distance of the beginning air—and all done spontaneously, often improvising to a tune they had never heard until that night. This is why, "down among the Catholics," in culture and imaginativeness, they claimed superiority to the people in the "Big House," as they called it contemptuously, to the "gentry"—a word they contemn deeper than any other.

I have a stone-breaker friend in County Roscommon. He sits all day by the roadside with his hammer, breaking large rocks into smaller stones. His is an epic task, and he wears eyeglasses of close wire mesh, through which he views the world from a refreshing vantage point. By chance, a great Anglo-Irish residence near where he was working one particular day had lain vacant for more than a decade, as the family struggled through intestacy's furor. He could see the Great House distant across the fields; he sat on his pile of stones near the disused gates.

One day, a strange and pompous gentleman, obviously long separated from a hunt he had been following, trotted his horse down the roadway where my friend labored.

"Stone breaker," he called imperiously, "have you seen the gentry ride this way?"

"Sir," answered my friend with his hammer and his wire spectacles and his dust-covered face, "ten years ago they came out that gate over there, they went down this road—and they never came back."

Charles O'Brien reported fairly—even though his descriptions read oddly like those of a visitor. His impressions have the same kind of objective ring that was sounded by many who visited Ireland when the century's unrest caught the world's attention. Often the travelers who visited went home and wrote in simplified terms.

Many addressed the weather first and foremost. William Makepeace Thackeray, in his *Irish Sketch-Book* of 1843, found more rain than he had ever seen. He was generally sour about everything, including modes of transport: "The traveling conveyances are arranged so that you may get as much practice in being wet as possible," he reported.

A French visitor, anonymous in the Paris newspapers, summarized the land difficulty thus: "No tenant farmer struggling to keep his lone donkey in rented grass could feel easy at the sight of his Lordship's stable of twenty horses galloping across thousands of acres. Magnify that divide all across society—in food, in clothing, in medicine, in every other aspect of life—and it becomes plain how a seedbed of rebellion got planted and cultivated. Revolutions are born when the drudgery of life aches from serving the grandeur on the hill."

Other writers—many from abroad—made the same societal observations as Charles O'Brien, though not perhaps as intimately. They confirm his version of the divisions. And they also underscore his sensitivity to the most crucial ingredient in Irish history: the sense of passionate social and political feeling.

At the beginning of the twentieth century, this was a volatile place. Savage upheaval lurked just below the surface. The island seethed like a swamp of crocodiles. All Irish people, no matter what their stripe, knew that there was a violent balancing going on. One day, the bailiff of history must surely come to collect.

Thomas Carlyle, who had a massive literary output, often brought his summaries to a sharp point. "The whole country," he wrote, "figures in my mind like a ragged coat; one huge beggar's gabardine, not patched or patchable any longer." And when Ralph Waldo Emerson saw the cliffs ahead of him in the Atlantic, he observed, "There lay the green shore of Ireland, like some coast of plenty. We could see towns, towers, churches, harvests; but the course of eight hundred years [of occupation] we could not discern."

So far, I have written little of the country I travel, my native land of Ireland. It behoves me to include some brief description of its geographical beauty, lest for some unknown reason in the centuries ahead, Man becomes so profligate or uncaring or so needy as to destroy famous aspects. It is, I believe, also the function of the historian to generate an awareness of the terrain in which the events of his narrative have taken place.

In a previous description of my young life, I recounted my father's recitation of the Seven Wonders of Tipperary. For the purposes of this little digressive essay, I pluck at random the Weir at Golden. In truth, it does not exist at Golden, but a mile and more down the river, at a place they call Athassel. And in greater truth, I do not pluck it at random—I choose it deliberately because of its founder's name. He was William de

Burgo, and the ancient Norman family became, in settled Irish time, Burke.

As you may imagine, having known the place since my childhood travels alongside Father, I returned to Athassel more than once, in order to contemplate whether April had originated here; and I fondly imagined taking her and her dear father on a tour of the beautiful place.

The limestone ruins of this great monastery glow white in the summer sun; and I have seen kingfishers flash their lightning blue in the willows across the river.

Who sleeps in these ancient tombs? It is known that more than one de Burgo lies here, deep within the priory walls. The outline of the cloister still stands, and the marks of the great altar. I have walked in the original channel, from which the monks (it is said) diverted the river to make themselves a little island; I have stumbled upon the rough earth that sets out the foundations of the town that once protected the abbey.

The best view may be had from across the river, from Mr. Dalton's land. Also, I much enjoy riding along the riverbank from the south, anticipating the moment when I see the broken arches of the dignified, empty windows. When I have ridden through, I then receive the extra pleasure of proceeding by the river until I reach the weir.

As a boy on a summer night, I could hear from my distant bedroom window four miles away the swishing noise of this water flowing over the little wall, and it sounded most clear when the night was calm and the river high after rain. On a summer day, all is pleasant turmoil in the foaming waters; and there is tranquillity in the dark water where it pools before falling over the weir.

I have known much peace there.

When April Burke (very likely a de Burgo) left the O'Brien household on that October Monday morning, she took with her a letter of introduction from Bernard to a law office in Limerick city, thirty miles to the west.

In 1904, Stokes and Somerville was owned by a father and son,

Henry and Stephen Somerville, with a partner, Richard Stokes. He was a government lawyer specializing in the new land negotiations.

The company can still be traced. On the death of Henry Somerville in 1917, the firm merged with Kavanagh and O'Keeffe, a practice with offices in Limerick and Kilmallock. Fifty years later, a young lawyer from Clare by name of Prunty, with plenty of money, bought Kavanagh, O'Keeffe, Stokes, and Somerville. He, naturally, put his name ahead of the four others, and the people of Limerick gave it the shorthand name of Prunty's. That is how law firms have traditionally proceeded in Ireland.

Liam Prunty gave it teeth; he loved to litigate. And, oddly for such a tiger, he also loved legal records, and this practice had an especially absorbing history. Back in the staid old days, it had once dealt principally in land registration, rights of way, and testacy.

In 1998, when he was sixty years old, Mr. Prunty announced that he had at last completed the formal cataloging and cross-referencing of his firm's entire archive. It reached back to 1790, when the first Stephen Somerville, freshly home from France, hung out a shingle in Limerick (and lured clients with tales of the guillotine).

Still on Catherine Street, the firm now owns three adjoining tall houses. Today, their clients come from European Union agribusiness, and from the American firms enjoying Ireland's tax holidays. Among the soldierly lines of filing cabinets, Mr. Prunty knows immediately where to find the Tipperary Castle case. He's a lanky man who lopes down the long room.

"Locally they called it the 'April Fool's Case' to begin with," he says, "because her name was *April* Burke, and because everybody, Catholic and Protestant—the whole place—told her she was a fool to take it on. But take it on she did, and it lasted seven years. Seven years—1904 the first note was sent to the court, and the judgment came down in 1911. That was fairly typical. And like a lot of land cases, nobody got paid; they all said, Let the government pay for it. But some people did well out of it."

The lawyers of the day placed newspaper cuttings in the files. Mr. Prunty, to preserve them, has had them photocopied.

"This case, this had all eyes on it. If it was today it'd be on the television twice a week and once a fortnight, as the saying goes. See? The news-papers were on to it from the start."

On Wednesday, 25 October 1905, *The Irish Independent* carried a report:

> The case has finally opened in the High Court to decide the own-ership of one of Ireland's most renowned houses. Tipperary Castle, with its magnificent residence and four thousand acres of prime farming land, is being fought over by three contenders: an En-glishman, Terence Burke, who alleges that he is the natural descen-dant of the last owner; Mr. Dermot Noonan, a barrister from County Tipperary, who claims that the estate was put together from stolen ancestral lands and that he knows the rightful histori-cal owners of each acre; and the Crown, who wishes the land dis-posed of to the highest bidder under the Wyndham Act. It is expected that the case will last several years.

In each file that he hobby-archived, Mr. Prunty wrote a brief sum-mary of the suit. He usually clipped his précis to the copy of the verdict, which he placed on the top of the case papers—judgments, contracts, all relevant documents. Since the Tipperary case remains one of the biggest events in the history of the firm, his notes run longer on it than on most of the other lawsuits. He wrote several pages, and included asterisked ref-erences to the evidence transcripts.

To anyone interested in the case—and in particular from the point of view of someone reading Charles O'Brien's "History"—Mr. Prunty's summary is thrilling. It's full of depth charges, which he detonates one by one.

"The likely outcome of April Burke in Chancery," begins his note,

> lay obscured in doubt and argument. Tipperary Castle had been vacant and the lands fallow since the sudden and intestate death in 1858 of its owner, Terence Hector Burke. Mr. Burke was the sev-enth successive inheritor of the Tipperary property, which he ex-panded.

He died of natural causes at the age of fifty-six. Colloquial evidence that he had been married to a lady of reported ill-repute was mentioned in the Judgment, but only for the purposes of discarding as irrelevant. An earlier claim had been made upon the house and lands in 1880, by a lawyer from Bristol, a David Birmingham, representing clients whom he refused to name. The claim fell, as the solicitor withdrew rather than uncloak his clients' identity.

A second claim followed from the same firm in 1904, and proceeded to the same conclusion for the same reasons; again, the firm of Birmingham and Bale told the court they required the protection of anonymity, and the learned judge denied it.

There go the first two detonations. The court heard an allegation that the mysterious and beautiful actress April Burke the First had been "a lady of reported ill-repute." Mentioned in passing, and legally "only for the purposes of discarding as irrelevant," that would explain Oscar Wilde's fleeting reference to Sarah Bernhardt: "Even though I do not wish to dwell upon this, she had something of Miss Bernhardt's background, or so it was said."

This needs some caution. Many actresses were sometimes—and inaccurately—described in repressed Victoriana as "of ill-repute." But the divine Sarah had indeed been a whore before she trod the boards. Had, also, April Burke the First?

Secondly, the applications from Bristol—who initiated those? Charles, on his early morning Somerset walk in June 1904, saw the Gambon woman who lived in the Brook House, Mr. Burke's Mater, as he called her, board a carriage for Bristol, dressed as though for an appointment. In short—who knew what about the Burkes and Tipperary Castle?

The next segment of Mr. Prunty's document opens up the train of events:

In January 1905, Terence Theobald Burke, of Alexander Street, Westminster, London, made an application for "the Grant of Possession of Tipperary Castle, Ireland." The Courts of Chancery in

London properly sent it to the Irish courts. Through his daughter, Mr. Burke engaged Mr. Henry Somerville of this firm. As solicitors are not allowed to plead before the High Court, Mr. Somerville instructed his son, the barrister Mr. Stephen Somerville.

Upon the receipt of the application in the Irish courts, the case opened (in October 1905) and preliminary arguments began; searches were commenced. In March 1906, the case was adjourned owing to the death of the original claimant; and in October 1906, his daughter, Miss April Burke, of the same London address, described as "an assistant in the British Diplomatic Corps and a junior Lady-in-Waiting to the King's daughter, Princess Maud," was advertised to the court as the natural claimant-in-succession. She furnished in evidence her late father's Last Will and Testament.

Saturday, March the 17th 1906.

Dearest Kitty,
I have to tell you of sadness that I never before knew [wrote April to Mrs. Moore]. Two days ago my beloved papa departed this world; and I am writing this to you, my dear friend, knowing that I have no person to whom I may speak my grief.
On Thursday, a messenger came to me in my office at Whitehall, bearing a note from our maid, Mary. Her note begged me to come home, as Papa had "become stricken." I went to Alexander Street at once and found Dr. Fleask there. Papa sat in his chair, as he always does, but he could not speak; nor did he acknowledge me. Dr. Fleask gave it as his opinion that Papa had suffered an apoplexy. "Nature's stroke of ill-fortune," as the doctor said.
We carried Father to the day-bed in the library and laid him there. His pallor frightened me; and with the purple around his mouth, which was sagging at one corner, I became afraid. At the

same time, I saw his face as it must have been when he was a little boy, all tender and clear in the complexion.

Dr. Fleask tested Papa again and again with the question "Tell me your name, sir," and when Papa made no reply, Dr. Fleask said, "Tell me who is this young lady?" but again Papa did not respond. He tried to keep his eyes open, but the eyelids drooped and fluttered.

There was nothing to be done at that moment, and Dr. Fleask departed. I sat there all afternoon, watching Papa. Each time he breathed differently, I started—in fear and in hope. Mary made some beef tea, and I attempted to get some between his lips; but he had not the capacity to draw it in. I talked to him all the time, and I told him of his own dearness to me. On his face came no sign, ever, that he heard me.

Now the night came in, and we brought as many lamps and candles into the room as Mary could find in the house. But they merely lit his passing—because at a few minutes before six o'clock, his poor body gave a great surge, as though he would rise from the bed. Mary shrieked, and I held Papa's hand tighter. He made a second surge, and then he sank back. His eyes opened for a moment, but they lacked direction; they closed again as he subsided.

I felt his hand grow cooler, and a breath whistled from him, and a tear formed at his eye and rolled down his cheek, and I knew that I had lost him.

My dearest Kitty, I ever reserved my warmth for Papa, and now I regret that I did not tell him how I loved him. This morning, the cobbler's boy came with Papa's repaired boot and I all but fell down with grief in the hallway.

On Tuesday we shall have the funeral; and I must prepare to comport myself in the way that he taught me. There will be Tennyson to read, and Shakespeare, and the Revd. Donne.

After that, I must take over the legal matters regarding Tipperary. I do not know what sort of face I must turn to the world. As you alone know, I am driven by fear; I fear everyone. We have talked before, you and I, about the brisk face that I show—but it is the only face I know. I tremble inside all the time, and Papa knew this—he

kept me "up," as he called it. Must my fears now take me over? My
dearest Kitty, please forgive my distraught tones.

> *Your bereft but still affectionate friend,*
> *April.*

Mr. Prunty's files have been meticulously constructed. He put everything in linear order by date. Thus, his summary observes, "In October 1906, Mr. Stephen Somerville, K.C., made a successful application to the court for an interim "caretaking" order, so that the property might be protected from possible marauders, and so that a farm plan might be drawn up to prevent the fences and pastures from falling further into the weeds of disrepair."

In other words, when April Burke got her hands fully on the case—that is, seven months after her father's death—she approached it with her customary vim. Once her father's funeral was over, she began the necessary rearrangements of her life that would optimize her attention to the lawsuit. She kept the house in London open—but now she turned her face west, to Ireland and, as if anticipating a life to come, began to insert herself into Anglo-Irish society.

Thursday, the 26th of July 1906.

My dear Robbie,
Yes, please come to Bantry—the Atlantic is so wonderful just now.
A squall yesterday which drove marine oddments up onto the sands.
I walked for an hour this morning, and was the best beachcomber;
I found scallop shells, jellyfish, gray, wrinkled driftwood, and a
wonderful seppe shell—or "cutting-fish," as they call it here.

Shall I expect you by Sunday, the 5th? If so, you shall renew your
acquaintance with an interesting person! You recall that my lovely

friend Mr. O'Brien had developed a perfect passion for the young woman who attended poor dear Oscar? Well, she is to be a house-guest of Doty Bandon's at Castle Bernard; she is coming over for her great lawsuit—she's seeking what she claims as her "birthright," Tipperary Castle. Nobody here believes her; they think her a charlatan, and she has behaved dreadfully to my Mr. O'Brien. I am firmly among those who hope that she loses!

Castle Bernard is very merry. The Bandons seem to make grandeur intimate—how I wish that Oscar had known them. So as you see, dear chum, lots of ding-dong gossip awaits—hurry-hurry!

Con molto amore,
Mollie.

Saturday, the 4th of August 1906.

My dear Kitty,
In haste. Shall we meet at Limerick? If you designate a hotel, we can have tea. (Do they have tea in Limerick?) I should like you to meet my Mr. Somervilles, father and son; they are my protectors among the law!

Speedily,
April.

SUNDAY, THE 16TH OF SEPTEMBER 1906.

Charles came home on Friday evening. He says that he means to stay some time. When Bernard asked about ailing patients, Charles said they are all "in a good way." At times I have thought how safe to be ill, were Charles the attendant healer. He cares so much.

Although he has not said so, I know that he has come to be with Euclid. This morning, he helped Euclid into the pony-trap. It took a long time. Euclid glowed after their drive. They went to Golden and saw Athassel again, which Charles enjoys.

Onward from the autumn of 1904 I have little to say of Ireland's events in general. Naturally I observed them as they occurred. Our island moved smoothly through the reign of King Edward the Seventh, and grew increasingly passionate about self-government; the talk of Home Rule replaced and surpassed in heat the debate on land reform.

In fact, the whole country burned with a nationalistic flame. Enthusiasts for the revival of the Irish language held many and vigorous meetings, and when I look back now I can see that the whole country was talking itself into a ferment that would one day boil into revolution.

As a "nation" (which we now increasingly called ourselves), we revisited our glorious past of myth and wonder; we reminded ourselves of our ancient poets and our many Gods and our brilliant artistic virtues. It often became heady, and Euclid became quite a specialist in ancient Irish paganism. He demonstrated how our mythical past had indeed been a matter of fact, and told us that we must observe what had happened—because in the workings of the past lay the clues to the future. And he told us, with Father's encouragement and to Mother's delight, that we would soon again become brilliant.

On the third of October 1904, as I have reported, I saw April and her driver turn their faces to the Limerick road. That she had been in my home, under our roof, between our walls, still dazed me with delight; now she departed and I believed that she would return. She did, and in circumstances that in time brought great turmoil.

It began with a letter from London, in spring 1906, to my mother. April wrote to tell that her father had died; it seemed that a stroke felled him, but she had the comfort of being present at his death, and she wrote movingly of how she missed him. Immediately, I wrote to her conveying my sincerest condolences; I had had little time to acquaint myself with her beloved father, but in that period I came to like him as much as a fellow might in so brief an acquaintance. In truth, I missed the dear man from the proceedings of my mind, as I had much looked forward to seeing him again, perhaps on the grounds of the castle that he might one day walk as of right or, as I have said, touring with me through the ruins of Athassel, burial place of de Burgo earls.

I had remained within reach of Ardobreen in the weeks after April's departure; in case she needed my attentions again, I wished to travel no farther than a day's ride from Limerick. During that time, I attempted in vain to gain the opinions of my parents as to whether she might prove a suitable and lovable daughter-in-law. Mother said she needed "greater knowledge of the girl" before she could essay such an opinion, and my father said she reminded him of how Mother looked at that age.

Euclid told me that I must be "firmer" with April, and when I replied that Father seemed to show no such firmness with Mother, Euclid said in his darker tone, "Different field, different beast." I still do not know what he meant.

That summer passed in short journeys to outlying counties, and one long journey to Donegal—a matter of some weeks. A priest in Bundoran, who had been Mr. Egan's patient and was much given to working in the garden, had written to me complaining of the itch. I stayed with him many days until it vanished (my treatment was a mixture of sulfur powder and pig's lard). Riding through Ireland in August had been exceptionally pleasant, and I saw many harvests, drank many ales in celebration; home again, I resumed my shorter journeys.

One Saturday in October 1906, I arrived home from Templemore and a patient with the gout (which is cured by drinking a boiling of ragwort, and eating a porridge of oatmeal, each three times a day) to find a letter from London awaiting me. Mother sat with me as I opened it; I have it here, as I have all April's letters to me.

Dear Mr. O'Brien—
Or "surely" (as you say in Ireland) surely must I not call you
"Charles"? For all the goodness you have shown me I may assume
your friendship, may I not? Your letter regarding Papa's death moved

me, and showed me how dear you feel in your friendship to me.
Therefore I begin again, this time with "Dear Charles."

    I have written to your mother my thanks for her condolences too,
and I have asked her—as I ask you—to extend my gratitude to your
father for his sound advice regarding the law and Tipperary Castle.
Acting upon your father's words last year, I engaged Mr. Somerville's
practice in Limerick, and as the newspapers have reported, they
agreed to act for my father in the matter of this estate.

    When Papa died, I became his sole legatee, and as an early step
I petitioned the Courts that the property be placed under some good
care. The petition was granted on condition that a Caretaker be
appointed, and to this end I took the liberty of suggesting your name.
I know nobody else in Tipperary and I understand too that you
harbor deep feelings for the place, and that is how I know that it
will be in excellent hands under your watchful eyes.

    Mr. Somerville has told me that he will shortly write to you (and, as
he said, be pleased to address a son of Mr. Bernard O'Brien) with
greater details than I can furnish now. As you may judge from this letter,
the suit has already been entered upon with the most serious intent.

    May I include you in my expressions of thanks for all you have
done and are about to do?

    Yours with gratitude,
    April Burke.

Mother asked me whether she too might see the letter; she read it
without comment, other than the question "Do they mean to pay you
for this caretaking?" In my delight I protested that I should not expect or
accept payment.

The law truly does move slowly. Next September—of 1907, almost
three years after April's first visit—a sealed packet arrived, heavy with
brown wax, postmarked "Limerick" and addressed to me at Ardobreen.
It contained a detailed "Letter of Appointment" and some keys bearing
ancient labels. Court papers indicated that permission had been given to
appoint a "Responsible Overseer" to the property and a Court Order

made to that effect. (This resulted in Euclid for many days addressing me, and referring to me, as "R.O.")

I had not waited for the official authority. In the intervening months, I had ridden over to the castle many times, most particularly in the winter months. At no time did I take any steps to exceed the curiosity of a passing stranger or to anticipate my coming powers.

Each successive visit persuaded me further of the castle's thrall. My father believed my mother a truly beautiful woman because, he said, "Every time you look, her face is different—that's the sign of true beauty." I had observed the same with April—and now I saw it in this place that I hoped would become her (and my) home.

Whether in morning light, or through drifts of noontide rain, or early evening fog, which floats a foot above the ground like a gray magic carpet, this estate gave off enchantment. I liked nothing better than to sit on Della, in the exact place where April and I had first dismounted, and look on the walls, the battlements, and the wonderful vista down to the bridge and the lake.

SUNDAY, THE 29TH OF SEPTEMBER 1907.

Today we rode with Charles as he opened Tipperary Castle. I have had few days in my life when my feelings changed so. At first, I felt angry at his being used. My son was born to take care of people, not ruined estates. Then, when we all sat on the old terrace, I felt the peace of the place. Charles has spoken much of this. I knew today what he meant. At last, when we entered the house, I was marvelously overwhelmed. Never have I known such magnificence.

But that is not the point. I have known other Great Houses, including Aunt Hutchinson's and, in London, Mrs. Wilkerson's. And, of course, the Countess of Athlone's London house in Mayfair. But I have never seen a house with such feeling in it. The ornateness that we can still see did not bring that. Nor did the beauty of the cut stone. Nor even the colors employed.

There is an *emotion* in the house, a care, a warmth. I must not raise my hopes too much for my son. At the same time I must give him wonderful praise for his feelings about this house. He has been so praiseworthy in his instinct. I applaud his judgment.

At one moment today I looked at him. He stood on the terrace, inspecting with a shrewd and tasteful eye the house that he once hoped might one day become his. That girl is not his worth by a long chalk. She is not his measure and has little of his character. I know that each crow thinks her own crow the whitest, but my elder son, with his fine shoulders and his mane of hair and his pleasing and willing-to-please face, was always beyond her merit. Yet I do not know how to tell him that. He disparages himself so readily, so often.

The Irish mansions didn't suddenly begin to rise above the landscape. They weren't a direct product of English colonization. Many of them mutated from the castles of the Norman barons, whose similar buildings can be seen today in Ireland, England, and Wales. But even before the raising of their ramparts and towers, they had forerunners.

The Irish, as did the Scots, built themselves what are now called "fortified houses." In Tipperary and the other counties of Munster, many fine examples can still be seen. Some of them have kept their height but lost their heart, and they stand in the fields, gaunt and ruined. Others have been "restored" as hotels and conference centers.

Tipperary Castle, from all the available documentation, began as one of those fortified houses. Terence Hector Burke did not, as Oscar Wilde had mistakenly believed, build it from the ground up. In fact, it's more the case that he became the last in a line of Burkes who had expanded and decorated their residence.

In time—and Oscar got this right—Terence Hector Burke added the theater. As his predecessors had done with other wings and sections, he built it so expertly that it looked as though it had always been part of the house. In essence, it became the last phase. Tipperary had grown from the original fortified house into a great Anglo-Irish mansion.

My appointment as "R.O." did not specify my tasks, except in the vaguest terms, and so I took it upon myself to define my duties. The keys opened their locks at first turn—excellent craftsmanship to work so well after a disuse of more than half a century. I had brought candles, and the Somerville letter contained detailed instructions as to how I should open shutters all along each passageway. Entering through the servants' halls, I let in light with every few paces that I took.

Nothing had changed in this house. Dust lay everywhere, but matters had been left as though the occupants had donned their coats one day and walked out. On a small table in the annex of the servants' hall sat a mug, an old candle, and some burnt matches. The mug, when I picked it up, left a ring in the dust.

When I had opened all the shutters down in this wing, I stood and looked at everything—the walls, painted yellow; the sensible cornices with less adornment than I knew I should find in the main house; the benches painted brown, now gray with the dust. No coats hung on any of the hooks—no hats, no cloaks, no ulsters; when the servants left, they must have known that it might be forever.

In the kitchen, a giant table stretched down the middle of this long room; on shelves and in cupboards sat the great pots and crocks that had serviced the food of the house. From the servants' quarters, and the kitchens and pantries (which I did not yet open), the main passageway led to the central hallway of the house. Here I had some difficulty; this passageway had no windows, and to illuminate my way I had to depend upon the light coming from the windows that I had opened far behind me. I passed through two heavy doors, and finally, with only a glimmer to help me, found myself in the main hallway.

The windows here gave greater problems, and dust fell upon me like gray snow as I drew back the long, heavy curtains. I then found the iron handles that, when turned, opened the shutters and, with the same ease as the earlier locks, the first shutter opened, then the second. I was covered with dust—but I had let in the first light in the main hall of the house for more than fifty years.

Whatever I had imagined I now abandoned. The walls had been composed of beautiful cut stone, which reached to a height of approximately four feet, and above that the hall was paneled with marble. On the cornices and all across the ceiling had been placed the most ornate stucco that I had—or still have—ever seen. As far as I could make out, it seemed eccentric, with some of the richer styles overlaid by simpler motifs; for example, in one corner a large bird with detailed feathers protruded from the wall, grasping a branch with leaves in its beak, while beneath was slung a great plaster chain. In another corner, a proud figure of a "Victory" of sorts surged forth like the figurehead of a ship. A great marbled staircase wound upward from either side to a balcony; the stairs could allow six people abreast.

And the hall could accommodate a ball with an orchestra. It went through from one side of the house to the other, and through the north-facing windows I could see our chimneys and the wood. On the other side, the westering sun suddenly came through the clouds and shone straight in to light a ceiling as ornate as Versailles, pink and gold and turquoise. In that radiance too, however, dwelt a sadness; a wide section of the central medallion, populated by lions, tigers, and other great cats, had broken off. In truth, there was much frightful damage elsewhere.

All had been caused, my father had long ago told me, by vandalism, by would-be thieves; local opportunists had tried to steal the flashings off the roof—to sell to munitions fabricators for making bullets. As one man had wrestled with a particularly dense chunk of lead, it had broken away in his hand, exposing a ceiling underneath, which is where the water poured down in time.

However, the man had then slipped on the smooth lead and fallen to his death outside. This had strengthened the aura of bad luck in a house already stained with the reputation of loss and pain, and the gutters and lead flashings thus escaped further depredations.

Through the gap in the ceiling, the once and former grandeur of the private apartments could be glimpsed. They evidently had had much delicacy, much exquisiteness; but, sadly, the years of rains through the holes in the roof had caused very considerable damage, and much of the other plasterwork lay beneath layers of black and green mold.

It was clear that the true state of the castle could not be judged without a tour of the building. Consolingly, it was plain that whatever restoration would be required, the place retained its basic magnificence.

I opened the padlock on the bars of the front door, but no matter how I hauled and pushed, I could not move the great door by an inch. It still had damage. I could not climb the staircase, and I could not enter any of the rooms that radiated from the hall. All the doors had swollen, and everywhere destruction had spread. Looking directly above my head, I could see the ribs of the walls to which plaster had once adhered; long, wide reaches of plaster hung loose. As I moved about, some of this stucco began to flake loose; a piece fell in the hallway behind me. Smaller and lighter than a coin, it would have hurt nobody, yet it could have brought others down in its wake.

Although my activities were necessarily limited, the house came alive again. Working steadily where I could, I threw back every shutter, casement, and door that I could reach, and I let the world bring its healing light and air indoors. Now I could survey the damage to the house, which proved even more extensive than I had anticipated.

The main staircase, with all its wide marble, was incapable of bearing the weight of a person; but by a rear and undamaged stair I was able to reach the upper floors. In all the corridors, in the gallery, and along the rear passageways, I found damage. Boards had rotted and begun to fall down; in many places I could see through the timbers to the floors below. One of the ornate painted doors to the gallery, which had romantic woodland scenes, hung askew; its companion had lurched from the topmost hinge. On the frayed chairs along the gallery wall, many of the seats crumbled to my touch.

I could not gain access to the greater rooms upstairs but, through open or fallen doors, I could see four-poster beds whose canopies had fallen, and exquisite armoires—which bravely seemed to have withstood the assaults of the decades. Through one door several yards away, I looked into a nursery—

and at once recalled how Mr. Wilde had told of the mysterious actress showing the new father his son's nursery before she disappeared. I reflected that I
had long ago vowed to find the basis of that story, to solve the mystery. Now
I felt that I never would; the journey to Somerset had proven too opaque.

Eventually, in that first week, I attempted to enter as many downstairs
rooms as I could (the upper floors felt too dangerous). The more recent
construction, such as the theater and the rebuilt kitchens, had stood up
well—but the older parts of the house, the dining and breakfast rooms,
and the three drawing-rooms, showed much damage. Green mold and
fungus spread everywhere, obscuring the details on the plasterwork,
much of which had begun to crumble. When I contrived to climb up
and reach a cornice in the main dining-room, the stucco cluster of grapes
came away in my hand, with the damp smell of decay.

In the ballroom, I found the greatest contrast—the most beautiful
room had suffered the most severe damage. Its stucco peeled; its plaster
cornices sagged or lay on the floor in piles. The marks of ancient cascades
from water damage all but obscured the beautiful turquoise and pink
paintwork. Some of the chairs along the wall, where at one time merrymakers had rested, now leaned or fell like dead, once-golden dancers.

At the end of the first week, my assessment revealed that more than
two-thirds of the house required substantial renovation; in fact, no more
than three servants' bedrooms above the stables had escaped damage. All
hangings seemed perilous. I dared not tug at a velvet curtain and took no
risks with walking across floors; I trod everywhere by the wall, where I
knew that joists rested. But many joists came into view beneath rotten
floorboards, and from their condition I understood that they would have
to be replaced before any new floor could be laid. My inspection was a
journey of pain and excitement.

SUNDAY, THE 22ND OF MARCH 1908.

At breakfast this morning, and yesterday, Bernard read no
newspapers. I asked why. He answered by making an appoint-

ment to see me here, in our bedroom, "secretly," he said, for eleven o'clock. When we met, he told me that all the newspapers are telling of Miss Burke's marriage in London last Wednesday to Henry Somerville's son.

"I did not wish Charles to see," Bernard said. But who is to tell him? Shall I? Or his father? Or the world? He is certain to find out. Perhaps he already has heard? And does not wish to say? This afternoon he went off to the castle.

Now we shall have some fixing to do. Must he continue working unpaid for this young woman? In how many ways can she break his heart?

Shall we send him abroad for some time? He talks of buying a motor-car. Della can travel no more. Indeed, I fear that he will lose her this winter. Charles says that he does not wish to break in a new horse. Bernard says he should buy one of Dan Dwyer's younger mares; they are well turned out.

Oh, what shall I do—about everything?

Tuesday, the 24th of March 1908.

Darling Mollie,
Now we have something to talk about! In The Times *there was a notice, very brief, announcing the marriage (on Wednesday last) "quietly" of "April, only child of the late Mr. and Mrs. Terence Burke of Westminster, to Stephen, eldest child and only son of Mr. and Mrs. Henry Somerville, Ballinacourty House, Limerick, Ireland."*

"Well-well!" I hear you say, perhaps followed by "the scheming rodent!" (which, as I believe, was your more recent nomenclature). You may not like her, my dear, which I think a shame—I find her perfect—but you must agree that her attorneys now have a true interest on winning her case? No? Of course! And she has no money—so what better means could a pretty body devise of addressing the hideously expensive process of the law? You must

admit to her shrewdness, Mollie, and you must admit that I bring you the sweetest of gossip!

So—be not surprised if she is found strolling the halls of her "birthright" ere long. In fact, Doty Bandon told me in August that your rodent was all but inviting house-guests for next summer.

Oh, I hear that Bosie was rejected by several hotels in Belgium. I feel sorry for him; the world may loathe him, but he is dying for the love and loss of Oscar.

Keep me posted, Mollie dearest, on the nouvelle *Mrs. Somerville. Perhaps she'll be in Paris at New Year!*

Your fondest friend—
Robbie.

The "decent" period of mourning in a family was, traditionally, a year and a day. April Burke married two years after her father's death. And six months *after* she asked Charles to caretake the property.

Other than the official record of their firm, no documents exist about the Somervilles. They had come into Ireland some hundreds of years earlier, as had Amelia Goldsmith O'Brien's family. But Limerick is a gossipy city, where memories are long, and the family, though now extinct, is well remembered.

Henry Somerville, the old man, had a pleasant, harmless reputation. A useful oarsman at Oxford University in his youth, he became at the age of seventy-five one of the prime founders of the Shannon Rowing Club in 1905. He paid for most of the fine new clubhouse. Other than that, and a Christmas Day swim across the river and back every year, he lived an unremarkable and blameless life. He married late and had one son (a daughter died in infancy).

Of Stephen, a little more was known. He was born in 1875, and was therefore seven years older than April Burke. A brilliant law student, he graduated early from Trinity College, Dublin, and went straight into practice at the Irish Bar. He became the youngest barrister in history to rise to the senior level of King's Counsel—"K.C." That's how he had the stature to lead the Tipperary Castle case.

He had a big, black beard and a bad name. Two complaints against him can be found in Irish Law Society archives. On both occasions he was accused of assault. No charges were brought, even though one of the allegations was investigated at some length. A sum of damages was agreed, and the case was hushed up.

The plaintiff, a thirty-year-old woman, identified only by initials, described "a drunken attack and attempted violation." In the other case, which had much less documentation, the words "repeated, violent attacks while drunk" are mentioned.

Nevertheless, at the time that he met and married April, he was enjoying a brilliant legal career. And he must have had something going for him. Flair, charm, individuality, style, great force of personality—these were the hallmarks of the Irish courtroom lawyers of that (or indeed any) time.

For April, it must have seemed perfect. Stephen Somerville, the most sought-after bachelor of the day, was six feet two, dashing, rich, and on the rise. And he could win her lawsuit for her. Plus, his uncle became the judge in the case, which might not be completely harmful.

As for Stephen—he now represented a client who, if he had anything to do with it, could soon own one of the most beautiful and potentially fertile properties in Europe.

My life as a healer taught me many lessons, among them the fact that, from time to time in Life, a stranger giving advice may alter one's own course—as Mr. William Butler Yeats did when he advised me to go to London, seek Miss Burke's father, and pursue my suit down that pathway. Mr. Yeats came back into my life when I was the Responsible Overseer at Tipperary Castle; and the words he spoke to me had a long-lasting and in time transforming effect.

I remember the morning so clearly—a fine Tuesday in March, a true spring day, with pleasant warmth, even though we were promised rain.

The gates at the entrance to the avenue now opened easily, yet I was always surprised when I saw a visitor. Usually they came on foot or on horseback; that morning, a full landau arrived, and even at a distance I recognized Mr. Yeats, with his great mane of hair and his tweed cloak and his large spectacles.

He had the reputation of being a diffident man, awkward in company. I found him delightful. With gestures he directed his driver to take the carriage along by the terrace to a point where he could see the fullest view of the castle's facade. There he stopped, sitting and looking. I, at the front door, waited a moment to see whether he would emerge for a deeper inspection. But my patience gave out, and I walked down the terrace and greeted him.

"Good morning, Mr. Yeats. Welcome to Tipperary Castle."

To my astonishment, he remembered me. I was just about to tell him my name, and remind him of my visit to his home in Dublin, when he stretched out his hand in greeting and said, "Mr. O'Brien."

I laughed and asked how he came to be here. He told me that he was driving from Limerick, where he had been staying, to pay a visit to his old friend the Archbishop, at Cashel.

When I offered to give him a guided tour of the place, we began to walk and I pointed out everything that I felt might appeal to him. He was consumed with interest, and soon we reached the spot where the best view is to be taken. As I pointed out to him the Rock of Cashel in the distance, he held up his hand for silence. (I talk a great deal when I am nervous.)

After a few moments, Mr. Yeats said, "This place has an importance to me."

Expecting a continuation of his thought, I said nothing. He waited for a moment, then spoke again:

" 'He bore her away in his arms,/The handsomest young man there.' "

I knew that he was quoting from one of his own poems, "The Host of the Air," and I murmured the refrain from it: " 'And never was piping so sad/And never was piping so gay.' "

He looked at me with his intense eyes and he said, "Thank you, Mr. O'Brien," and again lapsed into silence.

After a few moments he said, "Show me as much of the house as you can."

We went inside; I was delighted that, being the same height, we walked shoulder to shoulder. I took him by safe routes across shattered floors, beneath rotted stucco, up the rear staircases, and eventually we came back out through the servants' quarters.

Strolling up to the terraces, I said to him that I much admired his work in the arena of Irish lore. He became very animated and asked me what I enjoyed. I asked whether he would care to hear the full, complete version of my tale of the magic deer and we stood there, in the sunshine, as I told it. He was delighted with it, and said so three or four times, and asked me whether I would write it down and send it to him (which it has since been my pleasure to do).

As we walked up to his landau, he said, "What do you know of the plans for this place?"

I told him of the lawsuit, remarking upon its likely complexity. As he climbed into his seat I said, "My hope is that Miss Burke will win the place. Her father, whom I came to know—at your advice, sir, if you re-member." He nodded. "Well, he passed away, and now Miss Burke is his sole successor. My hope is that she and I will marry and we will settle down here and renew the castle and the lands."

Mr. Yeats looked at me in the most peculiar way, a long, penetrating stare.

"Is that your hope or your definite plan?"

I said, "Both."

He said nothing, merely looked again at the facade of the castle. Then he reached across the carriage's polished side and shook my hand earnestly.

"Good-bye, Mr. O'Brien. Meeting you the second time was even more pleasant than the first—and the first meeting was very agreeable."

But he did not tell the driver to move on. Instead he sank back in his seat and seemed deep in thought. I waited, my hands clasped behind my back like an obedient boy. Then he spoke:

"You told me, during our long talk when we last met, of something Oscar said. What was it again?"

I quoted: "Be sure to keep beauty preserved."

Mr. Yeats nodded. "Mr. O'Brien, I didn't say so earlier because I was afraid of breaking the spell of the place—but I was here before; I was visiting Cashel and I rode over one day. One empty, beautiful summer day. And that poem you so kindly quoted—I got the idea for that poem here. So the place is important to me. And it's important to you."

I said, fervently, "Oh, it is."

Mr. Yeats said, "Make it the most important part of your life. It has enough beauty to warrant that. If you do that, if you take that step— you'll not fail. You'll get everything you wish for. It might not happen in the way you think—but, Mr. O'Brien, you'll keep beauty preserved. I know it."

He shook my hand again, this man of whose aloofness people complain; he tapped the driver on the shoulder, and they drove away. The last I saw of them was the horses turning the corner down by the bridge and Mr. Yeats's hand in the air, waving as the landau disappeared into the trees of the avenue.

From *The Nationalist & Tipperary Advertiser* (published in Clonmel every week since 1890), in its edition of 28 March 1908:

"On Wednesday evening, Charles O'Brien, of Ardobreen, Golden, was found lying on the roadside near the old entrance to Tipperary Castle. He had been shot twice, and neighbors reported having heard gunfire some hours earlier, but attributed it to fowlers, known to frequent the area. As this newspaper goes to press, no reports have come to hand regarding the gentleman's condition."

SUNDAY, THE 19TH OF APRIL 1908.

What is to become of us? Three days after Bernard and I avoided telling Charles of Miss Burke's marriage, Charles was shot. We know not why. We know not by whom. He was struck in the leg and the neck by heavy bullets.

We have been putting together the pieces of the incident. Charles was seen by neighbors as he rode down from the castle to the main road at past four o'clock. It had been raining heavily. The same neighbors saw two men riding by and then heard gunshots. Then Charles was pitched from his new horse, Maudie, who died under him. She was killed when the bullet passed through Charles's leg and into her heart.

At five o'clock and again at six, I had been asking myself why Charles had not come home. Had he decided to sleep in the castle tonight, as he sometimes did? At some minutes before seven o'clock, we heard a commotion in the yard. Our neighbor Mattie Hogan came to the door. I answered the knock and I saw that Mattie looked stricken. On his cart behind him I saw Charles's boots sticking out.

With Mattie came a man who introduced himself as "Harney." He had heard the gunfire and kept on his own journey. By some mysterious instinct, he chose to return, though he did not need to (he had been going home). Harney (as, he said, everyone calls him), found Charles. And, seeing the neck wound, he lifted Charles's head to keep the wound closed. This probably saved Charles's life. Another passer-by then roused Mattie Hogan, who has the nearest house to the castle gate.

We set out in the long car for Tipperary and dispatched Mattie for Dr. Moran. Harney rode with us and kept up Charles's head. Charles still bled.

When we reached the hospital we found that the wounds were not in themselves mortal. His damage rose from the fact that he had lain there for some hours in a cold, wet ditch. Today he continues to lie ill in the Tipperary Hospital. We do not know whether he can live. Bernard says the gun must have been a Mauser. And, he believes, Mausers usually kill. Charles was fortunate, so Bernard says.

"Fortunate?" I am distracted. Fortunate to be shot? Fortunate to lie in repeating fevers? He has not lost his leg, as we feared he might. The neck wound may take his life. It grows septic constantly. Everybody has tried to help. I have sent a man to bring Mr. Egan to the hospital.

On some days Charles is lucid, on some not. He tries to recall what occurred. He saw two horsemen, he says. And he had seen one before, on the road to Bruree some years back. The men rode by him. No challenge was issued. Then, when they were behind him, he heard the gunshots. He says that he heard them before he felt the bullets. At first his leg, then his neck "stung." And he heard hooves galloping but recalls no more than that.

I have been sitting with him night and day. Bernard has made me come home tonight. Perhaps if I write it down, it will take away my anxiety. We thought that Euclid would die when he heard. He is less able to sleep than usual, and now he grows very weak. Harney has promised to ride here every day and tell me of Charles. It seems that Harney is remarkable. I do not know who he is. Bernard says he comes from Urlingford, in Kilkenny. He is twenty years old, mature, and unusual. I believe that he saved Charles's life. He believes so too, and as a consequence has become devoted to Charles.

What has come into our lives? What malign force has placed itself in our midst? I do not wish to hang blame around any person's neck—and I shall not do it. Tonight, I am exhausted, and full of tears that I have not yet shed for my two sons who have never grown up.

Tipperary Castle's long, officially secured closure told everyone that the estate had become a major inheritance issue. The grief-stricken Terence Hector Burke had not left a last will and testament before his wife vanished. If people had any knowledge—no matter how vague—of a son and heir somewhere, the property would be frozen by the government. Anybody laying claim to the estate would have to offer proof of family lineage, and thereby hope to establish title.

Over the decades, various claims came in, from chancers and hopefuls. Some claimed distant kinship, or said they had "verbal contracts," or showed forged wills. All had to be investigated, and the issue of title to the place became delayed and delayed. Many of these documents became matters of public record, because increasingly it began to look as though the estate would inevitably pass into public ownership. For this reason, government law officers had to take an interest.

As a result, the affairs of Tipperary Castle built up into a famously large official dossier. The legal files, still available to be seen, would stand more than six feet high if piled up together. They contain a few surprises—and one chilling shock. It comes in correspondence between the Royal Irish Constabulary and a Dublin firm of lawyers who at one time represented the British government's interests.

The letters reveal that the trio who assaulted Charles O'Brien in Limerick in December 1900 had meant to kill him. A "contract," as it would be called today, had been put out on him, and by people who meant what they said. Astute, wealthy, prominent, and capable, they had hired others to do their killing, as the rich usually do. Charles had no knowledge of it, would never have guessed it, and therefore remained unprotected.

4

My name is Michael Nugent. No, this is not a new voice in this tale—I'm the author of the "commentaries" on the writings of Charles O'Brien, and I've chosen this moment to reveal myself. I'm the one who discovered all the letters and newspaper reports, met Mr. Prunty in Limerick, received his permission to search his files—and found Amelia O'Brien's journal.

In fact, I'm the person who also bought the oak chest, cleaned it, opened it up, and in time donated it and its contents to the county library. I had long known of its existence; it had a kind of small mythology attached to it, among the people who had known of it.

It was presumed to be hiding somewhere in our county. In the end I found it by chance. And somehow, in one of those odd things that life delivers from time to time, I'd always known that I would find it, since the day I was alerted to look out for it.

I can't claim that I at first felt unusually arrested in any way by the contents. When I began to read the "History," I certainly found it interesting. As it went on, I felt it compelling for what it was. This, I thought, is a good self-portrait of a somewhat untypical nineteenth-century Irishman who had a decent sensibility and, when he was being objective, a clear eye.

Also, I knew the locality, and I recognized the names of the places; it all had a familiar ring. And I wondered whether it would make a diverting lecture for the Clonmel History Group. Or maybe I could turn it into a paper for the annual publication of the Tipperary Historical Society.

And it chimed with my interests. For most of my adult life, I taught (and with some passion) history and English literature to boys between the ages of twelve and eighteen. So, in the interests (I thought) of spontaneity, and for my own amusement, I began writing commentaries on Charles O'Brien, and his life and times, before I finished reading the entire text.

Then, as I read, I found myself being drawn in further and further—and for reasons that I could not quite explain. I stopped writing simple glosses on Mr. O'Brien's narration and began to step closer to him—all without quite understanding why.

Before long, I began to recognize that I was being completely taken over. When I came to the shooting incident I raced ahead to the end—because I now knew that I had some connection to this story. The attempted murder of Charles O'Brien was part of my childhood, a story that my mother told me as a secret, never to be divulged to my father (I will come to that presently).

My "unmasking" of myself at this moment comes about because from here onward my involvement becomes too dominant to permit anonymity. It can't be otherwise. I know how the story ends, and its ramifications spread far wider and go much deeper than the "History."

In a way that has shocked me beyond measure I am involved with the lives of Charles O'Brien, the O'Brien family, and April Burke. As a result, almost everything in my life has been altered, including the way I now have to perceive myself. It has been nothing less than a profound shock.

When I realized this, I had some difficulties in deciding how to manage the material. At the outset, while writing the commentaries, I had been expecting to do no more than merely follow the document's chronology—filling in the background, illuminating the historical details, that sort of thing.

But once I had begun to uncover the background to the story, I couldn't be content with that anymore. This "event" in my life—which is what it had become—had changed its character. I went back and read what I had written and I saw it in a different light. Dry, dispassionate comment would no longer be adequate, because now this was my story too.

Therefore, everything that I, Michael Nugent, write from now on comes with the hindsight of having read Charles O'Brien's entire document. And—such an important "and"—from the moment I introduce myself here, everything has been written *after* completing my own verifications and inquiries.

I decided after much thought to resort to what I know best—I began to behave as a teacher. "Master the subject," I told myself. "Lay it out in a clear and benign way. Make it easy to survey. And to assess."

To accomplish this, I decided that I would begin by fleshing out Charles's life. In a sense, he drove me to it, by saying, "Be careful about me." As I began to delve and find relevant material, it became essential to apply it to his text, as a kind of extra commentary, a corroboration of what I had been feeling and observing.

By the way, there is nothing in Charles O'Brien's "History" that gave me any clue to the eventual full story and my place in it. So—how much of my response was instinct? I can't tell. But I do know that once I decided to widen my inquiries, I hoped—with an earnest, arresting hope—that I would end up in possession of a text capable of teaching me something extraordinarily valuable.

And I did. What's that old saying—"Be careful what you wish for?" It's fair to say—and I'm smiling with pleasure and irony as I say it—that nothing I have ever read has changed me so profoundly, or mattered to me as much, as Charles O'Brien's "History."

Delightfully, that is what I, as a teacher, always sought to do: to improve, to elevate, to matter. I *loved* teaching. Not only have I always considered it a noble profession, but my heart used to pound with excitement on Monday mornings as I walked to the school.

How could it be otherwise? I taught Shakespeare, for heaven's sake! And the poets of the world. I taught the campaigns of Napoleon, the unification of Italy, the American Revolutionary War, the fall of the Roman Empire—I taught the great events of the universe and the great literary art of Man.

That was a privileged life. How many people gain the permission to earn a living by striding through great works and universal events and pointing out their wonders?

Now—though perhaps not on a cosmic scale—I was going to do it for myself, and I became so delighted at this prospect that I began to feel selfish. But I laughed it off. What could be selfish about it? Nothing! I live alone, I would trouble nobody, and I wanted something to fill my days.

Not for a moment did I suspect that this would become the most astonishing and rewarding thing that had ever happened to me. It brought shock, of course, and anger, and some deep sadness wafted in. But at the end of it, nothing would ever look—or be—the same.

When I decided to examine this entire matter as deeply as I could, I began by walking some ground—the woods in Dundrum, where the Treece eviction took place. I got my hands on old land maps, found a fence post, saw the ferns and the red bracken that also grew there in 1869, when young Charles O'Brien had sat in the pony-trap with his father.

It gave me a glorious feeling; I thought that I had stepped back in time. And I felt that an adventure had come into my life, that I could reach out and touch the past. I could almost see those "hundred or more, white-faced and grave" people who came to witness. How I wished I had tossed a shovel in the car so that I could excavate the ground where I reckoned the cottage had stood.

Next, I set out on my first documentary searches. I knew very little about "research"—indeed, I had always been slightly in awe of the word. In my own career, I merely visited the official Department of Education texts, extracted information and beauty from them, and passed it down to my students. But now I was obliged to do what the big boys did, the major academics. I didn't yet know where to begin.

One day, not long after the visit to the woods, I went to Dublin to lunch with a friend. She took me to the National Library. I had never been in the building before; it's one of the better relics of empire. People at small tables with green-shaded lamps pored over big, leather-bound objects. These turned out to be volumes of newspapers.

Library reading facilities were much less formal in those days—no passes required, or people vouching for one's character. We approached the desk, and my friend—who is a librarian—asked for *The Limerick Reporter & Tipperary Vindicator* for 1864 on my behalf.

Naturally, I knew what I was looking for—I had recently read Charles's version, after all—and I soon found it: the report on the case of leprosy. A girl by name of Mary Hurly had caught the disease from washing a sailor's clothes. Charles O'Brien had called it up as his first memory. He reported it accurately—he had the crucial bit, the date in his young boyhood, right. And the spelling of her name, which more commonly has an "e": "Hurley."

When I was teaching history, I tried to make it come to life. I liked to make it vivid for my classes; I liked to think that all history began as oral history—we could talk before we could write.

Now, in front of my eyes, I had an objective proof of a subjective event. Charles reported the oral version as told to him by his mother's housekeepers, and here, in the newspapers—journalism being the first draft of history—was the written account. (Which also raised an interesting question: Which informed which?)

Let me pause at this moment of revealing myself and clarify the sequence of events. Charles O'Brien met April Burke in November 1900; he was forty, she was eighteen. Four years later, after many failed letters, he traveled to London, met her father, told him of Tipperary Castle, and went with him to his boyhood home, the Brook House, in Somerset. The following morning he saw the lady who lived there board a carriage for Bristol, on an appointment—in all probability—to see her lawyers. That was in June.

In October 1904, Miss Burke came to visit the O'Briens, to see Tipperary Castle, and to hire lawyers—and the previous month a firm in Bristol put in a claim upon the estate. The case never got very far in the courts.

Next, in late October 1905, the newspapers reported the opening of the Tipperary Castle title hearings in the Irish High Court; and in March 1906, Terence Burke, April's father, died.

Six months later, she announced that, as her father's inheritor, she had now taken over the lawsuit. She was granted a caretaking order by the court, she asked Charles to accept the task, he agreed, and the keys arrived in September 1907.

In March 1908, April married Stephen Somerville; Charles's parents knew of it within days—Charles never tells how he heard of it. The poet William Butler Yeats came to visit the castle, remembered Charles, and was obviously puzzled at Charles's hopes of marrying April. Charles observed that when he stated his hopes of marrying Miss Burke, Yeats gave him a "long, penetrating stare." Yeats must have heard of April's marriage: he relished gossip, and he had just been in Limerick, where every Protestant knew of the marriage.

(Incidentally, was Yeats, in some indirect way, also attempting to tell Charles that April had married? The poem that he mentioned, "The Host of the Air," deals with a girl who is taken away by evil folk at the moment of her marriage to the man who loves her.)

Finally, Charles was shot the following day by the mysterious horseman who once semiassaulted him. Twenty-five days after the shooting, Amelia O'Brien made the entry in her journal—and now we meet a most significant figure in the story.

Joseph Patrick Harney, the young man who found Charles on the roadside, who came to the O'Briens' door that night, was born in 1888, the only son of the Crown Surveyor for County Kilkenny. His mother bore three other children, daughters; due to the family's salaried comfort, each of the four Harney children survived.

All received as good an education as could be had, meaning that they passed into schooling beyond the age of fourteen—which made them comparatively rare. Two sisters became nuns, one a government archivist in Dublin.

The Harney family seems always to have been well documented (as befits the children of a man who surveyed, and kept records). Their only son kept up the practice and left a personal archive, including an oral account that covered key phases of his life.

His earliest photographs show Joe Harney with a shock of black hair squinting into the sunlight. He wears a Sam Browne belt full of ammunition, and holds a rifle across his body like a soldier about to present arms. No uniform; this is a slim, tense man in a floppy tweed suit and boots; the photograph was taken in 1919, when Joe Harney was fighting in the War of Independence.

His role in Charles O'Brien's life became profound. Harney once said that because he had been raised in a household of women (his father traveled often), he grew up with "more than the usual quota of common sense." He might have added affection, gifts of friendship, and loyalty. When he attached himself to Charles it grew almost immediately into a deep and involved commitment.

Their relationship began in the days after the shooting. Harney took it as his personal duty to become the communicator between the hospital and Ardobreen. He wrote daily notes to Amelia. He watched over the doctors. He became Mr. Egan's assistant in the healing of Charles.

Mr. Egan wrought miracles. Harney brought him in at the first opportunity, as a visitor late one night when Dr. Moran had finished his last round of the day. The "little quack," as Amelia (kindly) called him, stood at the bedside and exchanged a touching greeting with Charles.

Harney charmed a nurse into undoing the dressings on Charles's neck and leg, and Egan looked grave at the sight of the wounds. The next night he came back, bringing with him some ancient soda bread on which mold had formed, like a green invader. Egan scraped off this unappetizing matter and applied it to Charles's wounds, while Harney stood guard over the door in case the nurse returned.

Within days, Dr. Moran began to profess himself pleased at the progress of the healing, but no sooner did one segment of one wound recover than another part became infected. This continued for eight or nine weeks—"two steps forward, one step back," as Harney put it in a note to Amelia; and then a day came when Charles, much healed, went home to Ardobreen.

Harney went with him and began to stay with the family, on and off, for some time. He helped in the yard; he read to Euclid; he drove Amelia on visits to neighbors and friends. Most of all, he became a companion to Charles, and the two men, the thin, amusing twenty-year-old and the brawny, thoughtful, and often anguished forty-eight-year-old, talked for hours and hours, often until dawn.

To Harney, Charles confided every detail of his feelings for April Burke. For instance, he told Harney, but never recorded in his own writings, how he had been almost forcibly ejected from Oscar Wilde's presence when he began to sketch the man a few days before his death.

Wilde had begged him to stop, saying that the likeness could only prove dreadful. But Charles pressed on until Turner, Wilde's "English" friend (as Charles called him), took the pad from Charles's hand and asked him to leave the room.

And Harney was there too, in the warm days of early June, when Amelia O'Brien visited her son in Tipperary Hospital and told him that "Miss Burke has married."

Amelia's journal for that night contained only this entry: "I told Charles today. It has been hanging over me. Until now I felt he was not well enough to know. He took it silently, said nothing. Not a word. Just gazed at me with those great big eyes. But he looked at me as though I were someone he had encountered at the end of the world."

After she finished, Harney told Charles and Amelia that he knew Stephen Somerville. "Not as an intimate or a friend," he said, and Somerville "never would be either of those." Harney had met him because Somerville had a cousin living near Harney's aunt in Kilkenny city, and Harney's aunt was the biggest gossip in the county. "She had a mouth as wide," he said, "as the mouth of the river Shannon."

Harney also told Charles and Amelia that Stephen Somerville was what we today call an alcoholic, a dipsomaniac. "And a bad drunk, at that, a violent drunk." (All this information comes from Harney's oral history.)

"I thought I'd buck Charles up with this information. His mother's eyes glinted for a moment—no love lost between Mrs. O'Brien and the new Mrs. Somerville, I thought, but Charles became distressed. He said, 'That's dreadful news; I wanted her to be happy.' Then he hesitated for a moment and said, 'She'd have been happy with me.' And he said little else.

"I walked to the hospital door with Mrs. O'Brien. My goodness, she was an attractive woman, with captivating eyes and the nicest, sweetest nature you'd ever find. She was in her sixties, yet I could so easily have fallen in love with her myself, and I only twenty. She put her hand on my forearm and stood to face me. 'Harney,' said she, 'do you think this will grow Charles up?'

"And I said, and I meant it, 'Mrs. O'Brien, do we want him to change from the kind of decent man he is now?' And said she back to me, 'I want him to be less hurt by life.' And off she went."

All in all, Joe Harney had strong values; they included a deep belief in his country's right to govern itself. And interestingly enough, even at that age, he had begun to understand the importance of recording his country and his own place in it.

With this in mind, and at his request, his sisters began to take down an informal record of his young life. Although there's no evidence as to whether Charles had confided in Harney about his own "History," their record keeping did demonstrate a shared value in the necessary observation of their own times. (As a history teacher I find this irresistible.)

From Joe Harney, too, we get a new portrait of April. In July, when he came home from the hospital, Charles felt well enough to return to his caretaking duties at the castle, especially now that he had Harney to assist him. He didn't go there every day—just often enough to check that no doors had been breached. If a rainstorm or a high wind had caused damage, he wanted to be aware of it. And he had also been given instructions to check that the neighboring farmers had their animals under control.

In September, almost fully recovered, Charles slipped and fell in one of the upstairs corridors. He reopened the wound on his leg. Mr. Egan couldn't be found, Harney wouldn't let Charles attempt to heal himself, and Dr. Moran took him back into the hospital.

While he was there, April came to see him. Her new husband waited in their hackney car outside—Harney saw them from the hospital window. He also noticed that April never mentioned Stephen's name, even though the man had traveled with her and was sitting outside. This is how he described that afternoon to his sisters:

"I heard the commotion—the window was wide open. When I looked down, I guessed right away and I thought, Is this the woman everybody's talking about? There she was, being helped down from the car by her husband, and a hospital porter, and a passing gentleman, and some lady. She was one of those people who gets others to buzz about her. Is that a gift? I don't know. I said to Charles, 'I think you have a visitor.' He knew by my tone whom I meant, and the expression on his face went between thrill and fear.

"Moments later, she swept into the room. She had the same excitement about her that you'd get from seeing a tremendous bird. Of course I saw at once why he had fallen so hard for her. She looked like his mother, only lovelier, if that was possible. Oh, she had a swing to her, that competent briskness; she didn't walk, she strode, and she had the best eyes of any woman I have ever seen. Brown as the earth, with a fleck. And that rich hair that she had.

"I always notice what women wear—that's what you get for growing up among women. And she was wearing a gold jacket and green skirt. The jacket was cut like a man's coat, almost military shoulders. She had a very light, long green-and-gold-striped silk scarf flying from her neck.

"And she had a black handbag, a purse, of crocodile skin. She put it down on the end of the bed, ran both her hands through her hair, brought the scarf under control and, said she, brisk as a breeze, 'Well, look at you, Charles O'Brien—you *have* been in the wars.'

"That was it. Very upper-class English accent. Not a 'Hello' or 'How are you?' or a thing. He said, 'You look beautiful.' Said she, this woman who, that afternoon, I can only describe as a running commotion, 'Aren't you going to congratulate me?' Charles said, 'I hope you'll be very happy.' Said she, 'No, not that—congratulate me on finding you. I didn't even have to go to your home.'

"Charles asked her how she'd known he was in the hospital, and she said that she had been dining with Lady Mollie Carew, who had now come back to Limerick from her summer sojourn in Bantry. 'I can't think why you and that woman are friends,' said our visitor. 'She's almost common.' And she sat down, on the chair that I had automatically pulled out for her.

"The visit didn't last long. In fact, it was over within minutes. A brutal visit, too—she had scarcely settled on the chair when I heard her say, 'Now. Business.' Next thing I heard the words 'I want you to testify on my behalf. Just tell the court that you always knew in your heart Tipperary Castle was meant to be mine. You'll do that, won't you?' That was what she said.

"I knew full well that Tipperary Castle meant the world to Charles. We talked of it often. He felt he belonged there, that his soul was there. And, of course, we'd discussed the possibility that it might have been O'Brien ancestral land a thousand years ago. The ghosts of race memory and all to that. Now here was this English lady asking Charles to secure it for her and her new husband—who was not a native Irishman. Protestant name, Somerville.

"Charles, ever the gentleman, said, 'Of course,' and said, 'I understand,' and 'Indeed—' but she cut him off. 'Good,' said she. And that was that. Not a 'please' or a 'thank you.' He nodded, in that grave sort of way that he had—it reminded me of an elephant, a big nod of the head. And then she said, 'By the way, I'm sending in a new caretaker. We need somebody there every day.' Then she was gone. She grabbed the crocodile bag, upped, and went.

"At the door, though, she looked back, just for half a second, and if I hadn't known Charles's story, I'd have sworn it was the sort of look any man would want to get from a woman. Especially a woman as beautiful as that. What kind of a look was it? It was a look—a look . . . well, a look of longing. And, I'd say, admiration. Then she was gone.

"Charles—what a hammering that poor man had taken—he looked at me, crestfallen. 'What did you think of her?' said he.

"All the evidence I had seen and heard suggested that I shouldn't like this woman—not like her at all. But, to my surprise, that wasn't the case. I liked her a whole lot, and I immediately saw the tragedy of the business, because even on my short acquaintance I was able to confirm one thing to my good satisfaction: that she was the perfect woman for him. There was an air between them—even in that short and somewhat harsh meeting, there was a rightness to the two of them together. A kind of a spark.

"So I answered Charles's question something like this: 'You'll probably be surprised to hear that I liked her very much.' And I added, 'Ask me again tomorrow and I'll see how she stays in my mind.' Needless to say, he did ask again, and this time I said, 'I like her even more today.' And said he, 'So I wasn't wrong to have fallen for her?' Said I, 'Not at all. Quite the opposite.' I meant it; I mean it to this day. She was twenty-two years younger than he, and they were perfect for each other.

"But I was only twenty, and what did I know of love or anything at that age? Strange business."

So passed the spring, summer, and autumn of 1908 for Charles O'Brien. In his lowest fantasies he couldn't have expected such turmoil, such roller-coaster fortune. First, he's installed, even if only caretaking, in the castle and estate to which he feels he belongs spiritually. The assignment makes him happier than he has ever been. Next he is suddenly wounded by persons unknown, and drifts toward death.

Then, after coping with the depression of humiliation that follows a physical assault, he is again struck down. He endures week after week of fevered infection. But he recovers, fights it off, and acquires a new, sparkling, resourceful, and admiring friend.

Then he hears the news that the woman he so desperately wants to share his life with is now out of his reach. She has—dread thought—married another. It seems never to have crossed his mind that she might. And finally, she appears to use him even more blatantly than before. This time, however, his helping her will cut him out of his own dreams. And then, in a savage payoff, she fires him from the task that he loved with all his heart, and was doing for no remuneration.

Given what we know of his romantic excitability, we could assume that Charles was in a much worse condition than he was when he first fell for April and was rejected by her. And we may assume that he went down somewhat under the blows of the world. After the encounter with Yeats (which took place the day before the shooting), no entries appear in the "History" until the end of May 1909.

He doesn't give the date; we can guess at it from Amelia's journal. In a cursory entry that remarks the weather ("unseasonally cold") and the growths of the spring ("good after all the rain") she observes briefly that "Charles and Harney have embarked upon a journey. They have made it mysterious. I mean—they have not told us where they are bound.

Charles merely said that he had 'some people to see.' But Harney will be a good companion for him."

Charles's next entry begins discursively. Then we discover the reason for this mysterious journey. He wants to visit people on whom his cures might not have worked. And he wants to find out whether one of them, out of revenge or hostility, shot him.

When, in childhood, I wished to be helpful, as children do, I worked alongside the various people on the farm. Inside, I watched Cally and Mrs. Ryan cooking and baking. Mrs. Ryan's daughter taught me how to pluck a fowl. When older, in the open air, I assisted by fetching the cows from the fields for the morning and evening milking.

In those days, Jimmy Hennessy and Dan Danaher, who tended the dairy cattle, showed me how to wash a cow before milking and then how to milk. And in time, I learned to enjoy the dairyman's position, which kept my head pressed to the cow's flank, as I squirted the milk and listened to the pail ring with each thin white jet.

Sometimes, when I came home from my healing travels and took leisure at Ardobreen, I liked to return to these practices. They calmed me and brought me back into a safe world. Perforce, I made few observations toward my History for the year 1908 and part of 1909; I spent fourteen months in the county Tipperary. For reasons too painful to discuss, I required peace and quiet. Suffice it to say that some assailants wounded me.

But one night, into my life stepped the man who would become my dearest and most faithful friend, Joseph Harney. Now I had found a companion, a clever and interested human, who would travel with me when I healed my patients.

It will be valuable to describe him. He is tall and thin, with a beaky nose and hair that flops. I had the impression that he had read every book that was ever printed, and he could draw extensive and accurate quotations from his copious memory. Nothing tired his mind, which inquired into every separate thing that he encountered. His speech was slow and clear, with little exaggeration of accent, which is generally true of the Kilkenny people.

I never saw in him any expression of uncontrolled anger; he was peaceful and he calmed everybody. In his most unusual characteristic, he could both think and act. Not many can apply a thoughtful survey to the great matters of the world; fewer can deal with physical matter. Joseph could do both; he could fix a bicycle wheel or consider whether Plato would gain a place in Ireland's political systems.

He elicited favorable responses from both sexes; indeed, I never saw a man so liked. Once, I asked him to define his deepest ambition, a daring question to ask any man.

"To become a man of no ill will," he said without hesitation.

"Where did you learn such a thought?"

Joseph said, "When I was twelve, my father gave me a large book about Abraham Lincoln. It contained many essays written by people who knew him. That was all I needed."

I can here confirm one aspect of Joseph Harney's quality. When I found that I was becoming generally short-tempered and impatient, I was easily moved to distress. Every time this manifested itself, Joseph—if present—made me "sit down and think." He said, "It only takes a minute. Take out your watch, look closely at it. Follow the passing of a minute." His advice proved beneficial, though sometimes I required many minutes.

In mid-1909, Joseph Harney and I set out on a journey. We had five destinations, all determined by me, and in different parts of the country. Sometimes, a cure will kick back upon a healer and his patient, with sad and regrettable outcome. More than once, I had been reproached by family members in a place I had previously visited, because my attempts to heal had not met with success. Hostility had been expressed, and I had thought it best to remove the irritant—namely, myself.

Based upon this experience, I deduced that it would not be good to leave such a hostile connection unappeased. Searching my memory, I found five occasions where the most bitter feelings might be harbored. Without telling my parents, I decided that I must confront each of those families where I knew resided the deepest animosity to me. I invited Joseph to accompany me.

When we began to travel, he gave himself a job to do—he was the one who planned the stages of the journey, where we would stay, how many miles a day we would cover, and, most important of all, our mode of transport: we rode bicycles. Harney taught me to cycle (he insisted that I call him "Harney"—said it made me sound like a gentleman with a manservant), and I mastered it immediately; he was an excellent teacher, and off we went.

After two days, we reached our first place of inquiry. The MacDonaghs lived in south Offaly, in a stone house with a slate roof; they had a small farm, and the father of the family had been a quarry worker. Dust from the stones he quarried had caused him sharp respiratory problems, and I had visited him upon a request from his brother, whom I had treated successfully for a chronically uncertain stomach (sweet warm milk, with honey, every night before retiring).

For the poor respiration I had prescribed balsam; but where I had shown him how to inhale the treatment in warm water, he went further; he drank it, and became so distressed at the taste and the gastric burning that he suffered a heart attack and died. As I had remained in the district, attending to others, I went to the funeral and was urgently accosted by his sons. I defended myself, but as I departed, the elder said to me that he would seek me out and kill me—"if it took ten years." As the sinister Bruree horseman seemed to resemble this family, I had wondered whether a kinsman of some sort had been employed.

Harney and I decided to approach this house at eventide; he told me that he had a plan—and that it necessitated him entering the house first. He did, and I waited outside with the bicycles. A dog came and wagged its tail; I must admit that I felt apprehensive.

A long time passed. Harney came out, pulling the door closed behind him.

"We'll travel on," he said.

But I said to this boy of twenty-one, "No. I must see them."

He looked alarmed. "Don't do that. I didn't get a good result."

I started to walk to the house.

"Come with me," I said. "We can't have this."

I knocked at the door, opened it, and stood there.

The family sat at their evening meal—the widow MacDonagh and her two sons and a daughter; the house had a dismal air, and seemed poorer than before. As I walked in, the elder son rose.

"Do you know what's coming to you?" he shouted.

"Please allow me to speak."

He would have none of it; he took a sickle from a hook on the wall and came toward me, swinging the implement.

Harney stepped in front of me and held out his arms like a supplicant.

"Here! Listen!" He got their attention, though they glared the coals of Hell at me. "Two things. First of all—do you think this man killed your father deliberately? If you do, you're all eejits. Second thing. If he's harmed—ever, by anyone, anywhere—I'll harm you." Enraged, he pointed to the son with the sickle. "And you won't know when it'll be. It might be next year—or when you're sixty. But I'll do it—myself. Now sit down and offer us a cup of tea like decent people. What kind of hospitality is this? We came a long way to see you."

This threw the family into confusion. Mrs. MacDonagh, in her black, rose to the occasion and turned to the dresser for two cups and saucers (the family was drinking from mugs); her daughter moved to make room at the table; Harney fetched a chair for me. We sat down, in total silence.

I waited to see whether someone should speak. Soon, oppressed by this, I cleared my throat—and received a warning glance from Harney; I subsided. The silence continued—then Mrs. MacDonagh spoke.

"Big auction here next week."

Harney, quick as light, asked, "Oh? Whose is it?"

The younger son answered. "A Gallagher man. His wife died; he's going to America."

Harney looked at the older son, who still had a seething air.

"You should buy that place."

Mr. MacDonagh said nothing—but I saw his eyes flicker.

"Does your land adjoin it?" asked Harney.

"Our bottom field hits their big meadow," said the younger.

"That's the thing to do then," said Harney.

The older son spoke, quick and sullen. "You need money to go to an auction."

"There's banks," said Harney encouragingly.

Mrs. MacDonagh listened to all of this, and I saw that she had a yearning to her—she wanted her sons to prosper.

"We know no banks," said Mr. MacDonagh again.

"We do," said Harney. "Isn't that right, Charles?"

I did know banks in Tipperary, and in Limerick; my mother's family had strong banking connections. But I knew no banks in Offaly, and I said so.

"But you can introduce this man, can't you?"

That night, I marveled again at Harney and his skills. At twenty-one, I was awkward and uncertain; he seemed capable of any situation. The MacDonaghs responded to him; by letter we performed introductions to the National and Royal banks. Some months later, we heard that they had bought another farm, not the one at auction—there had not been the time; but they had taken the next step in their lives.

"Always try to turn something bad into something good," said Harney.

He established of a certainty that no MacDonagh had ever pursued me, they attained a kind of forgiveness of me, and on we rode, on our bicycles, with our side-panniers and front baskets, through driving rain and in lovely sunlight. In each of the other four households where we visited, we found progressively less hostility; indeed, we found warmth and welcoming attitudes. Much of this may be attributed to Harney's friendliness, his refusal to let rancor float upon the air. When I look back upon it now, it feels like a journey of true progress.

I believe that we are witnessing, in the pages of his account of his own life, a man in the throes of changing. Charles O'Brien, remember, began his "History" by wishing to change. He wanted with all his heart to make himself irresistibly appealing to the young woman by whom he had been smitten. From this point in his text, it soon becomes plain that he was beginning to undergo a maturing process.

For years he had ridden around the country like an innocent abroad. In comparison with the works of other observers, including those of more formal historians, his general observations of his society were accurate and valuable. Where he seemed out of true came in his judgment of his own life, on which he seemed to have a poor hold.

He adored his father, yet we learn from his mother that his father reciprocated that love less than fully. Charles saw himself as upstanding and dashing, yet he had to be told to wear clean shirts. He blundered onto the stage of Anglo-Irish politics with the unfortunate incident of Parnell, where he was used like a simpleton by the British press hostile to Parnell. And he chose for the love of his life a woman who rejected him completely.

In the love affair, though, something may have been right. If someone as sharp as Harney thought that April Burke would have been ideal for Charles, then he can be assumed to have had some accuracy in his view of himself—even if he wasn't totally aware of it.

We also know that he found out one major fact about himself. He could be at home, feel at one with the world, in Tipperary Castle. Yet that raised the stakes for his life and his good management of it, because he was, as yet, no more than a bystander in that drama (although he did make a significant contribution, to which we'll come in a moment).

His reaction to misfortune—of which he tells us little—is fascinating. Suddenly, instead of languishing, he does something more than brave. Without giving the full details, he sets out to find the people who might have shot him. No fear does he express that this time they might finish the job. Instead, he finds them all, faces them, and sits down with them.

Unfortunately, Joe Harney is not on record regarding that extraordinary journey he took with Charles O'Brien in the summer of 1909. His view of it would have been compelling—especially given what a different picture we get of Charles through Harney.

Charles was as selective as any historian. Whatever his protestations of the integrity essential to the record he was keeping, he tells us only what he wants to tell us. He glosses over his injuries, and the subsequent illnesses and fevers. And he paints April in a kindly light no matter how cynically she used him. But Harney fills in Charles's outline.

And, fortunately, Harney was in court for Charles's evidence in the Tipperary Castle hearings. Charles himself never reveals that he was even there.

Yes, I got dragged into that case. Well, the use of the word "dragged" is excessive; I went along willingly, because my great friend Charles O'Brien was giving evidence. It was May, I remember, not long after Easter; the year was 1910, I'm fairly certain of that. I was over at the O'Briens' house on the Sunday. Charles was never any good at asking any favors for himself—it was his mother who said, "Did you hear that Charles is called as a witness in the case?" She didn't even need to specify—it was known as "the case." So that if you said, "Any news of the case?" everyone knew what you were talking about.

I knew what Mrs. O'Brien was hinting at, so I said, "I'll go with you. When is it?" And Charles of course demurred.

"Tuesday," said his mother, and she told me afterward that she was delighted that I'd go.

He was called the minute the court sat on the Tuesday morning. Which was unusual in those cases—mostly they began with legal arguments over knotty points that came up the previous day.

We spent the night before in a hotel near the courts, and Charles and I sat up until very late, discussing not so much what he would say as how he would say it. He was fifty that summer, but he was the youngest and least confident fifty-year-old—man or woman—that I ever knew.

I remember saying to him, "You have a wonderful gaze. It's very truthful. And it'll stand you in good stead, because you're supposed to speak your evidence to the judge. So just look at him and he'll believe you."

Then we worked out something that could have got us into trouble! I was to sit in the public gallery, and if Charles saw me putting my hand to my forehead, he was to slow down. When he got agitated, he always said too much and spoke too quickly—through nerves, I expect. And I wanted to be able to send him a reassuring sign that would help him to slow down.

It worked perfectly, and everything went very well. For a start, he dressed elegantly; he had a dark suit of clothes, and he wore a blue striped shirt with a white cutaway collar and a black-and-white-checked tie with a little diamond stickpin. And he had a sober waistcoat. He looked magnificent—the hair was still powerful, he had a look of Beethoven to him.

But he needed something to help him—because the way he was treated in court would have rattled any man. First of all, he was examined and then cross-examined, as happens with most witnesses, unless they're experts who don't need to be challenged. Now, in all such cases, the person who does the examination is the lawyer who's supposed to be on your side, then comes the cross-examination, from the opposition, and that's supposed to be hostile.

In this case you'd wonder which was the more hostile, because, of course, the first part of the questioning, the supposedly benign part, was done by Stephen Somerville, April's husband, with his black beard cut like a spade. He was so hostile to Charles that the judge intervened, and I thought he was going to ask him, "Whose side are you on?" He was rough! I can remember his first question—more of a remark, really.

"Mr. O'Brien," said he, "it is not customary for men to wear jewelry in court."

He was referring to the tiepin; he said it with a smile, but you could feel the barb. Everybody looked up, Charles looked over at me, I put the palm of my hand to my forehead—and Charles turned to the judge.

"My Lord," he said, and he had this great, polished Tipperary accent and, of course, perfect courtesy—he got it from both parents—"My Lord, I was not aware. And I'm wearing cuff links. Do they count as jewelry?"

Of course he knew that the judge and all the other lawyers were wearing cuff links—everybody did in those days. The judge laughed—and he was a bit of a sour old bugger in his way—but he laughed.

"Mr. O'Brien," said he, "you have drawn the most appropriate form of attention to the ridiculousness of your barrister's remark."

You see, the judge did a number of things there: He relaxed the witness. He pointed up Stephen Somerville's nonsense. And he reminded Somerville whose side he was supposed to represent. By the way, Miss Burke herself wasn't in the court that day—which surprised me.

Charles acquitted himself very well. After a while I was able to stop passing my hand across my forehead and sit back and enjoy the spectacle. Charles was dignified. He was thoughtful. They couldn't rattle him. When my old friend Dermot Noonan got up, he did his best. He was fighting to get the land into official hands so that people could buy it. I was taken aback by his attitude. He was antagonistic. And he was, I have to say, nasty.

He tried to dig into the relationship between Charles and April, but Charles didn't get caught. He just answered the questions as though he were a gentleman—which is exactly how he came across, and exactly what he was. Dermot's a tough man—but he couldn't shake Charles.

I've always believed that Charles won that case for April Burke, which, given the circumstances of the time, was very ironic. Like all great cases, it happened in one exchange—and we knew that it had happened. It came late in the second day, when Dermot was really stuck into Charles.

Dermot said to him, "You know this property—these lands, this house—better than anyone in Ireland, is that not so?"

Charles said, "Perhaps. I have certainly spent more continuous time there than anyone I know."

You see, Charles's answers were so reasonable and well mannered that you couldn't figure out whether he was answering for his own side or the other's.

"So what is your opinion of the place? I mean," said Dermot, "you're a well-traveled man, you hobnob with the aristocracy."

"I believe it very beautiful," said Charles.

"Is it the most beautiful you've ever seen?"

Charles turned to the judge. "My Lord, beauty is in the eye of the beholder, and it would be invidious to make an unfavorable comparison with other houses, in so many of which I have received great hospitality."

The judge himself owned a fine place in Wicklow, a house and estate of which he was known to be proud, and he nodded in grave agreement. And then came the winning point.

Dermot Noonan said to Charles, "Whom do you believe should own this house and land?"

Said Charles, "The party who will most preserve its beauty and usefulness for this country."

Said Dermot, "Why is that necessary?"

Charles took his time in answering; he turned to the judge and said, "My Lord, I believe that in the years to come, no matter what way the history of this country bends, Tipperary Castle and the gardens—they're a matter of world beauty."

Now, this unsteadied Dermot, and he was then jostled by the judge, who told him he must ask questions to elicit facts, not opinions.

So the next question was "And why do you think Mrs. Somerville"— he laid emphasis on the "Mrs.," to unsettle Charles, I suppose, to needle him—"why do you think she's the one who could do that?"

Charles had his answer ready. "Well," said he, "up to now all the local people have ever tried to do is damage the property. They try to break into the building. Or they steal grazing, they turn their animals in there unlawfully. The first act of Mrs. Somerville's was to appoint someone whom she knew would take close care of the place. I believe that if she owns it, she will turn it into a national treasure."

There was something very convincing in the way he said it. No drama, no great legal clinching point—just a steady conviction. His evidence came across as, well, irrefutable.

The final paragraphs of Mr. Prunty's note on the Tipperary Castle case assemble everything neatly.

"Months of delay and counterclaim had already stretched into years, and in 1911, the case was decided before Sir Michael King-Hamilton. The learned judge gave three lengthy disquisitions, one toward each side of the argument. First he dismissed the Crown's right to disperse the house and lands by sale. The learned judge said that he understood the great national interest in the case, given the recent direction that Irish lands had been taking 'back into native hands.' And in any case, the Crown had never taken any rights over this—still private—estate.

"Then he dismissed the claim by Mr. Dermot Noonan, a self-proclaimed member of Sinn Fein, who, via the provisions of the Wyndham Act, sought the property's 'rightful return to the people of Tipperary from whom it had been taken by Plantation in the year 1587.'

"In his dismissal, the learned judge made comment upon Mr. Noonan's 'meticulous and even scholarly Research, going back hundreds of years—some of which, it has to be said, eventually came to rest in that land where no proof may be adduced, the Land of Myth.'

"Finally he addressed the 'fresh inheritance' of Miss April Burke of London, who in the meantime had become the wife of Mr. Stephen Somerville, K.C.

"The learned judge likened her lawyer's presentation to 'a mystery and its attempted solution.' Family trees had been climbed and their branches shaken and their roots pulled out, scrutinized minutely, and stuck back in the ground. Valiant efforts had been made by Miss Burke's lawyers, who 'trod the avenue of probability with great determination.' Miss Burke herself had been a 'more than sincere witness' in the decisions that would affect her own destiny.

"She had also provided her late father's sole family heirloom—a drawing of the property in Tipperary that had been given him as an infant. The judge said he had taken 'personal care' to assure himself that the drawing was indeed an accurate likeness of the property, that he was satisfied on the point. He must also acknowledge—in the spirit of the law, he said, if not the letter—the power of such a piece of evidence in the family's belief of their rights to this property.

"Without the under-strengthening force, he said, of long-standing family beliefs and traditions, Society, in his opinion, would collapse. He felt 'obliged to point out' that all Irish people depended upon family beliefs in the pursuit of their rights to their land.

"In his conclusions, the learned judge cited only two passages of evidence"—these were asterisked by Mr. Prunty in the transcripts—"and they came from his section on Miss Burke's claim. The learned judge drew upon this evidence to adduce the integrity of Mr. O'Brien's testimony. He said that Mr. Noonan had defeated his own case by, in effect, trying to prove opposites: that Miss Burke (as she had been at the case's outset) had sufficiently poor character to use Mr. O'Brien in a misleading way, and would therefore prove base enough to lay false claims. Yet the rejected suitor, who, Mr. Noonan hoped had good reason to despise her, had testified with great strength as to her 'natural connection' to the estate.

"In eventually finding for Mrs. Burke-Somerville, and in awarding her costs and compensation for Chancery's neglect of the house in its vacated state, the learned judge garlanded his Judgment with caution. The final paragraph of his Judgment reads: 'I am aware that I am standing on grounds more fought over than anything in the Bible, capable of igniting more fire than Vesuvius. And yet a bridgehead must be established. We own what we know we own, and the knowing forms a central claim to what I may define as Notional Title. If Notional Title can be supported by evidence of any kind—even evidence that has been clouded by the mists of time and unrecorded circumstances, and by the furtiveness of the past—if such cloudy evidence points toward Notional Title, then, as in this case, I feel sure that the law must behave as in Nature, and observe the principle of Natural Home. And so, Notional Title becomes Natural Title.' "

The two pieces of evidence asterisked by Mr. Prunty run as follows in the transcript:

Mr. Stephen Somerville: What made you believe in your and your father's rights to this property?

Miss Burke: It is something that I simply knew was right from the moment I heard of it.

Mr. Somerville: How old were you when you first heard of Tipperary Castle?

Miss Burke: I believe about ten years old.

Mr. Somerville: And when you went there—at, I believe, the age of twenty-two?

Miss Burke: I felt that I had come home. It is something that I cannot describe.

Mr. Dermot Noonan, cross-examining: How closely did you observe Miss Burke's demeanor on that day?

Mr. O'Brien: Very attentively.

Mr. Noonan: Which is why you have felt able to tell the court that she seemed "so at one"—your term—with Tipperary Castle and its land?

Mr. O'Brien: She seemed wonderfully natural when there. And it is my belief that she had never been in an Irish field in her life. She lived in London.

Mr. Noonan: You were in love with her in those days, were you not?

Mr. O'Brien: Yes.

Mr. Noonan: And therefore biased in her favor, surely?

Mr. O'Brien: Justice must always supersede love.

Mr. Noonan: But you are prepared to give evidence in her favor?

Mr. O'Brien: If honest to do so, yes.

Mr. Noonan: Are you still in love with her?

Mr. O'Brien: That is an entirely improper question. She has married.

5

The estate of Tipperary Castle was awarded to April Somerville in 1911. All over the county few people talked of anything else. The archives of *The Nationalist* in Clonmel show the coverage—page after page, week after week.

Opinion split three ways. The Anglo-Irish welcomed somebody who had married one of their own: now those who wanted to stay on in their estates felt strengthened. Moderate Irish people felt perhaps that some kind of ancestral justice had been done to the name of Burke but also felt a little cheated at the entry of a Somerville—a Protestant. And republicans, dreaming of independence and the recovery of all ancestral lands, fumed at the loss of thousands of rich acres.

By now, Joe Harney had gone to Queen's College in Cork (today, University College Cork). And Charles distributed his life between lingering at home, visiting and staying with various friends, such as Lady Mollie Carew, and—far fewer—bouts of travel as a healer.

During weekends, Harney took the train to Tipperary and stayed with the O'Briens, even when Charles had gone elsewhere. On vacations, though, he traveled with Charles, and his company may have been enjoyable, but it must also have proven distracting. The evidence—or lack of it—suggests that Charles compiled little observation of the country's social and political life during that time. Nor does he seem to have made any significant contribution to newspapers or journals.

It's not as though he lacked matter to report or comment upon. Ireland raged with talk of Home Rule or the possibility of a republican insurgency. Europe—and the world—fretted about the probability of a war declared by Germany. Both issues had a synergy, because Irish activists saw in the likelihood of a war a chance to put on pressure and achieve, as a beginning, Home Rule.

Given all of this material and, as we have already seen, Charles's liking for discussing the events on a large stage, his silence seems peculiar. The answer comes in his mother's journal for Sunday, 25 January 1914. By and large, her weekend entries were her longest; this was an exception.

> It is over. The dread that I have carried for more than forty years has arrived. Its cargo will become the weight I bear now to my grave. We buried my beloved son on Friday. In the rain and sleet we lowered him into the ground. I am unable to sit or stand. My heart is screaming. It is against the law of the world that a child should pre-decease its parents.
>
> Poor Euclid, how I shall miss him. When the hour comes tomorrow that I should wake him from his afternoon sleep, and give him a cup of tea—what shall I do? It is ten o'clock and the night outside is quiet. I shall not sleep. Nor will Bernard, who is speechless with grief.

As this is a History of my own life as well as of my country in my time, I shall here acknowledge my brother, Euclid. He passed away on a January day when we all sat with him. I have seen patients die, I have seen them struggle to live, despite their mortal ailments, and I have seen them slip away as quietly and swiftly as a fish into a dark pool. Euclid lingered; he rallied—two, three, four times. If he knew that he was passing from us, he did not say.

In the previous few years he had grown frailer by the month, then by the week; and since Christmas, by the day. Seeing his condition, I had not returned to the road. In the second week of January, Mother asked

Father and me whether we should place Euclid's bed by the fire in the larger drawing-room—what we call the Terrace Room—because the long windows give out onto the terrace and thence with a view to the wood. That day, with much effort, we moved a spare bed to a place near the fire; and a day-bed into the room, also, where I lay many nights, talking to him, telling him "tales from the road," as he called them. I carried Euclid downstairs on the day we moved his bed; I have carried five-year-old children who weighted heavier.

He had, Mother now says, ailed since birth. Food never sat well with him; he picked here and there at his plate, he ate like a bird and not a beast. Thin since infancy, he never gained a continuous robustness. I recall no more than two summers, and those not in succession, when Euclid looked strong and healthy, and even then, the impression came principally from the sun's tanning of his face.

We have never known the name or cause or root of his ailment. I believe that he had a weakness since birth, that he lacked a density of blood. He was born into a household where his three family members bulge with energy—and he was granted none.

But he had the grandest soul. He had wit, humor, quickness, and a fire in his heart that, had it warmed his body, would have taken him upright through life. I believe that he was undermined by his own puzzlement at what ailed him, and that he railed at whatever denied him the same physical force as his father, mother, or brother.

He attempted to compensate with deliberate oddity in his demeanor, and with out-of-the-ordinary intellectual inquiry. Too poorly always to join a college or university, he surrounded himself with books—of all kinds, on all manner of subjects. To Euclid, the discovery of a new fact was as a gemstone to a lady; it thrilled him, he turned it this way and that, to let the light shine on it, and he carried it with him proudly, his beauty enhanced by showing it to the world.

I believe that he decided to die. The new place to lie, close to the heart of the house, rather than remote in his bedroom, seemed to elevate him for a time. He much enjoyed the flames in the larger fireplace; he found the influx of company exciting—because those who called to the house now engaged with him, brought him news. Perhaps we made the move too late—many years too late. Had we sacrificed the Terrace Room earlier, would the energy of the world, as it came to our door, have kept him alive?

But I believe that he had already taken his decision.

He told nobody. On the Sunday, I was sitting with him at two o'clock in the afternoon. The fire blazed; Mother and Father had driven to Holycross, where our long-retired and now ancient housekeeper, Mrs. Ryan, had fallen ill. Euclid took a little soup, no more than a spoon or two, and he had said little all day. Then he spoke.

"What do you offer for a pain in the chest and arms?"

I asked him, "Show me where."

"It's been here"—he indicated his left shoulder and upper arm—"since Thursday; it keeps coming back."

I said, "Let me get my bags."

Euclid shook his head. "I can't take anything. My mouth, my throat—I have no way of doing it."

I helped him to sit up a little, but after a few minutes he said, "I want to lie flat."

Those were almost his last words. Mother and Father returned soon and did not need to be told. Their eyes, when they turned to me, were filled with darkness; it is a sight I have seen often, the sight of fear entering a person's soul when they know in their heart that a loved one is going to die.

Did we sleep, any of us, for the rest of the week? I think not. If I went to bed any night, I woke again after an hour or two—and came downstairs to find Mother or my father, or both, sitting in the shadows thrown by the fire. Mother read to Euclid; he liked Tennyson and Coleridge, and I heard "on either side the river lie/Long fields of barley and of rye," and I heard of painted ships on painted oceans.

We were all present when he went. He had been lying quieter and quieter, taking no food, sweating a little. At eleven o'clock in the morning, he raised a hand to his left shoulder, said, "This hurts," and then sighed. He did not move or cry out; nor did his throat rattle. None of the things of Death came to his bedside; he merely went away. Father rose from his chair by the fire and spread his hands out from his body, opening and clenching his fists, opening and clenching, and blinking his eyes.

And Mother said, looking at me with eyes wide open as though in surprise, "Now what will any of us do?"

Eight months after Euclid O'Brien's death, the Great War began, in September 1914. All summer it had rumbled. After the Serbs had assassinated the Archduke Ferdinand, and the Austro-Hungarian Empire declared war on Serbia, blood began to seep across the jigsaw of Europe. Germany invaded Belgium, and England called for all to rally in the defense of small nations.

In Ireland, the call was accompanied by a seeming promise of Home Rule in exchange for enlisting. There was also the fact that the army was, at least, a job. All in all, around three hundred thousand Irishmen died on the green fields of France. In terms of population, that proportionately represented nearly five times the number of men that England lost. Home Rule never came.

Almost regardless of their age, Irish farmers' sons had turned up to enlist, as had laborers, mechanics, policemen, doctors, clerks, fishermen, bankers, plowmen, bakers, lawyers—and Charles O'Brien. He told Joe Harney that he had "come adrift when Euclid died" and did not know what to do with himself.

Harney tried to stop him. He had successfully dissuaded many other men. Harney had his own reasons for not wanting to see Irishmen join the British army. He knew that any man in a British military uniform was about to become a "legitimate target" in Ireland, according to plans in the pipeline for a rebellion.

Charles, nevertheless, went to the school in Golden and met the recruiting officers. According to the records, he was turned down for military service because the shooting had left him with a slight limp in his left leg—and, a secondary reason, because he was "much too old." He doesn't record his effort to enlist. Instead, at that point in his writings, he curiously recounts an earlier experience, the point of which becomes clear only later.

When I reflect upon the great changes I saw in Ireland, I am bound to record a remarkable, daily, and distressing occurrence. Riding here and there, I often saw individuals and, sadder still, entire families on the road, laden with baggages, sometimes on a cart, sometimes walking. Always I knew their business, yet always I asked—and always I received the same answer: they were bound for the emigrant ship.

I know that had I kept a count, the numbers would run to many, many thousands. It occurs to me now that the reason I have not discussed them earlier is on account of their commonplaceness—I saw them all the time. Near the great ports of the coast, they grew more numerous. Once, I rode into Galway from the east and I might have been attending a funeral procession, so singular was the line of men, women, and children trudging to the ships. This sight—and this is what I mean by commonplace—had been familiar to me all my life.

Overriding the protestations of his mother, Charles O'Brien decided, in the spring of 1915, to emigrate to the United States. Amelia argued that he had no visible future there, whereas if he stayed at home, at least he could live on the farm. It's clear from her journal that she even suggested that he study medicine at the Queen's College, Cork. Given some connections there, and an ability to pay a handsome fee, age would be no barrier.

Joe Harney had completed his studies. He worked in Dublin, a junior civil servant in the government land registry. This gave him less time to visit the O'Briens or be a companion to Charles. Amelia wrote Harney an anguished letter, which stayed in his family's possession:

> *He says that he feels Ireland a desert now, with Euclid gone, with April lost to him, and you permanently at work. He won't take over the farm—he says he is not a farmer, that he has no feeling for it, much though he loves our fields and our animals.*

But his decision has been a sudden one, and I feel that he has another reason, too painful to share. Now that "she's" living in the castle, he sees "her" many times a week, always in the distance. He rides to the village. He has seen her in the town. He has to hear her being addressed as "Mrs. Somerville." And they have never, so far as I know, conversed.

Although he doesn't speak of her, I know that in his heart he has never let go of her—and we have all heard of such attachments. In Charles's case, I am certain that it will last for his whole life.

Lately, he must have suffered new distress, because the talk locally is that such work as they have begun on the repairs of the castle has gone badly. Most of the workmen have fallen out with Mr. Somerville, who is drinking heavily and arguing with the workers. It has been stop and start and stop again. They say that, instead of progressing, their restoration has gone backward—that fresh damage has occurred owing to carelessness. Or—who knows?—malice. This must appall Charles. I am sure that he knows of it, because everybody else does.

Harney replied to Amelia, saying that over Easter he would come to Ardobreen. But Harney's train was delayed, and Charles, deciding that Harney was not coming, left. His father drove him to Tipperary, where Charles caught a train to Limerick.

Later that night, Harney arrived, just as Amelia and Bernard O'Brien were preparing to go to bed. She describes the moment in her journal: "Somebody hammered too hard on the door. Bernard said, 'Harney.' I said I doubted it. Bernard said, 'He's excited.' We looked out of the window. It was Harney. I went downstairs and let him in. He seemed very agitated. As he had not eaten, I led him to the kitchen. He ate some cold chicken. Carefully, to take account of his state, I told him that Charles had gone. He jumped up from his chair. 'Oh, my God in Heaven,' he cried. I calmed him—or tried to. Then he stood in front of me, almost shaking.

"Mrs. O'Brien," he said. "I heard it on the train. Stephen Somerville was killed. In France. In the war. He went there as an officer last week and was killed his first day out."

That was Easter weekend 1915—to put a date on it, Easter Sunday fell on 4 April. Euclid had died, leaving behind, by the way, a massive fortune in investments; he had spent most of his life writing to stockbrokers and banks, and almost without exception every investment that he made paid off in multiple percentages. But Charles had reached a point where he'd decided that there was nothing left for him in Ireland.

To add to the pain of Euclid's death, everything connected with Tipperary Castle wounded him. April, very much the lady of the manor, all furs and servants, was the talk of the place. Yet so remote was she from Charles that she might as well have been in Alaska.

And to cap it all, he was now hearing that the work on his beloved castle was going badly wrong. Stephen Somerville was drinking heavily, taking shortcuts, ordering inferior materials, and refusing to hire the best craftsmen. In other words, Somerville had not only stolen the woman who was Charles's heart's desire, he had stolen Charles's principle of trying to preserve beauty.

As a sensitive man with a deep sense of responsibility, Charles must have been cut to the heart's core. He still thought of himself as the natural warden of the place. He had nowhere to turn—so he might as well leave.

One man's crisis is another's chance—even an old cliché can have truth. (It was recognized among the Irish republican agitators who called for armed rebellion when the Great War broke out, saying, "England's difficulty is Ireland's opportunity.") On that Easter Saturday, Joe Harney came down from Dublin at Amelia O'Brien's invitation, heard en route that the "drunk in the castle" had died in the trenches—and realized that the one person who could prosper from this development had gone.

Harney and Amelia O'Brien sat down. Bernard did not appear (a fact that will have later, unpleasant significance) and figured between them where Charles might still be found. He might have had a head start, but Harney, from the depths of his affinity, felt that Charles was still in the country.

Always capable of heroic effort, Harney borrowed one of the farm laborer's bicycles. That Easter Saturday night, Harney rode the thirty miles or so into Limerick. He had no light on the bicycle, he knew the road only moderately well—yet he kept going.

At five o'clock next morning, he knocked on the grand front door of Lady Mollie Carew's house in Pery Square. An irritated man—the butler, but Harney didn't know it—tried to shoo him away. Harney shouted through the letter box that he'd break into the house if he had to. The butler eventually opened the door.

But the bird had flown. Charles had left the house at nine o'clock the previous evening for a sailing to New York on a pre-dawn tide at four o'clock.

He that has found a faithful friend, Mr. Yeats told me once, has found an elixir of life. One morning at dawn in the year 1915, my faithful friend Harney appeared, in unlikely circumstances. In a rowing-boat—and he had never rowed before—he took me from a ship that was leaving the port of Limerick. It became a commotion, with crew assisting my luggage to the rowboat, and passengers looking on, not knowing whether to cheer or commiserate.

Only a man as resourceful as Harney could have brought that off; some mechanical difficulty had held back our departure, and before we could get fully under way, Harney was alongside, hallooing. I do not know what he said to the mate who heard his request—but I do know that I forfeited my ticket (I was bound for the New World).

In the rowing-boat, as he pulled the short distance to the Shannon's banks, he told me why he had come for me.

"I believe that you have an important part to play in the life of our country," he said.

"For this you intercept me?" I asked.

"And for more than our country's good," he said, very serious. "For your own good."

"Might I not have judged what could be good for me?"

And he answered, "Somerville's dead. On the battlefields of Picardy."

I know that I said quickly, "Is April safe?"—and immediately understood that her husband must have joined the defense of small nations.

"Now you know why I intercepted you," Harney said.

We spoke little more for some time. He tied up the boat where he had found it, on the Shannon's banks; he roused a hackney man to take me and my bags—he rode a bicycle alongside—back to Lady Mollie's house, where we had breakfast and much excited talk.

In the midst of their speculation, I reminded my two friends that in all respects April had thoroughly rejected me. I said that I did not understand why they now believed my chances had so improved, and I told them bluntly that I felt sincere reluctance in approaching her.

They countered with opinions in which they almost matched each other. Lady Mollie said that, after Somerville, I would prove a wonder to the young widow, if only in the relief of being so different and so decent after "the lout" she had married.

And Harney said, "Why do you think Life has given you this opportunity?"

I disagreed, saying, "All that has happened is that a man has been killed. How many are going to die in this war? Each death can't signify a dramatic possibility for someone else."

The same hackney took us to Tipperary, and I was received at Ardobreen with elation. Harney was hailed and praised by Mother; and the rest of Easter passed in delighted peace.

On Monday morning, Mother said to me at breakfast, "Please shave, Charles, and dress in your finest. We have a visit to pay."

I knew that she meant the castle, and I balked; Mother overruled me.

"We are neighbors and we shall behave as such."

"I may prefer to wait outside."

"You are representing your father, who cannot come."

At this moment, it is appropriate to reveal how the war had taken over lives in Ireland. Several of the Great Houses had closed down; practical reasons dictated this course. Many of their laborers had been encouraged by the owners to enlist, and had gone off cheerfully to a thankless death in the savage mud of France. The landlords, whether at home in England or still on their Irish estates, gave space to distinguished families fleeing Europe, or arranged rosters of tasks for their estate workers and friends, such as the making of uniforms. Anglo-Irish gentlemen who were of age felt it a duty to offer themselves for the King against Germany's Kaiser, and that is how Stephen Somerville became an officer in the ill-fated British Expeditionary Force, under General Haig.

I drove the pony-trap to the castle. My father had not yet succumbed to the temptation of a motor-car, but the Somervilles had; a blue-and-gray Dunhill sat by the terraces. I had heard about it but never seen it, and I liked it at sight. The domed brass of the headlamps reflected the blue of the lightly clouded sky. Mother saw my glance.

"We cannot afford it," she said, and chuckled—which meant that Father had already been discussing it.

She reverted to briskness and said, "We shall not stay long, and we shall not talk about ourselves."

A woman of enormous girth opened the door; she wore a maid's uniform of black and white and had very short coal-black hair, cropped close as a boy; I recognized her accent as Galway.

As we stood in the hall, I surveyed the early attempts at work and felt my heart clench with disappointment. No debris from rain damage had been cleared; and timbers to be used in restoration and renewal had been piled high on top of the rotted plaster. I could see no workmen, and no evidence of work—and yet I knew that April and her late husband had been living here for some years. Perhaps such work as had been done had been directed to the upper floors.

In the clear acoustic of those open rooms, I heard the Galway maid say, "Mr. and Mrs. O'Brien, ma'am." Then I heard the crisp footsteps that I had known since the streets of Paris.

At the far end of the ruined hallway, April appeared. She wore unrelieved black, a dress with a high black collar and a hem at fashionable mid-calf, black hose, and black shoes. In her hands she held a pen as though she had been writing.

Mother, ever the ice-breaker, said, "Good morning, April"—in that friendly, irresistible way. "Do you remember me, Amelia O'Brien? And of course you know Charles."

I had taken off my hat, and I made a slight bow. Now I began to assess myself. Was my heart beating? Did my mouth go dry? Do I still think of her every day? I heard myself give an inward groan; and I know that I blushed. However, April—this cold girl, this organized, hard-minded, and brisk young woman, this assured and beautiful young widow—crumpled. She stood there, ten or twelve yards away, and began to cry. No noise came from her lips, no wail; she held the back of her hand over her mouth and tears flowed down her face.

Mother, her handbag over one arm, went toward her. The women embraced, and April wept on Mother's shoulder. I could scarcely believe it; this ran counter to every impression of April that I had ever carried. Never had it occurred to me that she had any flexibility of emotion; never did I think that I should see the day when I would watch anything but determination in her face.

As she sobbed, Mother looked over at me and with a swift nod of her head indicated that I should leave. I stepped to the door and concentrated my gaze on the distance. As the foliage had not yet come back to the trees, I could see a little of our pink walls, Captain Ferguson's wood, and the Beech Meadow.

Around the castle, however, I saw disorder. Supplies of building materials had also been piled on the stone terraces, and rain had seeped into some of them, rendering them useless. Two cords of timber had been leaned against a window; one had slipped, breaking a pane of glass. On this fine morning I would have expected visible industry all around the place; instead, two workmen sat on the bridge parapet far below. No energy came from that quarter.

I cannot say how long I stood there, waiting for Mother. When she came out she beckoned to me.

"I think she needs listeners."

We went in and saw April standing at the door where we'd first spotted her, at the far end of the great hall. She gestured and we followed, picking our feet carefully over debris. Soon we found ourselves in the butler's pantry, which seemed to have been restored to some functioning, and we sat down. As yet, I still had not spoken. She must have felt some embarrassment of me; when she spoke, she addressed Mother principally and gave me no more than the occasional glance, too brief to be inclusive.

"I want to tell this," she said, "and I want to tell it no more. Already I have told one friend in writing, but I need to hear myself speak it." From that moment, only she spoke.

I did not want Stephen to go. He made the decision, and I think I know why he did it—too much drinking. He thought if he became an officer, with a purpose, and the company of men—it might help. Before he went, it had become unsavory here. I was incapable of dealing with his tempers, and sometimes when he wandered out into the fields at night, I did not know whether he would come back. More than once I went looking for him at dawn and found him lying asleep at the bottom of a sunken fence, or down in the lower garden, disheveled and stained. There is nothing that I dislike more.

When the war broke out, he talked and talked of asking for a commission. He wore me down. At first he went to London in September, in the first few days, when there was scarcely any fighting. He came home, said they weren't ready for him, he was to go again at Christmas. But when Christmas came, he was too drunk to pull himself together, and he finally got to London at the end of January. They gave him some sort of assignment at a desk, and he chafed at it. Four weeks ago, they let him go to France.

I had a letter from him. He was delighted with himself—how can a man be happy at war? And he told me about a song. They were all singing it, he said, and he was the only one from Tipperary.

On the tenth of March, a Wednesday morning, I woke up here with a dreadful headache. And I knew that Stephen had died. I told nobody, but I got Helen, the maid, to drive me to the station. I took the boat to England, went to London to the war authorities, and they had no such dispatch. As far as they were concerned, Captain Stephen Somerville had gone to Béthune with the Royal Irish Rifles.

I caught the train to Dover, but I was stopped there by officers, who would not let me go to France. Back in London, the authorities told me that Stephen was in Armentières. Day after day, I went to the military offices. "Do you know of a Captain Stephen Somerville," I asked over and over; and I used all my old friends and colleagues to try and get news of Stephen.

One afternoon, an officer to whom I had been introduced by a family friend sat at his desk and pulled lists from his attaché case.

"Madam," he said to me, "all I can do is look at this list. If his name is not on it, you can call yourself lucky."

But of course his name was on it, very high up. They told me that Stephen was one of the first to die on the first morning in Armentières—one of the first of thousands. And it was on the morning of my dreadful headache. I said to him, "Thank you." This officer was about twenty-one. I must have said "Thank you" many times, because he took my hand and offered to help.

"Can you find Stephen? Can I take him back to Tipperary?"

He shook his head. "Madam, they must rest where they fell. Until things settle—until matters are clearer."

I began to walk. No idea where, or for how long. That was when I heard the song, that dreadful song, in the night; they were singing it, because I walked past British soldiers outside public houses, and they had this song that Stephen mentioned in his letters, and I have the words in my head and the tune; I can't bear it.

Everybody born in Tipperary has been saddled with that song. When my wife and I traveled, we always got the rejoinder "It's a long way" when we said where we came from. It was written by an English music-hall song-and-dance man who had never set foot in Ireland—Jack Judge. He had Irish grandparents.

Somebody in an English pub after a matinee made a bet with him one afternoon. Could he write a song for the evening performance? Nearby, he overheard a man giving directions to someone, saying, "It's a long way to Lancaster," and he won his bet. Everybody born in Tipperary knows that story.

But the song haunted the men of that frightful war, young men who came back aged, came back gassed and shattered, came back splintered and lame. I knew an old Great War soldier here in Clonmel. He told me that he had stopped going to pubs.

"Mr. Nugent," he said, "now and again, with drink on him, some fellow will start a singsong. And sooner or later someone'll sing that bloody oul' song and I'll start crying. I hate it."

As I think I've made clear, when I walked the Treece land, and then found the "leprosy" entry in that 1864 newspaper, I sensed that I was being enchanted a little by Charles O'Brien and his world. Very shortly after that, I recognized that I was irretrievably caught up. I embraced it with open arms. And, as is now clear, I told myself, "Follow every stream to its source."

Béthune lies not much more than an hour from the English Channel coast, southeast from Saint-Omer, which lies southeast of Calais. This is old Picardy, where, in another old war song, roses are shining in the silvery dew. I went north from Béthune, up toward the Belgian border, looking for the country before Armentières. Now the cemeteries began, rows upon serried rows of white crosses, and I was asking myself, Why are you here?

The answer had several components. I had agreed with myself to dig into the story as deeply as I could. Already I knew that Charles O'Brien was an unreliable witness—and, indeed, that he meant to be. He deliberately left out significant information. What else can you say of a man who puts an entire life change in parentheses, and in seven words: "(I was bound for the New World)"? Above all, I have a powerful belief in the spirit of teaching.

Teaching is about the truth. It's about the truth of the knowledge that you're conveying. And it's about the truth of the effect that such knowledge can have. When I was teaching Shakespeare, I wanted the boys to know that Hamlet behaved in an ugly fashion to Ophelia. But I also wanted them to know that he had been, as we say, "blackguarded" by his own father and mother. His father asked him to become a murderer. And his mother married the man who killed his father.

I'm merely citing this as an example. In the same spirit, I went to France. I felt I needed to see Stephen Somerville's grave, to hear the bolt click home. If Charles, in his text, was less than forthcoming, I would compensate for that. Teaching is—or should be—about the whole truth.

To put it in a more concise way: I knew that my reason lay somewhere between checking on a man who had told me to "be careful" about him and getting a deeper grip on this slowly unfolding drama.

Stephen Somerville is buried in the military graveyard at Estaires, among Australians, Canadians, and New Zealanders. His inscription is simple: "Captain Stephen Somerville, Royal Irish Rifles, La Bassée 10th March 1915."

Official sources say that Captain Somerville died when the Germans returned fire. They had been holding firm on the La Bassée ground for some time and were not about to be driven out. The English bombardment that aimed to shift them was the biggest ever in any war up to that point (soon, of course, to be exceeded by excess in the three years still to come).

Some of the local oral history will tell you that many of those who died in those three hellish days in March were killed by their own shells that fell short or malfunctioned—today's euphemism is "friendly fire."

Around these villages, if you ask, the local people will show you little hills out in the fields that seem no more than ordinary mounds of earth thrown up eons ago by glacial deposits heaving across the world, as the ice slunk back to the poles or the oceans.

But they have before and after photographs of these hills. And they will point out to you how more than a few were twice, three times bigger after the war than before. When you look puzzled and ask them, they shrug and say, "*les corps*"—the bodies buried inside those hills.

Incidentally, nobody could be more interested than an Irish history teacher in the fact that the general in that battle was Sir John French— the same man who later took disastrous charge of the British campaign against the Irish Republican Army.

Back in Ireland, the widow Somerville had several choices. She could sell the estate and return to England. Or go anywhere, rich for the rest of her life. Or she could lease most of it and hope to collect rents. Or she could stay; she had enough capital to restore and develop the place.

Each option posed problems. If she sold and left, what would she do with her life? Become the quarry of fortune hunters? If she stayed and leased, would she be able to collect all the rents due to her? By now, tenancy of any kind had made the Irish irredeemably truculent. And if she stayed—how would she handle such a huge project?

April closed her mouth firmly as she finished speaking of the song. She had become a little frantic as her story gathered pace; now she held her head higher, and I saw that she looked at Mother with almost a stare. Would she likewise look at me? She did not; she was trying to gain control of herself, and she made herself be still. In a moment, her eyes again began to fill with tears, until they held shining pools—which then began to slip in sheets down her face. When next she spoke, her voice had calmed.

"Papa had a saying; he spoke it every day. *De mortuis nil nisi bonum.* Of the dead say nothing but good. I speak it every moment to myself. And I am trying to let the next thought take me over and stop the worst thought, the *nil nisi* thought; there's so much that I want to say, but *nil nisi* won't let me. And so I try to get to the next thought, but I can't. Is that how grief works?"

Mother said, "We lost Euclid. He was the dearest boy. Since then I have made errors every week in the farm accounts. For months my letters bore the date on which he died and I didn't even know it."

I had not known of this. Mother had never mentioned it—indeed, we spoke not at all to each other of our grief. I said, "Since he died, I go out into the world every day without my watch and have to come back for it. It's as if I wished Time itself had halted so that he could still be with us."

As I had not spoken until now, my words seemed to echo, and I recalled how much I had liked overseeing this building, and speaking aloud to myself, and hearing my words boom.

Mother looked over at me. "I did not know about your watch."

I replied, "Nor I about your farm accounts."

Mother turned to April, who was regarding me closely for the first time. "So you see, here we are, all in pain and grief. The best we can do is move on to the next thing."

April threw out her hands in a hopeless gesture. "I do not yet know what the next thing must be."

Mother said, "It will choose itself—and it will come and tell you."

TUESDAY, THE 6TH OF APRIL 1915.

The window is wide open and not a breeze comes through. Bernard has gone to bed but does not sleep. I hear Charles walking across the floor of his room—across and back again, across and back again. There is a floorboard that creaks each time. If I listened hard, I could count his steps. I know when he turns and retraces.

We had showers of rain this afternoon, from the west. Four lambs were born last night.

I shall go against myself. Against my former feelings. I shall become the friend of young Mrs. Somerville, if she will have it—and I believe that she will. But I shall not do this for Charles's sake. It is easy to see that his passion for her has not dimmed. I think the opposite is the case. But I will not meddle in that. No, I shall do it for her sake. No young woman, no matter what her faults, should be left with such burdens.

Tomorrow I shall write to her. I shall tell her that she must come to me for tea and I shall go to her, each week, turn and turn about. And we shall do that until she sells Tipperary Castle and departs. As I believe she soon will.

Before Amelia O'Brien could write her proposal, a letter arrived from the castle; it consisted of one sentence: "Although I am certain that he might not wish to do so, would it be possible to ask your son if he would call on me next Saturday?"

That was all; no mention of the visit, the condolences, the shared grief.

In Charles's account of the condolences meeting with April, there's a lot to read between the lines. A major impression emerges of April's mixed feelings. The *nil nisi* remarks suggest that she was caught between sincere grief at the loss of a husband and what she wanted to say about Stephen's behavior—but was prevented by convention. Almost certainly she had never discussed him with anyone. I have seen all the letters between April and Mrs. Moore, and no mention was ever made of anything untoward.

Nor, on the other hand—not even in the first flush of marriage—did April ever utter the predictable sentiments of an Edwardian young wife, such as "I have married the most wonderful man" or "Stephen is proving to be an excellent husband."

To Mrs. Moore, she makes one or two remarks, along the lines of "the bliss of Tipperary on a summer evening" or "you should have seen dawn on the terrace yesterday." But her comments always refer to the house and grounds, and never to the matrimony.

We can assume that Charles rode over to the castle on the Saturday, as invited. He kept no record of the meeting. We do not know from him or from April what was said. Nor do we know how he and April reopened their dialogue—or, rather, opened it; they had never had one.

And we do not know whether she made apologetic remarks (if she felt she needed to), or whether he again declared his love, although it seems likely that his mother would by now have advised him against any such approach.

But much can be divined from the fact that, a short time later, on Monday, 19 April 1915, Charles opened a "Daily Ledger" in Tipperary Castle and made these (and many more) entries:

"Still workable: 88 balks of oak; 10 balks of beech; 22 balks of ash (stable-yard doors & boxes); all balks 8 ft. by 4 inches by 2 inches; 160 planks of beech; 58 planks of maple; 300 pine; all future planks where possible 10 ft. by 18 inches (will accept 12 inches); nails to be determined—too numerous to be fashioned here?" (He also opened full and formal accounts ledgers.)

Sometime later, he told Harney about that first meeting alone with April. Charles said that by the time he got to the castle he was shaking like a leaf, and that he stumbled as he climbed down from the pony-trap, and almost fell. To his astonishment, "she was trembling too," and they sat in the sunshine on one of the low parapet walls of the Long Terrace.

Neither seems to have said much at all when they met, and after a silence "I opened my mouth to speak, but she held up a hand." In other words, widow or not, she was still in control.

"April said, as a question, 'You love this place?' and I said, 'How can I disagree?' To which she said, 'Will you help me rebuild it? The house and the gardens? And the land? I have been told that I have all the money that will be needed.' Harney, I was astounded."

Charles then asked what she had in mind when she used the word "rebuild"—whether she meant to bring it up to a good, usable standard or whether to restore it to its former glory.

"Then, she captured me again. She said to me, 'What was it Mr. Wilde said about preserving beauty?' I caught my breath, and pressed her on the point, and she said, 'Italian marblers, French painters, the best English carpenters, the great Irish stuccodores, the finest farm stewards.' Naturally, I said that this would cost several fortunes. And then she told me what she was worth—and she could have rebuilt ten Tipperarys."

In September, April wrote to Mrs. Moore, who had just paid a visit:

"Kitty, to think that I should now be sharing in your high opinion of Charles. I am amused that you recall that letter from Paris. Who could have believed that such a wild creature should be concealing such a greatly capable man? Papa tried to tell me, but I would not listen. Now Papa must be smiling."

During that year, Amelia O'Brien made many entries in her journal. But she mentions Charles or April so rarely that it must have been deliberate. She discusses her own farm, her husband's poor breathing, notes the passage of the late Euclid's birthday (she put flowers in his empty room each year) and Charles's birthday, on 21 June. But she makes only a few passing mentions of Tipperary Castle.

"Now we have Italians staying in the village," she wrote. "A father and two sons. They have come to work on the Hall and Grand Staircase." And: "Charles has gone to the train in a great welter of excitement—his foreman carpenter arrives from Bristol today." And: "Who is this new man, my son? How he is flourishing! Is he going to dazzle us all with his energy? With the brilliance of his judgments?"

It's possible to read the journal as though Amelia might have been holding her breath, watching to see if anything might develop between her son and the beautiful young widow in the castle. But her entries also suggest that she was determined to make the world roll on. In fact, she includes a greater number of housewifery details than was usual for her.

"Mrs. Tobin has stopped adding baking soda to the washing. Doesn't she know it makes the clothes softer?" And: "I taught Mrs. Tobin today to soak the candles in salt and water. To reduce the candle wax dripping. She told me I should tell Father Cantwell for the church candles. 'He'll give you a special blessing, ma'am.' She looked at me as though I needed a special blessing." And: "I again polished Euclid's boots today. It is a way, I suppose, of not missing him unbearably."

The next entry from Charles resumed his "History." This time, we learn that in the latter half of 1915, the restoration work had slowed down on account of the weather, and he had a little time to spare. Now we begin to see the "new" man. From the moment he took over the restoration of Tipperary Castle, his words convey a newfound strength.

꩜

After not much more than a year under way in the war with Germany, it had taken a heavy toll on Ireland. We were persuaded by Mr. John Redmond that were we to support King and Country we should be writing our own docket to Home Rule. Long had we known what Home Rule would mean—our own parliament in Dublin, our own laws for our own people.

I was in a cleft stick. How I should have loved to have been traveling Ireland, to hear the many views that I knew were being expounded. As a country, we were dividing cleanly into three simple factions: those who wished revolution, even if bloody, and they included my dear friend Harney; those who believed that we must continue to seek the peaceful direction of Home Rule (and my parents had declared for Mr. Redmond, as they did for Mr. Parnell); and those who desired the status quo—that Ireland remain a territory of the Empire, fully governed by the Parliament in London; in this position April placed herself.

And I was divided because much as I longed to, I had no time or freedom to explore these divisions up and down the country. For the time being, I had changed from healing the people to healing this great estate of Tipperary, and I must confess that it was proving more absorbing than the nation itself.

Perhaps my earlier experience as the court-appointed Responsible Overseer made it natural for me to be the one who would steer the estate through its recovery. April had decided, with the influence of her husband's great bequest, to make Tipperary Castle her permanent—indeed her only—home; she sold the house in London. I accepted her invitation to renew my oversight on the property, to manage the estate back into life.

The work soon began; I divided the requirements into four categories: the House—meaning restoration of the exterior and interior fabric to the pristine brightness of its originality; the Contents—repair of the many hangings and pieces of magnificent furniture; the Gardens— cleaning and refurbishment of the Parterre, the Knot (almost vanished beneath wild growths), the two pavilions (known as Major and Minor), and the herbaceous borders that ran in lines hundreds of yards long from the Terrace down the Eastern Steps to the riverside; the Land—full use of the four thousand acres, which entailed the determination of proportion between arable and livestock, and the eventual purchase of herds and flocks.

My earliest steps in this mammoth task had to account for two things: work already undertaken, along with the supplies so far purchased to that end, and the long search for those who would accomplish the most beautiful repairs. I needed men who knew stucco better than anyone, plaster experts who could reconstruct freehand the great designs of the house, or who knew how to make molds in the rooms in which they worked. And I required the same standards in stonework, whether masonry or carving; and men who painted like angels; perhaps above all, I needed superb carpentry.

At the end of my first week, when I had made all these assessments and began to measure the range and size of the tasks facing me, I sought April. Our conversation was brisk and clear; she added admirable sharpness to each point. I gave it as my opinion that, were we to get a good proportion of what we needed by way of craftsmen, labor, and materials, we saw an eight-year-long prospect facing us.

I think that she was a little dismayed by this; but I counted out for her the likely duration of individual renewals—the Grand Staircase would take, I believed, at least two and a quarter years to restore.

She wanted, she said, to become a full partner in all of this. It was her wish, she insisted, to learn everything about her own house: how the stone was cut; how the marble slabs were quarried in Kilkenny and Italy; how the magnificent birds with their corbeled beaks were made out of plaster, how their brilliant whiteness would be achieved in the making.

We discussed, at her initiative, how I should be compensated. In previous times I would certainly have said that the work, the service of her wishes, would provide reward enough. Now I held my tongue; she offered a good stipend, and I accepted. Also, I had the common sense to understand that I would surely fail if I attempted to do it all under my own sole leadership. Therefore, I agreed with April that I needed a very competent assistant, a man with the potential to deputize for me when I must be away somewhere, hiring, purchasing, or simply learning from other Great Houses how I must proceed. She freed me to choose whomever I wished, and I invited Joseph Harney. He readily gave up his job and began with me in the first week of June.

Here I must add that Harney cautioned me when I asked him. He said that "events" might overtake his role in the house, but that he believed these matters would in the long term prove to our benefit. I knew that he was party to political affairs, and I knew too that were a rebellion to come—as many expected—he would be in the thick of things.

And I should interject a dark note. When I came back to the property, some workmen still hung around in that first week, including the pair that I had seen sitting on the bridge when Mother and I came to condole with April. For a week or so, I took no action. Then, one day, as I was examining the collapsed stalls in the stable-yard, I heard one of these fellows greeting a newcomer.

They knew each other well—but they did not know that I was within earshot. As they exchanged bantering pleasantries, I looked out through a hole in some planks—and I saw that the man who had just arrived lacked a finger on one hand. This was the lout who had accosted me on the road to Bruree; and I suspected, but without being able to ascertain it, that I had seen him ride by on another unpleasant occasion. I burst out of the stable, he saw me—and ran.

When I asked the workman who this fellow was, he answered me sullenly that he did not know. I dismissed him instantly (and his sole colleague left that week). As to the man who ran away—there was nothing that I could do. My mistake was not having challenged him and his insolence on that day when he snatched Della's reins from my hand. But I vowed that were I ever to meet him again, he would feel my knuckles.

In 2003, the Irish government published the proceedings of a study group set up to examine the country's "heritage," which meant, the document said, "built and natural heritage." Here is the second paragraph from the Foreword:

"The built heritage includes a wide range of structures from terraced houses to thatched cottages, bridges and boundary walls to canals and castles, but the 'Big House' has a special place in Irish architectural history. Once considered not to be part of our patrimony, these magnificent eighteenth and nineteenth century houses, built by Irish builders, are now increasingly valued for their architectural significance and for the wealth of superb interior decoration created mainly by Irish craftspeople."

In 1915, when Charles O'Brien began restoring Tipperary, under the ownership and patronage of April Burke-Somerville (as she soon began to call herself), no such official body had been attempting any such care of the existing mansions in Ireland. Many of them had fallen into poor repair, and not until the mid-twentieth-century founding of the Irish Georgian Society, led by Desmond Guinness of the renowned brewing family, had anyone taken the matter seriously on a wide scale. Charles, therefore, was well ahead of his time, to judge from his own text.

I began as I had hoped—with no workers hired; nor did I seek any until Harney took up his duties. He told me that, to begin with, we must be "men of charts," and he showed me what he meant; he built a chart of each job, like a family tree, and he bade me do the same. Where my chart would take account of work required, and the guessed-at length of time it would need, his chart was to place the appropriate numbers of essential workers on that particular task.

Take the smallest example; the front door would need the following craftsmen: two carpenters, a Master and an experienced carpenter to help him; a Master Blacksmith, who would remove the hinges, repair what could be mended, and make new hinges if necessary; and a farrier's assistant to make the nails to the required length and thickness dictated by the Master Carpenter and Master Blacksmith. Thus Harney and I ran twin charts for each separate task, and I am pleased to say that by the time that he and I had completed our main charts, which was in the middle of October, and had begun to hire those people whom we could reach, we felt that we had taken command of the task.

The weather helped a great deal. I might not have believed that stonemasons would come to work in winter; but we had no early frost. And I would have refused to believe that a thirty-three-year-old, tall, and beautiful English widow would don the roughest of clothes and work alongside the hardest of men. On the first day of October, Mr. Higgins, the Master Stonemason, arrived to take up work. I had already traveled to his home in Hollyford in the hope that I might hire him. He told me that his great-grandfather Jack Higgins had personally cut the great capstone over the front door—which his great-granduncle Peter had then carved so exquisitely.

When he began to work that first morning, I accompanied him and told him that April (whom I introduced) would hope to assist. He never questioned; he merely looked at her and said, "You'll have to put that hair away. There's dust." She and I understood him; she would work as a man, as a laborer, and learn about stone from him.

I waited a little, as I sensed his first lesson about to begin. Sure enough, he said to her, "There's silk and there's tweed and there's canvas. Stone's the same, and you have to decide what it is when you're cutting it."

He then took her on a tour of her own house, pointing out the silk, the tweed, and the canvas—the door and window reveres, the main facades and cornices, and the sturdy buttresses. Within a week, she was on her knees beside him, steadying the strong planks he used to frame and hold the stone he was cutting. He showed her how to use a chisel, how to find the grain on a stone and go with it, where not to cut across the stone's own formed trend.

On the Saturday evening of that week, I met her in the Great Hall, from which I had had a great deal of the debris carted away. I myself was on my knees, looking into a hole beneath the floorboards to determine whether the cavity ran all the way down to the cellars. She walked to me, and as I stood up, I saw that she swayed. Although ready to catch her should she fall, I made no such move. She steadied herself, with a hand against the wall. I saw that she was exhausted; the impression may have been increased by stone powder in every pore of her face and a gray ring of dirt that ran around her forehead beneath her hairline, where she had taken off her head-covering.

Our relationship had been straightforward: we discussed castle matters without difficulty; she liked Harney and was easier with him than with me. In the presence of all workers—of whom we soon had a small army—she addressed me as "Mr. O'Brien." When alone, she called me "Charles." Now she said, in a worn-out voice, "I think I'm going to call you O'Brien—when there's nobody else around," and she smiled at me.

I did not respond to the intimacy; I nodded—gravely, as had become my custom. Since we had begun this great task together, I had taken care to dwell always on the business in hand. We had no personal conversation of any kind; I inquired into nothing other than how she saw this wall, that floor, the other tree or shrub. I had determined to keep farther from that flame than I had been in the past, when I was severely burned by it.

"So, O'Brien," she said. "I shall try to scrub this"—she gestured at her face and hands—"my own house from my own skin. Not that I shall ever remove it."

She passed on, into the rear of the house and, I supposed, to the rooms upstairs that I had long ago indicated as potentially habitable for herself and her bridegroom.

What was it like in those first six months, working next to the woman for whom I had so fiercely expressed my passion, both in my life and in these pages? And what was April like? I received no practice at saying anything about her; Mother, in that time, never asked a question about her, about my feelings—never made an inquiry into anything but the work, in which she was deeply interested. Consequently, these next sentences will be my fresh impression of April, and of her place—if any—in my heart.

Fifteen years had passed since I first saw her. She and I had traveled through many events since then. We had both known failure and bereavement; she had lost her father and her husband; I had lost dear Euclid, and I had been attacked—nothing so lowers the spirits as assault. By all accounts she had failed to bring her husband into decency—having married him, as people speculated, so that he could help her to acquire the estate. And I had failed to make a mark on the world that would impress her—would have impressed her enough to think of marrying me.

Where our lives had touched, we had been without success toward each other, even at the level of friends. That she had gained more from me than I from her might seem, on the surface, to be true. She had garnered my good offices for the protection of the estate that she would inherit, and it was widely believed that my evidence in court had gone a considerable way toward helping decide the findings in her favor. Before the end of it, she was married; I lay in a hospital bed; and she soon dismissed me from her life and my usefulness in it. Those are the superficial impressions that any observer could not be faulted for noting.

I take a different view. By asking me to oversee her estate, she released me into the world for which I felt I had been born. When, on winter days, I walked those empty corridors alone, I somehow knew that I had come into my true life at last. I was no longer uncomfortable with myself; I did not feel like an awkward man trying to show the best face to the world, and yet afraid that no person would value me.

In short, I had been given a great gift by the woman whom I had been unable to wed. Now I believed it my turn to repay—by the restoration of her wondrous inheritance. Thus, I decided that I would not trouble her with remarks as to the proceedings of my heart. Certainly I had been fearful—fearful of meeting her, fearful of being in her company. Her rejection of me, and the curtness of it—these had wounded me greatly each time, even though I tried not to feel them. I mourned her father when he died; I had been so looking forward to what I felt would grow into a delightful relationship. And the many questions that had been raised by the proceedings in court as to how much the Burkes knew about Tipperary and when they knew it—I decided to let them lie.

SUNDAY, JANUARY THE 23RD 1916.

Charles came home today. We had a good talk. Bernard went out to look at cattle. Charles tells great stories of the castle. We debated much as to how he should have a great mural painting restored. Charles says that he and he alone will de-

cide. "And not April?" I ask. "Oh, I may consult her," he says
airily.

Harney arrived later, for supper. He is such a wonderful
young man. And he loves Charles as Euclid did. He hangs on
everything that Charles says. While Charles bathed—he says
that he is permanently stained from the castle works—Harney told me of Charles *in situ*. How he knows everything that
is to be done. How even the Master Craftsmen defer to him.
How he commands the suppliers and the workers. How his
taste is appreciated by the Italians, the French, the English
carpenters.

I did not ask the main question (re April). Nor shall I. I
shall wait until I am told. If there be anything to tell. There
may not be—but I cannot believe that my Charles has
quenched that flame in his heart. It would have been like
putting out the furnace at the core of the earth.

Every summer morning I rose at half past five, dressed, and set out on a
walk of the nearest grounds. I walked the walls, inspecting any work in
progress, and when a full circuit of the castle had been completed, I then
walked through the gardens. Here I encountered a delight every day of
my life, with birds, small animals, and fresh growths. When the cleaning
of the gardens got under way, the journey became even more delightful,
as the gardeners disclosed nooks, some of them containing classical stat-
uary that had been long hidden by overgrowths. They found topiary, in
the shapes of birds and triangles and rabbits, and two wonderful circles
that led to a small, hitherto overgrown maze.

And when they had begun weeding, and had torn away grass from
underfoot, they revealed excellent paths of brick in herringbone patterns,
and white gravel, and in one case large round stones that made it feel like
walking on cannonballs. I was inclined to think that, of all the work on
the place, the garden clearances and renovations gave the greatest pleasure.

After the gardens, I went on a tour of the four sunken fences that border the house at a distance. (Some call a sunken fence a "ha-ha," and Mother tells me that the name comes from the surprise. A sunken fence consists of a deep trench, one side of which is a vertical wall of stone. This provides excellent fencing but does not obstruct the view, and when one sees it one is inclined to say "Ha-ha!" in delight at the surprise or discovery.) And when I came back from the fourth ha-ha, I walked along the western shore of the lake, onto the graveled path that led to the bridge, and climbed the Laurel Steps (they number fifty and are overhung with laurels) up onto the Terrace. From there I surveyed the entire property, and I could see clear down to the village.

So far, the reconstruction of the outer fabric had taken precedence, with the roofs being the most important. I had teams of men build structures all along the parapets, so that shelters could be raised over existing holes in the slates. When Harney and I got down to the task of finding the best builders, we first sought roofing experts. Without a sound covering there would be no point in beginning interior work. To my surprise, it took only a matter of weeks to secure the worst damage against any kind of weather; this made us very free to consider our next steps.

After breakfast I began to walk each job, usually with Harney, sometimes with April too. As the work went on, I saw April less and less during the day; she moved from one section of the project to another, working alongside craftsmen and laborers, acting as an assistant, hauling, tugging, lifting, asking no concessions for being a woman or the owner.

I saw her with the stonemasons, the carpenters, the men on the roof—she toiled as an equal, and since her first stonemasoning experience, she had learned to cover her hair as tightly as possible. One morning over breakfast, Harney, to whom she spoke a great deal more than she did to me (but I did not invite or encourage much exchange), asked her why she chose the route of, he called it, "hard labor." As he said, she could be sitting back, the lady of the manor, and watching us all sweat.

April looked at him as though he had said something unutterably stupid.

"This is my life," she said, a trifle shortly. "This is what I do. I breathe.

I eat. I sleep. I do this." She said it in such a way as to close down all argument.

Later, I reflected upon her words: "This is my life." What did she mean? Either she had been stating, *"Laboro, ergo sum"*—"I work, therefore I am" or "What I do, I am"—or she had been saying that since she had turned her back on London and won the estate, she had now embraced this as her true existence, where past and present became as one. For this I admired her further.

Usually the tour of the various sectors of work took some hours. I talked to every Master Craftsman, every foreman; I asked them questions, I established their problems, their needs. Of course I was interrupted all the time, typically by new deliveries, many of which proved flawed—either wrong materials, or inadequate to the task, or not at all what we believed we had ordered. Constantly, too, Harney and I dealt with problems among the workers. At the busiest moment of all the work, we had close to three hundred people on the estate, and the hammering and the measuring and the arguing and the whistling and the singing made it a pocket universe unto itself.

In the late afternoons (lunch occurred on the move), I conferred with the Master in charge of each area. Mr. Higgins always provided my first conference. In age, he deserved this, and more than that, he merited it in importance; to him I looked for the securing of the entire property structure, and to him I looked for apprehension of how the job would eventually turn out. He was a small man (I've observed that stonemasons can be a stocky breed) and he said little; he had a nasal speech, and a great shyness—rather than look directly at me, he rolled his eyes upward as he spoke.

At his waist he wore an enormous belt, very wide at the back, which he pulled tight when addressing a significant block of stone. Much of his work had to do with "patching" the walls, where mortar had loosened the joints of the cut-stone blocks—this puzzled him; he put it down to water damage. When he patched, he and his men chiseled out the section minutely and measured the space over and over.

As I first watched this, I became impatient; Harney stayed my tongue.

And then, when I inspected the first patch—and at Mr. Higgins's invitation I climbed his ladder to look at close quarters—I could not tell where it began and ended. From the ground it seemed as if the castle wall had never changed; it was almost miraculous.

According to the Irish Georgian Society and the government of the republic, "at the beginning of the nineteenth century, a time synonymous with country house building in Ireland, there were approximately eight to ten thousand landed proprietors in a population of around 5.4 million people. Possibly around one third of these were absentee landlords who resided more or less permanently outside the country. The remainder lived in country mansions, which they had built on their core estates. It is difficult to determine with certainty how many country houses there were in the twenty-six-county area [the modern Republic of Ireland] at this time, but the number certainly ran into thousands."

Obviously, their standards of construction and decor varied. Not every Irish Great House resembled or excelled its English, Scottish, or European counterparts—but their very existence speaks to a triumph of taste and cultural ambition. And logistics; when Charles O'Brien began to restore Tipperary Castle, at least he had the railway and an improved road network by which goods could be delivered with some safety.

He also had better luck—unlike Lord Cloncurry, who, a century earlier, had been developing his estate of Lyons House, near Dublin. The ship bringing his Italian and Greek masterpieces back to Ireland foundered and sank in Killiney Bay, a few miles from the Irish shore.

To speak of improved amenities, however, might sound like a belittling of Charles's efforts. With no telephone, he had to rely on letters and the word of those supplying him. Therefore, his courage in ordering, sight unseen, and having faith in his suppliers was considerable. Also, he had a time factor; the virtue of patience must have been his greatest requirement.

What interests me over and above the details, however, is the rise of the new Charles O'Brien. I've looked back many times through his text to see whether there's a first appearance of the emerging man. It's difficult to find.

Yes, there is a man of sensitivity in those historical and personal narratives. Yes, there is a man with the capacity to care deeply—not just for a woman with whom he has fallen in love but for his "patients." And yes, there is a man who takes a profound interest in the world around him. Who else would have bothered to ask two farmers about their love of land—and extract such lyrical responses from them?

But the man who took over this great restoration, who supervised the taste, who hired and fired, who conducted himself as a leader—this is a different creature, long removed from the ham-fisted man at Oscar Wilde's deathbed.

Now we come to the first connection between Charles O'Brien and me.

My father, John Joe Nugent, came from a large family. He was the third of eleven children. As he often explained, in his position he had to fight every step forward, with the older siblings keeping him down and the younger ones trying to push him out of the way. A cheerful man, he liked company, especially men with memories.

When he married my mother, tongues wagged. Of different stock, a Dublin merchant family, her parents believed that she had come down in the world. She married a man without a profession (her father had been a surgeon), and she went to live in a country town.

After the wedding, she and my father made a small but curious pact. In certain arenas of her life she would continue to use her maiden name, Margery Coleman. I never knew the motive behind this. But my mother's aunt, Betty Coleman—who, in the quirks of a large family, was only a year older than my mother—told me once that it had something to do with "your mother wanting to hold on to something of what she came from."

In many ways my mother did not fit in. Her earliest hobby had been photography—unusual, to say the least, for a girl in Ireland. She had made a study of what was happening in the field abroad. And she had saved to buy herself the best and most appropriate equipment—all of which she had in her possession when she first met my father, on a train from Waterford to Limerick.

The number and weight of the bags in her luggage caught his attention. They fell into conversation. A romance began more or less immediately, and they married within a year. My mother often told me that she would like to have had more than one child but was very happy with the one she had—which is music to a small boy's ears.

One day, when I wasn't yet ten years old, a local man got shot—by accident—on our street. My mother heard the shot and rushed out. The man lay on the pavement, bleeding heavily. He had been taking his gun off his bicycle when it went off. My mother knelt beside him and held his head up until help arrived. The man survived, and later we were told that the act of holding his head up had saved him. The bullet had lodged in his neck.

I marveled at this. Nothing as exciting had ever happened. That night, at bedtime, I asked my mother how she'd known what to do. She told me that "a dear friend" had once been shot in the neck over near Tipperary, and that a man who'd heard the shots came back, and kept her friend alive by raising his head to close the neck wound.

When that—not necessarily conclusive—evidence came back to my mind, I then recollected something else. Long before she died, my mother and I had spent many Sundays, especially in winter, sorting and cataloging—in our amateur way—her huge collection of photographs, which amounted to a minor history of photography in Ireland. Her earliest work had been on glass plates.

As I read Charles's text, I began to recall a series of photographs that she had taken in Tipperary. They showed teams of workmen and craftsmen, all photographed on the same day, at a castle. And then came the clincher, where I married Charles's text to my mother's photography.

She had taken a series of pictures that turned out to have great historic importance. Several years before I was born she had been in Dublin throughout Easter 1916.

As had Joseph Harney, and as had Charles O'Brien—who devotes a long passage of his text to that epic week.

When I first conceived this History, I made clear my awareness that I lived in an important historic period. Indeed, I knew that I was living through several moments of definition; the land agitation gave way to serious land reform, with the Wyndham Act making sure that no farmer need feel forced to be a tenant all his life. Then came the Great War, with its postponement of Home Rule for Ireland, meaning that many young men had gone to die in return for a promise that would now never be kept. In short, I lived in a country where something of importance seemed to happen every day. One day, history came to touch me directly.

Ever since I met Joseph Harney, I had known that he carried rebel fire inside him. We spoke much of politics, and he gave no quarter in his belief that political freedom came only from military force. We never argued this point, Harney and I; my own plea went toward never having violence, but my pacifism had not been such that it stopped me trying to go to war.

Admittedly, I had been swayed by the promise of the Home Rule that Ireland would be granted in exchange for our soldierly support. When that self-government never came, despite the numbers of Irishmen who died in the hope of it, I felt more sympathetic to Harney's idea—but I always believed, as I still do, that debate will always have to take place, so it might as well come first as last.

Harney worked demonically hard at the castle restoration. He took no time off, didn't want to; occasionally he visited his family, over in Urlingford. No matter what time he came back—we both slept at the castle—there he sat at breakfast next morning, bright as day and busy as a bee, full of plans and opportunities. So it was that I felt shock—but not surprise—when, on the evening of Saturday, the 15th of April 1916, Harney came to me and said quietly, "I have to go away for a time."

My heart quickened—and he knew that I knew.

"Don't ask any questions, Charles. I'm better if you don't."

I walked with him as he rode his bicycle down to the main gate. As he climbed on the saddle and began to turn the pedals he said, "I'll be back. I don't know if it'll be soon. But—if I say I'll be back, I'll be here." And off he rode.

A week and a day later, on Sunday afternoon, two ladies appeared in the driveway. On a beautiful afternoon I was standing at the end of the Long Terrace, using the low wall as a table while I calculated the wages needed for the coming week. Matters had been under tight control, and month after month Harney and I had been able to tell April that the entire task was costing no more than we'd assessed—and often less.

The two ladies with their bicycles came shyly along the avenue, having dismounted out of respect. I assumed them to be local girls seeking employment—people came to us every day looking for jobs—or sightseers or relations of some of the workers whom we had billeted on the estate. When they saw me, they conferred—and then with some determination put their bicycles carefully aside and made their way to me.

They approached straightforwardly, with no hesitation—two young women, one with dark hair, one with red.

As they drew closer, I said, "I know who you are."

They did not laugh; nor did they smile. One said, "You're Mr. O'Brien, aren't you?"

Their solemnity worried me.

"I am. Is everything all right?"

The older said, "Well, we don't know, and we don't know what to do."

And the younger-looking one chimed in, "Joseph's gone to Dublin. A fellow came to the house this morning looking for him. When we told him Joseph was gone, he said, 'Doesn't he know it's all off?' That's all we know."

By dint of questioning, I discovered that Joseph had long been a republican volunteer on the understanding that if an armed rebellion were to take place, he would be in the front line. Rumors had abounded that "something" was going to happen—but the "something," said the Harney sisters, was supposed to be canceled, and if Joseph didn't know, they said, "mightn't he be walking straight into a trap?"

I had long suspected, from Harney's demeanor, that some plans had been drawn. He received letters, and once or twice men came to see him; he met them down the avenue, much talk took place, and the men returned the way they had come. I never asked questions, and he never told me information; I assumed that he was part of some plan or other—

rather, it is more accurate to say that were he not part of some plan or other, the other plotters must be fools not to have engaged him.

"What do you want me to do?" I asked these now-distressed girls.

They looked at each other. "Can you get him back?"

The younger girl said, "He'll do anything for you."

"But I don't even know where he is."

"We know," they said in eager voices, and they told me an address on Northumberland Road, Dublin. I knew that I could find it—and I said that I would try. Both girls came with me to the kitchen, where Helen made them tea; for once she remained good-tempered, and they knew many people in common. I found April; she did not wish to meet the girls. When they had gone, I told her that I must go to Dublin to find Harney, that I feared he might be in some danger.

She said, nonchalantly, "I presume everything is in order."

That was all; she said nothing else.

The Easter Rising (as I taught in school so often) began in confusion. It ended in tragedy, was reborn in defiance, and concluded in triumph six and a half years after it began. There had been confusion among Irish republican activists and disagreement as to the timing of an armed uprising. But the principle had been accepted. England, weakened and distracted by war, had a vulnerable flank to the west. All going well, Germany might prove a valuable ally if it saw the Irish also declaring war, and if it had begun to gain ground in France and Belgium.

However, only a small percentage of the country had the slightest interest in an armed rebellion or anything like it. Many Irish hearts had been broken already by the Great War. The reports coming back from the mud and blood grew worse and worse. Battlefield names—Ypres, Loos, Verdun—these became chants in a dirge. The fallen men had been volunteer soldiers. Nobody wanted more death.

Friction within the republicans reached a head just before Easter Week. One faction assumed that it would attempt to take the city of Dublin. Another believed that the action had been called off. Both happened. Just over a thousand armed men occupied key buildings in the center of the capital. Some thousands more around the country never shouldered a gun.

By the late afternoon on Easter Monday, 24 April, the rebels had barricaded themselves inside the General Post Office and several other establishment buildings. Other, smaller groups of rebels watched key Dublin avenues. These were men mostly without uniforms, country boys, with disparate guns, little ammunition, and a day's rations—sandwiches made by their mothers, sisters, and wives.

SUNDAY, THE 23RD OF APRIL 1916.

Charles is staying here tonight. Tomorrow he will go to Dublin, he says, to find Harney, who "may be in some kind of trouble." He aims to catch the train. Other than a worry for Harney, Charles looks splendid. I told him what I hear: That the castle work is excellent. That the craftsmen would do anything for him.

He asked my opinion. We talked about the stonework, the carpentry. He asked about his father, whom he hasn't seen for some time. It always seems that Bernard is out when Charles calls.

Should I be worried that Charles goes to bring back Harney? Fewer than two years ago I should have been frantic; not tonight.

Today I dared ask the Question. Charles only said that "April works very hard. The men respect her. I don't want to distract her." I told Charles that she comes here now and then, and we talk. In the past he would have blurted, "Does she speak of me?" Not now. I wonder what is going on in his head.

The train had many people on board, returning to Dublin after Easter. It seethed with rumors that burst into the fire of fear as we neared the city. Outside Kildare, we were stopped a long time in one place; nobody knew what was happening. One voice said that Dublin was in flames from the river to the hills; another said that the English soldiers had been routed, and that a new flag flew over the Post Office. Out of a genuine excitement there grew a sincere dread; many people hoped to turn back but could not leave the train.

We started again, shuddering, halting, and running for some miles, but very slowly—and then we stopped again, for a long time. The train fell silent, with whispered conversations here and there, and now we drew away again, and the evening darkened. As I did not reach the city until several hours later than I had hoped, my intention—to find Harney, take him to a hotel, and then catch the morning train home with him—was thwarted. On Monday night, I found myself on the street at Kingsbridge station, being told by a soldier at gunpoint to go back where I came from.

I found a night's lodgings in a boarding-house at Islandbridge, a mile's walk from the train. There, nobody had gone to bed; the household sat at the table as I ate, and people came and went, all bearing excited news or asking fearful questions. An impression began to form of the day's events and the condition of the city.

It seemed that small parties of armed men had marched to many points and announced themselves as the "Irish Republican Army," the new governing force of the city. In the General Post Office at Sackville Street, they had run up a rebel flag; and in broad daylight, the "Army Commander," a gentleman named Pearse, had proclaimed Ireland a republic "in the name of God." Some gunfire had been exchanged, but in general it had been agreed that the British Army had been taken by surprise—because most of its officers had gone to a race meeting out in the countryside.

In my bones I knew that Harney would be installed deep within this hurly-burly. His reliability made it likely that he would be at the address his sisters had given me; it seemed that I would have to look for him in the very thick of things.

I was excited—apprehensive too, but mostly excited, as must be imagined in a man who once had set himself to write a History of his own country in his own time. As I lay down on the tiny bed in the box of a room, listening to the hum and murmur of talk that still went on downstairs, I reflected that, two years ago, I should not have approached this task in anything like so confident a frame of mind. And I reflected further that I had received an incomparable gift from April Burke, the wife of the late Mr. Somerville. She had made me competent; my desire for her respect and love had indeed raised me up and improved me.

Next morning I set out at seven o'clock; a passing bread cart (with a silent driver) took me to Kingsbridge, where I had last night disembarked from the train. Knots of people waited there; piles of luggage suggested that they meant to quit Dublin. One man told me that the city center had been rendered impassable—"Barricades everywhere. Those bloody Sinn Feiners, why can't they leave well enough alone?" Others also cursed "the Shinners."

Mr. Griffith's "Sinn Fein" movement had by now, of course, caught much of the nationalistic imagination, and people saw no difference between his political activism and the Irish Republican Army's militancy.

When I had walked along the river some distance, I met the first barricade. It is important to describe my appearance; I had specifically dressed like a well-to-do business gentleman, black frock coat, hat, etc., in case I had to deal with officers. As I reached the barricade, a soldier halted me, gun aimed.

"Where is your commanding officer?" I asked.

A blond young man appeared.

"Are you in charge here?"

"What is your business?"

I said, "My practice is my business. I need to reach it."

In the distance I heard gunfire; and I saw smoke rising from buildings. No people walked anywhere—the streets had emptied except for soldiers.

"No chance, I'm afraid," said the young officer. He looked apologetic and respectful; my attire was having the desired effect. "Where did you want to go?"

"Close to the Post Office," I said.

He shook his head. "We have a siege there," he said. "We've already had casualties."

"I stayed with friends in the country last night. Shall I be able to get home?"

"Depends where home is."

I said, "Northumberland Road."

"No trams, I'm afraid. Wait here, Doctor."

The young officer returned. "I can get you part of the way—one of our chaps is going to Merrion Square."

As he escorted me to a nearby vehicle, he said to me, "My father's a doctor. I'm supposed to be in France."

The first two days of the Easter Rising had about them an aura of stalemate, of action yet to happen. Nobody had accurate information. Rumor distorted everything. The British government, engrossed with the war in Europe, reacted slowly.

And at noon on the Monday, Patrick Pearse, a barrister, teacher, and poet, had the freedom to stand in the street outside the General Post Office, which his men had commandeered, and read the Proclamation of the Irish Republic.

Those who saw this event—now an iconic moment in Irish history—recall chiefly the scattered cheers and jeers, and the strained, pale look on Pearse's face. He knew that he was taking hundreds, if not thousands, of men into a blood sacrifice.

Not all of the streets were closed. The official response was as sporadic and incomplete as the rebellion itself. Over wide areas of Dublin, life continued as normal. Children spent their holiday week as they always did, playing in the streets. On Tuesday morning, people returned to work as they found it possible. Newspapers appeared, and milk trucks and bread vans made their rounds. The city had not yet heard enough to make it feel threatened.

Reinforcements had been called up from other garrisons in Ireland—

by train from Belfast, on foot from barracks nearer to Dublin. And in England, troops were scraped together. With scant munitions, they took the train that would carry them to the boat that would put them down on the Irish shore.

Charles O'Brien's ride in an army vehicle brought him to Merrion Square, childhood home of Oscar Wilde. From there, he had a walk of ten minutes or so to the address he had been given on Northumberland Road. Neither he nor anyone else knew, on that Tuesday morning, whether he would have safe passage.

Although I believed that I knew my way, I asked an old lady whether Northumberland Road lay straight ahead. All around me seemed peaceful.

She replied, "What are you goin' there for?"

I said, "I must meet a friend."

"Well, there's fellas up there with guns. And the Shinners—aren't they after locking themselves into Boland's Mill, so they are. I hope they all get shot."

"You don't sympathize?"

"Ah, what are they, only corner-boys? Louts, is what they are. Disturbin' the peace on us." Her sweet face became harsh.

"But they see it as a fight for freedom?"

She said, "My daughter, she has a husband out in France; he's in a uniform, so he is, not some coward firing guns from behind a wall. He's fightin' for our freedom, so he is."

And she went on her way.

From that corner of the square it is possible to look all along Lower Mount Street to the beginnings of the red brick and leafy peace of Northumberland Road. I stepped out into the roadway, and nothing did I see other than some boys playing with a ball. I walked on, without the hint of what was to come about in the next few days.

On Mount Street Bridge on that glorious morning I looked back to my left at the hulk of Boland's Mill. Nothing seemed untoward; I saw no activity—but nothing occurred on the streets either. Nor did I see any soldier, nor a gun of any kind; and Northumberland Road was as quiet as a smile; indeed, the loudest noise at that time came from my rapping on the door-knocker of No. 25.

Nobody answered. I did hear footsteps, however—and I knocked again. After a metallic scraping sound, the large brass flap of the letter box was pulled back from the inside, and a gun-barrel appeared.

A voice said, "What?"

"Is Mr. Harney here?"

"Who wants him?"

"His friend Charles O'Brien."

Nothing happened; I had produced no response. The gun-barrel remained in place. I waited. After several moments I knocked again.

I must have waited thirty or forty minutes; then I knocked again, with particular force, and shook the door so hard that I obviously dislodged the gun wedged inside. (I had long concluded that the gun's owner had left it there as a threat.)

Footsteps came striding, and the door whipped open.

"In—quick."

Two men stood in the hallway. The one at the rear held a gun; the other picked up his rifle from the floor.

"Joe's asleep—he was on watch all night."

They led me upstairs and introduced themselves: "I'm Jimmy Grace, this is Michael Malone. Sit in there, and we have to ask you not to move."

We had come to an upper-floor drawing-room, with two long windows overlooking Northumberland Road; a third window in the side of the room faced south. I believe that I immediately understood the objective—and it had probably been decided by Harney. Troops arriving might possibly come along this road, the main artery from the port of Kingstown, which continued broad and easy into the city center. This house would provide an excellent ambush point.

Lace curtains hung down over the windows; by moving them aside slightly I could see directly into the houses across the road. As far as I could ascertain, no other ambush was prepared; directly opposite, a girl in a maid's cap and apron walked here and there, restoring sheets to a bed. In another house, a gentleman sat in a chair, reading a newspaper.

Michael Malone said to me, "Here, for now, you have to do everything you are told. So—step back from the window."

He said it pleasantly, and I found a chair deep inside the room.

"Who's in command here?" I was careful to voice the question in no pejorative way.

"Commandant Harney. Otherwise we'd have shot you." Mr. Malone did not smile as he spoke; Mr. Grace remained silent.

I sat in that room for three hours; other than the two men, nobody came or went. At a quarter to three, they gave me bread and tea. And at three o'clock I heard the familiar footstep coming down a nearby staircase; after a whisper in the hallway outside, Harney entered, beaming.

"How did you get here?" he said, obviously delighted.

"I came to fetch you."

"The girls?" He grimaced.

"Yes."

"I thought they might," he said. "They tried hard to stop me."

"So they sent me"—and we both laughed. "What's going on?" I asked.

"But you must have heard?"

"Not about this place. There are guns in the city."

Harney said, "We know that reinforcements will come in along this road. Our job is to stop them. Or delay them."

I said, "Come on. Come out of here."

He shook his head. "Can't do that."

"Joseph—I promised your sisters I'd get you out of Dublin safely."

He laughed. "But you didn't say when you'd do it, did you?"

"Come on."

"No." He held out his hands. "I can't. This is my command. Here— I'm a soldier."

"All right. Where do I sit? What can I do to help?"

"You don't sit, you lie down, in the next room, under the bed."

I said, "This is nonsense. If we leave now—"

Harney held up a finger. "Charles—I'm not leaving here. And I can't let you leave now. You could get shot."

I abandoned my attempts to persuade him. Harney left the room and came back a short time later in uniform—a full military tunic in soft green, a soldier's breeches, and a hat with one side pinned up in a slouch. Diagonally across his body he wore an ammunition belt. Now he had become someone else.

"Volunteer Malone, secure all. Volunteer Grace, check again all windows and doors." He beckoned to me, and I followed.

In the next room—smaller and toward the rear of the house—the shutters had been drawn tight and mattresses dragged against the windows. Other bedding covered the floor.

"Stay here. There's food and drink. Until I come for you," he said and shook my hand.

Strangely, I did get a night's sleep, deep and sound. It is my impression that one or both of the other men slept in the room also, but my sleep was too deep to confirm this. I awoke at six o'clock to a silent house, and I drifted back to sleep in the room that would stay dark, no matter how high the sun. An hour or two later, I had bread, cheese, and milk, and then I sat there, not knowing what to do. The morning drifted on. I could hear men talking but saw nobody; the walls in these new brick houses had been densely built.

At eleven o'clock, activity in the front room seemed to intensify. I heard heavy boots pounding, objects being dragged across the floor, and dull metal clanging. Then, once again, the same grave silence fell. Somewhere in the far distance a child laughed.

This silence lasted for a long time; I know that it did—I could scarcely take my eyes from my watch.

At twenty minutes before noon I heard something new—a faint rhythmic sound that did not come from inside the house. I pressed my ear to the door of the room, trying to divine what I could. The sound increased, steady and firm—the sound of military boots in step. I had never heard troops on the march and was surprised at the even fullness of the sound, a dense, rhythmical tread, faster than I'd expected, and heavier. No sooner had I remarked upon this to myself than it was blotted out by a new and more savage sound: the men in the room at the front of the house had opened fire.

They fired in a specific routine—one: pause: two: pause: three: longer pause. I calculated that they fired through one window after another, systematically and regularly. One. Two. Three—I began to count: five seconds, I reckoned, between each gun. And when that sound had established itself, I became able to distinguish sounds from outside. First came shouts, barked orders. Intermingled with those, I heard screams, then more shouts.

And—why had I not been expecting it?—the gunfire increased fourfold as the soldiers on the street began to fire back. A new force hammered into my locked and darkened room—the sound of shattering glass from the windows near Harney and his men. This was followed by repeated thudding sounds, and I knew that these must come from bullets striking the adjoining wall. A hell of noise was born, full of cracking and splintering sounds, full of booming and tinkling, punctuated now and then by brief sharp whines, which I took to come from ricochets. I crawled away from the door, spreading myself as flat on the mattresses as I could, and reached the comparative calm of the wall farthest from the one adjoining Harney and his comrades.

There I lay, heart pounding, trying to divine the course of this pitched battle from the weight of fire. I cannot tell how long this activity went on; my concentration did not extend to looking at my watch repeatedly. Could it have been an hour? Perhaps—and more. At one point, all matters escalated and the firing from the next room reached an almost unendurable pitch of intensity. Downstairs I could hear a sudden great hammering on the door. Bullets pierced the woodwork, then whistled into the hallway and expired, and I reasoned (if that word may apply in such heat and fear) that the military must have tried to breach the door. But Harney and his comrades had fortified it the previous night with furniture, and now they seemed to change the angle of their fire to address this attack. Their heavy rifle shots (I could easily distinguish them from the army's gunfire) sounded closer to the front walls of the house, and I presumed that they had begun to aim downward, because the hammering on the door soon ceased. Later I discovered that the soldiers—from the Sherwood Foresters regiment—had indeed tried to storm the house.

Through the wall, I could also hear the bolts of the rifles clanging and clicking as the three men reloaded; they seemed to have plenty of ammunition. Upon the retreat from the front door, comparative calm returned. This was followed by a sudden burst of firing from inside the room, a shout, and a sudden bursting open of my door.

Harney beckoned, Grace stood close behind him, and I saw Malone lying face down beneath one of the windows. I knew that he was dead— I know not how I knew. We crashed down the stairs and into a rear scullery, and from there by a side-door into the yard of the house next door. The three republicans had so pinned down the Sherwood Foresters that they had been unable to surround the house. And the army had taken dreadful casualties—close to three hundred soldiers died.

Harney, bent double, led us to the rear of a long garden. Past a small glasshouse, he opened a door onto a deserted lane; he and Grace no longer carried guns. He tapped Grace on the shoulder: "God go with you."

Jimmy Grace kicked open a locked gate facing us, and went into a garden leading away from Northumberland Road. When I last saw him, this freckled boy, he was climbing a high brick wall fifty yards away. Harney and I stood there—he in uniform, I in my best suit, both of us covered in plaster dust. He had blood on his cheek from a glass splinter; I had a bloodied hand and shirt-cuff, from some piece of glass—I remembered not where.

"I need a coat," he said, "and you have to go."

"Yes," I said, "with you."

He looked at me. "No point arguing, I suppose?"

I shook my head.

Behind us we could hear the soldiers firing sporadically at the house. We began to run through a series of lanes; I slowed him down—he was more than twenty years younger than me.

In Percy Place we found a woman carrying a bucket of water to her basement home. We followed her down the stairs. She became immensely alarmed and, screaming, slammed the door in our faces. On

Mount Street, we knocked at two doors; when they saw Harney's uniform they swore at him and shut the door. We found refuge in the little church at the end of the street—and there we sat, breathing heavily, trying to determine our next move. Simultaneously, Harney and I took out our watches—almost two o'clock.

Harney said, "It'll be dark at six; we'll stay here until then."

As I nodded, still short of breath, we heard a fearful noise, followed by another, and another.

"Artillery!" said Harney.

Time would tell us that the authorities had sent a gunboat up the river Liffey, and it had begun to shell the center of the city.

We barred the door of the church from the inside and stayed there until darkness fell. Nobody troubled us. We both slept, taking it in turns; in sleep, Harney's face returned to boyhood. When he woke, he might have been recovering from a country walk.

"Do you think," he asked me with a grin, "that God will mind if I wash my face in holy water?" and he went to the baptismal font and scrubbed his face vigorously; I followed suit.

Harney planned, he had said, to get to Boland's Mill; we could reach it in about ten minutes, and he believed that we had lanes enough to hide us.

Once again he asked me to go home to Tipperary: "You might get killed."

And once again I refused, saying, "So might you."

Our journey to Boland's Mill became a haphazard thing of slinking in the shadows of lanes and running in bursts across wide streets. I think that we were fired on once, but we saw no concentration of soldiers anywhere. We could tell from the light in the sky that a great part of the city was aflame.

Harney led, looking back for me at every stage. Our last move took us from a street, down steps to the canal bank, and we ran by the water, in darkness and mud, not knowing where we were going but seeing the hulk of the mill ahead. As we stopped under a bridge, trying to divine our best way forward, a huge searchlight illuminated the mill building.

"They've surrounded it," said Harney.

"Which means," I said, "that we can't get in."

But we did. Harney knew that along the canal wall, beneath the surface of the water, ran a shelf of stone. I lowered him until his feet found
it; the canal water came up to his breastbone. He crouched to show me
how we would travel, and we walked along that stone shelf, doubled so
low that my face touched the cold, slimy water many times.

The mill had been built to the canal, for the easy carriage of goods.
We could hear soldiers' voices not more than a few yards away, but they
were not looking for two men sidling like crabs under cover of the canal
wall; they were more likely watching for besieged rebels trying to break
out.

And "besieged" is how we found the place; the canal left us close to a
double door for loading boats, at which no sign of life could be detected.
Now and again, a shot went over our heads as we squatted, trying to figure out where we could break in while the soldiers fired randomly at the
mill. Harney rose to the challenge, crept forward along the canal's shelf,
and soon we tumbled onto some kind of high platform, a dock for loading. Judging from the random army gunfire, we had reached the blind
side of the mill.

There we lay for several minutes, recovering. Soon, I crawled along
the wooden floor of the dock, followed Harney up some kind of steep
stairs to a door, and found myself behind him in a half-lit passageway,
outside a small office.

Far beneath us, in the dim lights of a few candles, spread a remarkable
scene. Men sprawled everywhere—all over tables and long benches, by
the racks and storerooms. Few wore uniforms; most had guns. At windows and by barred doorways, others crouched, weapons at the ready.

I felt as though I were alighting from the sky and looking down on
some extraordinary occasion; I remember the silence, punctuated by distant gunfire; and I remember the way the men not guarding doors and
windows sat in orderly stillness. Some had food; many simply looked
ahead; a few dozed. The dimness made it impossible to gauge the number of people—Harney thought a hundred, I thought fewer.

As we stood there, soaked and now beginning to shiver, the door of
the office beside us opened. An immensely tall man with spectacles

looked at us; I recognized him immediately—I had met him in Bruree, in the house of my dear consumptive patient.

Harney saluted; they shook hands. Harney made an introduction: "Commandant Eamon de Valera."

I said, "I know."

Until Sunday we stayed in the mill, under the command of "Dev," as everyone called him. Men lent us greatcoats until our clothes dried—and then we got drenched all over again when a shell hit a water tank far above our heads. The capacity to fight back from inside was much more limited than I had seen on Northumberland Road. This building restricted opportunities to fire; ammunition supplies had almost run out; and any gunshot from within had begun to draw massive retaliation.

All next day, shells pounded us over and over—and then we learned that de Valera had raised a rebel flag on the building in the hope of diverting fire from the civilian streets of the city farther in. (The strategy had limited success; by Friday the British troop reinforcements had begun to shoot on sight—men, women, and children.)

Those were days of terror—and of no little wonder. Every roof, wall, and foundation shook every minute of every hour, or so it seemed. Men grew old in front of my eyes. I made it my business to speak to many, knowing that I should soon be sifting this astounding time for the purposes of my History. Few admitted to an age of more than twenty-two or so; these boys and young men, from shops and offices and farms, had one thing in common: an imbued and unshakable desire to have their country governed by its own people.

Given my own knowledge of Ireland, I knew the families of many. One told me that I had cured his whooping-cough when he was a baby. Another recalled how I had comforted his grandfather when the gentleman was simply too old to carry on. When the word went around that I healed people, I grew much in demand—but I had no materials and no facilities. I helped as best I could with cleansing and dressing wounds, and for many there was little that I could do.

By Saturday we knew the full desperation of our conditions. We were surrounded on all sides—even from the water. The gunboat that had been shelling the city was now turning its full attention upon us; soon the building would be destroyed around our heads. We had no food; we had desperate wounded; we had bodies.

On Sunday I saw Harney deep in conversation with de Valera, who had not been in the building. Rumor had it that Dev had taken several men and occupied another building nearby, and that thus we were gaining ground. Untrue; and now he and Harney broke away—in agreement, to judge from the nodding of heads.

Moments later, Boland's Mill surrendered. We walked out into the world, ragged, exhausted, and unknowing of what was to come. Would they mow us down with their guns the moment they saw our faces? Not far from me, a young man began to cry, and he pointed ahead; aimed straight at us, and attended by two soldiers, stood a barbarous-looking gun with a belt of bullets feeding into it. I stepped left until I walked beside the young man.

"To get you," I said, "they'll have to get me too."

He calmed down. Up ahead strode de Valera and Harney; within moments Harney disappeared, taken into an army vehicle. I tried to break from our ranks as they took him—he and I had earlier been separated. But a soldier knocked me back into line with the butt of his rifle on my shoulder and I had lost my best friend.

It was the bloodiest of weeks. The heart of Dublin lay in ruins. British artillery pounded it and was answered only by small-arms fire. All the main buildings around the river Liffey were reduced to blackened, smoking hulks.

Boland's Mill held out until the end. The General Post Office had already surrendered, and the Poets' Rising, as it would soon be called for its many poet-soldiers, died fast. Every republican activist who could be found and identified was rounded up and taken into custody. With no moral support except from one another, the rebels were ordered to lay their arms in piles and were marched along the streets, derided by the civilian population.

That night, every rebel aged eighteen and younger was told to go home. The remaining men and women were piled into jails and makeshift detention centers within garrisons across Dublin. Under orders, the army and police then arrested over three thousand people believed to be members of the IRA or Sinn Fein. Most were released within weeks. In the final sifting, just under six hundred men were deported, many of them to a prison camp in Wales called Frongoch.

However, the worst had yet to happen. The rebellion came to an end on the afternoon of Sunday, 30 April. On Tuesday, 2 May, a series of secret trials began—of those whom the British authorities believed to be leaders. No lawyers represented those on trial, and nobody was allowed to speak for them. In any case, not one of the men or women on trial would have pled not guilty.

Fifteen death sentences were handed down, and the executions began. My own father, John Joe Nugent, politically aware during that time, told me he knew nothing of what was going on. When news of the executions broke and when the word got out as to how many men were killed and in what way, the mood of the country changed to one of deep and angered sympathy.

The killings had been grisly. Firing squads of riflemen stood feet away from men who refused to wear blindfolds. Heavy bullets tore them to shreds, and then the officer in charge applied the coup de grâce bullet—to the head. Of them all, the execution of James Connolly drew the most outraged responses. He had been severely wounded in the General Post Office, where he'd commanded the socialist Irish Citizen Army. As he was unable to stand, they executed him in a chair. Thus did the Poets' Rising, observed at first hand by Charles O'Brien, become a success.

The British officer accepting the Boland's Mill surrender singled me out; somebody must have pointed to me. I was told politely to go back where I'd come from, and my insistence that I wanted to find my friend Mr. Joseph Harney carried no weight. As I stood there, a portrait of dishevelment, my clothes in ruins, exhaustion and grime lining my face, I saw Mr. de Valera. Two officers were confronting him, and a conversation was taking place. I walked over to him, but was not allowed to get close. All was confusion; I could hear him trying to argue for the release of his men, saying that if not released, they should be treated as war prisoners.

He gained no advantages for his men—nor for himself; he was summarily led away, accompanied by an armed guard. At that moment, I saw a distinctive young woman, in age not more than a girl, step in front of Mr. de Valera. She had curly blond hair, and her clothes and bearing suggested good family background; she hauled with her a camera apparatus. To a bright magnesium flash—which startled some—she took a photograph of Mr. de Valera. Other photographers stood there too, and many of the "de Valera surrender" photographs became famous all over the world.

The young woman said to me, "Who is he?" and I told her Mr. de Valera's name, and his role in the Mill. Our conversation went on, and thanks to her good offices I was able to recover myself and find a place to sleep. Through her, I was also able to arrange a change of clothing, and eventually I gained some composure after such an extraordinary week. However, I was quite unable to eat for two days, and for a month afterward I found myself trembling many times.

Next morning at ten o'clock, I made my way to Dublin Castle. Some soldiers halted me at barricades, but I was able to persuade them of my neutrality, and on I went. The city lay ruined, with bodies still lying in the streets. I have often heard it said that it is the civilian population that tells the world when a battle has ended. Now I saw the pathetic sight of families peering at corpses, hoping that they would not find a loved one who had died. No corpse that I saw wore a uniform; these dead included old men, young men—who seemed not to have been armed—women, girls, and I saw two small children. I was glad that I had eaten no breakfast.

At Dublin Castle, I asked to see the highest authority in the land. Obviously I did not expect such a wish to be granted; but I did meet a gentleman whose office, when I was shown into it, manifested a significant position. I used my mother's name and connections to introduce my inquiry: I wanted to find Mr. Joseph Harney, from whom I had been separated in the events of the week; he was supposed to travel with me to Tipperary Castle that very night.

The respect that I received was very considerable—until I returned, as bidden, at four o'clock that afternoon. The same gentleman met me in the hallway of Dublin Castle and told me that my friend—"Harney," as he called him—was in jail in a rebel uniform, and would be court-martialed sometime in the coming week. By exerting considerable pressure, I was able to establish that Harney had been sent to Kilmainham Jail, and I went there forthwith.

Nobody would allow me to see Harney. Nor would they confirm his presence there. I waited a distance away from the prison, trying to make myself as discreet as possible. At six o'clock, in the dusk, some warders appeared, their day's work over. I followed two of them to a public house, where, presently, I joined them. After some drinks I learned that all the prisoners would be tried within the week. When I asked what sentences might be expected, one man drew his hand like a knife across his throat.

Next morning, some banks opened and some city shops. I presented a letter of credit and bought myself some clothes; then I paid a call on Mr. Yeats. He accepted my profuse apologies for arriving unannounced and seemed pleased to see me. During some excellent tea—which he himself made—he plied me with questions regarding Tipperary Castle, and clapped his hands in delight at my progress reports.

Then we discussed the events of the past week, and I described to him some of what I had seen on Northumberland Road. We commiserated regarding the awfulness of it all—and I told him that my treasured friend and colleague had been caught up in all this. Mr. Yeats knew the gentleman at Dublin Castle, and had been a dinner guest at his house; he now gave me a letter, which he read before he sealed. After an introductory remark, the letter said, "Mr. O'Brien, with whom I understand you are already acquainted, has excellent—and truly non-political—reasons for requiring the safe conduct of his colleague Mr. Joseph Harney. I would deem it a personal favor if you would do all in your power to assist."

At Dublin Castle, they would not allow me to see the gentleman—but the name of Mr. Yeats got the letter accepted. I waited outside. At one o'clock, the gentleman in question appeared, to take his lunchtime walk. I allowed him to see me walking along Dame Street toward the castle, and when he did not turn away as he saw me, I knew that Mr. Yeats had gained some purchase.

We greeted politely and he said, "An inquiry has gone through at a high level. That is all I can say."

I replied, "Thank you. And may I deliver in person Mr. Yeats's warmest compliments." I added, as well, an invitation to see the work in progress at the castle, and we parted as gentlemen. I never saw him again; and I did not find Harney.

All week I haunted Dublin Castle and Kilmainham Jail. Dreadful word began to seep through of unjust trials and frightful executions. Ten men had been shot, we heard, then twenty, thirty, fifty—they were killing them hour upon hour. The rumors grew frantic. In the earliest morning light I went and stood at the prison walls. Others had gathered, small, sad bunches of people, women in black, praying aloud. We winced, each one of us, and we shuddered as we heard the volleys of shots from behind the walls.

At last I had nothing left to do but go back to Tipperary. I made a plan to go home by train on Friday, stay with my parents, and on Saturday return to the castle. On Sunday I would travel to Urlingford and meet Joseph's family.

That plan never fell into place. I went home as planned, and Mother waited at the station. When I showed surprise to see her, she told me that she had met every train from Dublin since Tuesday, the day on which they first heard news of the rebellion. I took the reins and we talked and I told her of Harney and what had happened; I did not include details of my time in the house on Northumberland Road.

When we neared home, Mother said, "We must go to the castle first."

I know every line on my mother's face; I hear every nuance of her voice.

"What has happened?"

"It's best to let you see."

From the avenue all seemed normal. And from the Long Terrace all seemed normal—except that no workman could be seen, and many liked to work on after the day's end. We walked to the main door, which stood open.

"Go inside," she said.

The castle interior had been attacked with fire. Where the recovered paneling had so recently been shining, there spread wide holes whose edges still smoldered a little. Not all of the timbers had burned through. One of the two new doors had been all but destroyed; the other had not caught fire.

"April?" I said—and betrayed my concern, which neared panic.

"Safe," said Mother. "She received some burns on the hands and arms trying to put out the fire."

"Serious burns?"

"No. And nobody else was injured. But—everybody has fled."

Mother told me the story. On Wednesday morning, as I witnessed the extraordinary gun-battle in Northumberland Road, three armed and masked men came to the castle. They ordered everybody out of the building—including April and such workers and craftsmen as were there—and said that they were restoring this castle and all in it to the land whence it sprang. And they announced that anyone working on this castle henceforth would be shot on sight. One of the raiders could then be seen spreading some flammable liquid all over the ballroom floor, and then the main hall. He lit it and the armed men departed. Amid much fear, the workers drifted away. Only two people would go into the flames with April—the Master Stonemason and the Master Carpenter.

7

Charles, though exhausted, describes how he "reached for vigor and energy." The burning, now two days past, had done all the damage it was going to do. He needed to establish the human damage. Helen, the bad-tempered housekeeper, emerged from the kitchen, and Charles's text says that he "allowed her to speak the rage that everybody felt."

When she had calmed down, she told him that April had gone to Mrs. Moore's. The Italians might not yet have left the country, even though they'd threatened to do so. Mr. Higgins and Mr. Mulberry had stayed in their lodgings in the village. The two of them had come up to the castle together each morning. They had secured the damaged areas against collapse and told Helen that they awaited "further orders."

My oppression at the loss of my beloved Harney now had this new weight added—but my thoughts fell quickly into a straight order, which I proceeded to follow.

The main depredation had been directed at the fresh repairs, as though the arsonists sought to destroy the very principle under which we had been laboring—the restoration of a former glory. They had splashed with oil the beautiful ancient panels in the hall and then held matches or flaming rags to them. This achieved no more than wide scorch marks across the painted details, the destruction of one full panel, and half of another door; evidently they had hoped that when the rest caught fire, the flames from the wood in the panels would add ferocity to the fire.

As I walked through the house, their method became evident to me. Leisurely in their vileness, they had taken enough time to set several fires here and there. As well as the hall they had attacked the ballroom, the library, the dining-rooms, and the three drawing-rooms. In each place, they had heaped piles of books and chairs together on the floor, then doused and lit them, hoping that the planks would then come alight too, and thus attack the fabric of the house. As in the hall, many of the fires had been set along the walls, also in the hope that the flames would lick up along the panels and spread.

But they seem to have known little about setting such fires—they had even tried to start one on the marble of the Grand Staircase, where it had simply died. I did not yet know enough about marble to tell whether it had been damaged permanently, but the snow-white Carrara balusters along one flight of steps had blackened entirely; and two wooden props that the Marchettis, with Mr. Higgins's help, had placed under a marble parapet for temporary support had all but burned through, and the long slab leaned perilously.

The raiders had not continued upstairs; all their efforts had been aimed at the main floor. The worst damage occurred in the Library, where three stacks of books had burned completely through. Again, we had good fortune here; most of the books had heirloom status and the leather bindings had prevented them from blazing—that is to say, the leather halted the flames and thus obstructed a larger conflagration. That would indeed have threatened the entire house, but it was contained within a series of dozens of little fires.

We had been fortunate (if I may use such a word about an attack) in that the castle's original sturdiness resisted the lick of the flames. Indeed, in one section, where an old carved column rose from floor to ceiling as an ornamental support for the library shelves, the flames had succeeded only in making a little blackening.

I went down to the cellars; no fire had penetrated there. In fact, anybody entering the cellars from the western doors—that is from the butler's pantry—would never have known that there had been a fire in the house. Only the smell of burning told the story—it hung all over. I have been told that much of the fear related to a house on fire comes from the sense of smell; this odor permeated every place and, I thought, every object. The old window hangings now reeked of it, as did the remaining books on the library shelves—what should we do with those? They reeked too; perhaps the airing of the coming summer days would help, or the frosts of winter.

I stood in the Great Hall, looking through the north and south windows. On this spring day, with its gently sailing white clouds, I allowed myself to breathe for a moment. In the past, I should have shrunk with the inward moan of a querulous child asking self-piteously, "Why me?" Now I gave a grim smile, and commented to myself on the force and pace of my life. Mount Street, Boland's Mill, Dublin Castle, Kilmainham Jail—no more momentous week could I ever have spent, and nothing in my life had prepared me for it. Then I began to assemble my priorities—though my heart still ached for Harney.

First, I would take Mother home; then I would tackle a horse from the farm, ride over to Knocklong, and find April at Mrs. Moore's house. I would hear her plans, and then I would ride back to the castle and find my workers. How I needed Harney now; he would have taken such efficient charge over so much—above all, his local intelligence would have set the measure of how seriously we must consider the threats that the arsonists made. In this, I was as a blind and deaf man; other than Harney, I knew nobody in the republican movement, or where to find them.

April, when I saw her, proved admirable; as with Helen, anger had taken her through the difficulty. The Moore house, a fine, gray stone building with tall windows, sits in trees at the end of a curving avenue. One may observe the house from the road and, as I approached, I could see two ladies standing in the doorway, their faces turned to the last of the sun. Even from a distance of several hundred yards, April was easily identified; beside her stood little raven-haired, plump Mrs. Moore.

The bandages shocked me, and I did not trouble to hide it. April's hands, including all the fingers, wore white swathes to the elbow; her face had suffered no burns. Her hair, uncovered at the time, had singe marks, and the very lowest reaches had been burned; she had managed to beat out the flames before they reached her neck. In doing so, her palms had been burned—and before that, her arms and the backs of her hands had suffered when she'd tried to save books in the Library.

When I questioned her as to the time she'd spent among the flames, she diverted me and talked about the mason and the carpenter and their heroics. Neither man, fortunately, had received any burning, nor damage of any kind, other than distress at the vandalism to their work. I released the anger in her by asking about the arsonists—and in doing so heard the details that I fully expected.

"Three of them came," she said, "and they felt no necessity to wear masks or disguises. One of them is easily recognized—he has a finger missing."

I asked, "What exactly did they say? Helen says they threatened everybody."

"Helen rushed at them; she hit one, and kicked another until I pulled her back."

My view of our housekeeper took another positive leap.

"Do you believe their threats?"

"They're scum! Cowards! I'm certain they knew that you had gone away. How did they know that? And I'm certain that they would never have come near the place had you been there. How is Harney?"

"I have much to tell," I said. "But I want to see those burns."

Somewhat to my surprise, she readily agreed to let Mrs. Moore and me unbandage her hands and arms. Again, I did not hide my response; she had been burned badly. One burn had a wide black edge—a charring, which is the worst sign of all; I feared permanent scarring. Mrs. Moore told me that they had put an ointment of chamomile leaves on the burns, but it seemed to have had no effect. We repaired to a landing upstairs, and I asked Mrs. Moore to have her housekeeper fetch me a pan, some spoons, buttermilk, three eggs, and some honey.

It did not take long to bring the mixture together. I painted it gently on April's arms and hands; she never flinched, though I observed tears in her eyes when I had finished.

"Now comes the harder part," I told her. "You must sit motionless—

or certainly as still as you can—for the next three hours, until I take this off."

As someone who spends her life in perpetual motion, she frowned, but agreed. Mrs. Moore invited me to stay the night, as darkness would soon fall. I accepted, out of weariness as much as anything else—I had scarcely slept all week, and the train in the morning had been most uncomfortably packed with people fleeing Dublin. It seems that every person in Dublin has a country cousin.

Three hours later, in advance of dinner, I removed the loose cheese-cloth with which I had covered April's hands and arms. Touching her filled me with a rare kind of joy, notwithstanding the circumstances, and for the first time I began to feel freedom from the burden of Euclid's death, and the loss of him. To my surprise, I could already report progress, in that the black charring had reduced. April saw this too, but said nothing—she did cast a significant glance at Mrs. Moore, who smiled. In those days I watched for any and every sign of April's approval.

At dinner I sat on one side of her; Mrs. Moore sat on the other, and we helped to manipulate food to her fork. Finally, she gave up and began to use a spoon. My chief advice had to do with preventing the blisters from bursting. From across the table, Dan Moore, whom I had never before met, commiserated in a gentle and altogether decent way. We talked not at all of my week's adventures; when asked about Harney, I side-stepped. Nor did I offer any details about Dublin; I indicated that the city had been closed to all but the military.

When it came to bedtime, I surprised them.

"There will be no more dressings," I said. "Tomorrow morning, I will again paint the burns with egg white, honey, and buttermilk. When I have gone, peel it off after three hours and make sure that the skin gets air. Keep a towel nearby. If any blister should break, cover the mark with a thin layer of honey"—and I demonstrated. "But tonight you must, I fear, sleep with your arms thus." I raised my arms above my head, and everybody laughed.

Next morning, after attending to my new patient, I set out for home. We made an arrangement that April should return to Tipperary when she felt ready—and that I would come to Knocklong again in the meantime.

Our parting had friendliness and humor in it, although the gratitude for my care was expressed solely by Mrs. Moore—whose husband then walked with me to the gate.

"Will you be calling on the constabulary?"

I said, "I don't know. Last night, when I awoke for a time, I tried to gauge the best measure."

"Awkward," he said. "You're supposed to tell them—but that's probably more dangerous."

"What would you do?" I asked him.

"I'd find 'em and shoot 'em. One at a time. That'd stop the rest of 'em."

Charles O'Brien saw more of the Easter Rising than most people in Ireland. It never turned into a countrywide rebellion. That first weekend, some units of republicans—the "Volunteers"—reported for duty here and there throughout the country. But they met, hung around, and disbanded. They had all been waiting months for something to happen. It was on. It was off. It was on again, it was off again. Finally, the main action took place only in Dublin, because the commanders there defied general orders and set out on their own.

A minuscule percentage of the population supported the republicans. The country had become so wedded to the promise of Home Rule that Irishmen equally passionate in that cause threatened to bear arms against the Volunteers.

When it became clear that an armed rebellion was under way, the British authorities declared martial law. Then they used it to license atrocities. In the days and weeks after the Rising, soldiers shot people at sight in the streets of Dublin. Old and young civilians, totally innocent of all rebel connection, were simply mown down.

In response to this barbarism, Irish opinion began to turn, especially in the rural counties. Then came the deaths of the fifteen leaders—and the tide turned completely. Trying to keep officially silent on the names and numbers of the executed had proven futile. There's no such thing as a secret in Ireland; the dam leaked fast, with all the details. James Connolly, shot in his pajamas, in a wheelchair, was the last straw. The country began to boil.

Day after day, as a horrified people raced to the morning newspapers, Charles waited to hear whether the name of his friend had been included. By the middle of May, London knew, from Irish and international reaction, that it had made an error. It had given Ireland a bunch of martyrs. And Charles had not as yet found Joseph Harney's name among them.

As to the arson at Tipperary Castle, it had no connection to Easter Week; that, presumably, was the cover for the operation. And it belonged in no republican policy of that time. But it still drove stakes of fear into the hearts of the Anglo-Irish. They assumed that the attack on April Somerville's estate would prove part of a nationwide movement against them.

In the years just ahead, their apprehensions would turn out to be somewhat correct. A couple of hundred mansions were gutted by deliberate fires—reprisals to military outrages. By then, the arsonists were seen as freedom fighters, and their activities became the War of Independence.

And that guerrilla campaign, fought in fields, on riverbanks and mountainsides, from behind ditches, on bicycles, along village streets— that was the fire that spread from the General Post Office in Dublin and the horrific execution yard in Kilmainham Jail to every county and parish on the island.

Deliveries of any sort to the castle were a leisurely business—we had a long avenue, and for the driver or carrier there was much to see at the end of it. We received many callers every day but, in the days after I returned, I awaited nobody so eagerly as the bearer of mail. I watched all day—we could see visitors coming from afar; and the next best thing to seeing Harney would be the arrival of a letter telling me that he was safe. The newspapers had not included his name among those executed, but I refused to depend upon that. Despite Father's faith over the many years of my childhood, I did not believe that I should ever reliably uncover the most crucial personal information in the pages of any journal. (Thus did my attitude change after the incident with Mr. Parnell.)

Therefore, when I'd left Dublin, I'd implored the young photographer whom I had met outside Boland's Mill to gather news of all those in Kilmainham Jail—the living and the dead—and send it to me in a letter. She gladly agreed to do so and refused all compensation that I offered, with a distinctive gesture at the memory of which I now smile: she turned her face away playfully, like a child being disobedient. True to her word, she faithfully gained access to all that I needed—and did so, I gathered, by the expedient of wishing to photograph the prison governor. As pretty as one of her own pictures, she soon teased from him the names of the executed men and wrote them to me.

My eye, when I opened that letter, raced down the page, skipping from name to name: Eamonn Ceannt, Thomas Clarke, Con Colbert, James Connolly, Edward Daly, Sean Heuston, Thomas Kent, John MacBride, Sean MacDiarmada, Thomas MacDonagh, Michael Mallin, Michael O'Hanrahan, Patrick Pearse, William Pearse, Joseph Plunkett. I never stopped to count; I knew when I had reached the number of fifteen, and—such joy!—no trace of Harney's name. The photographer told me in her letter that "there are to be no more executions; all others arrested are either being freed or taken to prison camps, mostly in England and Wales, where they will be held, it is said, in the interests of public safety."

Just before the letter arrived, I had been prizing away a charred piece of wood from a library shelf; now I blackened my own face as my hands wiped my tears: Harney must be alive! I sent Helen to Ardobreen with the good news, and she came back with a note from Mother: "He had too much life in him to die now." That morning I knew that, sooner or later, he would come home; sooner or later I would see him again. Twice more that day I found myself close to tears—of relief, now, as I no longer had to imagine Harney, with that quick, restless mind, that endless curiosity, facing a firing squad.

Charles described my mother as I knew her. Her blond curls went slowly white. And all her life she had that sweet, playful way of turning away her face like a child when she didn't wish to accept a gift or a compliment.

Reading his description of her thrilled me. It also gave me pause. When she told me about the neighbor whose head she'd held up after he accidentally shot himself, she also said, "Don't mention this to your father."

I, of course, said, "Why?"—as small boys do.

She said, "I'll tell you one day."

And she did. In my teenage years I asked her whether many boys had pursued her when she was young. She said there was only one that she had ever liked. From her description, it must have been Charles O'Brien. She said he was big and generous, with what she called "the manners of a gentleman"—always important to her.

I said, "What happened to him?"

My mother laughed a little and replied, "His heart wasn't available. But your father has never known that he existed. I've never talked about him."

As this must also be considered a History of what has impressed me, I shall add a brief account here of my Master Carpenter, an Englishman of Italian origins, Mr. Mulberry. He stands six feet tall, as lean as one of the planks he has planed. His brown eyes take in every knot and gnarl; he runs his hands over a piece of wood as a mother runs a hand over her child's face. "Measure twice, cut once," he says; and he measures with more fuss than a seamstress, cuts with more care than a surgeon. No problem can defeat him; he surmounts and surpasses. His love for his work, his dedication to it, his zeal for the beauty that he can wrest from wood—these have as much importance to him as faith to a priest, beauty to a girl.

Mr. Mulberry speaks little, has a liking for humor, protects his tools like a bear her cubs, thinks before he acts—and then acts splendidly. When we first met (I received an introduction to him through Lady Mollie Carew) and he journeyed to the castle (at my expense) for our interview, I thought we should not be friends. He sat in my "office" at the castle and asked penetrating questions: Did they originally use local timber and are there trees still standing in that wood? Who knows what glue was used? How far is the castle from the coast? (In other words, where is the nearest shipwright?)

I answered as best I could, and Mr. Mulberry, with no expression on his face, wrote all my answers in his notebook. It was easy to divine his line of thought; this was restoration, and he wished to use original materials or those related to them, and he knew that shipwrights have the best resources of all who work with timber.

When he had finished his rigorous examination, he put his notebook away and stood to his feet. He said, "I will take the job, but when it comes to the carpentry, everybody has to do what I tell them. Understood?"

He said "Understood?" often, and I came to know that he used it when matters felt difficult to him.

Of all the people who worked on the castle, I watched Mr. Mulberry and Mr. Higgins most closely, as I felt that they had most to teach me. Chalk and cheese though they seemed, they became the firmest of friends, and I believed that their closeness, which lasted all their lives thereafter, was born of the shared principle that work must always be superb. Those men had earned the title "Master"; they believed deeply in their own work, they spoke a pride in the apprenticeship they had served—with much praise for the men who'd taught them—and, if a little impatiently at times, they willingly instructed those around them.

Their merit became evident when I returned from seeing April at Knocklong. I debated with myself whether I should ride on past our gates to the village and find them. Instead, I decided to go to the castle first and seek them later. I need not have paused to think; both men awaited me. They had already ascertained through the drumbeat of village talk that I had returned from Dublin.

I walked with them in and out of the damaged rooms, and through their eyes I saw the charred, blackened expanses with a new disgust. Their anger suffused their faces; both men flushed quite red, and their

concern peaked their eyebrows, furrowed their foreheads. When we had
completed our tour, I sought to reduce that anger and change it to energy; I asked them where we should begin. Sure enough, the inquiry set
them to work, and by two o'clock we had a plan: cleansing, scraping, ordering new materials, and then reconstruction.

Next, we addressed our greater difficulty; as we all agreed, it was the
finding of workers who would return, or begin anew. This debate went on
for some time, and we resolved it in this way: I would inquire of my father's farmhands, find names and nominations; they would reach out to
such of their workmen as they could find. They had my permission to say
that from now on the castle would be guarded with guns, day and night.
Furthermore—and here I lied—I had taken the precaution, I told them,
of speaking to republican connections in Dublin, where I had gone to
seek Harney, and they had assured me of protection, should I ever need it.

Soon, matters improved further. When it became known, through
rumor and reluctant officialdom, that the activists who had been arrested
after Easter Week had been taken to prison camps in England and Wales,
it naturally followed that they must be allowed to receive letters. I established that Harney had been taken to the north of Wales, and I wrote him
a long, conversational letter, telling him news of the castle and its troubles
and how we were bringing everything under control again. As I prepared
the envelope, Helen the housekeeper told me that her brother, Eddie, had
also been taken there. I added a P.S. asking Harney to find him.

By the end of the summer, we had all but cleansed the fire damage
and were ready to repair it. No arsonist came back to trouble us, and I believe that I understand the reason. In my letter to Harney, I had described the burning, told him what the raiders had said, and worried for
the safety of April—and for Helen. In not so many words, I wanted to
give Harney as much emboldening as possible—not that he ever needed
any—to help us from afar.

And then, late in the year, under a December sky of milky primrose
light, came a wonderful day—though, in truth, a day of mixed fortunes.
Helen, not a creature who should contemplate a speed greater than a
saunter, came puffing up the Long Terrace to me, almost running, almost
shouting.

"Oh, sir, oh, sir"—and she had not enough breath to finish.

"Easy, Helen. Take your time"—but her force so shook the air around us that all the workers stopped to look.

"Sir, they're here, they're here!" she cried and burst into tears. "Eddie's home, and Mr. Harney's with him, sir, they're *here.*"

It became my turn to run—and I found Harney in the Ballroom, looking all around him.

I said, as though to a stranger, "May I help you, sir?"

He laughed and spun around.

"The minute I turn my back," he said, "everything falls apart."

We did not embrace, we did not shake hands; that was not our way. The tears in our eyes did not fall; as they evaporated, I began to show him what had been damaged. He shook his head over and over.

"I don't understand it," he said. "I simply don't understand it. But—it hasn't happened since?"

His question contained more than a little severity; I had calculated accurately by writing to him.

As we walked, we talked; he told me about the camp. It had contained Germans captured in the war, and when he'd heard that he and the other Irish republicans were being sent there, he'd felt great relief; he'd known then that they would have prisoner-of-war status.

I asked, "Did you travel alone today?"

"No. We came in at Cork, and now I have to go on home."

As he spoke, two other men appeared, and he added, "These were my traveling companions."

One, I deduced, must be the brother of Helen—he had the same barrel shape, round head, and pug nose; the other was our erstwhile visitor and my courtroom interrogator, Mr. Noonan, who, as he walked toward us, was deep in laughing conversation with April—which was how my fortunes grew mixed that day and afterward.

Old IRA men in Tipperary often stated, "Frongoch freed us." The saying had a double edge. First you were expected to understand that they had been released from the camp. But what they really meant was that Frongoch bred the guerrillas who took up where Easter Week left off. More than seventeen hundred men were sent there. Most had some connection to the idea of armed rebellion—and those who didn't soon caught on.

Inside the camp—later nicknamed "Sinn Fein's University"—they created a regime. The teachers among them set up classes, with much history and politics. Their intense worship already had a zealous Catholic base. They spent hours every day exercising; they drilled like soldiers on a barracks square.

Most crucially, they heard military theory. They acknowledged the central fact that had been driven home during Easter Week: they had no chance whatsoever against a standing army of the size and firepower available to Britain. But they did have assets that might prove invincible. They had a countryside in which thousands of men could hide, and an indigenous population now sympathetic enough to hide them.

So, in Frongoch, they agreed upon a style of warfare that we Irish subsequently claimed to have invented—the rural guerrilla. With variations, they drew up a strategy that would be called "Flying Columns." Small active units—perhaps no more than a dozen men in any one of them—would be drawn from as many parishes and villages across the country as they could muster. With basic arms, such as rifles, handguns, and, where it could be managed, a machine gun, they would attack local garrisons and ambush military transports.

This strategy became famous as a means of empowering the powerless. Some historians claim that Chairman Mao emulated it, as well as the Vietcong. Many agree that it defined the French Resistance, a claim supported by the fact that the word "maquis," which the French called themselves, means scrub or scrubland—from which the *maquisards* materialized to attack German convoys.

Among the Irish, its chief proponent became the revolution's—and the country's—greatest hero of all time. He taught his guerrilla tactics in Frongoch, when he came out he began to organize it, and later he led it. His name was Michael Collins—and he was the next visitor to Tipperary Castle. Later that week, he came looking for Harney. Incidentally,

Charles never describes whether Dermot Noonan stayed on, whether he
ate a meal at the castle, or when he left.

I walked with Harney to the main gate; he took my bicycle and would
"report back for duty," he told me, "next Monday, the first of January. It's
a new week, a new year, and a new era." I watched until he rode out of
sight; few pleasures in life have been greater than seeing Harney safe and
well after all he had been through. He did not look thinner or plumper,
he did not require a haircut or a shave—he looked exactly the same.

When I asked if the incarceration had affected him, he said, "There
were people who made it good." One of those people arrived at the castle on Friday the 29th of December.

I did not know who he was—but I knew from the moment I saw him
that he was remarkable. He alighted from a motor-car which stopped
halfway up the avenue, at a place where it is wide enough for a large,
wheeled vehicle to turn around. Wearing a gray homburg hat and a
gabardine coat, he walked quickly. Work at the castle had eased down a
little; I had given many of our workers some days of holiday, on account
of inclement weather and so that they might enjoy Christmas—and thus
I alone saw him arrive; I stood in the now splendid main doorway.

He walked straight to me and held out his hand.

"Mr. O'Brien"—a statement, not a question.

I said, "Yes," and he said, "My name is Mick Collins and I'm looking
for Joe Harney."

"He went to see his family in Urlingford. He'll be back here on Monday."

Collins looked past me and all around. "So this is the castle?"

"You know about it?"

"Joe talked about it all the time. I teased him about it—keeping alive
the imperial past."

He laughed, and I said, "Is that what you believe?"

"May I see the place?"

He stood about five feet ten inches, a very handsome fellow, quick of speech, a Cork accent. As we walked, he looked at the rooms minutely—and I surveyed him.

Back in the hallway, he asked, "Is the woman who owns it here?"

I shook my head. April had gone to visit my mother; they had become friends, and tried to meet frequently.

"Well," he said, looking around. "I have two thoughts, and they're both right. On the one hand, this place was built on the backs of abused tenants, whose unjust rents paid for it. On the other hand, it might be owned by foreigners, but we're the ones who built it. Irish skill, labor, and genius built this place." He pointed to the stucco fruit clusters on the injured cornices. "See them? I bet they're Stapletons. Not an Italian name, nor a French one, but Stapleton. An Irishman."

I said, "I'm very aware of all that—it's one of the things I like about my job."

"Well, it'll all be yours one day."

I shook my head. "No. Not at all."

Long ago, I had begun refusing that hope, stamping down that aspiration.

"Joe Harney says you're going to marry this woman here. He says it's like watching two stars spinning around each other."

I said, firmly, "Mr. Collins, that will not occur."

He walked away from me and came back again.

"Come here to me," he said.

To my astonishment, he grabbed my forearms and began to wrestle with me. Such strength! He was laughing, and I got over my surprise, went along with it, and laughed also; we wrestled and tugged, hauled and heaved all around the castle hall, that big echoing place and not a soul to see us. Finally, I gripped his hands behind him in a way that he could not break and I heard myself say like a schoolboy, "Give in."

"Never!"

"Give in."

"No."

"Give in," I said, "or it's the floor for you."

He laughed, his arms sagged, I let go, he turned around, and we shook hands.

"Mr. O'Brien, can you fire a gun?"

"Why do you ask?"

"You can guess."

I shook my head. "No. Nor will I."

Michael Collins said, "I must go; I have a man waiting for me."

"But you haven't had a drink or a bite to eat!"

He said, "There'll be other times."

And there were other times, many other times, and I relished them all, no matter what difficulty accompanied them, and in common with the rest of the country I wept on the day he died. He was twenty-six years and two months old the day I first met him; I shall always be glad of that moment, overjoyed that I subsequently saw him so often, and deeply sad that I shall never meet him again.

Michael Collins became a walking legend, a living myth. If he had actually met all the people who said they knew him, he would never have got anything done; he'd have been shaking hands all day, every day. But my own father did meet him; he knew him through a cousin married to one of Collins's cousins.

My father didn't like Collins. He said that Collins "scared" him—although he did acknowledge the legendary coolness of nerve, said to be Collins's chief feature. And when I was a boy, my father told me a story of his own days as a young railway clerk in Dublin, where he worked for some months of 1920.

One summer night, in Sackville (now O'Connell) Street, he ran into a military cordon. He had to wait behind the barricade, as did everybody else. As he stood there, my father saw a man nearby, holding a bicycle. My father told a story well.

"The man saw me, strolled over, rolling the bike, and he said to me, 'You're John Joe Nugent' and immediately put a finger to his own lips, indicating of course that I shouldn't reply, 'And you're Michael Collins'— which is what I might have done, except that I wouldn't, because he was the most wanted man in Ireland; there was a reward of ten thousand on his head, and big 'Wanted' posters of him everywhere, on every wall in the city.

"Before I could say to him, 'What are you doing here—are you out of your mind and all these soldiers everywhere?' he says to me, 'Would you ever hold this bike for me for a few minutes?' and he handed the handlebars to me. I grabbed them and he walked off toward the buildings where all the soldiers were going in and out like bees in a hive.

"The next minute I saw him, on the steps of the Gresham Hotel, and he was talking to the officer in charge of the military action. They were laughing like old pals, and it was the first time I found out that sweat can flow down from under your arms—it was like two little cool rivers down my sides. And then I saw Collins strolling back toward me, the hat on his head, the gabardine coat on a summer's night.

"He took the bike back from me. 'Thanks, John Joe,' he says, and I says to him, 'In the name of God, are you out of your head? What were you up to?' And he says to me, 'I had to find out what the soldiers were doing.' And he winked at me, and he leaned forward, and he whispered, 'And d'you know what they're doing? They're searching the Gresham Hotel for me.' And off he goes. That was Michael Collins for you. Cool as a lake."

Collins turned Ireland—or, rather, the British authority in Ireland— inside out. After the internment in Wales, he developed in practice what he had taught there in theory. He built guerrilla squadrons all across the country—each county had its Flying Columns. And he assembled other hit squads that devastated British intelligence and killed their agents. He saw Ireland's nosiness and gossip as guerrilla assets—with the right contacts, he could uncover any plan. And in propaganda terms he capitalized upon every British atrocity and reprisal; his supporters reported and published them.

Perhaps his outstanding achievement was his capturing of men's loyalty. Collins assembled his unconventional army in a country where respect for authority was considered close to treachery—because all authority was British. This ran so deep that common cause didn't necessarily guarantee automatic obeying of orders. But Collins's men would have gone through fire for him. As they did, and all their lives—and I met them and spoke to them—they would say with quiet pride, "I was a Collins man myself." There were more than fifteen thousand of them on active duty. All told, he mustered another sixty thousand "helpers" out of a population of three and a half million.

Collins called himself a soldier, not a politician. Yet he took part in the eventual negotiations that brought the War of Independence to an end. Then we shot him, his own countrymen, his political rivals, in the civil war that followed.

My parents often spoke of "the day Michael Collins died." Both had occasion to be out of the house, and traveling. My father got off a train in Limerick and saw people kneeling on the streets, weeping. Three counties away, in Kilkenny, different city, different province, my mother saw the same. Each said afterward that they knew, without asking, what had happened.

In the summer of 1917, with the work fairly bustling onward at the castle, and an army of human ants fetching and carrying and toiling, April asked me to take her on a tour. By now I had learned to drive the motorcar, and so had she. Her arms had healed wonderfully, and when she had come back to the castle, in early summer 1916, Mrs. Moore had come too. Together, we'd kept bathing the burns with egg whites, honey, and buttermilk, and when the new skin grew back, we saw no scars of any kind.

However, for a period of more than three weeks in July, April took to her bed with a curious but strong influenza, which interfered with her breathing. I feared tuberculosis. Our wonderful predecessor at Ardobreen, the oft-naked Captain Ferguson, had planted eucalyptus in many varieties, and I filled bowls with their crushed and pounded leaves, poured boiling water upon them, and steamed their essence in April's bedroom. Slowly she recovered; but for some weeks she remained frail and scarcely moved out of doors.

The tour that she had requested took us to six Great Houses. She had written ahead to each, and had previously known most of them through either Dan and Katherine Moore or the Somervilles. All replied, all invited us to stay, and we set out on an itinerary that would last about eight days.

We had glorious weather. I loved driving the Dunhill, and we took Jerry Hallinan, the mechanic, with us; he sat behind on the high, overhanging seat as we sped along the road. Sometimes, though not every day, we saw another car, and we always halted on the roadway to talk and compare experiences. And when we stopped in a village or town for lunch, we were immediately surrounded by people of great curiosity and interest; Jerry enjoyed being the main actor in this little drama as he explained the wonders of the engine.

Our tour took us to three counties; we paid one visit in Waterford, two in the county Cork, two in Limerick, and one in the North Riding of Tipperary. When she first asked me to accompany her, April also gave me the reason. She said that she wanted to reassure the other owners of houses such as Tipperary of her intentions to stay and play a full part in the life of her estate and of her new country.

"It is, after all, the land of my ancestors," she said.

Although I suspected that she also wanted some education in how to run a Great House, I made no comment. Since her return to full health, her zeal toward the castle had not diminished, as I sometimes feared it understandably might have done. Instead, it had redoubled. She now flung herself even more intensively into every task in the place, and Harney remarked to me more than once on her energy, and her boundless interest in every aspect. We admired her greatly for it, and liked to be surprised by her, as we were when we first witnessed this city girl's—this *English* girl's—capacity for understanding how we might stock the fields with cattle and sheep.

She came to every fair and market with us, as we slowly bought herds and flocks. She it was who engaged both of our stock managers—the cattleman and the sheepman. She personally took over all the establishment and management of the piggeries, and she meant, she said, "to be feeding a thousand pigs by 1920." (The buildings for such farming, the byres and sties, had been in place, we calculated, for at least a century and a half; they had been built solidly and needed little repair.)

We agreed that we would start our tour with the house farthest away, and so we set out for Curraghmore, the estate of the Marquis of Waterford. I had some apprehensions as to such griefs as we might encounter along the way. In the middle of 1917, the news from the war in Europe had already appalled us beyond endurance, and every village and every estate was losing men of every rank and class.

I knew something of Curraghmore; it had been the subject of a Euclid "research" many years before. That winter, he had taken a decision to let his hair grow down over his eyes, then had it cut in a neat fringe that hung like a black curtain upon the bridge of his nose. As ever, he'd rationalized it.

"You have heard what people say—that the eyes are the windows of the soul. I do not wish people to have such easy access to my soul—and besides, I can see their eyes from behind my curtain of hair, which gives me the advantage of them." Whereupon he would flick his heavy fringe.

During the previous summer, in a different phase, he had taken a decision never to smile again—because somebody had told him what a charming smile he possessed. I remain thankful that he abandoned that posture; when Euclid smiled the sun came out.

He had not at that stage decided how he wished to spend his life (in time it would emerge sadly that he had little choice in the matter). If asked, he would reply, "I am a student of mysteries." Indeed, he did spend a very great deal of time studying mysteries of which he had heard or read—and Curraghmore and its legends came into his curriculum.

The Waterford estate lies in as lovely a countryside as you will find in Ireland, with the river Clodagh watering the place. We drove in from the main road at about eleven o'clock in the morning. So sheltered is this private valley of Lord Waterford's that, it is said, the leaves of autumn cling until Christmas. As with Tipperary, the house may not be fully seen until the avenue curves out of the trees and into the open plain. The effect is altogether magnificent.

On account of its windows, the building gleams like a cube of light. If each of the four walls has three stories in height, and each story has seven windows, I add that up to eighty-four windows, many of them ten feet high, all reflecting the sun across Lord Waterford's five and a half thousand acres.

"More land than Tipperary? Hmm," said April, and she frowned.

The sixth Marquis was not present—"war work in London"—and his aunt met us, a large, tall woman of great, imposing style. She wore a red fez.

"You were married to that drunk, weren't you?" she said airily to April as we climbed the steps, and such was Miss Beresford's vivacity that she gave no offense. Some years older than my mother, she looked at me as a butcher looks at a carcass. Turning to April, she raised an eyebrow.

"Convention forbids what I want with *him*," she said, and affected a wicked shudder.

In the hallway of the house, she whistled on her fingers like a huntsman. Three dogs raced down the stairs, and the smallest, a terrier, jumped into her arms from ten feet away. Miss Beresford wore a garment of black that resembled a military tent, which seemed—when I looked closer—covered in dog hairs.

She showed us the high rooms and their paintings and sculptures; and deep, dark furniture, on which sat glorious pieces of crystal glass from the nearby city.

"A Quaker fellow started this glass-making," she said in her lazy drawl. "From England. And there were some brothers, I forget their names. My father gave them all some money, and from time to time they gave us glass. That is all."

We sat to lunch at a long table. She fed the dogs from her plate, and called to a prowling cat, "Get out, you bitch, you're getting nothing here until you start bringing in some mice. Earn your keep!"

We ate and drank a good meal, and even though I had many times been in the houses of my parents' Anglo-Irish friends, and Mother's relations, I had not visited so grand a residence. It took my breath away, as did this strangely magnificent lady, and I observed how calmly she lived this life of wonder. She wore giant rings of crystal in her ears and talked with the ceaselessness of an engine.

It became clear that April found her delightful—and the regard was reciprocated. I might as well not have been there—except for the fact that now and again Miss Beresford would narrow her eyes, look down the table at me, turn to April, nod to indicate me, and lick her lips, saying, "Oooooooooh!" Somehow she accomplished this without the slightest possibility of offending.

She told us a little of the history—how the de la Poers had come here as Norman barons in the twelfth century and by "shrewd judgment" had not only maintained their place in this exquisite valley, but had actually expanded their holdings over the centuries. Then she looked at April.

"Now, did you get Tipperary justly—or did you fool them all?"

April blushed, and I said, "The judge in the case was more than—"

"I didn't ask you, handsome," said Miss Beresford. "I want it from the horse's mouth. The whole country said, my dear, that you stole a great march on us all."

April said, quite calmly, "Then the whole country is wrong. The whole country should find something better to do with its time."

Miss Beresford clapped her hands, and whinnied a laugh so loud that the cat jumped and the dogs grew nervous.

"Oh, that's my girl, that's the spirit. Anyway, whose business is it what your grandmother did? Whoops—the bladder."

She jumped from the table, with the dogs following. When she returned ten minutes later, she did so while loudly calling some savage imprecation down on some unseen person in a room off a corridor somewhere.

I had been looking all around the room—such opulence, such delight. When Miss Beresford sat down, I said, "This truly is a splendid house. It must be the finest house in Ireland."

She looked sideways at me to see whether I flattered her.

"There is a better one," she said, "and you damn know it. Your damsel here owns it."

Miss Beresford addressed April again.

"Work the land. Do not have tenants. I hope you do not intend to. You see—these people, I suffer many as tenants; they are dirty and lazy, and they will let the land rot."

"I mean to farm it all," said April.

"Now—the fire. Did you go and shoot the fellows who tried to burn you out? Only language they understand, you know—they're like the black fellows out in Africa, although thank God they don't go naked here in Ireland. That's the only benefit of a non-tropical climate."

April said, sweetly, "I believe your family has an interesting background."

Jerry Hallinan had regaled us with the story of a curse—in the shape of a dog who haunts Curraghmore, and who has been seen by many, with sworn oaths to that effect.

"Oh, you mean the curses? This place is thoroughly cursed."

Perceiving April's delight, she went on to tell a tale, but not about a phantom hound. The curse came from a widow who lived on the Curraghmore estate. She had one son, her hale and hearty breadwinner. But the young man had a resentment of the landlord and often stole milk, and apples, and straw for his and his mother's bedding. When the widow begged him to desist, he laughed her off. Being a woman of some ethics, she approached the landlord, the first Marquis, and asked him to discipline her son for these petty thefts.

Lord Waterford, however, according to Miss Beresford, his flamboyant descendant, "had a taste for excess, as do I, as do I. And, d'you know—he hung the youth. From the branch of a tree, a beech, I believe. Hung him like a sack of potatoes. Until he was, as you might say, very well-hung indeed." (Again came the great, sky-piercing laugh.)

When the shocked widow remonstrated, he cut at her with his whip—and in return she cursed his "seed, breed, and generation," and said that the next seven Lords of Waterford, beginning with him, would meet an untimely and violent death.

"And it's still up and running, you know," Miss Beresford added. "We've had gunshots, falls from horses, and other misadventures; one Marquis was eaten alive by his own hounds. I think there's only one to go—I lose count. God knows how he'll die."

Suddenly, something new occurred to Miss Beresford and she looked at me.

"Is your father Bernard O'Brien?" As, nodding, I began to reply, she said, "I think I know the fellow." Turning to April she said, "Loved the ladies, loved us."

Miss Beresford rose. "I will show you the rest of the house, dear. You"—she pointed a finger at me—"you can go to the stables."

I trusted that she meant I could inspect the horses, but it also sounded as though she meant that I should sleep there.

We stayed the night, and dined as we had lunched—at the long, long table in whose polished wood I could see my face. Through dinner, Miss Beresford began to fall asleep. Soon a maid arrived and assisted her upstairs, with April following.

I do not believe that we learned much of how a Great House is run—but April and Miss Beresford became true friends, and soon corresponded.

As we drove away from Curraghmore, she asked me, "Miss Beresford—is she what you would call an Irish eccentric?"

I corrected the term: "An Anglo-Irish eccentric."

The weather held up—dreamily golden days, with the hedges full of blossoms, and the wavy fields yellow with grain. We had planned our distances well, and we reached our other appointments in an excellent frame of mind. Soon it became apparent that, by comparison with some others of the Anglo-Irish, Miss Beresford might be counted the sanest person we met.

Lady Argus in Ballydaniel bathed her feet in her own urine every night—"to harden the skin." I wished that she had not chosen to do so in front of her guests. The Mountpatricks fought at dinner—not merely squabbled. Taking exception at some idea of her husband's, Lady Mountpatrick rose from the table and struck him across the head repeatedly with a book. He caught her by the ankle and pulled her to the floor—then resumed eating as his wife crawled back to her chair.

Sir Michael Cross—who had, it was said, a thousand guinea-hens on his lawns—introduced to dinner a young man who wore rouge, and Lady Cross remonstrated, "If Michael's catamite continues to steal from my dressing-room, I'll soon have no rouge left." Raising her eyebrows to April she said, "And if it were only the rouge"—at which point the young man, named Angus, began to cry.

The Shandons came in from a shoot about an hour after we arrived.

Lady Shandon saw us in the great hallway (where we had been much entertained by the disputes of the servants), came running up the steps, and almost fell. It soon became clear that she had been drinking heavily—though not as heavily as her husband.

"I don't know who you are, sir," he said to me. "I don't know the doxy with you, I've never heard of any of you, I haven't been expecting you, and as far as I'm concerned you can bugger off." At dinner he was charm personified: "Now tell me all about yourselves, my dears."

The remaining house had immense charm; Drishane will ever remain uppermost of that tour. Here, in a pretty setting where you can smell the ocean from the window of every room, we were the guests of the distinguished writer Miss Edith Somerville. Her books about Englishmen in Ireland, and their humorous mishaps at the hands of the roguish locals, had become quite famous; April had been devouring them. When we arrived, there was a contest as to which lady wanted to meet the other more, as Miss Somerville had known all about the Limerick Somervilles and the castle lawsuit.

I believe that I have never eaten so much bread and scones. Miss Somerville sat at the head of her dining-table, speaking of her deceased literary collaborator, "Martin Ross"—in real life, her cousin Violet Martin—as though the lady had not died two years earlier, in 1915.

The talk, as it often did, went to the Easter Rising. By now, many people knew that I had been in Dublin that week, and Miss Somerville said that she had wanted to be there herself, "with a gun in my hands—but I consulted my love and she said, 'Yes, but where shall you be each night, and how shall I find you when I come back from where I am?' So I stayed in Drishane."

So naturally did she speak these words that April asked me later whether Miss Somerville did indeed refer to a deceased woman—what had been their relationship? I explained that the literary partnership sprang from what would have been called a "romantic" connection, had one of them been male.

Drishane spoke many things to me—and, I would discover, to April—as to how Tipperary must be run. While reeking of literature and art, the house also sat on a working farm, in whose daily operations Miss

Somerville had immersed herself. In residence and acreage very much smaller than Tipperary, it gave us a feeling of what we might do. Brilliant visitors came often to Drishane. And not just members of the Ascendancy; the literary and artistic lions came too—Mr. Shaw had recently stayed there; Mr. Yeats was soon expected. Painters and dancers and great lawyers sat at Miss Somerville's feet and found her both challenging and adorable.

But it seemed to me that we had an advantage over every other Great House in Ireland, and one that we had not yet, through pressure of restoration works, examined in full. We had a theater.

My heart danced at this thought, but I refrained from raising it with April. All in good time, I thought. As we drove home, I found myself torn between two strong feelings: the excitement of this theatrical prospect and the apprehension lest some attack or other mishap had taken place at the castle. In the event, we found all in excellent shape, we were greeted as returning heroes, no bad news awaited us—and they had begun the restoration of the great mural at the western wall of the Ballroom, my own pet project.

If my mother, Margery Coleman Nugent, had been the photographer in Dublin who met and took care of Charles O'Brien at the end of Easter Week and later sent at least one piece of correspondence to him, why had I never heard of it?

That and other, related thoughts irked me when I first read these recent sections of Charles's text. I stopped reading—and I changed course; I began to rifle my memory. The first haul was as predictable as a trawler's— a lot of mundane stuff and one or two glittering, appetizing items.

You can't call my childhood life in any way remarkable. I would have liked more enchantment. For instance, some children have the feeling that they are adopted. They fancy that they came from Gypsies or some other exotic root. I didn't. My complaint was that our house was so small.

It wasn't large enough for the adventures enjoyed by children in the storybooks I read. We had no back stairs, no dark corridors, no stone-floored, mysterious pantries. I didn't have a paneled wall that might open any night and beckon me to sunny, magical lands. My ceiling was too low for me to fly around the room. The window wasn't a casement—a fairy wind could not blow it open. And anyway, it looked out on a little street, not into a garden dark with laurel bushes, where winding paths led to a glistening lake.

It's not that I didn't try; I did. But I didn't even have wallpaper. The walls were painted a dull beige, with a chocolate-brown door. I wasn't able to do anything about that.

How wonderful it would have been if my father had been carrying Michael Collins's gun. How thrilling if he had been a fire-eater. I'd have settled for a juggler or some mild card tricks.

But my mother had been this quick-off-the-mark photographer whose pictures of Easter Week became famous. Although I wasn't allowed to tell anyone, on account of her reticence, it was thrilling to know it.

I think my delight at her place in history imbued my teaching spirit. Earning a monthly salary in a small country town in Ireland did not keep me from all vividness. And, as her early career rewarded her all through her life, mine prospered similarly; I am proud of the excitement that I generated. To this day, I meet men I taught as boys. They single me out when they see me in town. Sometimes they call to the house with a small gift at Christmas. Always they tell me that they remember things I taught them, and how I made lessons come alive, that there was never anything they didn't understand. Some of them will recite from Dryden or Pope, or one of Shakespeare's sonnets. One man called his champion grey-hound Horatio!

When our only child died (of meningitis—she was four), we were showered with letters. And when my wife, Polly, died a few years later, of cancer, the funeral was half a mile long. That's what teaching gave me—because I put into it my energy and my sense of knowledge's thrill.

So—to summarize again: first I had a weird feeling that I belonged to these pages or they belonged to me, or should so. And then, at the shooting of Charles, I realized that I truly did have a natural connection to this text. The details of 1916 confirmed it; I simply did not know how deep the involvement went.

Nor did I know—or for a moment anticipate—that it went even deeper to April Burke than to Charles O'Brien.

As I read that description of my mother, and as I read that she had written to Charles, my searches intensified. No stone, I told myself, would not be turned; no stream would not be sourced. That's how I came to see the acres of the Great War's white crosses. And otherwise I'd never have come so close to Easter Week, whose every battle I have since traced. But those scrutinies—and their findings—were only the overture.

I shall now describe the events surrounding the great mural, over which I feel especial proprietorship. The Ballroom runs east to west, and the sunlight beams in through the southern, floor-to-ceiling French doors, which lead out to the Main Terrace and the Parterre. During all the works, I kept reminding myself that, one summer night, here in this Ballroom, guests would dance, and between dances stroll outside to take the air.

From the three drawing-rooms, three pairs of painted doorways—all fruits and flowers, nymphs and shepherds—open into the Ballroom; at the other end, the room concludes in a mighty wall. By comparison with my later scrutinies, I did little more than glance around me on that first visit as Responsible Overseer; too much debris prevented and discouraged me. In the following days and weeks, however, I left nothing unseen—and that is how I came to discover the mural.

I had no idea of its existence. On the day that I first took over, I concentrated on finding and assessing the safe places in the castle, and I did not discover the painting for four days. In fact, it took a specifically strong and directed beam of sunlight to suggest that the wall had not been painted a simple white; I ascertained it while wrestling with a handle on one of the tall doors, trying to determine whether rust had irretrievably eaten the lock.

Turning away, I looked down the Ballroom, and thought that I saw a phantom of some kind; certainly I became aware of a great presence. I have no propensity to spectral experiences; they interest me only for curiosity, never for belief. Yet, almost mocking myself, I looked again. No,

I had not been wrong the first time; yes, the room did contain a specter—a massive figure in the middle of the wall, whose scarlet and yellow garb came faintly through what I had taken to be white paint.

Down the ballroom I walked, trying not to mask the sun's beams. I touched the wall, and soon realized that the "white paint" was, in fact, a kind of mold that had formed all over the wall. It took the form of a stiff white powder, coating and obscuring everything; the tunicked figure behind it proved simply too strong to be contained.

With the utmost care, I began to brush away the caked powder. I am proud that I had the sense to do it down low, in one corner, a tiny patch at first, where any damage that I might cause would not easily be perceived, would not leap out at the eye. The powder was stiff; it needed my pocket-knife, with which I took even greater care than I had done with my hands and fingernails.

Under the caking (caused by dampness on top of paint, as I later learned), lay a mural of brilliance and vivid color. It had as a theme Odysseus the Wanderer, Homer's great hero, but at that moment all I could discover was a scrap of purple cloth, which seemed part of a gown or cloak, and the paw of a small animal, perhaps a dog.

While the light was with me, I walked along the wall, peering as closely as I could, in a fair state of excitement. I soon established that the mural ran the entire width of the Ballroom wall, and from floor to ceiling. By placing my face close to the moldy coating, and glancing askance along the face of the wall, I could see a little more of the painting—and it looked magnificent. Immediately I vowed that however it would be done, that painting would one day be restored, its genius shown to the world, and perhaps even its painter identified and hailed.

I supervised the reclaiming of that mural myself. For two years I searched the world for the best restorers. The war in Europe undoubtedly hindered me, but at last I found my man—or, rather, my man and his wife. They came from France, from near Avignon—Serge and Claudette Lemm. Both spoke good English, she more than he because she had spent some years in Scotland. In their late thirties, quiet and elegant, they had met on a church work in Tuscany and had since restored many wall paintings in French houses.

That August day in 1917, when we returned from our tour of the Anglo-Irish Ascendancy, the Lemms had arrived and begun work. They had raised a high platform all along the Ballroom wall (with great care they had covered the floor with layers of burlap), and they had also hung two great sets of sheets. The inner sheet, of strong muslin, protected the mural itself, and they would take it down carefully every night, carry it like a corpse to the exterior of the castle, and, far from everything, shake it gently, to release any powder that had adhered to it. The outer sheet, of heavy coarse linen, hid them and their platform from prying eyes.

I exulted that they had begun, and every Saturday I climbed their platform (the only one permitted) to examine the postage-stamp-sized area they had uncovered and refreshed that week. They worked in silence, but no oppressiveness hung about them. Each time they saw me, they smiled and continued working—good, shy people who went on to achieve an outstanding result.

For the remainder of 1917 there is little to report. The war grew more dreadful every day; we had now lost sixteen men from our small parish. When the two sons of one of our carpenters perished, April rendered a touching requiem. She had been working in the theater; by now all the doors had been returned—with no great effort—to their full function; and she had opened everything wide. As I had done for the general works, she had opened a ledger for the theater alone, and had listed all that she conceived of doing or that needed attention. In this, Harney helped her particularly; I could see that they had become friends, and I much enjoyed observing their closeness.

When the news came through that the Nealon brothers had perished (with the British Tank Corps, at the battle of Cambrai, in the north of France), April came to me. She suggested that we "gather all the men when they stop to lunch, herd them to the theater, and remember, with some poems, Mr. Nealon's two sons."

The occasion moved all present. Mr. Nealon, usually a talkative and fidgety man, had been silent and hunched since his dreadful bereavement. Now he thanked us as we showed him in advance the words that we would read: a passage from Tennyson's great requiem, "In Memoriam"; Harney would recite, in Irish, "Kilcash," a poem about a great

Irish house not far from Tipperary; and I would speak a short verse that Mother had read at Euclid's funeral; "How shall we mourn the ones we love? / With banners, praise and singing; / And in the skies, far up above, / We'll hear their voices ringing."

The stage had been swept of all dust and the musty curtains rolled far back to each side, out of sight. All these workmen sat on the faded turquoise-and-gold chairs of the auditorium, afraid of embarrassment at their rough clothes, and stiff with bewilderment at such emotion.

But they changed; Mr. Nealon, of whom I knew little, had been sitting with us on the stage, out of honor and respect. When Harney had finished speaking, Mr. Nealon stood up and, by prior arrangement with us, sang a song which has recently become very popular around here, by name of "Danny Boy." I feared mawkishness, but Harney quelled me, by telling me that the song portrays a father mourning a son. The audience of my workers soon joined in—and thus did we put on the first performance in the theater of Tipperary castle.

A couple of months later, two rockets would crash into Charles O'Brien's life. Of one he writes openly, and he goes on to devote a sizable chunk of his "History" to it. The War of Independence began, and it affected the life of Tipperary Castle. But he never wrote a word about the second—at least not in the text. In 1918, April fell in love with Dermot Noonan. He had been calling often to the castle, on republican business with Harney.

It began in secret—but Ireland's a fish tank. In September 1918, Amelia began to mention it in her journal: "What is going on? Why does Charles have to suffer so?" In December, April confessed it to Katherine Moore and asked advice: "Tell me I'm not mad, Kitty."

And in December too, Charles himself wrote one heart-searing letter about it to Harney. With no preamble, no pleasantries—Harney had gone home for Christmas—Charles launched into the subject with a howl of pain.

Dear Harney,

Help me. I am destroyed. All my secret dreams—of which you alone
are the keeper—are broken into bits. Yesterday, at ten o'clock in the
morning, I saw April coming out of the Narrow Wood. As she
climbed the field by the edge of the trees, she looked behind often,
and she also had a task to adjust her skirts and other clothing.
Indeed, she stopped for some time until respectable again. I was
about to ride down to where she walked when, emerging from the
wood on the other side, came your friend Noonan.

By the first days of February 1919, I knew in my heart—and remarked
as much to Harney—that war had broken out in Ireland. It began simply enough when, a few miles from Tipperary, members of a Flying Column ambushed some policemen in order to grasp the explosives that
they were escorting to a stone quarry. Two policemen died, the explosives
were seized, carted away, and hidden, to be used in making bombs—and
the authorities declared reprisals. From that moment Ireland was at war;
and I knew it from the changed pattern of events, the drama of which
came to rest in Tipperary Castle on many quickened nights.

To begin with, Michael Collins visited. He came to meet Harney, and
when I first saw him again, I extended to him the facilities of the castle
and offered to have him stay. He refused.

"That won't be good for you or for the great work you're doing here,"
he said. "The less that's known about me coming here, the better."

Harney, standing beside him, agreed.

As time wore on, I understood what he meant. Mr. Collins's visits to
us had been, in essence, for planning operations; strange, rawboned
young men often arrived in his wake, and went into quiet meetings with
him, walking the fields in the distance. (Indeed, when the strangers
began to appear before he did, I knew that Mr. Collins would not be far
behind.) Harney told me that this pattern was being repeated all over Ireland, and I soon came to know that for the years 1917 and 1918,

Michael Collins had toured the land, preparing and putting into shape a guerrilla army for a fearsome war.

At their mutual insistence, I introduced him to April. I had not wished to do so in case she became implicated in any way. He displayed exemplary courtesy to her, complimented her upon the style and magnitude of the enterprise that she had undertaken, and apologized for distracting some of her colleagues from the castle works. I had expected him to give a speech on the perfidy of the English—especially when he heard her accent—but he did not. Early in 1918, for example, he commiserated on the dreadfulness of the German war; and he spoke to her with great interest and passion of France, and Paris, the glories of European continental life.

"All our future lies there," he said. He quoted from the Reverend John Donne: "No man is an island, entire of itself; every man is a piece of the continent, a part of the main"—and April told him that she had read it aloud at her father's funeral.

To which Michael Collins replied quietly, "This is in general a time of funerals."

One day late in 1918, an encounter took place that changed our lives at the castle for some time. Harney approached me and asked if he could speak to me privately. When I went outside with Harney I saw that Mr. Collins had arrived, and with him a squat, black-eyed, powerful-looking man. His name was Dan Breen, and in time he would become one of the most feared republican guerrillas in the country. It was said that if the soldiers came to search for him and his mother put out his boots by the door—indicating that he had come home for the night—the troops retreated, prepared to say back at the barracks that they had not found him. He never went anywhere without two revolvers.

We walked a long way from the castle without speaking; I could always trust Harney to know when silence should be observed. Soon, Mr. Collins spoke to me:

"There will be operations starting around here. Violent events. Men will be looking for shelter."

Harney and Mr. Breen said nothing; I waited.

"I'd bet that the castle has bolt-holes of all kinds," said Collins. "It'd be very easy for men to hide here."

Still I listened.

"But if the British Army came to know that you were hiding men on the run—the consequences could be severe."

I said, "How severe?"

By now we had halted, out in the high fields to the south; far away, I could see the thin ribbons of silver water flowing down the sides of the mountains.

"You could be shot. And Mrs. Somerville could be shot—although I'd doubt it; she's English. But you'd be blamed."

"I'd be shot?"

Mr. Collins said, "I think so."

I said to Harney, "What do you think?"

"They'd shoot you, Charles. Or put you on trial, and then hang you."

Mr. Collins added, "And they might even set fire to this place—although I doubt that too. This is the kind of building they think they're here to protect."

"Well," I said, "this needs mulling over. And I have to put it to Mrs. Somerville."

Mr. Collins said, "We have reason to believe she'll agree."

Dan Breen said, very roughly to Mr. Collins and Harney, "How do you know he'll not hand us over? He's not exactly what you'd call a patriotic Irishman, is he?"

I said to him, "I can't let that remark influence my decision."

Mr. Breen, angry, said, "Which means you're not going to do it."

"I have only one worry—and that's for my workers."

Mr. Collins said, "That's understandable."

"But," I said, "if there's a way in which people can be smuggled in and out with me almost the only one knowing it—"

Harney said, "All the operations around here will be carried out at night." And he looked first at Mr. Breen, next at Mr. Collins and said, "I told you he'd do it."

Then began a strange time. That afternoon, Harney and I donned the roughest old clothes that we could find and explored the castle's basements and foundations. We discovered that provision had been made in the original building for more extensive cellaring and storage than had been finally constructed. Long crude rooms stretched underground, with strong if rudimentary stone columns supporting ceilings that had held up well over time.

Though filthy, and in some places damp, and altogether dark as a mine, these long honeycombs felt safe—and not a sound of the outside world could be heard. As we had reached them by a steep staircase of almost twenty steps, we knew that we must have come a long way underground.

We returned to the surface—the subterranean cloister was reached by a door at the rear of the butler's pantry—and began to pore over such original plans as we had found. On one drawing of the house and grounds, Harney saw a little pennant, which seemed to have no relevance to anything. It stood out in the countryside, halfway to the lake; according to the drawing, it formed part of a sunken fence.

Immediately we set off; we already thought that we knew what we had found—and our delight was confirmed. Almost concealed in the ha-ha, and artfully so, was an entrance to a passage. We wagered that it would lead to the underground apartments we had recently explored, and we were right.

Harney hand-picked two men from among the castle laborers, and they worked for some weeks making the door even more obscure, and the underground rooms safer and drier. We installed tables, chairs, sleeping-bags, and rations; and we told nobody, and we never discussed it except when the two of us were alone. Inside a month we had built a refuge that would have housed fifty men.

Although I made it Harney's responsibility, I checked the progress, usually by myself. One day, I found that some of the chairs now had pleasant cushions, and that books and old periodicals had been placed beside the chairs and sleeping-bags, and that canvas sheets or burlap had been laid on the tables, where men might eat.

When next I spoke to Harney, I said to him, "A nice touch, the reading matter. And the cushions."

He looked at me, puzzled. "I was going to compliment you," he said.

I said, "I didn't do it"—and he knew that I told the truth.

Immediately we knew who had done it—but we resolved not to raise it with her.

Again, we have the selective "historian." April obviously contributed to the hide for the men on the run because Dermot Noonan—and his men—would be using it. And that's how Michael Collins knew that April would agree to the scheme. Charles must have known that, in the eyes of Collins and Harney, Noonan had the status of Dan Breen. Noonan led IRA units, and he planned attacks and raids. In 1919, as with Breen and Collins, he became one of Ireland's most wanted men.

The poster issued by the army at the time carried a physical description of Noonan. More flattering than Breen's—whom the army writer described as looking "like a blacksmith coming home from work"—Noonan's called him "a clever fellow; carries himself like Napoleon, cocky as a sparrow, and speaks like an educated man, therefore doesn't sound at all Irish. Dresses like a gentleman."

They printed a grainy old photograph. With his thick black hair flopping down either side of a middle parting, he looked like a young professor.

Noonan's mind had a razor's edge—quick, legal, and witty. In conversation or argument he matched and then outclassed most people. He won most of his cases, often quoting from ancient laws in their original Latin. Although some thought him cunning—Bernard O'Brien called him "too clever by three-quarters"—his passion for his country and its cause could not be doubted.

When leading his guerrillas, he recited verse inspirationally: "There they laid to rest / The seven Kings of Tara," he would intone and then say—either intimately or passionately, depending on the size of the group he was addressing—"We are the descendants of those seven kings. When Saint Patrick came to Ireland, every family was a kingship. That was taken from us—and we must take it back."

For all his shortness (five feet six), women flocked to him. He had given himself a past with some mystery. When he was a student in Spain, it was said, a wealthy duenna had killed herself for love of him. And although we have no proof of it, it seems highly likely that he had approached April Somerville about using the castle as a hiding place for his men.

Michael Collins himself inspected the castle's underground refuge. He came in one night by means of the hidden door in the sunken fence. When he stepped from the passageway into the darkest of the cellar rooms, Harney and Charles waited to greet him.

According to one reminiscence that Harney gave, Collins asked, "Has Dermot seen this?"

Harney replied, "Not yet"—and Charles turned away.

"I could see," said Harney, "that he hated the idea of Noonan hiding here. And I knew that although Charles had not declared himself to April, he viewed Noonan as his rival for her. And there's no doubt that Noonan saw Charles as his main obstacle to winning April. Did Noonan have a vested interest in winning April? Of course he did. If he won her—well, he'd be the master of Tipperary Castle, wouldn't he?"

Once again we hear not a word of this from Charles. But, as seen through his "historian's" eye, we do get a rivetingly clear picture of a local guerrilla unit at work.

In truth, I had not prepared myself for the complications inevitable to the business of sheltering fugitives. "On the run" became a famous and controversial condition in Ireland from early in 1919 to July 1921. Many young men all over the island lived on the run from the authorities, and I will take a moment here to discuss them.

As I believe I have made clear, violence will never be a part of my life. I will never use it to make statements on behalf of my country or myself; killing and maiming my fellow-man seems futile and wrong. It may be said in this matter that I am splitting a hair—did I not do all but collaborate with the men on Northumberland Road and in Boland's Mill? And I will answer that I was attempting to save my friend's life by involving myself in his—and my country's—passion. Curiously, Harney did not seem caught up in violence; so matter-of-factly and yet proudly did he approach the task in hand that he seemed no more and no less than a committed man undertaking a solid day's work. Harney, in those circumstances, had a simplicity of purpose to him, a straightforwardness that brooked no discussion, let alone argument.

Now, in the men of the Flying Columns, I was to find identical simplicity. They did not call themselves "revolutionaries" or "freedom fighters"—nothing like that; they said that they were soldiers, hoping to rid their country of a power that should not be ruling them, a foreign power that had no historical or geographical right to be there. That was their position, nothing more but certainly nothing less.

Who were these men? As they would not wish their names known, or indeed any record effected of their identities, I shall speak of them in careful generality, and seek to give an overall impression of the unified nature of their company. And then I shall attempt to say even more about them by the simple expedient of describing in detail an action they undertook. I learned the account of it from them, in many hours of questioning and conversation; it is the story of an action taken not far from the demesne boundaries of the castle by a dozen of these youngsters one moonlit night. Which is what they were mainly, youngsters—no wonder they were referred to as "the boys."

First, who were they? A young, Irish rural Everyman, fresh-faced and awkward, that's who they were; some of them seemed barely to have commenced shaving. Most had the compelled shyness of the Irish country lad; if asked a question their cheeks reddened, and they looked to the floor and mumbled—until a friend spoke up, sometimes with a joshing word. Then they felt free to talk. Their coloring came from Ireland's national rainbow: many had freckles and red hair, some were blond, others dark as Spaniards; yet others had complexions of sunburn no matter what the time of the year.

They wore boots—some had no hose, some wore homespun stockings—and jackets of tweed, with dungarees beneath. None had been schooled beyond fourteen years; a few had not even made it that far before quitting to work for some farmer somewhere; and the few wages they took home at the end of a week eased the family burden. One or two had the softer hands and faces of clerks, working in government positions at the post office or some other such institution; their clothes had something of the town in them.

A fixedness of purpose united these young men. I saw them in our "underground," often weary after an incident or on fire with apprehension before going out that night on active duty. Every man carried a gun; none allowed it to leave his personal vicinity. Some had learned the capacity to relax; others were strung as a coiled spring; still others responded to the "life or death: you choose" circumstances of their lives by sleeping during all the time that they spent in the castle bolt-hole. As to food—most ate ravenously, a few not at all, unable to guarantee that they would not soon afterward vomit it all up again.

I see them now, in the gloom of the maps and candles—I see them lying about like figures in a painting or a blurred photograph. They look warily at the artist or the lens, and yet they have a firmness of gaze. Some wear tweed caps, sometimes with the peak turned backward. They seem both innocent and experienced, both eager and worldly-wise. Their faces have open expressions, as though they wish to be seen as staunch.

A few smoked cigarettes or pipes, though we discouraged that when it was reported from the fields that some puzzling aroma of tobacco could be discerned above the ground between the ha-ha and the castle's stable-yard—in other words, on a line directly above the hiding-place. It took Harney to point out that there must be ventilation shafts everywhere—otherwise they should all have suffocated. Sure enough, we found the ventilations on the blueprint—tiny marks, almost indiscernible, as if meant only for the man who made the drawing.

Once or twice in the early days of the cellar's operations, I happened to be there when men came back from an "action," as they called it. They seemed extraordinarily heated and, walking among them, doling out mugs of hot tea and bacon sandwiches, I was the one who pointed out to them their good fortune to bear no wounds. That changed somewhat the night of the Tankardstown Ambush, as it came to be called. Here is the account that I pieced together from all the reports I was given by the men who took part. It has the value, I believe, of typifying an IRA Flying Column's action in the Irish War of Independence.

All the towns of Ireland had garrisons from which British troops patrolled the countryside. After the IRA guerrilla campaign began, the army undertook search-and-arrest missions to "capture the gunmen," as the official brief said. On any given day, truckloads of soldiers left these barracks and ranged through the surrounding parishes, stopping and interrogating people, sometimes making arrests, sometimes attacking a village in reprisal for some lethal action that had lately taken place.

In truth the soldiers had a rough time of it; they sat hunched in trucks, riding along narrow, bumpy roads lined with hedges, from behind any one of which might come a deadly fusillade at any given moment, fired by an enemy they could not see. To add to their misery, the open trucks had to be covered with chicken wire; this had the dual purpose of allowing soldiers to poke out gun-barrels and return fire (or open fire, as they did—and often—on innocent passers-by) and at the same time protect them from any bombs thrown, which would merely bounce on the chicken wire and roll away.

The soldiers, with a few exceptions, seemed no older than the IRA boys. They often came to the castle, and I was astonished by them; many were no more than loutish English, Scots, and Welsh who'd thought they were being sent to fight the war in France, and who did not know how to adjust to Ireland. One or two officers seemed to have a sense of decency—and then they divulged to me that the men under their command (as the entire country now suspected) had one thing in common.

Owing to the war, and the consequent shortage of military personnel, the British Government had opened the jails. Provided he would put on a uniform and go to Ireland and fight the IRA, every rapist and robber, every murderer, thug, and villain in an English prison would be freed. They gave them uniforms of khaki trousers and surplus police tunics, which were black—and they became known as the Black and Tans, or "Tans" for short. Officially they had the name of "Auxiliaries," and troops of them augmented depleted regiments, such as the Northamptonshires, who occupied part of Tipperary.

It became known through a local girl working as a cook in the Cashel barracks (Collins's tentacles ran everywhere) that trucks full of soldiers would travel at a particular time one night from Cashel to Kilshane. Harney laid his plans. One of his men, the son of a nearby farmer, had the ability to ride his bicycle very fast, whereas the poor condition of the roads forced army lorries to go slowly. Harney delegated his "scout" to wait in Cashel until he saw the trucks leaving the town.

Earlier in the day, at a declivity, a dozen members of the Flying Column chose their positions behind the low wall that bordered the road. They elected to remain on one side only, because a hundred yards or so behind them, the fields became dense with trees and scrubland. Across from them, they had parked and propped a farm cart that they proposed to draw across the road on a rope when the trucks came within earshot—and after the scout had bicycled through. He had been briefed to raise his cap according to the number of trucks.

Came the night, crisp and clear with a great, bright moon. At about seven o'clock, they heard the rumble of the lorries and soon came the scout, fast as the wind on his bicycle. As he passed the IRA positions, he raised his cap—once, twice, three times: three lorries full of soldiers. When the scout had cycled over the rope and passed safely on, the Flying Column men hauled the farm cart out from the gateway into the middle of the roadway, where it lurched to a halt and tipped down on its shafts.

Over the rise came the first military truck and down into the hollow, but it did not see the cart until too late to warn the others. The driver dragged his wheels to a halt, as did the two drivers behind him—and the Flying Column opened fire. On "aim" and "fire" orders, three groups of four men simultaneously attacked the three trucks.

The first soldiers who died were shot in that opening hail of bullets as they began to leap from the trucks. Those who lived had waited a moment, then jumped when the IRA took time to reload; some soldiers crawled under the trucks, and some died there; others then took cover in the ditch across the road from the IRA and returned fire. The military could not assess how many men were attacking them, so fierce was the IRA assault.

Flying Column members burned their fingers that night, as their guns grew hot. Of their twelve rifles, five jammed or locked in some way—and each of the IRA men to whom that happened resorted to handguns. Harney, I was told later, saw an officer on his feet in the middle of the road, revolver in hand, not taking shelter, blazing away in the direction of the IRA and shouting at his men to come and join him and advance across the road. None did; Harney jumped to his feet and with his own handgun shot the officer.

The gunfight went on for twenty minutes, and then, one by one, the IRA ceased firing. In each group the youngest men slipped away first and dissolved into the trees. Soon, the army noticed that the IRA firestorm had declined and, on shouted orders, began to hold their fire. When the firing ceased entirely, they presumed—mistakenly—that they had killed all their assailants. Cautiously the soldiers rose from their positions and, trying to see their officers' gestures in the moonlight, in the shadows of the trucks and the dead bodies, they began to advance. An officer led the way, and the twenty or so soldiers remaining charged with him, firing as they went.

But nobody returned fire. When they cleared the low wall, they found only open space; their attackers had melted into the night. The officers took a decision not to follow into the trees—for all they knew, a greater ambush awaited them there. It did not; Harney, ever mindful of his men's safety, knew when to be satisfied with a victory. He had given the order that everybody, once they left their positions, was to make for the castle; the distance to us, in a straight line across the fields, was just over a mile.

Harney had two casualties, one not serious, one more dangerous. A boy from Mooncoin who had come into Tipperary because his parents would not allow him to join the Kilkenny Flying Columns had taken a flesh wound to his face. Just below his left eye (his right eye, as he explained to me, had been sighting his gun), a bullet had ricocheted and caught a chip of stone from the wall, which had hit him. Very sore, and bleeding heavily, he endeavored not to be hysterical.

The other injury posed greater problems. One of the oldest men in the Tipperary IRA (in his early fifties), had taken, we believed, a bullet in a lung. Harney and one of the youngest members had carried him across the fields; he was, they said, "spraying blood every time he breathed." We laid him on a table and stripped him to the waist. The bullet had almost passed through him; when we wiped the blood away, we saw the blackened, neat hole where it had entered, and at his back we could actually feel it beneath a bruise.

I had placed some of my healing stores in the cellar, and we decided to bathe his wound as much as possible with a eucalyptus mixture in hot water; but it was clear that he was bleeding heavily, and so I needed cloths of all kinds. When I went up to the castle, I found April in the kitchen, planning the meals for the next day. (We fed daily lunch to more than a hundred people, which enabled us to "hide" the food for the men in the cellars.) She asked no questions, and I saw her fetch a hat and coat. Presently, I heard the car engine, and the Dunhill left the castle grounds, its lamps like twin moons.

Within two hours, a doctor had arrived—a Dr. Costigan, unknown to me except by name and repute. In those days, we never knew who sympathized and who did not, and trying to find doctors so early in the guerrilla campaign gave us considerable pause. To my surprise, the doctor's coat and shirt were already covered in blood—and he told us (April did not come down to the cellars) that he'd been hit by flying glass as he'd left his home, that three truckloads of soldiers, said to contain many dead bodies, had arrived in Tipperary and were looting the town and attacking buildings.

Thus did the War of Independence reach deep into our lives in Tipperary. The doctor took out the bullet and stanched the flow of blood. He stayed all night; the man recovered—and the other casualty, the boy, said the doctor, would have "a wonderful scar" to talk about for the rest of his life. The boy did not look displeased. As to the other ten men who had been "out," as they called it, they sat quietly, Harney their leader among them, some chattering lightly to each other, some silent and alone. All cleaned their guns. When asked to recount their individual experiences, it became clear that each man thought he had effected a number of serious "hits." Yet when the newspapers reported the incident, they said that three soldiers had died, and none of the remaining fifty-seven had been wounded.

The Tankardstown Ambush became famous. It has been described as "a textbook IRA operation." Time would tell that twelve soldiers had died on the spot, and two more died in the hospital—a huge success for the Volunteers of the Flying Column. Sixteen more ended up being invalided back to England, many with severe wounds.

However, the British army was not alone when it came to distorting facts; Charles O'Brien bent a few details too. To begin with, the operation was conducted by Dermot Noonan, with Joe Harney as second-in-command. And it was Noonan—according to Harney—who asked April to find a doctor for the wounded man.

She had the perfect cover. With her accent, classy bearing, and posh motorcar, the soldiers and police would never query her presence in Tipperary. Nor would they stop her from bringing a doctor to attend one of her staff out at the castle.

From the Irish Folkore Commission's extensive section on the War of Independence, here's a relevant extract in Harney's oral history account of Tankardstown:

> We always knew when we could go no further. Ammo told us; each man fired about a hundred and twenty rounds that night, that's rifle fire. Small arms—well, I know that I reloaded my revolver four times. And more than ammo told us—if the enemy was still active at the site, and we hadn't put everybody away, there was always a moment when we knew we wouldn't get any more penetration. Tankardstown was like that—on both counts: ammo and penetration.
>
> So, as previously briefed, we pulled back. The rule was always the same: youngest volunteers first, officers last, unless we had severe casualties. Whether fatal or wounded, one officer—usually the second-in-command—and the youngest volunteer took the fatality or the most seriously wounded. That night, we had to carry one man, Michael Fitzgerald; he took a bullet—it clipped the tip of his lung.

A bright night—in fact, a very bright night. The fight had been tremendous; we were all nearly deaf for a while afterward, and I had a burn on one finger. We pulled back and the cover was excellent. A thick, low mist hung over the ground to a height of about three feet, and then, as soon as we got in among those trees, we were as safe as houses. And by weaving across the countryside, we were able to stay more or less under cover until we got to the castle. You see, that's the great advantage of guerrilla warfare—the military wouldn't dare follow us. They wouldn't know where we were; they'd have been terrified.

Dermot Noonan was the last to leave—I knew the sound of his gun, he was still blasting away when we had been gone more than a quarter of a mile. Then, when his gun went silent—there was always that anxiety that he had been hit. I only relaxed when I saw him again. He was very amusing about his height—he used to say they could never hit him because the blades of grass came up over his head, or he could hide between the stones in the wall.

That night, he led like Collins himself, out in front, his eyes like lamps. And he knew, Dermot always knew—he said to me back at the castle—that we got at least eight of them and maybe more. And then, as if he hadn't enough adventure for one night, he climbed into the car with Mrs. Somerville, who owned the castle, and it was he who persuaded Dr. Costigan to come out and look after Michael Fitzgerald. And saved Michael's life. Dermot knew Dr. Costigan from some law case or other.

In his own text, Charles never discussed this, never mentioned Noonan, even though, in the cellars below the castle, Noonan was the one who held the debrief. Charles skated over that detail too—all he said is "When asked to recount their individual experiences . . ."

In short, Charles avoided any mention of Dermot Noonan, who had become one of the most significant figures in the drama that lay beneath the surface at Tipperary castle—the drama of Charles O'Brien, almost sixty years old, still passionately in love with this rich English widow, who now, in 1920, was thirty-eight.

That's one way of putting it. And when I began to read between the lines of this text, and began to find my researches augmented by such extra texts as Harney's reminiscences, and Mrs. Moore's letters to and from April, and the contradictions between what Charles did and did not report, I decided to research "Mrs. Somerville" some more.

I went back to Dublin to see the portrait that I had earlier described in my commentaries and sat in front of it for a long time.

The first time I saw it had been by accident. Long before I'd heard of Charles O'Brien, my librarian friend in Dublin, Marian Harney, had told me that the Scullys, a family of bad landlords in Golden, had given paintings, furniture, and books to Trinity College, which owned land in the north of the county. That is how Sir William Orpen's painting of April came to hang in Dublin.

Heredity fascinates me. From the moment our daughter, Elizabeth, was born, I scanned her day and night, face and feet, body and soul, for any resemblance to me. When Orpen painted "April Somerville, London 1912," she was thirty. What could I learn from her face, from that dense, shiny fair hair? (Mine was never like that; dense, yes, but black, and as a boy I wore a heavy fringe, which at times almost came down into my eyes.)

Did April look fierce? Or unfair? Or spoiled? She had a shapely nose—retroussé, delicate. On I went, tracing one characteristic after an-other—mouth, jawline, hairline, ears, neck, as if searching for clues to her character.

I rose from the chair on which I had been sitting and walked forward to look more closely at the portrait. Then I stepped back and viewed it from another angle. From over there, back to here, forward a pace, back a yard or two—I looked and looked.

Unbeknownst to me, I was being watched. A man at the end of the corridor was taking books from a briefcase and putting them on a shelf. I heard him before I saw him.

"It's only an Orpen, for God's sake."

I swung around. He spoke again.

"You're not looking for meaning, I hope?" He came forward, a touch ir-ritated. "I have to see what you're looking at? Orpen was a stupid bugger."

Right in front of me he stood, blocking my view of the portrait. He too put his head this way and that. Then he looked back at me—and the puzzled expression on his face died.

"Oh, I'm sorry, it never occurred to me that it'd be a relative. You a Tipperary man?"

"Yes."

"This is a Tipperary picture."

"I know."

He introduced himself: "Henry Lisney. Not the auction people—they're the ones with the money. I'm an art lecturer here, nineteenth and early twentieth century."

I introduced myself, as well, and asked, "How much do you know about this—I mean, about the woman, too?"

Henry Lisney looked at the portrait. "Not much to say, *truly*. Society commission, husband probably. Orpen never gave out much information; this for some reason came to Trinity in the nineteen-*thirties*. What was she, your *aunt*?" Henry Lisney had a speech habit of emphasizing the last word in every sentence.

I said, not a little astonished, "Why do you say that?"

"Oh, God, don't tell me it's your *mother*!"

"And why do you say that?"

"Well," said Henry Lisney, "you're the dead spit and image, as they say."

"What?"

"We never see where we resemble our family. Jesus, my dear man, I can't even recognize myself in *photographs*."

"Where would I find out more?"

"If it was Lavery, it'd be easy." (Sir John Lavery was the other famous Irish portrait artist of the period.)

We chatted a little. I told him about Tipperary Castle, and about Charles O'Brien's text. Henry Lisney paid close attention; for a bellicose and opinionated man he proved a good listener.

"So how did your, ah'm, relative—" He pointed to the portrait. "How did she get involved?"

"Well—she was the chatelaine, so to speak. And I have no evidence that she's in any way related to me."

He snorted. "I have! The best evidence is the evidence of your own eyes. That's why we use the term 'eye-witnesses.'"

Henry Lisney told me that Trinity College had photographed every piece of art in the collection, and he promised to send me a transparency of April's portrait. I gave him my address.

On the drive home, I laughed. Now, if it had been a portrait of Charles O'Brien and if Henry Lisney had said I looked like Charles— I might have begun to think that Charles and my mother had had a little fling sometime.

One of the points about teaching is this: it makes you driven by text. You depend on the printed word for every handhold. In full flow, you sometimes walk the tightrope of imagination. But always, always you return to the text. When I got back home I began a long haul through Charles's "History" for what I might have missed.

Overall, he drew an odd picture of April Burke. First comes the moment when she steps on the small chair in Oscar's bedroom to straighten the picture that got skewed. Other than that momentary eye contact, she gave no impression of being aware of Charles for as long as he was in that room.

At the funeral, she physically recoiled from him. And it seems clear that when she feared he was stalking her, she used her connections to have him run out of town—no small matter in the liberal days of fin de siècle Paris, where the Irish were popular.

He next met her at her father's home in London. She had—probably deliberately—stayed out at lunch in order to avoid Charles, about whom she had been told overnight by her papa. When she did find him there, drinking with her father, she threw him out.

In all of these descriptions, Charles did not shrink from describing her behavior—a curious decision. Given his undoubted passion for her, might he not have wished to portray her in a more idealized light? I answer that to myself by saying that his reports of her arose from his innocence—he didn't understand how she came across in his text. But—I'm not sure . . .

In fact, she is almost kind when she first mentions Charles. In that early letter to Mrs. Moore (the reply has never been found), she contents herself with calling Charles "a strange man—a big Irish fellow, with, I confess, a light in his eyes and a deep voice."

April comments on his "well-trained manners"—but of course she also says, "I am given an impression that he may be quite dangerous." Touch of racism, too—nothing new in that.

Now the mysteries and contradictions begin. On the one hand this woman is depicted as cruelly rejecting. In Charles's mother's journal she's "icy" and "conniving"—you could hardly use stronger language as a woman in Amelia O'Brien's generation. Yet when her own father dies, April falls apart with grief and insecurity in her letter to Kitty Moore.

Here's another point: when Oscar Wilde told April the story of Tipperary Castle and the death of its owner, April professed to have no knowledge of it. And when Terence Burke went with Charles to Somerset, he had already declared himself astounded by the fact that he might own a great estate in Ireland.

Yet in evidence during the High Court hearings, April said that she had known about Tipperary Castle and their possible connection to it since she was ten years old. And she said too—in fact, won the case on it—that she had found, and known that she had found, her natural home. So at the very least, do we have here a tribe of deceivers?

And what about the fact that, after strong rejections, she blandly asks Charles to caretake the castle? And then marries Stephen Somerville—which copper-fastens her chances of winning the case? Did she know in advance that Somerville was a violent drunk? Did she care? In another contradiction, when Amelia shows tenderness during April's bereavement, April collapses into the older woman's arms.

The text by itself had already told me that I was seeing a difficult woman. Ancillary reading made her complex. Even though I felt that I recognized and understood everything she did, I had to wonder at Charles's judgment. And then came Noonan.

8

SUNDAY, JANUARY THE 25TH 1920.

Things have become so difficult for Charles. His heart breaks while his castle builds. As the works proceed excellently (everybody praises his orderliness), his life falls into turmoil. This love affair between April and the bantam Noonan is now turning out so scandalously that I cannot write of it here. I do not wish to see such matter in my Journal.

Our lambing has started early. We had two last night. Bernard believes we shall have at least two more in the next day or so. He thinks it is all due to the rain. We have one lamb in the kitchen, in a box by the fire. That used to be Euclid's job—only then he would not let go of them!

I sent a note to Charles. He needs to spend some nights here. But he has written back to say that he cannot.

We had ever believed that the most beautiful and difficult works should be left until the end. Also, we had agreed—April, Harney, and I—that the house's jewels could be summarized as the Ballroom, the Great Hall and Grand Staircase, the great Odyssey mural, and, above all (in every sense), the plasterwork, the magnificent stucco details that adorned every wall and ceiling in the formal parts of the building.

In the last days of 1918 we had already been able to calculate how long it would be before the stucco work could begin. And in the last days of 1919, I commissioned the stuccodores; since it has died as a trade in Ireland (how we mourn the great Stapletons and Wests), I found four Italian brothers who had worked in, among other places, the Vatican halls in Rome.

Three years, the Paglalonis told me—three years to repair these damaged plasterworks and put them back in place. I was jubilant; I had watched their careful perusals of everything that they must approach, and I had expected a span of ten years. With so much damage, we had all despaired of ever achieving the originals—and then I watched the brothers at work. No one else that I can envisage could work so precisely, with such comprehensive energy, and so fast.

We gave them, as they requested, vacated sites in which to work (with the exception of the Ballroom wall with the mural). They began by spreading black fishermen's tarpaulins on the floors, on which they laid every piece of plaster, large and small, beneath the place on the wall or ceiling whence it had fallen. (We had preserved everything in numbered and listed boxes.) As they did this, they talked to each other all the time, in unusually slow speech—indeed, every syllable that they spoke seemed at odds with the speed of their movements.

As for their delicacy! No man handled a pearl from the sea as tenderly as a Paglaloni caressed a piece of stucco, be it the head of a great bird or an as yet unidentified crumb of plaster that turned out to be a grape or a flower bud or a bead.

I watched them closely as they assembled the pieces on the ground, and then surveyed the prospects of elevating the existing pieces to their sites above. Each brother took command of a sector of the stucco for that wall, or that ceiling in that room or corridor; and when they had worked through the assessments of the linear pieces, they investigated each cornice. The simplest pieces had been placed on the flat wall; the corners of each room held wonderfully elaborate displays—of cornucopia or fruit trees or great blossoms or creatures; and in the middle of the ceilings spread the great medallions with dramatic stucco creations in relief. In the Ballroom we had a Neptune with ocean billows and tridents.

It seemed to me as if they must make all new material; that was not so. For example, inside the heads of birds, inside the bunch of flowers, the Paglalonis found the baskets of wire supports built and placed there by the original plasterers, as the little cages over which they draped their beautiful designs. When first I saw these structures, I felt that it was like looking into the broken hearts of the birds and the other creatures. Now these fortunate little beings would have their hearts restored, and they could again parade their beauty before the world.

For long times before, I had been enjoying almost daily conversations on my own pet matter, the mural in the Ballroom. Our French contractors, the Lemms, had advanced to a most interesting phase of the renewal, and had also expressed some surprise at what they had uncovered. The limestone of which the castle walls had been constructed had, they declared, proven a friend to the mural. They had found considerably less damp than they had expected, and the coat of congealed powder (as I had described it) had actually given the mural some protection. Much of their early labor, they said, had been the careful removal of this concealing white cake.

"All such work," Claudette Lemm said, "where you want to uncover beauty—it has mistakes, it must have. We made a mistake by not removing all of the white mask in the beginning, really. But we feared that it would expose the painting too soon. Then we changed our decisions, and we have been able to move ahead, really."

On the morning that the Paglalonis arrived, Madame Lemm showed me the point of revelation that the mural had reached—Odysseus's torso, and much of the mural's upper half. I cheered so loudly that the Italian brothers peered in; when we beckoned them to come and see, their delight exceeded mine. I did not grasp what they said, but I heard "Fragonard," and "Watteau," and "Delacroix." The Lemms stood by, smiling, and when the Paglalonis left, Claudette beamed me in conspiracy.

"That was why we showed them, really," she said. "To set them the standard of the house."

"Were they discussing who painted it?" I said.

"Yes. They are wrong. It is not Fragonard; it is stronger. And we do not think that Watteau came to Ireland. It cannot be Delacroix, we think; he is not born when this was painted, really."

I said, "Do you know?"

The Lemms looked at each other. Claudette said, "We think it was Vien."

"Vien?"

"Yes. Joseph-Marie Vien."

I said, "A moment—I want to find Mrs. Somerville."

April came to the Ballroom shortly afterward and viewed the mural with much pleasure.

"Do you know of Vien?" I asked. "A French painter."

April directed her answer to Claudette.

"Father or son?"

"The Elder."

They nodded, so pleased that she knew.

Serge Lemm said, "We know that he painted some murals outside of France and Rome, but we do not know where they are."

April said, "Do his dates fit?"

I said to the Lemms, "We think this part of the castle was built between seventeen-sixty and seventeen-seventy."

Claudette Lemm said, "Then his dates fit. He was born in seventeen-sixteen and famous by the age of thirty."

"But this is so exciting!" April exclaimed, and then walked from the Ballroom, passing me without a word. I saw the look from Claudette to her husband. Amid all that beauty and discovery my heart sank, because I knew that they pitied me.

From the Harney oral depositions:

We all had a fair idea of what was going on. I often overheard the workmen talking about it—workmen gossip like old women. Besides, after a while the "lovebirds"—as the workmen called them—didn't bother to hide it.

You can imagine the bind I was in. Dermot was my friend and comrade-in-arms, and Charles was my deeper friend and comrade in life.

I thought about interfering—my own mother told me that I should put a stop to it, that I should tell off Dermot, and what was he doing anyway with an Englishwoman, if he was such a little patriot? But, as I said to her, each of them wanted the other, the pair of them's free as the air, and Charles had made no move toward April.

That was the point where I had the most difficulty. I knew what was in Charles's heart—and it was unfortunate that I was the only one who knew. Charles had told me that for as long as he didn't see April or hear her voice—all those years when he never heard from her—he could handle it all. Ever since he came to work alongside her, though, his heart had been bursting every day.

So he had made a plan—which was very like Charles. He figured it like this: In 1920, when we had hit the last heights of the castle works, he was sixty years old. Her father, he told me, would have been sixty-six had he lived, so April—who talked about her father every day—had been in the habit of loving an older man.

Somerville had been seven years older than she was, and there was thirteen years between herself and Dermot Noonan. Charles was twenty-two years older than she was. Mind you, Charles was a very youthful man; most people took him for forty-five or -six, that quick walk he had, and all the energy.

He also reckoned that the main work on the castle would finish around 1921 or '22. If all went well, he said to me, he intended to take April on a long tour of what had been restored. He was then going to tell her that he had seen it all as a labor of love—from him to her. And he was then going to ask her to marry him.

You see, they actually got on very well. I was at most of their meetings; in fact, I saw them together more than any person on earth. And I have to vouch for the fact that they were a natural pair. They never argued. One never deferred to the other, one never overruled the other. They worked it out from the point of view of common sense.

I always said to Charles that he and April would make a great couple. He knew it, and I think that she did too. But when he showed no enterprise toward the capture of her heart, as they say in books—she turned away. And the only reason he didn't approach her earlier was because she had turned him down so hard in the past.

Talk about a tragic time! There we were, rebuilding this beautiful house, this magnificent palace. And running a lot of Tipperary's war from the castle at the same time. And there I was, watching my friend Dermot, and I already knowing that in this case—and not for the first time—he was being more opportunist than sincere.

The everyday conduct of that love affair was very severe on Charles. He'd meet April and me in the morning for breakfast—if she came down that morning—and he'd know by the dreamy and tired look of her that she'd been up half the night with Dermot. Maybe they'd gone out in the car somewhere, nearly daring the soldiers to arrest them.

Dermot had, in a way, turned her into a kind of Irish freedom fighter—or that's what she thought. She was in love with the whole romantic notion of it. I mean—I saw them one day down in the Narrow Wood and Dermot showing her how to fire a Colt revolver, a gun with a kick to it that nearly knocked her down to the ground.

She loved Tipperary Castle, she loved the countryside. And now she was in love with this romantic, handsome, clever guerrilla leader, who was going to be an important man when the freedom was won. Perfect for her. Out of a novel or a storybook. And for Dermot—well, there's no need to spell out what was in it for him. By then, he and Charles no longer spoke to each other.

I said to Dermot one day, Listen, said I, shouldn't you be civil to him? Dermot just laughed. Naw, said he, he has no guts.

When I sat back and reflected, that trip to Trinity College would not let go of me. Twice I had gone back over the text, to try to make sense of April Burke's character. I knew that I must dissect her and her life, piece by piece. Difficult to do—she was long dead and her pathways had closed in. And when I asked questions locally—nobody seemed to know.

The footprints left by her and Charles were few and far between. Her traces had faded. Yet luck had been on my side many times since I began this exercise. So, I told myself that I might have some more luck—it usually runs in streaks.

My first step, as I've described, took me to the portrait. I think I went to view it as a kind of test, as a kind of question to myself: Is this worth doing? When the question had been answered—and in a dramatic way, with Henry Lisney's intervention—I had to find the next thing to do.

I began by dividing her life, or what I could divine of it, into sections: Ancestry, Birth and Childhood, Paris, London, Ireland and the Somervilles, and the other Anglo-Irish who knew her. My objective: to get as close to her as I possibly could. My method: to meet any and all of the people who knew her, and to track down every piece of paper that would tell me more.

Again, as when I began reading Charles's text, I didn't quite know why I was being so ignited. I put it down to instinct—and I was still amused that a stranger who'd looked at the painting with me had told me that I was her son. Before that, he'd said that she was my aunt.

There were, of course, other reasons. I had initially become fascinated with Charles, and although he irritated me from time to time, I found his story inspiring in some odd way. He had met my mother, and had even been helped by her to find accommodations in Dublin's most tumultuous week.

And it brought me back into a period of history in our own county when events took place that would have been powerfully interesting even on a world stage, let alone our locality. The contrasts caught my imagination—as a great building was being restored, it was housing the revolutionaries who were tearing down what the place represented.

And there was the intellectual reason: I liked teaching history because the past contains so many mysteries. Not as many as the future, perhaps, but more than enough to keep a retired teacher active in his mind and spirit. In short, I was enjoying this immensely.

The Ancestry gave me no problems. I accepted that April's father, Terence Theobald Burke, was born to the man who died of a stroke on the stage of the theater in Tipperary Castle, Terence Hector Burke. I then traced his lineage, and was able to draw a time line of the family in the estates at Tipperary.

The father of the apoplectic Terence Hector Burke was Luke, and his father, Henry Burke, had commenced the "building" of the castle in 1760—in other words, April was the fifth generation of these "modern" Burkes. I put the word "building" in quotation marks because there had already been a fortified house on the land.

Henry Burke comes across as the most powerful of the family—and the shrewdest. He was born in 1710, and I found a document (in the Bolton Library at Cashel) telling that "Henry Burke of Tipperary Hill, the same, did raise one thousands [*sic*] militia for His Majesty's use toward Scotland 1745 and became rewarded."

Meaning that he sent soldiers to King George to hurl against Bonnie Prince Charlie, was rewarded with (I assume) a parcel of land, and then expanded on his fortified house. Well, that was one question answered; I had always been puzzled as to how a family with such a Catholic name and background came to own a huge farm. No trace could I find as to whether an earlier Burke had switched to Protestantism.

Next, Birth and Childhood—and so to London, and Somerset House, repository of England's cradle-to-grave records. On 1 June 1880, Terence Theobald Burke of Orme Terrace in Mayfair, London, married Sophia Holmes of Alexander Street, Westminster, and Maiden Bradley, Wiltshire.

Now the stew began to bubble. When April's father married April's mother, he moved into her home. According to Charles's text, April told Oscar Wilde that her mother had died when she, April, was "very young."

True; Somerset House lists the death of a Sophia Burke, née Holmes, of Alexander Street, Westminster, *by drowning in March 1885*—three years after April's birth. Well, well!

Next I went to the British Library's newspaper archive in Colindale, North London, and endured hours of waiting—which proved worth it. From *The News of the World* for Sunday, 22 March 1885:

"Tragic scenes were observed at Westminster Embankment on Friday afternoon as the body of a young mother was retrieved from the river. Passers-by comforted the small daughter. The woman was seen by witnesses to have jumped from the bridge into the river, even as her child entreated her. The deceased, aged twenty-five, it was said, was later identified as the wife of Mr. Terence Burke, who lives in nearby Alexander Street and is a deputy brewer for Mr. Whitbread."

In other words: as a small child, but entirely aware at the age of three, April saw her mother walk away from her, climb the parapet of Westminster Bridge, and drop into the Thames. That could explain some difficult matters of personality, I expect.

Now came the blank spaces. In my lowest times I took comfort from Thoreau's remark that "most men lead lives of quiet desperation." Given the almost total absence of record, I can only assume that April lived in the care of her father through most of her childhood.

The parish registers at Westminster record the death of a Mrs. Elizabeth Holmes, of Alexander Street, in 1886, at the age of fifty-one. We can tell that she was a widow (the use of her given first name, "Elizabeth"), and we can assume that she was April's grandmother, who lived with them.

Next, a school record places April in "Miss Campbell's for Young Ladies of all Ages" from 1887 to 1899—twelve years, after which she shows up with Dr. Tucker in Paris. And after that she becomes more visible as she begins to enter Charles O'Brien's text, marries Stephen Somerville, and wins the court case.

Now I had at least a pathway of her life, and amid all the Tipperary sources—Charles, Harney, Amelia, Mrs. Moore—I had assembled an idea of who she was and what she was like. But at that stage I had come no closer to finding any connection to me. I was beginning to wish that I had never seen that portrait, and to wonder what fantasy had taken hold of me. Once again, I turned to that most reliable of witnesses: Joe Harney's memory.

Talk about getting caught in the middle. Charles talked to me every day—every day—about April and Dermot Noonan. He looked as haggard as a ghost. His jaw was sagging, he was gray in the face. I kept saying to him, "Listen, do your job," I'd say.

"But, Harney, I can't," he'd say to me. "I'm not doing it for *him*. Why should I? I did that before, I did it for that drunk, Somerville—and look what happened to me."

And I'd say back to him, "That's dishonest of you, Charles."

We were able to speak to each other as frankly as that. I mean—I'd have done anything for him. And I'd say, "You always told me that you were doing it for her."

And he'd say to me, "Yes. You're right. I'll try and remember that." And he would. Then after a few days he'd collapse again into the terrible pain he was feeling.

Mind you, the two of them were very blatant. Dermot, for all his good points—he was always inclined to strut a bit. He'd walk into the Gallery or the Ballroom looking for April, and you'd think he owned the place. Charles would be there, talking to the plaster men—we had these four crazy Italians, they were brilliant but mad as hatters, and Charles was always calming them down.

And Dermot would ask Charles, "Where's milady?"

He'd pronounce it in the old-fashioned way, "mill-adie," and Charles, cut to the quick, would give a polite answer—because that's what Charles was like. If he knew that Dermot was gaming him, he never said so. I tried to talk to Dermot too. Might as well have been talking to the wall.

I never tried to talk to her. It would have felt intrusive, and I liked her too much for that. And she never said a word to me about it. Anyway, she wouldn't have listened to me—she was too far gone for that; she was on clouds higher than I could reach up to.

What worried me, though, was the fact that we were building a tinderbox here—and I think that I was the only one who knew that. We had all these delicate works going on, with temperamental contractors, big decisions being taken every day, a red-hot love affair roaring like a fire in front of our eyes, and a cellarful of men with guns. I suppose it was what you might call an interesting time.

In the last weeks of 1920 and the first weeks of 1921, Harney and I made a thorough inspection and a deep, thoughtful assessment of all that had been completed at the castle, and all that had yet to be accomplished. We began with the house exterior, moved to examine the interior, agreed that it was too soon to assess all the furnishings and hangings repairs (we had established a great workshop in the stables), and then moved out again to inspect the gardens and the land. This inspection, we calculated, would require five days. Each of us, at my instigation, had distilled the castle works into a large notebook, and the final compilation amounted to the sum of all we had added, as one task uncovered another requirement.

Outside, and on top of the building, we checked every slate and (mindful of history) every leaden flashing, every chimney, every gutter and spout. All the roofing had been long completed, and had survived many rainstorms. When we descended, we scrutinized every external stone on the building. The great marches of the castle's facade now looked perfect; the buttresses and columns had a blue-gray gleam to them; all window reveres and all doorways and their arches had been repaired and cleaned; all "canvas, tweed, and silk" seemed perfect—and Mr. Higgins seemed not to have aged a day.

Inside, we peered at every inch of the Great Hall walls, and went down on our knees to feel the floors with our hands. Here, there had always been what seemed like an acre of stone flags, laid on the diagonal pattern, alternating between dark gray and white. Many had suffered in the long depredations, cracked, discolored, loosened; we'd replaced them, preserved what we could, and now the floor seemed like a geometer's plan.

Signore Marchetti, I regret to say, had aged a great deal—he had suffered a heart attack one Sunday, in his lodgings. I could not be found, and Harney had acquired a doctor, who told Signore Marchetti that he must do no more lifting and very little straining labor. The prevention from exercising his craft had aged him, I believe, more than the heart condition. Whatever limitations he had encountered in his life, he had not allowed it to show in his work. He and his sons had almost completed the Grand Staircase, and I could scarcely believe that they had authored such beauty.

Marble presents difficulties; it is not what it seems. Neither as durable as it pretends to be nor as resistant to the world's stains and leaks, it also offers risks to its cutter. A misplaced blade may strike a vein and the slab has been lost; or a fault may appear which destroys the very feature of beauty for which the slab has been purchased in the first place.

Here, however, we had been given the best of all possible worlds by this remarkable family. They walked with us as Harney and I ran our fingers over every lip and baluster, across each banister and tread. We observed the grains in the marble, and how they ran to their greatest felicity; we could see that no edge remained rough; we could see more than anything else that the Grand Staircase glowed like the moon, with its white flat surfaces, and its columns of Kilkenny green and black marble.

At the top, I said to Harney, "I want to walk down and back up again."

He, as ever, understood me, and we did so, lingering on both journeys, accompanied by the Marchettis. They seemed so anxious, until I said to them, as we stood on the landing that gives way to the upstairs of the house and the Gallery, "*Perfetto. Moltissimo perfetto.*"

The father and sons burst into tears and could look nowhere; Harney and I moved on, and for the next few hours, whenever we neared the staircase, we saw the Marchettis walking up and down, up and down the stairs, and talking to each other in great excitement.

Our stuccodores were deep in their task; the Lemms had uncovered and restored three-quarters of the Vien mural; I had said that I wished to look no more until all was ready to be revealed. And we spent the rest of that day marveling at the work of Mr. Mulberry. He attended every door and every floor, he had recovered, repaired, or replaced close to sixty doors, and we had long ago lost count of the planks in the floors. I believe that Harney, for his own amusement, extracted the figure from his records of the purchases, but I have forgotten what it was. Mr. Mulberry had also attended to the maple floor of the Ballroom, the paneling all over the house, the stage in the theater, and the wonderful racks for drying clothes in the eight laundry rooms. Now he walked with us as we asked him about everything.

He might have been teaching us. When answering a question as to how he had mended the dovetailing on a broken drawer in a bedroom armoire, he gave us a brief talk on the skills needed. Like Mr. Higgins with stone, he saw his materials, wood, in terms of other matter—in his case, he likened it to skin.

As he sent his hand along a table in the Gun Room, he said, "I wouldn't leave a wood surface rough any more than I'd shave myself poorly."

He showed us door jambs where he had inlaid pieces of wood for balance and correction of leaning—even though nobody would ever see them. "I'll know that they're there," he said.

And he'd repaired a table on which beams from a ceiling had fallen, cracking it clean across; we could not find the rift.

After Mr. Mulberry had ducked our shower of compliments we went to April. When we had finished our recital of what we had seen, she turned to me and said:

"So your time here is almost finished?"

Tipperary, December the 28th 1920.

My dear Kitty,

The warmest compliments of the Old Year and the best prospects of the New to you. What shall 1921 bring? By now you will have read about Lord and Lady Glendoran? The house is quite destroyed and everything in it burned to a cinder. How dreadful! I motored over there at once and saw an awful sight. Bartley stood amid the ruins in his dressing-gown, trying to find anything—any small thing, Kitty—that he could salvage.

He was quite demented; he took some minutes to remember me, and Louise said that he almost died of heart failure when the flames took over the roof. His stamp collection has been destroyed; he had it since a boy. He is heartbroken. It is a wonder that they did not die. They lost all their horses when the stables went up.

What shall we do? How many attacks have we had since summer? I have lost count, but it is more than a dozen. Perhaps you and Dan should get rid of the guns, as it seems to me that some of these attacks begin as a search for guns, and end in conflagration.

Here I believe that I am safe, and you know why. Kitty, my new love—he is a remarkable man. I may soon ask you to render me a great and lifelong service, but I shan't detail it in a letter. Indeed, it may come very soon, because I love such an impatient man! More informations anon.

The work proceeds apace, with many things almost completed. How beautiful we have made it.

Thank you for the geese. And the ham. And the meat pies! Were I to eat them all, I should be as fat as a fool—and that is something else on which I seek your urgent advice. Do you expect to be at home next Sunday?

As the works at Tipperary drew near completion, the labor army began to shrink. It had been immensely high. *The Limerick Leader* described the castle as "Tipperary's greatest employer after the Crown."

Charles, in one comment, says that on a particular day in 1918, the day that he calls "the Apex," Harney and he counted 371 people working on the castle restoration. He did not include April or Helen the housekeeper or Harney or himself.

No matter how much further money went in those days, that was an enormous payroll. Which raises a question: How wealthy was April?

The answer is: very! She paid for everything from her bank account. The estate generated no income until the first milk proceeds and cattle sales began, in mid-1918. How rich? According to Irish probate records, Stephen Somerville bequeathed to April, after deductions and lawyers' fees, a final sum of six and a half million pounds. A staggering fortune in today's terms, it could more than pay for anything she wanted to do.

Then, in 1917, her father-in-law, old Henry Somerville, died—stricken, it was said, by the death of his son. April must have smoothed him along very carefully too—he left her all his money. When everything had been liquidated, she received eight million from that bequest. In today's money, we can assume that she was a billionaire.

We can also assume that she had never known poverty. The borough of Westminster has always been residentially prime. April grew up among the well-to-do, went to an excellent (though now defunct) school, and her status as a young lady was defined by what she did next.

The British diplomatic service operated its own inner grace-and-favor systems. One obtained certain positions according to whom one knew rather than what one had learned.

To have been placed in the household of the doctor to the Paris embassy made a statement. Here was a girl from a good background who needed a way forward in life. Her father held an excellent—white-collar—position in a brewing firm. She was close enough to the cloth to warrant upper-class care.

Which raises the matter of April's other ancestry—April the First. After all, that was how the story emerged in the first place. Charles knew of the Burke connection to Tipperary Castle only because Oscar Wilde had met the actress. By now, neon arrows flashed at me—pointing to this shady lady.

It seemed sensible to begin with her son, April's father. I knew where he had—allegedly—been born: in Tipperary Castle, if Oscar's story was true. And I knew where he had been raised—in the English county of Somerset.

Like Ireland, England documents itself well. Unlike Ireland, valuable gossip is more difficult to come by. Not only that, Irish chatter knows no time limits. Here in Clonmel, I can have a conversation about an event of seventy years ago as though it had taken place last week. The English moved house too often for intimate continuity.

Therefore I had problems. I was searching for people known to have lived in Somerset one hundred years ago—and some of them were elderly then. I took the ferry from Rosslare to Fishguard, drove across Wales and over the river Severn into North Somerset. Gambon was the name I was looking for—anywhere near Yeovil.

Old tennis saying: "The ball bounces to the winning player." I struck gold (of a kind) on the second day—not on the name Gambon, but on a scrap of history from the house in which Terence Burke had been raised.

It hasn't changed since Charles first saw it, in June 1904—a stone house with its back to the world. The lane feels just as he described it: the steep hill and the view out to Glastonbury Tor and the Somerset Levels, where Coleridge walked. They've added some huge electrical pylons, which hiss and fizz sixty feet above the ground.

England being a land of gifted amateurs, the area has attracted excellent local histories. Trawling one tasty little volume (*Tragedies in the West Country—a Chronology*), I found a note that made me almost shout.

In 1878, an unnamed woman described as "an actress" jumped "spectacularly" off the beautiful Clifton Bridge, which spans the Avon Gorge in Bristol. Her address was given as the Brook House, near Shepton Mallet, in Somerset.

The public records and the newspapers gave me a little more. Her age was given as forty-seven, meaning that she was born in 1831. The newspapers carried a squib describing how two people had tried to stop her, but she, "excitable and inconsolable," told them that she was being "blackmailed." Coroner's records gave her name as "Avril Burke."

To knit it together (somewhat): "April" became "Avril," not an impossible error; Queen Boudicca has long been "Boadicea" due to a scribe's poor handwriting. If she was born in 1831, that would make her twenty-five when her son was born in 1856. (He was, remember, only four years older than Charles O'Brien.) The husband she abandoned, Terence Hector, died on the stage at Tipperary in 1858, leaving an infant son.

Oscar Wilde met the actress when she was older. He was in his twenties. Since he was born in 1854, he must have met her in her forties, in the year or so immediately preceding her death. It all fits.

Who was blackmailing her so fiercely that she jumped to her death? And what was the blackmail's leverage? That, like Sarah Bernhardt, she had been a tart? That she had—appalling disgrace to the Victorians—abandoned her child? And had now come back to "the stage"—i.e., still plying a whore's trade, as many still believed of actresses? An unscrupulous enemy could get mileage out of that.

My trail ran cold in Somerset. I didn't get to the rest of April the First's story for some time. But I did note that April Burke-Somerville's grandmother *and* mother had committed suicide. And in identical fashion, by jumping off bridges. That indeed must make for some rocky terrain in a person's psychological landscape.

Thursday, the 25th of March 1921.

My dearest Kitty,
Now I truly need your help. The "frights" of which we spoke in
January have come home to roost! Be not alarmed—I am overjoyed.
For double reasons—not only will I have the delight of a son or a
daughter, but I shall be married to a man who loves me, and whom
I love with all my heart. Nobody else knows but you and Dr.
Costigan, who is quite, quite certain.

I believe that the matter must be handled very discreetly—it is so
easy to get a bad name around here. But we have constraints owing
to my dear man's current way of life and, shall we say, the unusual
demands made upon him. Nevertheless, we shall make all haste.

My History, being also a personal matter, has permitted me much latitude. From time to time, a memory assails me so beautifully and so recurrently that I feel obliged to record it—as with my sojourns at Athassel Abbey (whose rushing waters I sometimes hear at night from here, if I walk out on the highest part of the gardens). In late March 1920, there was a morning in Tipperary that I shall never forget.

I rose before dawn. With spring promising to come early, I walked the immediate precincts of the walls, as I ever did, and watched for any unusual matters. That morning, I found one new cause for rejoicing: a great swan had come to the lake sometime since the previous night's dusk. We had wanted swans for some years now, and often talked about it; we made many inquiries as to where and how we might acquire swans; we had even corresponded with the Keeper of the King's Swans, who had not been helpful.

Now Tipperary Castle had its own swan, and I walked to the lake's edge, taking care to make no noise. The swan moved among the sedges some yards from me, as though seeking a resting-place; its serene gliding would calm the wildest heart. But I became anxious; swans require partners, I'd been told; if this swan did not find a partner, would he fly away? I have no explanation for the fact that I thought it male.

Up at the castle, I could scarcely wait to give the good news—but I breakfasted alone; no sign of Harney, which suggested some "activity" in the night; and for some weeks April had not been down to share breakfast. Indeed, I had scarcely seen her.

All day, I found myself walking over to the highest point of the terraces from where I could see the lake. I could not always glimpse the swan, but did see it often enough to ascertain its continuing presence. Of another swan I saw no sign—until near five o'clock.

The sun was beginning to set in a magnificent blaze, and long streaks of red cloud were setting the western skies on fire. I was in the gardens between the two pavilions, measuring with two of the gardeners how much ground we should need to break open for the planting of three hundred new rose-bushes. Suddenly a shadow darkened the air above our heads and there was a noise of wings. A huge swan, larger than the one I had seen, flew low over us in the direction of the lake.

I jumped back, in evident excitement.

"We're all right now," said Jerry Kirby, the older of the two gardeners. "We've swans."

All three of us made for a point from which we could see the lake below us. Sure enough, there on the waters, side by side, not touching but gliding close to each other, went two swans, white and calm as hope. My heart was filled with optimism.

Charles and I—we went through a fierce time. Think of what was going on. I was out every night with a gun in my hand, not knowing if I'd ever come back alive. By day I was helping to rebuild the beauty of the very empire we were hammering at. The man I depended on for my safety as a soldier, Dermot Noonan, was in the middle of a desperately passionate love affair.

And who was it with? With the woman who was the heart's desire of my dearest friend, Charles O'Brien.

And she was the owner of the estate that I had been working on for the past six or seven years and to which I was fiercely committed.

The war was raging across the country like a wildfire. Reprisals happened everywhere, and we hit back with counter-reprisals. What was typical was this: we'd hit a barracks or a troop convoy. In revenge, the Black and Tans or the regular army would attack the village or town, drag men and women out, and shoot them and burn their houses. And then we'd burn down a mansion where we thought the British were planning their campaign against us. Or where we thought—or often knew—the owners entertained the officers.

Now, through all of this, we hid men every night in the cellars at the castle. Charles O'Brien might not have carried a gun, or ever fired a shot in anger at a soldier—but he played his part. And he was one unhappy man. But he never pretended, he never changed his behavior from that civilized way he had. He had a good word for everybody. That work would have collapsed without him. And then, of course, in the spring of 1921—what beautiful weather we had that year—it was the worst time for Charles.

He knew—we all knew—without being told. I guessed very early, because I grew up in a houseful of women and by now my sisters were married and having their own babies. You can tell with a woman. The complexion changes. And she was old for having children. That's what my mother said—if she never had a child before, thirty-nine years old is no age to start.

Why do I dislike the word "melodrama"? Probably because there's nothing "mellow" about it—that's the joke I used to tell in class. I think I dislike it because whether you want to or not, it pulls you in. Now it was dragging me in.

I found myself telephoning a former pupil who works in the police forensics laboratories in Dublin. Could he test something from a century and longer ago for DNA? Of course he could. Feeling queasily melodramatic and more than a little foolish, I sent off some locks from the tresses of hair in the oak chest. And some hair from my own head. Why was I doing this? I had no idea. Instinct, again.

9

April, Harney, and I never spoke about the men who hid in our cellars. We seem to have believed by unspoken agreement that the greatest security lay in keeping silence. They proved no small task to us, and we committed many hours of labor and concern to their concealment and their welfare. Usually, we housed approximately twenty or so of these youngsters, whom I saw grow into maturity before my eyes. Boys came in along that dank, secret passageway from the ha-ha at the fresh age of eighteen; six months later they spoke with the wary restraint of men aged forty.

I observed them closely, and soon I could begin to single out individuals and distinguish them among their comrades. Three kinds of men (if I may simplify for the purposes of clarity) composed the Flying Columns: the hearty, the easily conversational, and the quiet. In each case, I believed that I was witnessing men who were responding with their spirits and tempers to the unusual circumstances of their current existence.

The hearty men laughed off dangers and joked with each other about the circumstances from which they had just returned. Men who sat down, ate and drank, and lapsed into quiet conversation seemed to feel the difficulty more severely—or were prepared to let it be seen on their faces, in their demeanor. As to the quiet ones—in time I learned that from their number were drawn the greatest marksmen, the crack shots. In short, those men killed more than anybody else.

On account of mild wounds that they had received, I was given opportunities to make deeper acquaintance with two of the quieter men,
and slowly I began to elicit from them, one at a time and never together,
their views on the lives they now led.

The first lived several miles away, in one of the county's prettiest villages; the second came from nearby, and his aunt had once worked for
my parents at Ardobreen. One night, attending to an eye with a splinter
in it (I bathed it with cold tea), I asked the first if he knew when he had
shot someone. He said nothing; so I asked him again, in a different way.

After a deep breath he said, in a kind of half-breath, "Ah, you do, sir."

I waited, keeping my voice soft, bathing the red eye.

"Is it something you see? Or, maybe, hear?"

"Ah, you kinda know, sir."

"Oh? Now don't move, I'm just going to dab this in here. You kind of
know? How would that be?"

He never answered.

When I plied the second one with questions, he manifested similar reluctance.

"Do you ever see a face?"

"Sir, well, I'd see a head, sir."

"But not a face that, say, you'd recognize if you met him?"

"I'd never want that, sir."

"Why wouldn't you?"

"Sir, it wouldn't be right; I'm supposed to plug him."

"You mean—you're there to shoot him, and you don't want to know
him?"

"Sir, my job is to plug him."

Even though I knew that my questions made them uncomfortable,
they seemed warmer to me thereafter. When I went down to the cellars,
one or other always had a cheery greeting for me—before he lapsed again
into silence, sitting quietly by himself away from the others. Neither ever
joined in the card games or the endless political discussions.

The postman brought a shock—from the DNA tests.

Without any question I, Michael Bernard Nugent, am descended directly from the person on whose head grew those locks of hair. I assume that the garments among which they lay belonged to the first April Burke. Now what do I do? Disbelief is my first ally.

For good reasons. I loved my mother, Margery Nugent. That quiet woman suppressed a great talent, because she became the wife of a railwayman she loved. Rock no boats. Shatter no glass. That is what she said to herself when she married. She told me so before she died. But I felt attached to her, and I still miss her. The spirit doesn't lie.

Then—doubt sauntered in, asking slyly, Shouldn't you have sent the DNA people something of hers?

My emotional metabolism has a kind of "time-delay" mechanism. If something awkward comes at me, I hold it at bay. And then, several hours later, usually the next day, I'm ready to take it on. That has been my main protection method over the years.

The DNA letter arrived at nine o'clock in the morning, I opened it, read it—and, finally, that night, I was strung out with agitation.

How can this be? Are they sure? I read and reread the little note that came with the printout: "Was it your grandmother?" The technician did add a caution: "I'm aware of the sample's age—but if this was in court, I'd have to swear to the highest probability of consanguinity."

My thoughts, my scrambled thoughts, went like this: That fellow, Lisney, Henry Lisney—he saw a resemblance. And: What do I do now, what's to happen to all the information of my life? Followed by: No, this can't be the case. And: Supposing I exhumed my mother? Or my father?

Then I returned to Charles O'Brien's "History," the cause of this difficulty. I was by now on my umpteenth reread and again coming close to the end.

Notwithstanding the mood of relaxation that pervaded the cellars in general, and sometimes the high degree of social ease—at times we had more than fifty men down there—I perceived one day a sharp evidence of their high training and alertness.

At ten o'clock in the morning, I heard the noise, and then I saw the lorries on the avenue. Five trucks of soldiers rumbled toward the castle, led and followed by staff cars. I ran to the cellars and told everyone; they scattered on their stomachs along the floors, hiding behind any object that they could use as shield or cover. As they crawled and squirmed, their little leader, who had once been our lunchtime visitor at Ardobreen, looked at me and said, in a loud voice, "Now who has betrayed us?"

I turned away and climbed the stairs back to the servants' quarters and with help moved the great food-safe back across the doorway. Helen the housekeeper brushed the floor in front of the butler's food-safe and moved a bench into a position nearby, lest the floor betray telltale signs.

Harney had disappeared; I later discovered that he had climbed into the highest part of the East Tower, which had long been prepared and armed for any such emergency. As the staff cars converged in front of the castle, the trucks halted too, and disgorged more than a hundred soldiers. All wore the uniforms of the appalling Black and Tans.

Two officers, one young, one senior, walked up the steps—and I walked down to meet them.

"Good morning, sir, dreadfully sorry for the trouble."

"Not at all," I said. "In fact, we're very glad to see you."

"You are?" He looked disbelieving.

I said, "I mean—my God, after all that's been happening. We knew Summerhill very well; Colonel Rowley was an old friend of my mother's. We're still shocked."

In February, a beautiful house in County Meath had been burned, to great dismay.

The young officer said, "Do you feel safe here, sir?"

"Who's safe anywhere?" I asked.

My greatest fear had almost paralyzed me—that April had become suspect in the eyes of the authorities.

"Where's the lady of the house, sir?" he asked.

I said, "I don't actually know; I think she may have gone to stay with Lady Bandon."

The officer looked a little perplexed. "You see, we wouldn't like to search the place without her permission."

I said, "Oh, I can give you permission—I'm her agent in all such matters. Here, let me help you—where do you want to search and for what?"

"We heard, sir"—the young officer did not quite know how to go forward—"we heard that gunmen hide here, sir."

"Goodness—do you mean on the actual estate? Where?"

The other officer had been watching me closely, and now he spoke.

"Well, they could be anywhere, sir, couldn't they? It's a big place."

I said, "Well, let's figure out where you and I would hide if we had to. Outside, there are the woods, and we also have three large groves. And inside, we have the cellars, and I can tell you all about them. In fact, I can do better than that."

Not far away, Mr. Higgins, our Master Stonemason, stood watching. He held no sympathy for either side—but I knew that he would understand my drift.

"This man over here—" I beckoned. "He knows this building inside out; he's restored all the stonework." I called him. "Mr. Higgins, these gentlemen want to search the cellars. Can you make it safe for them?"

"I can't, sir, and I won't." Mr. Higgins, walking toward us, heated up a little. "And, sir, I told you before—I'm taking no responsibility for anyone going down there."

To the officers I explained, "This place was closed for fifty years. There had been severe rain damage and a lot of collapsing. Mr. Higgins has had the task of securing all the underpinning."

I asked him again: "Isn't there some way in which they can inspect the cellars?"

Mr. Higgins said, a touch impatiently, "Sir, you told me to secure the western door with stone, and we did that. We never moved the ceiling that fell, and if you open that door—I mean, I can open it for you—but more stones will fall."

I sighed. "You're right. Was there ever an entrance from the stables? I'm most anxious to accommodate—"

The young officer cut in. "It's perfectly all right, sir. May we look inside?"

I led them, enthusiastically. They gasped.

I said, "I'm not about to let a bunch of IRA thugs with guns into this place."

They agreed with my point of view. I went across to say something to one of the Paglalonis, and I saw the officers conferring—which was what I wanted to achieve. When I returned they said, "If you don't mind sir, we'll just turn the men loose in the woods."

"Of course—and please stay for lunch?"

They smiled. "Can't, I'm afraid."

Their search lasted not more than an hour, and all they did was frighten the crows. I stood with Mr. Higgins and watched their cars and trucks drive down the avenue. Within minutes Harney had come to my side.

"How did you do it?"

"I didn't. Mr. Higgins did."

Mr. Higgins said, "No. He fooled them to the eyeballs."

In school I always said "War of Independence." And in English schools they say "Anglo-Irish War"—that is, if it even gets mentioned. My parents called it "the Troubles"—not to be confused with the more recent "Troubles" of the 1970s and onward.

By the spring of 1921, every city, town, and village in Ireland had been caught up in the first "Troubles." Due to lack of arms, the campaign could not be timed to coincide with the Great War, "England's difficulty." But the Irish republicans, including Collins and de Valera, believed—somewhat correctly—that they had nonetheless struck at a time when Britain was still emotionally as well as militarily depleted.

And once again, the British government became a valuable ally. If the executions of the 1916 leaders had swung public opinion behind the Rising, now the atrocities of the Black and Tans became a countrywide outrage. The men of the Flying Columns became folk heroes.

They proved impossible to fight. Any English regiment that came to Ireland had officers who understood artillery, and cavalry, and strategy, and the movement of supplies. How could they fight an enemy who might lurk behind the next hedge? Or who might not? Who might descend on them in a mountain pass or on a main road? Or who might not?

And how could they fight an enemy who, in some cases, was their employee? Michael Collins gained access to almost as many military secrets as he wished, because his supporters were the filing clerks and the secretaries and the errand boys of the men who drafted the British strategies.

The Flying Column volunteers passed into legend even while they were on the run. Ballads were made, poems were written, artists portrayed them. Most active in the south and the west—that is, in the best guerrilla terrain—they and their daring created problem after problem for the authorities, who had no experience of fighting like this.

Furthermore, the quality of the clashes when the IRA took on the army created a natural David-and-Goliath atmosphere. Twice in March 1921, the Irish public read of results that the army would rather not have released. In Millstreet, on the border of Cork and Kerry, the Flying Columns laid land mines that killed more than a dozen troops—and the Irish admitted to no casualties. Two weeks later, at Crossbarry, in Cork, over a thousand soldiers surrounded a Flying Column—and not only failed to capture them but lost over twenty soldiers.

Something new, and often disastrous, happened every day. Thus, the psychological war, too, was lost by the British. They first began to lose it themselves, when their policy of executions created Irish martyrs. Then each guerrilla incident became public, despite the official efforts at censorship.

To read the newspapers of the time, especially from an Irish point of view, is to ride a seesaw of brilliance and disaster. For every IRA victory in the fields, local villagers were almost certain to pay with their houses or their lives.

Nor did every one of Collins's units have unmitigated success. Joe Harney's archives contain a vivid account of an operation in which he was involved early in June 1921. Although it doesn't say so, it was to have a significant bearing on the life of Charles O'Brien, even though he was not involved. And on my own life.

We were told by one of our people in Dublin that a Very Important Personage would be on the train from Portarlington to Mallow on the first Tuesday in June. He was a general, a big prize. The orders were to capture him and hold on to him—a bargaining chip. I was given the job. We were told to keep him fiercely secure—and I thought, "The cellars."

A good decision, I felt; we meant to treat him like a prisoner-of-war—a lot more than our men were getting. I said so to Charles, and he was kind of amused: "A general? We're coming up in the world."

Dermot was away somewhere. I think that talks about a truce were beginning, and he was a very good negotiator. Since I can't separate out any of the things that I was thrown into at this time, I also have to tell you that he was getting married that same month to April Somerville, the Englishwoman who owned Tipperary Castle.

Dermot pulled all kinds of strings. Mrs. Somerville, she was taking instruction to convert to Catholicism—from what faith, I don't know, because I never heard that she had any religion. And the problem was—he was on the run, so where could they get married? It had to be in a church; I'll come to all that.

We set out in the morning to get the general, and everything went wrong. We knew the time of the train—but it was hours late. And they had taken a security precaution that none of us anticipated: they'd put on a long train that day and the general sat up in the front of it, so that when the train came in, his carriage always went beyond the station platform. That was to make it harder for anyone to get on board easily. And in the station we chose, Dundrum, his compartment was halfway into the woods before we could get near him.

There were eight of us, though we'd been promised some more Volunteers. We were to take the general down onto the tracks, through the engine sheds, and out the other side, where a car would be waiting. By the time the train came in, we were very nervous. No other men showed up, and there was no sign of a car. A few minutes before the train came in, the stationmaster tipped us the wink about the length of the carriages, and where the general would be sitting.

I told four of my men to get on the train at the platform, not to draw

guns but to head for the front of the train. I took the remaining three
Volunteers and we ran forward, crouched down below the windows so
the soldiers couldn't see us. Although there didn't seem to be that many
soldiers around.

When I figured which was the general's carriage, I sent two of my men
in the door at the back of it, and the remaining two of us ran up ahead,
and got on the train.

Straightaway, I saw him. He was sitting there not in uniform, and
with two or three other men around who were also in plain clothes.
There were two soldiers in uniform at each door.

When dangerous things happen fast, you see them slowly. I saw one
of my men die—he had come in at the back door of the carriage, gun in
hand, and one of the sentries shot him. That was the first gunfire. I still
had no gun out—but I drew it then. I got the first sentry, but I only
wounded him and he got off two shots before I plugged him. But the
man with me got shot.

At the same time, my second man at the back of the carriage got the
sentries there, and he also plugged one of the plain-clothes men who had
drawn a gun. I got a second plain-clothes fellow—and the third one almost got me. He let off one shot that missed—and I reached him and
shoved my gun in his neck.

Somehow I guessed that the general wouldn't be armed. But—you
never saw a calmer man.

"Don't shoot," he said, very levelly. "That's my son-in-law"—and indeed it was, although I didn't find that out for certain until much later.

"Tell him to put down his gun," I said.

"David—you heard the gentleman."

The gun hit me on the foot when it dropped. My second man picked
it up, and got the son-in-law out of the way.

"General Hogarth, I'm Commandant of the Third Tipperary Brigade,
and you have to come with me."

He stood up. "I rather thought that's what you had in mind, Commandant," he said.

My other four men—they couldn't get through. The train had been locked behind the general's carriage. So there we were, on a train that might take off at any moment, two of us with a top-ranking British general and nowhere to go.

The other four boys were clever enough to get off the train, run ahead, and square off the driver, threatening him if he attempted to get the train moving again. I couldn't get the general safely down onto the tracks and cover him at the same time—so three of my fellows grabbed him and helped him down.

Now—from the rear of the train we heard shots. I looked down the platform and saw a bunch of soldiers running toward us. They had been firing into the air, and I stood beside the general and held my gun to his head.

We walked him—remember, we were down on the tracks and our pursuers up on the platform—we walked him around the front of the engine, across the railway line, and into the engine sheds. The troops came after us and I kept saying to my boys, "No firing, no shooting."

And the general said, "Well, you seem to know what you're doing."

We got to the engine sheds—which were empty. It was a kind of strange procession. I was in front, quick-marching the general as best we could on uneven ground—he understood it straightaway and fell into step with me. Behind me, almost walking backward, came five of my fellows—I had not time yet to think of the two fallen comrades. And behind them about fifteen or twenty soldiers with guns aimed at us. On we went, across the floor of this huge shed, and a railway man ahead of us, one of our sympathizers, unlocked a side door.

I said to him, "Where's the car?"

He said, "She's over in the trees—she'll see you."

Sure enough, there was the car—and there was Mrs. Burke-Somerville, as her name still was, driving it. I discovered long afterward that she had prevailed upon Dermot Noonan to let her take part in some action. This was perfect for her. She wouldn't be stopped; if she was, she had an English accent and we were going to her castle. And she and the general would understand each other. What is it about some women that makes them want to be freedom fighters?

The car had a high seat on the back, outside—I think it was called a "dickey" seat. I was to sit up there, with a gun under the rug aimed at the general's head, in case we were stopped. That was the plan—but it never fell out that way.

We got to the car. The general tipped his hat to April; she had the engine running. The soldiers being kept at bay by my fellows couldn't see the car—which was round the bend on a wooded road. I stood back to let the general get into the car, but he stood with his hands by his sides, waiting for me to open the door.

Like a fool, I fell for it. I think I was seduced by his rank—I remember thinking, Yes, he's used to people opening doors for him. So I reached for the handle on the door and he elbowed me, elbowed my gun hand out of the way, and legged it. He ran surprisingly fast and he ran back the way we came. My fellows never saw him, I didn't shout, and I didn't fire—we were told to take him prisoner, and I started running after him.

Of course you can guess what happened. The minute his own men saw him they opened fire on my boys. But they hit their own general, and down he went.

There's always a hollow in a crisis—a space when you stand there and see everything that's happening. Or at least that's what I've found. And there was a moment that day when I saw everything. Six of us, a dead general, fifteen, maybe twenty soldiers facing us over his body. I shouted to April to drive away, because I didn't want her seen by the soldiers— there were about four other motor-cars in the whole county and none of them a Dunhill.

She razzed up the car. I was the farthest back; I got two of them. But they got all five of my boys. We only had revolvers and one rifle that jammed. And now there were six bodies—and more—on the road that goes into the woods. I ran; I saw the car in the distance and before it went around a bend and out of sight, I saw the windshield breaking—a bullet had hit it. My better thought was that the soldiers hadn't had a chance to see the car, which wobbled a bit, then straightened out and drove on. I thought, She's safe.

Dermot Noonan did all the planning for that Dundrum operation, and it was perfect. There isn't a square inch of those woods that he doesn't know; he was born there. Now his knowledge came to my aid, and I was able to escape and hide. The lateness of the train helped too, because it was soon dark. Once it was safe to start moving again, I left my hiding-place—a culvert up by the sawmill—and I got out of the woods far from the scene of the gunfight.

By midnight I was back at the castle—and that was my next shock. When I came out of the woods I took one of the bicycles that were always left for us at various places. The road home was quiet, I went by all the back ways, and when I cycled up the avenue of the castle, there was the car parked there, in the dark, blocking the avenue, leaning a bit to one side.

My first thought was that it had failed mechanically—and then I saw the driver's seat was all stained dark, and I knew it was blood. Never did I travel up that avenue faster. I got to the kitchens and Charles was there, pacing the place. He looked at me, said nothing, and pointed to the ceiling. Upstairs, there were Helen and Dr. Costigan attending to April, and the sheets were covered in blood.

What happened was this: When the windscreen shattered, a piece of the glass hit April on the neck and she thought she'd been shot. She also thought, from the huge gunfire, that I was dead. On the way home, in all the distress, she started to lose the child. And on the avenue, she hit a stone and couldn't get the car to move.

When she saw me, April grabbed me so hard she bruised my hand, and she kept saying, "I was already too old." I tried to console her and she said, "Now I'll never have children" and she'd look at the doctor, hoping that he'd say no, that of course she still wasn't too old to have a child. But he said nothing; why would he say anything?

That was one of the two worst nights of my life. I went back downstairs and I said to Charles, "You should be up there."

Said he, "She won't let me; she says this is all my fault."

I settled within myself that it was an error. This was the usual Irish official inefficiency that we all love to howl about. Presumably the age of the

DNA had confused the test. I telephoned my former pupil and thanked him and then engaged him in conversation. My nerves were still jangling, and I asked him casually what was needed for such a test. Then I thanked him again.

My mother's hairbrush sat in the untouched suitcase on top of my bedroom bookshelves. I went to the library, and on the Internet I found a company in England that does DNA tests for paternity and other legal or commercial reasons.

I telephoned. Yes, a clerk said, the hairbrush and its strands were fine. So I sent it off. By now I had long known that Charles's "History" had no such answers for me.

I was out in the fields with Harney in the early summer of 1921 when Mr. Collins came to us for the last time, and this time I saw a maturer man—a less excitable individual. He seemed to have aged since I'd first met him, in late 1916; given what he had been doing, a little of which I knew from Harney, the wonder is that his hair had not turned white. When I was a boy and my father told me tales of the intrigue preceding the Land Act, and the rebellions plotted by the bearded men in greatcoats who came to our house at night, he inclined to say that when "Ireland has her final revolution, Tipperary will be there at the finish." I told Michael Collins this, and he replied that he regarded Tipperary as "the intellectual breeding-ground of this war we're fighting." This explained his many journeys to the county.

His last visit to us took place a few days after a failed Flying Column operation. Harney had been detailed to lead seven men on Dundrum railway station and capture a general from the Dublin-to-Cork train. The general tried to escape and was accidentally shot dead by his own men; Harney escaped uninjured—except for his heart, which ached, he said, with guilt that he lived while his seven comrades-in-arms died. The failure sat heavily upon him; he'd fallen for a ruse of the general's, and he condemned himself gravely for it.

I knew of the operation beforehand, and even though wisdom after the event is an offense to the intelligence, I felt that the attempt should never have been made. The planning seemed lax—though Harney bears no responsibility; he merely carried out incompetent orders. Other than such inefficiency, and the sad losses of Harney's comrades at Dundrum Station, the war went well in our county. Mr. Collins told me of other major operations in which the Flying Columns succeeded against great numerical odds. He also hinted at diplomatic exercises.

"It seems that our timing may be proven right after all," he said. "I think they're war-weary."

He knew that Mr. Lloyd George, the Prime Minister, feared the funds flowing from the United States to the Irish republicans. Already a stream, they might become a torrent—and England had indeed lost its appetite for war.

SUNDAY, THE 12TH OF JUNE 1921.

I was born for dilemmas. My poor son—where is he left standing in all this? I must stop thinking of him as "my poor son." He will be sixty-one at midsummer and I will be eighty-five. Why is it I feel younger? Another dilemma.

It doesn't compare with what's happened. April, now my friend of six years, lost her baby. But she will marry the father, little Noonan. What can Charles be thinking? And still he soldiers on. He is garlanded with praise every day for the work at the castle. Maybe that is what keeps him going.

I hope he doesn't hear the things I said to April. She asked me if she should marry little Noonan. I'm too old now to mind my p's and q's. So I said straight out—No. Marry Charles, I said. His feelings will guard you forever. But she didn't listen to me.

Wednesday, June the 15th 1921.

My dear April,
My plan has changed—I shall come on an earlier train, and we
shall spend tomorrow night preparing your clothes—how exciting!
But I must ask—do you feel strong enough to go into it? My dear,
leaving you on Sunday, you looked so pale, and I kick at myself, I do,
for having let you walk so far, so long when we could have sat. But
I'm the servant, remember, the bride's maid, to do your every wish.

Dan understands the need for the minor key we're playing in,
and he doesn't mind not being invited; he mislikes weddings anyway.
But he sends you, he said, every good wish and he hopes for your
happiness.

Until Thursday noon.

With affection,
Kitty.

It took four weeks for the results, and they charged me heftily—because
I paid for three tests: the ancient lock of hair, my mother's hairbrush, and
my own hair. The lab technicians must have puzzled over this one. They
found no connection whatsoever between the two females. But they also
connected me to the tresses found in the theater at Tipperary. If I had already been engaged with Charles O'Brien and his uneven (to say the
least) April, now I was obsessed. I went back to my inspection of that
teeming drama.

It was a beautiful day. The middle Friday in June. I drove the car. She
asked me to, the night before, so I got the blood cleaned out of the seats.
And as she walked toward me, she said, "Harney, d'you think—" And
that was all.

She never finished the question. Mrs. Moore was standing at the other end of the Great Hall, not a lady I knew very well, but I knew enough about life to tell that she was very anxious. And that evening and next day she hovered over April, giving her all kinds of care and attention. Mind you, April had recovered well from the miscarriage—but she looked exhausted.

People have great natural tact—whether they know it or not. Nobody came out to look at us. We got April into the car out in front, and there was nobody on the terraces, and nobody in a doorway. I couldn't believe it.

You can guess what my fear was—that Charles would appear. If he did, there was no mistaking the fact that April was about to become a bride. No veil of course, being a widow—but she had a bouquet of flowers, and a hat.

Heavens above, did I look around! But—no Charles, no sign of him. I got them all into the car, and away we went. And then, just inside the gate, on a little hill from which you can peep through the trees, I saw him. He was standing there, watching us, just at the point where we had to slow up before going out on the road. He looked straight at me, and I at him. And when he turned his back, you never saw a man with a sadder pair of shoulders.

Well—if that was only the worst thing that happened that day. Because he was on the run, Dermot had arranged things very secretively. He got a priest in Cashel to perform the ceremony and to get over the problems of April not being a Catholic—he told the priest that she was taking instruction in order to convert. The priest was one of his men, anyway.

And then Dermot pulled his masterstroke. No church—too dangerous; anyone might see him going in there. And a bride would attract attention. At that time the Rock of Cashel was all but closed. You had to go up a dirty old lane to it, and nobody would see you, and Dermot knew—the legal brain—that the church on the Rock was still a consecrated church, and that people could legally marry there.

He hid nearby the night before, and we had arranged that I'd come in and tell him everything was clear. In the meantime, the two ladies would wear big coats to hide their finery, and they'd clamber up the lane and into the Rock area. The priest was to wait down the road until he saw us turn up the lane—it was all arranged like a guerrilla operation.

And it all went well. Dermot was there—he came out from his hiding-place and we headed for King Cormac's Chapel, one of the oldest holy places in the country. Now, he hadn't been in touch, and nobody had seen him since these arrangements were made weeks earlier. He asked me about the Dundrum fiasco—and then I told him about April, and her health, and what had happened to her.

He looked shocked and asked how she was. I told him everything about that terrible night in the castle. And I left him there, leaning against the wall, and went to get the two ladies. I was excited at being able to tell April that he was here, ready and waiting.

"Oh, Harney," said she, "you've answered the question I was afraid to ask."

She was obviously afraid that events might prevent him from showing up.

The priest arrived a few minutes later. Now the bridal party was complete—bride and attendant, best man and celebrant, and bridegroom waiting for us at the altar.

But when we got to the little church—no Dermot. I thought he had gone into hiding again until he was sure that the voices he heard were ours—that's what I'd have done—and I went looking for him. Well, I searched and I searched and never found him.

When I went back to the chapel, April was crying. Not out loud, just tears pouring down her face. We waited an hour and more, because that's what she wanted to do. But we could be waiting still—he never appeared.

Eventually, we all returned to the car. I gave the priest his offering—a man has to get paid—and we drove back to the castle. She never stopped crying throughout the whole journey, and when we got back there she disappeared and nobody saw her for weeks.

So, now I could conclude that I was not the son of Dermot Noonan. For which relief, much thanks. I met him once and disliked him intensely—

condescending and cocky little prancer—and that was years before I ever heard of Charles O'Brien.

Nor could I be the son of April Burke-Somerville, who could not now, after a severe miscarriage—and at almost forty years of age—ever bear children. But I was still the grandson of April Burke the First, the strumpet from County Limerick.

The human spirit can be damnably perverse. However distraught I was by the first DNA revelation, and further hammered by the second one, I was now disappointed. If I had been April's son, that would have given me, late in life, some of the sense of magic that I had always missed. I could have told myself that I came from that grand intrigue, and that both my grandmother, the actress, and my mother, the chatelaine, had been the objects of great, all-consuming passions.

Mind you, I would also have had to observe that both my grandmother and my great-grandmother had taken their own lives by jumping off bridges. So there I was. April did not marry Dermot Noonan. And I still had no explanation for the bizarre DNA results. I searched Charles's history, and I searched it again—and found nothing there. The mystery continued.

I worked like a demon, hauling in every loose end that I could find. Then I indulged in some unraveling of the text to make some more loose ends. And I chased them to their origins. After that, I began to check out the other hazy figures in this steam room.

Noonan did marry. Three years later, while still in his fifties, he found a different young widow with a large farm of land. A leopard doesn't change his spots. The wedding took place very conventionally, in a church. Why couldn't he have continued the flamboyance?

Whatever the complications, part of me wished that April could have married on the Rock of Cashel—one of the "Seven Wonders of Tipperary," according to Bernard O'Brien. It's unique.

From the grassy heights inside the enclave, the views to the north and west define the county. The view is of wide open fields, a ruined abbey, a sense of deep fertility, the high, blue sky, and those cloud formations that fascinated Charles O'Brien.

Inside, the buildings continue to engross me, even after forty years of guiding school tours around the place. The vaulted heights, the gray-white of the limestone, the ancient mason work, the smoothness of the cut stone, the hush—nowadays, I sometimes go there just to feel the place, to be part of it.

And I replay what it must have been like that morning—for this disappointed woman, rich beyond her dreams, her body in aching turmoil, still hunting for the happiness she had slightly touched when she lived as a girl with her father. She stood in the shadows of King Cormac's Chapel, an exquisite little twelfth-century Romanesque building whose construction had all kinds of mathematical orientation built into it.

And she waited and she waited for the man who'd lost interest in her once he knew she could not bear him an heir so that he and his family would then completely own the Tipperary estate. He had failed to get it in court, and now he was trying to get it by other means. I suppose she was fortunate that he didn't marry her and then kill her.

Through all of this, Charles kept writing his "History." But never a word of April's misfortunes does he record—no mention of the miscarriage or the aborted wedding. So much for the objective historian—selective again. But I remind myself in fairness that he did issue a warning at the beginning: "Be careful about me."

Many of his entries now merely illuminate details of the later work on the castle: a fight among the Paglaloni brothers; Mr. Higgins the stonemason marrying for the first time, at sixty-five, to a girl of twenty-three; the sudden appearance of a new Flying Column leader in the cellars; and some details of local visitors.

There's a general sense, by the middle of 1921, that he's not going to write a lot more. That sense would have come across even if one didn't have the physical advantage of seeing how few pages are left.

But when he does attend to the events that made it into the history books, he shows the same awareness of detail that he did when he was merely nine years old back at the Treece eviction—which now returns to him, with a shock.

Shall I write this History for the rest of my life? But shall longer days, if I am granted them, ever prove as engrossing as those which I have already chronicled? How I thank my father for the first such thought—that I should write down, as the witness, the events of Mr. Treece's harsh evicting. Father could not have known how being a witness would, in general, hold my life together—or in the particular, how that eviction would return to me as a gift. It was a gift that gave me a lesson that I might never have so sharply learned, and it came about like this.

After Harney's defeat in the Dundrum Ambush, he took some heart in the events up and down the country. The news from within the republican organization reached us days or weeks late, and then we would hear details that the newspapers never reported. I thrilled to the daring that men exhibited in ambushes and other raids; and, in common with everybody in the land, I flinched at the behavior of the troops. No wonder that Sinn Fein swept the elections in May; as one newspaper reported, "disgust cast the most votes," and it is true that revulsion at the army and the Black and Tans gave new support to the Irish Republican Army.

Discussing the rapid developments became quite a pattern with Harney and me. Each morning as we took a respite from the building work, he would tell me of this IRA operation, or that army reprisal, and I felt that I was living in the very pages of history.

One morning, down in the stable-yards, when we stood in from the rain and marveled at the continuing success of the cellars as a refuge, I asked about a new face leading the men.

"He's a fellow called Lacey," Harney said, "who is by all accounts fearless. He has been busy in these parts since early last year."

I had seen the chap but never spoken to him—and I marked how all the men respected him.

"What became of your erstwhile leader?" I asked, preferring not to use his name.

"He's not coming back," said Harney. "They say there are big talks on the way and he's in there."

I feared that Harney had been deliberately placed in a position of danger as a disrespect to me—so I asked the question that had been weighing heavily on my mind ever since the dreadful fracas with the general.

"Why was Dundrum chosen? It was unsuitable, was it not?"

Harney said, "He was supposed to lead it—and since he came back from Spain, he made it his business to know every stick and stone of the land around Dundrum."

At this, a cold feeling climbed my neck, and I remembered an early ghostliness that this individual had caused in me.

"Does he have a connection to the place?"

Harney looked at me, surprised that I might not have known something of common knowledge.

"Of course he does. His family was evicted by a landlord, right at the edge of the woods, near the sawmill. He was only a babe in arms. George Treece: a bad egg, by all accounts—your father must have known him. The evicted family emigrated to Canada. And, by coincidence, so did the Treeces."

Now my heart began to rend itself. All my days I had pitied that family; I thought of them frequently, and they had a most tender place in my feelings. Not long ago, Mr. Yeats wrote a poem entitled "Easter 1916" in which he mentioned one of the leaders as having "done most bitter wrong to some who are near my heart." In this he spoke for me too with that evicted family whom George Treece wronged.

How I remembered a mother lashed with a whip, and two boys come to her aid, and a man with one leg, and a house torn down; and how I thought that even a mind and spirit as yet unformed, such as that infant in his mother's arms, could not have lived through such a catastrophe and not have been somewhere, somehow, aware of the injustice—and would then have been reminded of it by family lore all his life. At the moment when I understood that I had seen the infant evicted grown into a man, I believe that I became a more understanding human being.

In the weeks immediately preceding this information, we had been living in a most precarious state. April, deeply unwell, had lately taken to her bed. As part of her poor state, she must have been distressed and terrified at the news reaching us every day from the other Great Houses. They were being destroyed at the rate of several a week. Lord and Lady Listowel were burned out, and the place that Lady Mollie Carew so loved, Castle Bernard, was burned to the ground. Lord Bandon was kidnapped (and later released), and while the place was blazing, Lady Bandon, Mollie's—and April's—dear friend Doty, stood in the flaming doorway and sang "God Save the King" while the arsonists looked on.

I waited every day for a gang to arrive, and unable to endure the anxiety any longer, I approached the new leader, Lacey, and asked him whether I must worry. To my relief he looked at me as though I were crazed (we were down in the cellars), and then turned to gesture at all the men behind us, eating, smoking, reading, playing cards.

"D'you think these boys'd let that happen?"

Then came the better news—the government instructed the army, which included the Black and Tans, that no more houses in Ireland's towns and villages were to be set aflame in reprisals for ambushes or other Flying Column activity. We had had significant destruction in our village the night of the Tankardstown Ambush; many young men were taken from home at gunpoint and shot, and the teacher's house was burned to the ground. Now, therefore, the counter-reprisals against the mansions would also cease.

I have lived such a profound life—I feel as though I have lived many lives. How happy were my days with my parents; and how beautiful and long the days of my childhood, with Buckley and his innuendo, and Mr. Halloran and his dwarfs, and Miss Taylor and her tears, and Mrs. Curry with her turkey's walk. And my lovely Euclid—I found many ways to honor him in my thoughts, and I was a fortunate man to have known such a soul. Of Mother—what can I say that will make a sum equal to her parts? She is now an old lady—but the youngest old lady I have ever known, and still so ordered and orderly.

And I have been in every parish and village and town in Ireland; I have healed people and made them well again, I have given them hope and they have rewarded me with smiles. I do not believe that there is a house in which I visited that I cannot be welcome again. My potions remain as efficacious as ever; I have never given up my interest in curing the sick, and I never shall. It is my sincere conviction that all human ailments may be rendered better, that all the frail may be made strong. In these pages I discussed a consumptive patient in Bruree, the village whence Mr. de Valera hails. Now she has three children and a husband who loves her more than ever.

My missteps have been my own, and there were many. But there came a day when they ceased, when I took command of a great project, and at the same time took command of myself. Few men ever are granted the capacity to seize such an opportunity. For the granting of it, I am indebted to the woman whom I have loved for more than twenty years, and whom I have loved whether she cared. On account of her presence in my life, I met the man whom I have come to love as a son—and would that I had a son, to tell him about my friend Joseph Harney. He is one whom I must account in this History as on the scale of Mr. Yeats and Mr. Parnell and Mr. Shaw and all the other remarkable people whom I have known, each one touched with greatness in his own way. This has been a fortunate life.

Everything in Ireland quickened that spring and summer. As a boy I heard the old-timers talk of the glorious weather in 1921. Its curiosity value paled beside the pace of events.

In December 1920, the Government of Ireland Act was made law in London. It divided Ireland into two electoral districts. The elections that Charles mentioned were held on 13 May 1921, to try to determine the Parliament of Southern Ireland. Of the available 128 seats, Sinn Fein took 124.

The election took place against a backdrop of daily violence. Michael Collins had cranked up the guerrilla war to a high pitch. On the one hand, his men were killing soldiers and policemen in significant numbers. And on the other hand, the forces of the Crown, frustrated and lacking battle plans, were committing worse and worse atrocities.

They shot in cold blood IRA Volunteers they captured, declaring that these men had been "trying to escape"—the phrase became a national jibe. They breached orders and agreements and burned down houses, villages, town and city centers. They opened fire on innocent people at random—and any soldier caught at it was declared by the authorities to be "insane."

The pressure on the government began to mount. No juries could be found to sit in the courts. Policemen began to retire or resign. The paid government officials began to tell their masters in London that not only was the country fast becoming ungovernable, their methods were exacerbating matters. On 11 July 1921, a truce was called.

We had to be careful. After all, those of us with guns, the Volunteers—we were still outlaws. The orders came through a few days later. Go home, but go carefully. Disarm, but hide your gun in a safe place. Stand down, but be ready to spring back into action.

The boys left the cellars at night. Charles knew when they were leaving, and he came down, to the very point of exit, and wished each man well.

Naturally, I stayed on. I wasn't in good form at all. The Dundrum thing still hung over me—I hadn't even been able to go to the funerals. But at least now I'd be able to visit the families. Seven men dead, seven families—I thought I'd never recover from it. In truth, it took me years, and I think I managed only by the expedient of becoming friendly with those families—fathers and mothers and brothers and sisters.

Next day, when all the boys were gone out of the cellars, Charles and I set about cleaning up. No small task, I tell you. We'd had a long run and a good run, we'd saved at least one life there, and mourned many others. We had to leave it clean as a whistle—you never knew in those days what was going to happen next. You had to be ready for anything.

And then we went back upstairs, and I began to get myself back into the life of the castle. Charles, without telling why, took me all over the place, and I knew that he was saying, "Welcome back."

It all looked splendid. How he brought it off I don't know, given how troubled he must have been by the events with April, and her baby that didn't get born, and her marriage that didn't get made.

I mean—if you looked up and saw those plaster cornices, and those birds with the berries in their beaks, and those great medallions with Zeus and Aphrodite and Neptune and Lord knows what else, and all of them restored and gleaming—oh, God, it was tremendous.

That very day, they were just beginning the last big job—the painting of the walls and ceilings. Charles took me down to the stables where Mr. Mulberry's workbenches used to be, and Mr. Higgins's stone sets, and he showed me where the painters—from London—had set up what almost looked like a laboratory. There was this long bench, and there were test-tubes, and boards with daubs of color on them, raspberry, and turquoise, and yellow like the sun itself.

"It's going to be as authentic as we can make it," said Charles. "What else have we left," said he, "but authenticity?"

I seized my moment.

"Speaking of authenticity," said I, "how is April and what are you going to do about her?"

I said it in a low voice, but he turned away from me. We walked out in the open air, where nobody could hear us.

"I don't know how she is," said he. "I haven't asked. She is safe physically—I know that. I've supervised the food that Helen brings her—but Helen is sworn not to tell her that."

He didn't continue.

Said I, "And the second half of my question—what are you going to do about her?"

His answer was very much like his spirit. "Today, I don't know—but maybe one day I'll know what to do. And if that day comes—I'll test things."

And, of course, as I and my family have ever known since—a day came and he did test things.

Harney's fighting days were over. So were Tipperary's—and Cork's and Kerry's and Dublin's and Limerick's and Clare's and everybody else's. The truce of July became the treaty of December. A deal was struck to divide the island. Six of the thirty-two counties remained loyal to the king, and the remaining twenty-six became independent, with our own government and official institutions.

The ink on the signatures still shone wet when the arguments broke out. De Valera, who had refused to take part in the negotiations, declared the treaty unsatisfactory because it left a British political and military presence in part of Ireland. Collins, one of the negotiators, said they had done their best to get a good solution. Civil war, vicious and incestuous, came in like a thug.

In most Irish history books, the name Michael Collins never appeared during my time as a teacher. When all the dust of the twenties and thirties settled, Collins's great rival de Valera became the ruler of the twenty-six counties and banned Collins's name from the histories. Thus are new nations born. And in England, no school that I know of has ever taught the full story of the British in Ireland.

Before the internecine upheavals broke out, the British troops began to leave. Here, Charles O'Brien outdoes all the history books, because once again he becomes the witness. It was just before Christmas 1921, and Joseph Harney was with him.

From afar, we followed avidly the Treaty negotiations in London. I thrilled to think that I had met two of the Irish delegates—Mr. Griffith, who never fired a shot except in print, but to great effect; and Mr. Collins. The countryside talked of nothing else; I think that Ireland could not believe its own eyes and ears that peace of a kind—of any kind—might come.

For those weeks, April became a sort of politician. She wrote to all her English and Anglo-Irish friends, including Miss Beresford, and told them not to feel so betrayed. To her Irish friends, who had supported the Volunteers, she spoke of the responsibilities of a new nation. Her intent, she said, was to bring both sides of her circle to terms with what had come about and with the future as she saw it.

A fresh zeal seemed to have seized her; she wrote long letters full of reasons why she had restored the house; and she invited her correspondents to consider that now Tipperary must be looked at in a different way—that it was a part of the past, unpleasant for some, but still full of meaning, and it would now make a great contribution to the new state's future.

Her energy had returned. But she did not feel sufficiently well, she said, to join Harney and myself on a journey to Dublin—a journey that had a specific meaning. We had heard the tales, we had read the reports—and at six o'clock one morning Harney and I left the house to drive to the North Wall of Dublin's port and see the British Army leaving Ireland.

Scarcely a word passed between us on the road. The car was new—a Singer—and even though we could have pulled down the top, we chose not to, and we wrapped ourselves like Eskimos. As we drove into the city, we saw no police, no military—just ordinary people going about their ordinary business.

We drove along Sackville Street, still in ruins after the Easter Rising shells—scarcely a building had not been destroyed. As we turned down toward the Custom House, we saw the sight that we had come for. Lines of soldiers marched in the street, line after line of them, laden with kit bags and with rifles shouldered. Along the pavements, a few people waved, and in many instances, men, women, and children walked purposefully along beside the regiment, talking to this soldier and that sergeant or corporal. I quickly understood what I was seeing—many of the men in British uniforms were Irish boys who had been sent here after France, and they were talking to their families about when they would next be home.

Harney said to me, "Turn back," and on the wide street I turned the car around; he directed me back across the bridge to the quays on the other side of the river Liffey. I saw what he intended—that we should get a distant view of the marching troops rather than find ourselves among them. First, however, we saw the ruins of Liberty Hall; as James Connolly's headquarters, where he and his Irish Citizen Army planned their strategies, it had been the first target of the British gunboats that sailed into Dublin Bay to quell the uprising Easter Week.

Now, as we stood on Butt Bridge, we saw the soldiers perfectly. They marched six abreast—at no great pace, because they carried so much. I had often contemplated what a retreating army looks like. The Romans ran south through Britain to their galleys at Dover, so great had been their urgency. Napoleon sulked in his carriage as he led what was left of his army while they lurched and staggered back from the ice of Moscow.

The British Army leaving Ireland had no bands, no swagger, just men marching. They were cheerful; they waved to the bystanders.

Harney said to me, "What do you think of this?"

I said, "It can be nothing but good."

Harney then said, "Oh, it's much better than that," and his voice had fervor in it thick as butter.

Two British ships stood at the dock—one of the Royal Navy and one of the Merchant Navy, and they had begun to march men aboard. Like Noah's Ark, the soldiers went in two by two.

Sometimes when historic matters are taking place, we do not necessarily make ourselves aware of that fact. That morning, by the river Liffey, watching those troops marching out of the land of my birth, I knew what I was seeing. Eight hundred years of domination and suppression, often unjust and frequently brutal, had come to an end in much of Ireland.

Harney and I stayed for some hours; then we went to Jammet's, and over potato soup and excellent beef I told him about Oscar Wilde, and the first April Burke.

After watching the troops withdraw, Harney went back to Tipperary with Charles just as the pro-treaty and anti-treaty factions were beginning to square off. The country still reeled from the sheer ferocity of Collins's campaign, and there were many wounds to lick, many bereavements to heal.

By this stage in his text, Charles has more or less abandoned the idea of keeping a rigorous historical chronicle. He was, of course, preoccupied with the castle, and that was the main focus of his attention; in his record of his life as it had now become, he kept detailed accounts of cattle prices, how much he was paying workmen, and so on, and he wrote less and less about contemporary events. Therefore, the first time I read the end of Charles's "History," I felt slightly cheated, especially now that I knew I had more than a passing interest in it.

For example, he completely omitted Noonan, who became a major figure in the politics ahead. How I wish that Charles had had the courage to tell us what he felt when all that was going on. I wanted to know his feelings as he saw the love affair burgeoning, and when he heard of the miscarriage—was that the first time he knew of the pregnancy?

Above all, what went through his mind when he saw her drive off, as he—and she—believed, to her wedding? And what did he think when she came home, jilted? Now, with my own identity at stake, and so late in my life, I knew I needed—vitally so—to learn more.

And my thought was: Two such luminous people as Charles O'Brien and April Burke must have left behind more of a trace than Charles's selective account. After all, Harney left behind what amounts to an oral history.

For starters, though, I already had a database nearer home. I hadn't touched my mother's photographs since she and I sorted them when I was a schoolboy. From time to time, I had promised myself that I would catalog every one and donate the collection to the National Library.

She had taken so many—before she married my father. Also, she had done quite an amount of sorting without my help. Perceiving her work as a matter of national interest, she had divided each category according to county. "Dublin" had the thickest files, but I went straight to "Tipperary."

In the file marked "People" I found nothing to help me—but I did in "Places." She'd taken about thirty photographs on the day they opened the restored castle to thank the locals for their help.

At the back of the file I found a newspaper—from *The Nationalist,* folded open to a page with the headline "Grand Time at Tipperary."

"It was a day long awaited," writes "Our Social Secretary,"

and hundreds of local people who had worked on the rebuilding were happy guests. Mrs. Somerville, radiant in a green frock, welcomed many local dignitaries on her lawns. Dinner tables inside the castle groaned under the weight of food, and John Ryan & Son, Vintners, Main Street, Cashel provided beverages. Mrs. John Ryan was among the guests, looking radiant in black.

At eight o'clock in the evening, with the sunlight still broad upon the fields and terraces, Mrs. Somerville ushered her guests along the southern walls, to some platforms and benches. The castle is equipped with a theater, but with one hundred seats it was deemed too small for the large crowd.

Mary Cody, aged six, danced jigs and reels, and a fiddler, Joseph Harney, played for her; the audience delighted in them. Her brother, James Cody, recited a poem, "Dark Rosaleen," and also received loud applause. Two ten-year-old girls, the Cody sisters, played concertinas dexterously; the concertina is a difficult instrument—but not in their hands. Mr. and Mrs. Cody (of Cody's Boots & Shoes, West Gate, Clonmel) were proud parents in the audience. Mr. John Coffey (of Coffey the Butcher), who is also a renowned local tenor, sang "Danny Boy." He was accompanied by his cousin Josie Cleary, on the violin, and were there extra sobs to be wrung from the song's mourning, she would have found them. The sun's dying rays fell aslant across the audience and bathed the people in shades of red.

Mrs. Somerville made what she called "a historic announcement." She declared that she was forming a troupe of actors, a permanent company, to put on plays at the theater. She said that local people whom she hired would be paid for their work, and would also get the benefit of being taught by famous actors, whom she intended to invite from time to time. Her words received many energetic murmurs of comment.

The Nationalist report includes many more names, notably of businesspeople who advertised in the newspaper. Charles receives no mention; nor did the Social Secretary make any observations on the renovations or the gardens or the food.

In his "History," Charles also reported the day. Though briefly, and with some reflection, he—as ever—added substance. Here, with some abridgments—he included lists of names—is an excerpt from his account.

My country in its adventures and tensions had been, in my lifetime, advancing toward the convulsion of rebellion, as I had been struggling with unrequited love. Ireland has now achieved the aftermath of independence, which, as I write this, has not yet reached tranquillity—but I believe it will. I myself have not yet reached out and grasped the inner peace that I seek—but I hope to do so one day.

Both my country and my spirit have been in need of ritual. First, the departure of the troops gave us a national reason to celebrate—our green island is now ours to throw open, to welcome in the world. And second, without, I hope, self-aggrandizement, here is my parallel with it: on the day in August 1922—let me give it full title, Sunday, the 20th—when April opened the castle to friends and neighbors, we marked a great joy at the completion of our massive work.

The Gardens had approached, in my view, perfection; already we received questions as to our inspirational planting, and requests from people who, having heard the rumors, wished to visit. Our restoration of Major and Minor (the two pavilions) made my heart sing at the sheer beauty of Mr. Mulberry's fretted carpentry. The swards of the terraces, when newly mown, looked like starched green linen.

On the morning of the celebration, I rode the land. Out across the fields, I gazed at our herds and our horses. We had developed excellent systems of paddocking and grazing in rotation, with the dairy cows and the beef cattle (mostly yearlings) fenced away from each other. Not so with the horses; I'd deliberately asked the ostlers and the stewards to achieve a good mixture according to age; as with humans, young horses need to learn sense from their elders.

When I came back, I walked from the stables into the kitchens—all restored, all staffed, and working as though there had never been a hiatus of nearly seven decades. As to the building, when Mr. Higgins had concluded his stonework on the exterior of the castle—several years had passed since then—he had come indoors and attended to the great fireplaces, all of which had been restored. I requested his caution to make them not so much to look like new—they still kept their patina of ancient fires from long-past winter evenings. Of these, his greatest task had been in the kitchens, where two gigantic fireplaces at either end had been in dire want of repair, right up to chimney level. Now the fires roared with the cooking of the food, and the fireplaces looked magnificent.

Before that reparation, however, I had asked our Master Stonemason to restore the bridge; it may well be judged the sweetest thing he ever did for us. I believe that he thought so too, because when it was completed, Mr. Higgins went out of his way every morning coming to work, and every evening going home, to stand on the bridge and stroke its cut-stone parapets.

Now, as I stood in the main doorway, waiting for the first guests to arrive, I looked not only at the bridge but at the restless willows above the water, the great placid beeches and oaks beneath the castle walls, the line of plane trees, and I admired—again—how they had been trimmed, and how their new growths gave forth the most pleasant feeling of safety.

Nothing, however, compared with the castle itself. From the slates, blue-black as crows and now shiny in the sun, and along the parapets and battlements, to the turrets, and then down along the great facades with their long, big walls—oh, what a place we had here! Privately I had said to myself: I will see to it that this woman has the finest house in Europe. And not only will it be so judged in the strength of its fabric—it will be hailed for the steady perfection of its exterior, and the daring beauty of its interior.

All around the Great Hall we had re-created what it must have looked like. Ancient drawings of the castle had helped us, and it took little imagination to see a king or a knight stride across here, and climb the angelic white marble of the Grand Staircase. The hangings, the tapestries with their great scenes of hunting—how they asserted their rights to be here.

I began a last walk through the great rooms. How had the polishers achieved such a gleam on the furniture? All the doors between the dining-rooms had been opened, the tables connected, and now we had one great banqueting spread; I guessed the connected tables reached more than eighty feet.

Every outer door on the southern side of the castle had also been opened to the paved terraces and rows of tables bearing the drink to be served. We had kegs and casks, beer, sherries, port wines; at least the paving-stones were now level, and people might not fall down, because here we meant that they would dance!

I walked along to the open doors of the Ballroom and went back inside the house. Four months earlier, Serge and Claudette Lemm had unveiled "my" mural—the saffron yellows, the coral reds, the green soft as our fields. I loved the scale: the house of Odysseus was mighty, yet intimate; by the tree in her bedroom, Penelope sat at her loom, weaving the celebrated garment.

At the unveiling I told April the story: With Odysseus away from home, suitors persisted in trying to win his wife's affections. He's dead, said some—the Trojan War killed him; he's no good, said others—he's not coming back. Penelope promised each suitor that she would marry him when she had finished weaving the robe on her loom, and each day she wove so that they could see her, and each night she unraveled what she had woven, so that she never finished.

In the mural, Odysseus has returned and strides his bedroom floor like a great-thighed hero; through the door behind him we see the bodies on the floors of his house—the suitors he has slain lie in their own gore. Penelope sits nearby, and she holds across her knees the robe that she has at last finished weaving; it is as blue as air, and the loom beside her is empty of yarn.

April looked at the picture for a long time, but she said not a word. Now I stood in front of it and feasted across its wide range: the horses, the dogs, a kitten playing with a leaf, a hand-maiden in an orange gown pouring shining water into a cauldron, a tray of food—Vien had painted a scene of a conquering hero standing in his own house, about to claim his woman. If I never do anything notable in my life, I shall at least say that I have had this picture released to the world's eyes once again.

No day had more sun as that great, celebratory Sunday. My mother stood with me—still as straight as a stick—at the door to the opened dining-rooms and watched the seated banquet begin.

"So this is to be the shape of the world," she said. Mother wore a black-and-white silk dress that day, and a great black hat with a white ribbon. People thronged to her, and she had a smile for everybody and an interested inquiry.

My dear Lady Mollie arrived—whom I had not seen in months, a fact for which she chided me.

I defended myself well; I know all her sallies—and then asked her, "But why did you not bring Mr. Ross? I should like to have met him again."

To which she replied with an answer that I had heard about others all too frequently in the last eight years: "He died, dear."

I said, "But I did not know? Was it Vimy? The Somme? Or—in Ireland?"

"Neither, dear. He never went to war; he didn't need to—he was able to die with no reason."

To which I said, "I'm afraid I have been so absorbed that I have missed much."

This somber news made a brief black plume in the air—but it was the only such darkness.

Weeks earlier, as we'd prepared for this day, I'd asked Harney the address to which I might send Mr. Collins an invitation. He'd looked alarmed and shaken his head.

"We won't do that," he said.

I asked why and he told me that, given the bitterness now mounting between those who supported the Treaty with London and those who believed that it gave Ireland too little, Mr. Collins might not be safe here. Tipperary had become rife with anti-Treaty forces—the "Irregulars."

"But we have no politics here," I said.

"No, Charles, but the people you invite—they'll have enough politics for everybody. That's not a subject to mention that day."

There came a moment when I walked away from the dancing and climbed up the highest of the terraces, from where, a few hundred yards distant, I turned and looked back. It looked like a gala from history. The dancers had not confined themselves to the Ballroom; they had, as we intended, whirled out onto the paving-stones outside the Ballroom doors, and as they flew and spun to the music, the bystanders applauded them. Everywhere seemed full of good humor. By the liquor tables, people stood three and four deep, and people of all stripes talked to one another; this was a day of the greatest gaiety.

In the midst of the dancers, I saw April. She danced with Harney and they danced excellently together, and I saw her throw her head back and laugh, and then reach in and embrace Harney, and then laugh again and then dance on, and I remembered Mr. Yeats's wonderful poem, that he conceived here—"And he saw young men and young girls / Who danced on a level place."

I shall write and tell him, I reflected, of April's "sad and gay face."

At three o'clock in the morning we still kept torches burning on the avenue. The Paglalonis, the Marchettis, the Lemms—they had stayed together at dinner, and as darkness fell, they came to me almost as a group, and each one said that they wept to think that the work had ended, and each one told me that never would they work on such a rewarding enterprise again, and each one brought me gifts, and I had not the words to thank them.

The Marchettis gave me a marble carving—and rendered me speechless when they told me its provenance: "The Signora's hands."

"The Signora?"

"Yes," they said, "the Signora Somaaar-veel."

Had they asked April to sit for them while they took casts of her hands? It appeared so, and the carving was a perfect replica. Gianfranco Paglaloni gave me a little stucco medallion of a horse—a replica that the brothers had constructed of the first piece of decorative plaster ever placed on the castle walls. Serge and Claudette Lemm gave me a charcoal drawing they had made of the mural's Odysseus: "For Monsieur Charles O'Brien—who knows of these things."

When everybody had left, and the last of our workers had gone to bed, and no sound could be heard anywhere, the first lemon stripes of dawn began to spear the eastern sky toward Cashel. I leaned against the door and looked out into the gloaming—full darkness seems never to fall on an Irish summer night. Another line by Mr. Yeats came to mind: " 'What then?' sang Plato's ghost. 'What then?' "

MONDAY, THE 21ST OF AUGUST 1922.

Why must Life so mix us up? I have great joy in my heart today at my dear son's triumph, and great sorrow—that I can never speak—at my beloved Bernard's despondency. Dare I say it to him? No. Then we shall have to address it between ourselves, and we are too old. Bernard sits by the fire all day. I know that he broods on the great wrong he has done.

Now it hurts him so. He could not share his son's triumph yesterday. He could not witness how our neighbors hail his son. He knows that some people who went to the castle banquet are aware of his dreadful truth.

Many times, I feel he wishes to tell me what he has done. I fervently hope he does not. For if he does, I shall have to cease speaking to him forever.

And does he not worry that Charles knows? And if Charles does not know, why does he not know?

Oh, I wish I had not written these words here. They despoil the memory of the great day that we had yesterday. Charles tells me that he and he alone chose the yellow that is painted on the walls of the Great Hall—and the raspberry on the Gallery's ceiling. He knows colors better than I do. I am so proud of him.

From Joe Harney's oral reminiscences:

It was three days, I remember, three days after the banquet in Tipperary Castle when I heard the news. What's that machine they ride at carnivals, what do they call it—a roller-coaster? Yes, that's it. There were still people cleaning up and putting the dining-rooms back together after that great party. In the village they were saying that there'll never be another as good—there couldn't be.

I was sitting in the sunshine outside the Ballroom when I heard it. What could I do but weep? I put my hands over my face and I just wept. In floods. That awful feeling we get in our chests—I can still feel it now, all these years afterward. Oh, God! When I thought of the times I had been with him, and how I looked up to him.

It was Charles who told me. A workman rode up from the village in a bad state. Charles didn't believe him—and then he did believe him. Just as Charles told me, April arrived and found the two of us in tears.

"Mr. Collins is dead," said Charles, and she sat straight down.

None of us said much to each other. She asked one question: "Does that mean our protection has gone?"

Who could answer her? I know that she wanted me to reassure her, but I was out of it by then; I was never going to make war on my fellow-Irishmen.

April nodded as if she understood why we didn't answer, and then she left us alone. When our grief thawed a little, Charles and I talked. We talked for ages—about the first time Charles met Mick Collins, about the clarity of his vision, about how tough he was, about the mistakes he had been making by killing too many of his own countrymen in this new conflagration.

"Did he really protect this place?" Charles asked me.

"Didn't you know he would? You let his Volunteers hide in the cellars." Charles often played the innocent—and I often stopped him from doing it. "And he liked you a lot. That's why he wrestled with you that first day. He only did that with men who impressed him. I always thought it was childish."

"But—April's right, those days are over, aren't they?" said Charles. "There are houses being burned again."

"Left, right, and center," I remember saying. I thought to burn down these lovely old houses was barbaric and stupid, and they were burning nearly one a night.

Charles sat there, and he said something like, "Well, they tried before." And he must have caught some look or shadow or something crossing my face—he was as quick as a fish when he wanted to be. He pressed me, and I tried to avoid it.

"That first fire—what was it? What caused it?"

I tried to avoid it, and he pressed me again.

"Harney, what are friends for?"

Well, he found out now. Very slowly and very carefully, I told him that the previous attempt to burn down Tipperary Castle had nothing to do with patriotism or anti-British sentiment or anything like that. It was the result of a conspiracy.

A bunch of local landowners whose properties all adjoined the castle decided they wanted the estate broken up. Then each of them could get some of the land. Charles's father, Bernard O'Brien, was one of them. When the Burkes, April and her father, came into the picture, these men saw the danger to their interests. Without ever telling Bernard, a bunch of them hired thugs to frighten off April, and everyone that had anything to do with her. That's how Charles got beaten up in Limerick—he'd told me all about it. And that's how he got shot, and how I met him.

In fairness to Bernard, he nearly lost his reason when he heard it. Who wouldn't? His son shot and nearly killed? But, mind you, he didn't call off the arson efforts, and he was the one who told the thugs that Charles was away Easter Week. That was when they set the fire in the castle.

Charles asked me about that too, and I told him—to soften the blow—that they had also threatened Mrs. O'Brien. I mean—these fellows followed Charles across the countryside here, and attacked him. They warned people off talking to him; people would go in and shut their doors if they saw Charles coming.

When he saw all this happening, Charles thought—and I did too when he told me—that someone had a grudge against him, that a cure had gone wrong or something. Sure, didn't we spend many weeks visiting people where he thought there might be an old enmity? There was no such thing—there were no old enmities. Unless you count his father.

So—I told him all this. I'd only found it out a few months before, from one of the Volunteers, whose uncle was one of the fellows they hired—a bad pill of a fellow called Donoghue, with a finger missing. He used to mooch around the castle, trying to see what he could steal.

What a grim morning that was. Our leader dead, shot on a roadside in his native County Cork, and shot by fellow-Irishmen, his former comrades. My friend here in front of me, white in the face at the thought of his father's treachery—the father whom he always talked about so warmly. And the threat hanging over us that all our work might be burned down any day or night now.

I could nearly see Charles's mind working. "I'm going to think," said he. A few days later he said to me, "Regarding that matter—I've decided." He told me that he was going to forgive his father—that he had already forgiven him. But he was never going to mention it at Ardobreen.

"He knows what he's done, Harney. That's why he hasn't been able to look me in the face for many years—that's why he was never there when I went over to visit Mother."

Then he made a joke of it. "Anyway," said he, "after Sunday night's party nobody will boycott me."

It seems a preposterous tale. Would a father endanger his own son? Bernard O'Brien hadn't signed up for harming Charles. Nevertheless, I felt disinclined to believe the story when I first read it. But it kept nagging at me. It had an uncomfortable ring of truth.

So I included it in my "Items to Research"—this was before I had been given Charles's mother's journal. And then I found a paper in the *Tipperary Historical Journal,* by a Trinity College lecturer in history, Joachim Ryan, who specializes in eighteenth- and nineteenth-century Irish land disputes.

Dr. Ryan described the existence of numerous such cartels as the Tipperary one, and he explained their motives as "partly shrewd practice, partly emotional."

"These farmers," he wrote, "had struggled through generations to keep the farms that they tenanted, had perhaps taken them into ownership though the indulgence of a benign landlord, and then sought to own more land in order to strengthen and secure their income. They had seen the political winds blow, and knew that land might be acquired through a variety of means: via a direct landlord-to-tenant sale, via a Wyndham Act sale—when they would have been negotiating with the government—or via a default sale, where fallow land that seemed to have no promise of being farmed, for legal reasons, might one day be purchased upon application to the government."

That's simple enough. Once the Tipperary cartel saw the Burke interest waxing, their only hope was to frighten people off. It didn't work. Charles survived and went on to his triumph. What a shield innocence can be.

But it still seems barely credible that neither Charles nor his mother would raise the matter with Bernard. Perhaps age really did count. Amelia wouldn't have wanted to end her days in acrimony. And Charles would never have brought that kind of turmoil into his family.

Therefore, Bernard got away with it. I wonder if Euclid knew—he seems to have missed little of what went on.

After the party, and the shooting of Michael Collins, Charles writes only one more entry. It's dramatic, and it closes the book, so to speak, in terms of his "History," and its brief last sentence brings to an end over twenty years of agony. Harney described the same event, again differing in some significant ways from Charles—but it was by no means the end of Harney's involvement with Charles. The date relating to the entry is not specified, but my own further discoveries put it at Monday, 4 December 1922.

On the night before beloved Euclid died, I had a dream which I cannot now fully recall; I know that it had a tipped-up cart, and a mountain of cow-manure by the doors of the sheds. Unlike many people, I set no store by dreams; to me they are wanderings of the mind that occur because the body is at rest. That dream also came to me the night before I was shot, when Maudie, my young mare, died beneath me on that wet and cold road.

Not long ago, the dream came back—a tipped-up cart in a yard with whitewashed walls by cowsheds. This must be a yard that I know, yet I cannot place it in my memory. It did not distress me, yet I noted that, as I say, it had appeared in the past when matters of moment came by. I wondered, but in a mild way, what might now threaten.

Next evening, I had my answer. It had been a curious day; we'd had unseasonal snow. I have rarely seen snow; forty miles away, our coast is washed by the temperate waters of the Gulf Stream as it climbs up the Earth from the Gulf of Mexico. But on this day we had a snowfall about two inches high, and we piled wood high upon the fire in the Great Hall.

Then we stood at the doorway—and returned many times—looking out at this wonder. When I refer to "we," I mean April, Harney, myself, and any number of people who came and went; we had a Miss Richardson and a Miss Hayes, seamstresses from Limerick, who had come to stay in the castle while they sewed vast masses of cloth to April's directives, for further draping the high windows.

At about half past nine, when April, Harney, and I had dined, I remarked upon the rising moon and, in order the better to view it, we strolled to the door. By standing just inside we could keep the heat of the Great Hall upon our backs, and the doorway had comfortable room for three people standing abreast. My shoulders almost touched Harney's (April stood on his other side), and I felt something curious in the air between him and me. It was almost as though he bristled, as a dog does when a fox or a foe is put up. Just as I was about to ask him, I heard the noise, and I heard Harney suck in his breath.

Down at the road, a vehicle of some kind turned into the avenue; we saw the big yellow eyes of its lamps sweep across the fields of snow. From Harney came a kind of grunt, and he moved as though to quit the doorway—but I halted him and questioned him by raising an eyebrow.

"Gun," he murmured.

I shook my head—and shook it again for emphasis. He looked into my face.

"Never again in here," I said.

"But—our protection?"

"Joseph, we'll protect ourselves."

Patient as a maid, the truck came unhurriedly up the avenue and soon arrived into the gravel square before the front door. News or feelings of some primitive kind had spread, and soon the Great Hall behind us had filled with people—from the kitchens, down the Grand Staircase (our two seamstresses), and from all corners of the house. They jostled for position inside the windows, and behind us at the door.

Out of the truck, eight men stepped down into the moonlit snow. Most carried guns; two, who came last, reached back into the body of the lorry and fetched great cans, filled, I presumed, with petrol or kerosene or some kind of flammable liquid. The men moved slowly, as though they had all the time in the world; each wore the "uniform" that I had seen so often in our cellars—the day-to-day clothes, the cap, the diagonal bandolier across the chest.

The pair with the cans of liquid knelt in the snow; from their greatcoat pockets they took wads of rags and began to lay them out in neat lines. One went back to the lorry and returned with, strangely, two pairs of crude fireside tongs. I heard Harney swear beside me; I saw April look at them as though mesmerized; I saw the cooks and the maids stare with horror, their round eyes dark with fear. One of the men beside the lorry spoke an order of some kind; the kneeling pair poured the liquid on two rags and lit them; they flared on the snow, and the arsonists picked them up on the tongs, one each, and held them out. The flares illuminated every face of those gunmen, and threw the shadows of giants on the castle walls.

At another order, a young man stepped forward, ahead of the flaming rags, and aimed his rifle at us where we stood in the doorway. Now the leader came toward us, and I heard Harney mutter a name that meant nothing to me—obviously he knew the man, perhaps a former comrade-in-arms.

"Get everybody out," the leader called.

Nobody moved.

"Once more—get everybody out." He did not seem agitated; he did not seem afraid or nervous.

We stood still, and at an order the young man with the rifle fired. I do not know what strategy they had prepared—perhaps he meant not to kill or wound any human. The bullet hit the arch above the door; I saw the chip of stone fly down in front of my eyes. My thoughts—how we seek refuge—went to Mr. Higgins, his beautiful cutting and polishing, and his words if he saw this bullet-hole.

Nobody moved—at least nobody that the raiding party could see; but inside the Great Hall, girls scurried and squealed in terror; how I felt for them. The leader stepped forward some more paces, and the men with the flaring tongs kept level with him; now they stood no more than ten yards from the door, and we could see their eyes in the dancing flames. Behind them, the moon stood low over the snowy fields.

"For the last time," called the leader. "Everybody leave this building."

We did not move—not Harney, not April, not I. The rifleman pulled back his bolt, the metallic sound clacking in the bosom of the castle's echoing walls. His leader spoke an order, and the rifleman lowered his barrel some feet. He sighted the gun even more carefully than the first time and squeezed the trigger. I closed my eyes. Beside me, the wall chipped as though a powerful wasp bit at it and moved on. Something fell to the floor behind me, inside the hallway, and I looked back; there sat the slug of the bullet, death's little black nose.

In the Great Hall, panic was breaking out, and yet we three, who had put this place back together after the ravages of time and enmity—we stood in the doorway, three figures of loving solidarity. I think we must each have sensed at that moment how much we had come through in a short time.

As the boy prepared his gun to fire again, the three of us left the front door, and calmly, in no hurry at all, we walked side by side to stand directly in front of the boy with the rifle.

As he could not now fire at anything—except the sky—without hitting us point-blank, he did not know what to do and glanced across at his leader for direction. The men with the burning torches also grew uncertain; their flames seemed less robust than before. Their leader wore a disbelieving look—and I think it had less to do with this flouting of his authority than with genuine surprise that three people could be so foolhardy as to walk unarmed at a squad of men carrying and aiming guns.

Nobody moved, and nobody spoke. One man accidentally dropped the flare from the jaws of his tongs. As he bent to pick it up, I heard April snap at him, "Do not touch it." The cool and educated English voice cut through the air—and I glanced again at the moon, which was brilliant and large.

Their leader stepped some feet toward where we stood—but he did not come near us; his men, whom we now faced no more than two or three

yards away, did not know where to look. The second flare-carrier dropped
his flames, and they fizzled out in the snow, leaving a black mark like a sin.
April broke our ranks, walked to the leader, and confronted him.

"Stephen Meehan, how dare you? How dare you come here?"

I felt Harney flinch. Meehan reached for his handgun; how had she
known his name?

"Put that gun away—or are you shooting women these days as well as
children?"

Harney beside me murmured, "No, stop, April, stop."

Meehan stepped back and screamed an order—in Gaelic. But nobody
moved. Again he reached down to his belt, and this time he pulled out
the gun.

"Put that back," April said in a voice so clear it could be heard on the
mountainside. She turned away from Meehan and addressed the men
who had not obeyed Meehan's orders.

"Listen! If you put this place to the torch—you are burning your own
property. This estate has been handed over to the new Irish state—for the
new Irish people to enjoy. It was built by the Irish. And it was managed
by the Irish. And it was repaired and restored by the Irish. Is that the respect you have for your countrymen?"

She turned again to Meehan and pointed an arm to the heights of the
castle.

"Your great-grandfather was the mason who built that turret." And
now she turned again to the men, standing transfixed in the snow. "If any
of you—any one of you—if you come from near here, then you are probably here because this place kept your forebears alive. Gave them work.
And will give you work—and your children. This estate is the largest employer in the county. Barbarians wouldn't behave the way you're propos-
ing to do. What has this to do with the Treaty, you savages?"

She turned on her heel, walked back to the castle, went in through the
doorway, and was swallowed by the yellow light of the lamps in the Great
Hall. Meehan, revolver in hand, half-made a step to follow her, then
changed his mind and walked away. The men with the guns sloped
toward the lorry, changed their minds, and walked down toward the
mouth of the avenue, where it disappears into the trees—and their young

marksman ran to catch up with them. Both of the torch-bearers climbed into the front of the lorry; one started the engine, and they drove away.

This left Stephen Meehan, and Harney muttered, "We'll not take our eyes off this fellow."

Meehan looked wild; the light caught his eyes' whites, and he stared at us in a fixed way. He began to wag the gun as though it were accompanying some remarks that he was about to make. Then, walking backward, looking at us all the time, he stepped a wide circle away from us and ran after the truck. The driver had stopped, obviously to wait for Meehan; Harney turned to the castle and made for the door at a trot. I, not knowing why, waited—and watched.

Under the moon I could have read a book that night; the reflection of the snows made it brighter. Meehan climbed into the back of the truck— but still it stayed, ready to enter the trees that overhang those reaches at the top of the avenue. I could see the men inside the truck—they sat like soldiers along each side; I could count them; I could see where Meehan sat, nearest the rear. But directly across from him there must have been a vacant seat—it wanted one more figure. As I watched, a man came out of the little beech grove, in what we called the Front Field, that leads down to the main road. He carried a gun, and even though he stumbled in the snow, I would recognize his walk anywhere. He saw me, and I am pleased to say that I believe he looked sheepish as he climbed into the lorry, and hammered the butt of his gun upon the floor as a signal to drive away.

When I went into the castle, I found a great pandemonium. People cried for joy and relief, and the talk had soared to a wild babble as those who had not overheard the moonlit exchanges sought the fullest version. Harney climbed a few steps of the Grand Staircase and asked for attention; then he told them what had happened.

Soon, everybody had dispersed. I told Harney whom I had seen climb into the lorry; he expressed dismay—and disgust. He asked what I had thought of "April's brilliant ruse," but I laughed and did not make a committed answer. Then I claimed April's attention.

"Find your coat," I said. "Come with me."

We walked together out into the night; Harney looked at me with astounded interest as we went—he always sensed things.

In the general scheme of gardens and lands, I had made sure that the proud spur of ground which gave the best view had been preserved, and it was a tolerable distance to walk. I had sat there often in the old days, on Della; it was the point from which April and I had surveyed Tipperary Castle on her first visit, in October 1904.

Now we climbed the slope, and when we reached the vantage point, I turned to look back; she turned with me. We both saw the same sight: a magnificent building, all parapets and battlements, with its windows aglow, and smooth smoke climbing from its chimneys; and we both knew the same thing—that love of humanity had made it so.

For perhaps five full minutes, each of us drank it in; neither said a word; we stood some feet apart, untouching. I broke the silence—with the words that I had written down, and memorized, more than twenty-two years earlier, and that I had spoken to myself in my own head every day of my life since then.

"I believe, as I have always done since we first met, that you and I should marry."

April said, "Of course we shall."

We walked back to the house in silence, and still untouching—except, I think, in our spirits. As I went in the doorway, I turned back and I looked at the great and inspiring moon with more delight in my spirit than I have ever known.

And now, I believe that I may consider this History complete. It is no more—but also no less—than the chronicle of a faithful and sometimes foolish man. I am aware that I have not done outstanding service to the art of the historian, but I have tried to render a fair likeness of my country as I have seen it.

In my own defense, should any reader find me wanting, I may only reiterate the need for care when Ireland and her story are considered: "Be careful," I have cautioned. And in my own praise—and you will know by now, whoever you are, that I am neither modest nor immodest—I simply say that I have done something many men do not. I wed the woman I loved.

⬧

Harney's account of that night runs to several pages. He tells the same story Charles did. And he adds much speculation as to the talk in the anti-treaty camp the next day about the failed mission.

From him we learn two facts. First, Stephen Meehan was shot dead a week or so later. He ran crazy with a gun, and his own men downed him. Second, and in many ways more interesting, Dermot Noonan quit the civil war that week.

Why? Harney speculates that "April's ruse" made him think again. Noonan knew that things would have to settle down; the civil war couldn't last forever. And if it became known that he'd tried to destroy— for no good reason—a treasure newly donated to the Irish people, his political future would carry at least a blemish, perhaps a blight. Especially given his personal history with the castle.

I was more concerned to see where Harney's account didn't match Charles's version. By now, I had a fair idea of the kind of difference I might find—and there were five in all.

First, the young gunman might not have been aiming at the door jamb with his second shot. Harney says that Charles had called out to him, "Why don't you shoot me, you brave fellow?" And he put his hands on his hips, and stepped forward to make himself a bigger target. As a consequence, the bullet missed—but we shall never know whether the miss was deliberate or the result of intimidation.

Next, the trio did not march out from the door in step with one another. Charles went out first; he stepped in front of Harney and April and marched straight at the gun barrel. The others followed, and Harney is honest enough to say that they did so only when they saw that Charles had closed off their possibility of being shot, and they'd observed that the men at the back hadn't primed and aimed.

Third, the flares did not drop from the tongs. Charles kicked them aside and stood menacingly over the two arsonists. That was why Meehan came prancing forward with his half-drawn gun.

Fourth, Charles grabbed Meehan by the arm and dragged him in front of April, where she delivered her speech—the words that clinched the evening.

And fifth—Harney also saw Noonan, and he started down the slope toward the truck to intercept him. Charles shouted to Harney to "go back" and Harney stopped—because he saw Charles "striding down like fury."

Harney moved again, though, and he arrived in time to hear Charles say to Noonan, "Never—never, ever—interfere in my life again." According to Harney, Noonan scrambled up onto the truck—"and he looked a bit whipped."

Finally, this is how Harney saw the later event of the evening:

"I was talking to Paddy Furlong, the butler, and I saw April coming down the stairs with her coat on. Charles was standing inside the front door in his greatcoat; he looked like a noble statue. They left the house together. I went to the window and I watched them, and they walked to a favorite spot of Charles's—on the crest just above the beginning of the Long Terrace, where the castle land is at its highest. Whenever Charles wanted to think, or to survey something—that's where he went.

"When they got there, they turned around to look at the house. I never took my eyes off them—I was inside the window, and they couldn't really see that I was watching. They never spoke that I could see or hear, they never touched nor nothing; they weren't even standing close together.

"After a long while, they started walking back down to us, exactly the same as the way they went up. But there was something different about them—something was after changing."

Thursday, the 14th of December 1922.

My dearest Kitty,
A note to tell you that I shall be away (in London) from tonight until Tuesday. I believe that you may guess what a good life now faces me—at last.

> *Yours affectionately,*
> *April.*

10

Needless to remark, the story of Charles O'Brien's life didn't end with April's short, excited letter to Katherine Moore. The wedding took place in a Westminster registry office—the governmental formalities separating Ireland from England hadn't yet extended to the recording of births, marriages, and deaths. No doubt April saw to it that all their papers were in order; that was what she was like.

He is described in the register as "Charles O'Brien, Gentleman, of Ardobreen, Golden, Cashel, County Tipperary, Ireland," and she as "April Somerville, Widow, of Tipperary Castle, Tipperary, Ireland."

When I first read Charles's final entry I was left feeling high and dry. What happened next? How long did they live? What became of them? Did they truly donate the castle and the estate to the new nation—or was that statement of April's no more than, as Harney called it, a "ruse" to stop the Irregulars from torching the place?

This "History" had hit me with three body blows. First there was the inexplicable emotional connection I felt to Charles, who seemed to be saying—and in my words—what I had been feeling about myself for most of my life. I'm not claiming that I felt that we were alike; he was big and dashing, I am small and withdrawn. But I nonetheless felt a warmth of connection to him. Inexplicable, I said to myself, but there we are; these things happen.

Then I discovered his connection to my mother through, initially, her photograph of Eamon de Valera at Boland's Mill and then her help to Charles during the week after the Rising.

Finally came the DNA reports—meaning that, although a great deal had been resolved in the story of his life, Charles O'Brien and his "History" had pitched me into turmoil. And even though I had set myself methodically upon a course of "research," I was no nearer to solving my own mysteries.

Of which I had two: one minor but intriguing and one major and crucial. I still had ahead of me the task of clearing up the path of life taken by the first April Burke. And because of her, I had to find out who I was.

In a little West Tipperary church called Kilfeakle I found the original marriage record. It was bland and blurred: "Terence Burke, Gentleman, of Tipperary Estate to Margaret Collins of Gurtymore, Parteen, Limerick." The date in 1850 is either (ink had run) 22 or 23 May. No Collins family, or trace of one, could I find in Parteen, but I did find Margaret Collins's birth certificate; she was born at Castleconnell (not far from Parteen) in 1828. (The newspaper reports of her death said 1831: had she—typical actress—lied about her age?)

My reasoning now ran as follows: calculate her age backward from her suicide. If she was already an actress in 1850, she must have begun her stage career earlier than the age of twenty-two. And I couldn't find the name Collins with any relevance in the places associated with her birth and marriage records.

Which probably meant that she had not come from a good family. So by the time she met Terence Burke she could have been a "working girl" for some years.

A miserable life—a whore's, back then. And it still is, I suppose (we don't have that many in this county, at least not that I know of). I assumed that she wanted to get off the streets, so she changed her name to April—more exotic—and became an actress (which didn't mean that she didn't still ply her street trade). And then I went looking for proof of my assumptions.

I found a newspaper notice of November 1848 telling of "Mr.

FitzGibbon's Celebrated West End Troupe" bringing its "Celebrated Repertoire" to Cashel. In the middle of the bill sat the name "April Collins—as lovely as Portia as she is tragically Juliet."

Hah! Oscar Wilde said that for "many months" after first seeing her, Terence Burke had pursued the beautiful actress. Now I had more or less nailed the meeting; Burke saw her, almost certainly, in Cashel, with Mr. FitzGibbon.

Other than the record of the subsequent marriage, I found no further information about her—until February 1855, when she crops up as "Mrs. April Burke" topping the bill in "A Theatrical Cornucopia" at the Arcadia Hall, Dublin. Her fortunes, it seemed, had improved. This newspaper report described her life during the run of the play:

> Mrs. Burke travels with a maid and a laundress; they stay in rooms on Ushers Island, with a view to the river and the green fields beyond. If too fatigued after a performance, she will not trouble to dine abroad; she will have food brought to her rooms and cooked there. She has marked preferences for guinea-fowl; pheasant is the only game she will eat; her meal often begins with a smattering of caviare. Sometimes she is visited by her husband, Mr. Terence Burke, the esteemed Tipperary landowner.

This was a rich lifestyle, and it was obviously supported and encouraged by her adoring husband. Time was running out, however. Soon the actress must return and keep her side of the bargain—breed children to ensure the succession at Tipperary. The trail, as they say, went cold. All I had to go on from here onward was Oscar's story.

But, since I was checking everything, I thought I'd better ascertain what I could. By a (not very big) miracle, I found Terence Burke's death certificate. Actually, what I found was the informal version, scribbled in the doctor's records. He was a Dr. Hennessy, and I met his fourth-generation descendant, who lives and still practices in the same house—the "Dispensary"—in Kilross, not far from Tipperary Castle.

Country doctors in the old days threw away nothing. They kept sheds full of old records that they perhaps hoped to get around to sorting one day. In there I found the certification of Terence Burke's death, and I found something else—the inscription "M/Y present?" Hmm.

"What," I asked today's Dr. Hennessy, "could that mean?"

After some thought and taking down of books, he said, "Possibly mercury."

"Isn't mercury poisonous? Was this suicide?" I had already found so much of it.

Dr. Hennessy said, "More likely he was using it for venereal disease. It was an old cure."

Now what did I have in my hand of cards? Here are some of the speculations I made about this woman—from whom, modern science had told me, I was descended.

When she met Terence Burke and married him, her life improved, and she no longer had any need to work the shady side of the street. But her past caught up with her, transmitted itself to him, and, unable to bear it, she fled. As a Victorian fallen woman, she would have seen the abandonment of her child and her life as atonement.

Or did a friend or family member know that she had walked a loose path? And was that person blackmailing her for money—and her only solution was to flee? I wouldn't have cared too much about any of this part of Charles O'Brien's life had it not been for the wretched DNA. There are times when science tells us too much.

When I drove away from Dr. Hennessy's, I went back to the church where April Burke the First had married. There was something I wanted to check on the register. Could I have got it right?

Suddenly, the story opened up, and I felt that I had found out everything I needed to know about April Burke the First. The path of research became a road to an answer—and a feeling of remarkable satisfaction, when I heard the pieces click into place.

In 1861, the "Prince's Theatre" in Bristol opened its doors, launched by a member of the famed MacCready acting family. The boy Terence Burke was four years old and living thirty miles away, with his mother in the Brook House. With them lived the lady whom Charles met with Terence Theobald Burke, the younger April's father.

The lady was not "Miss" Gambon—she was "Mrs." Gambon, née

Collins. Her name appears as a witness to the wedding at Kilfeakle church. Charles could easily have mistaken her name as pronounced "Miz Gambon" in the burr of the West Country. She had married a man called Gambon, who—according to Somerset records—died in 1860. If her sister went to live with her—and what would have been more natural if the boy was there?—an actress would at least have brought in an income. And now, of course, the actress was a respectable widow.

So here's the scenario. April Burke's husband dies. The actress goes back to work at the Prince's Theatre—which had a touring company. She works there for some years, builds an excellent reputation—and meets Oscar Wilde in Dublin.

Her son is growing up in Somerset, cared for by his aunt when the mother is touring. They never speak to the boy about his father. The guilt is enormous. And so is the fear that someone, somewhere, knows the nasty secret of the father's ailment, which they think may have killed him.

Now think of the date when the actress jumped to her death: 1878, the year in which the boy reached his majority. Did Miz Gambon blackmail her sister? Who was the inheritor of Tipperary? I felt the solution roll out in front of me. If the boy tried to get his inheritance, the aunt would have told all. But if he signed it over to his aunt—then she would take on the property or, more likely, sell it, now that land matters in Ireland were easing.

Here's the clincher. In September 1904, as we know from the court records, an application was made by a Bristol solicitor on behalf of persons unknown. In the details lay a little barb—"for the purposes of dismissal only." The doubtful origins of Terence Burke's mother, April's grandmother, were alluded to just sufficiently to discourage a gentleman from opening that can of worms.

Next, in late September, 1904, a freak influenza swept through the West Country of England. It took scores of lives—including that of Miz Gambon. April and her father went down for the funeral—probably, as they do around here in rifting families, to make sure that when they put her in the ground, she stayed there. At which point April and her father felt free to open the inheritance claim.

So far, so good—mere speculation; but, to leap forward somewhat, here is part of something written by April to Charles in the spring of 1923:

My father, as you may have divined, was at heart a timid man. He had been raised a timid boy, and chose to have little society outside the home in which he grew up; and he played with one or two local boys. When he came to London, he intended to pursue a similar pathway, and his marriage to my mother gave him some protection in this intent.

However, when she died so tragically, he withdrew even further than he had intended. We saw nobody, we visited not at all; to meet anybody outside my school or our immediate neighbors became so unusual as to be remarkable.

Imagine, then, how strange I found it to be confronted in our own drawing-room at Alexander Street by a most unpleasant woman. That is how I found out where Papa had grown up. He had always said "the West Country" in response to my many childish inquiries. Now I found the name of the house and the name of the place.

More rewarding still, I found that my quiet, dear papa had a spine. This visitor kept browbeating him—I could hear them from my room, to which I had been sent—and he kept resisting. He refused to sign something that she wanted. That was when I first heard the name of "Tipperary Estate," and I was ten years old.

This is the lady that you and Papa met in June 1904, and whose death a few months later released us to pursue my father's birthright.

One mystery was solved. The greater one faced me. If I was descended genetically from April Burke the First, what was her connection to my own mother? Or to me? I felt bucked up at my detective work—which is no more than the use of reason to dispel the irrelevant and inaccurate, and zoom in on the core.

Over and over, the words of Mr. Lisney kept at me: "the dead spit and image." I went out and bought a good magnifying glass.

My mother, Margery Coleman, got very sharp results with her camera. On the day of the Tipperary Castle banquet, she took pictures mostly of the inanimate—the stonework, a general vista, the bridge, a long view of the dancing, the swans on the lake. But when I looked through the magnifying glass at the one and only crowd picture she took, the faces were like characters on those medieval tapestries. Their noses even looked as big as those on Bayeux's great embroideries.

No sign of Charles—but April was there; she wore a dress with wide vertical stripes. She stood at the outer edge of the photograph, her arms around a man. I knew it could not be Charles; in no way did it resemble his description of himself. That was when I wrote to Marian Harney, and that is when the long, final unfolding of this story began. She wrote back immediately and asked me to come and stay in her house for a weekend.

Within eighteen months of that weekend in Dublin, I sold my house. I changed my life. My existence improved in ways that I could never have imagined. I ascended to, and stayed upon, a plateau where my view of life was sunnier. Although I had always kept it to myself, I had still grieved every day from my losses. No more, now.

Marian Harney lives in Monkstown, in the southern suburbs of Dublin, in a house that she inherited from her father. From the outside, it appears to be as small as a cottage. Inside, it has many large, pretty rooms, where the sun pours in. Built in 1865, it's a classically Victorian town villa, with two floors of levels below the front door, and a long garden, which she keeps superbly.

I arrived on a Friday afternoon. She'd told me where the key was, so I let myself in and waited in the garden. She came home at about six o'clock, poured drinks, and said, "Where do you want to begin?"

I told her "the story so far," and she listened with great attention; we were sitting at a wooden table. When I had finished she rose, said something like "Back in a minute," and she reappeared, lugging a suitcase. It was a particularly beautiful piece of luggage, solid leather, with reinforced corners; I guessed (accurately) that it had been made in the 1920s.

Memory uses strange devices. I remember the most significant moments of my life in two ways—either by what I was wearing or the weather at that time. When President Kennedy was shot, I was wearing a tweed overcoat and had been back at school to give two boys extra tuition—it was seven o'clock in the evening, Irish time. For this suitcase, I recall the weather—as balmy an early summer evening as I have ever known. In the distance, I heard a seagull's cry over the nearby sea.

We lifted the suitcase onto the table. As she thumbed back the round brass clasps, Marian said, "I have to warn you: some of this might distress you. But I think you should read everything that's in here."

She threw back the lid, this librarian, this woman whose life was spent managing repositories of knowledge. Inside stood rows and rows of packages, neatly held in rubber bands and with a card bearing the month and year in the front of each package. There were some other packages too: "Receipts" and "Doctor" and "Plantings."

Marian took out the first package, and before she handed it to me, she said, "When Charles O'Brien and April Burke came back to Tipperary as man and wife, they entered upon an agreement. They decided to write to each other, if at all possible, every alternating day of their lives—that is, he'd write one day, and she'd reply the next. It seems to have been her idea.

"And when they started it, they liked it so much that they didn't confine themselves to one letter a day. They often wrote five, six, seven letters, most of them short notes, with the occasional longer expression of affection or the clearing up of a memory or something. Here's the first package."

I opened at random.

Christmas Eve 1922
A long time ago, I said to you that I wanted to call you "O'Brien."
But I couldn't keep up the intimacy—you were too forbidding, too
distant from me. If we do what we talked about on the boat, viz.,
write to each other every day, then you shall be "O'Brien" and you
may use any name you like to address me.

Oh, O'Brien—I have so much I want to tell you.

> *By the by, the lower bolt on the first loose box on the right as you*
> *enter the stable-yard has come away from the wood of the door.*

I read the letter again, and I realized that Marian was watching my face.

"Have you read these?" I said.

"Every one of them."

I observed that April "doesn't quite stay on the point."

"All her letters are like that. Here's his reply."

Again, I read, and I found myself thrilling to the familiarity of the handwriting.

Christmas Day 1922

How well you have observed me in that I like being given "tasks."
I will attend to the stable-door bolt this morning. And I have given
myself other tasks. To watch over you. To try and be aware of what
you need before you need it. To let you weep out all that shame and
unsafety. To make sure your roof is ever safe and your walls are ever
sound, so to speak.

And today, yet again, I shall have the pleasure of your company.
All day. And then all night.

The same loops in the letters; the same brown ink; the same excellent writing paper; I turned the note over in my hand and held it to the light.

"This," I said, "is the man I know. She, however, is a revelation."

"They both are," said Marian.

I said, "What do you think of them?"

Amazingly, her eyes filled with instant tears. She shook her head and laughed.

"I'm not telling you. Ask me again when you've read everything in the suitcase."

I said, "What else is in there?"

"You'll find out soon enough."

"You're teasing me."

"No, I didn't mean to. What I'm saying is—well, there's Charles's mother's journal. Amelia O'Brien—that's very revealing. She doesn't write about him very often, but when she does it's always worthwhile. And her entries about the running of her house—I found those more interesting than perhaps you will. You'll love her—she was a terrific woman."

"Anything else?"

She went vague. "Yes. But the best way to take in the whole experience is by reading the letters first."

For that weekend, I did nothing but sleep, eat, and read from the suitcase. So much material—and I learned that even in the preservation of it, the differences in the two characters had been obvious. Charles had preserved all April's letters in sequence, and in numbered boxes, filed with delicacy and respect. She had kept all his letters too, but tossed into drawstringed silken bags, of the kind in which some ladies kept their nightwear. Marian had put them together.

"Typical librarian," I said, with admiration. "Unable to bear disorder."

"It's not so much not being able to bear disorder." She thought for a moment. "It's—it's the fact of the disorder preventing an interesting and instructive human experience from being recorded."

It seems possible that, one day soon, I will transcribe the letters, add a commentary, footnote them where necessary, and have them published. They may well amount to more than one volume. For now, I include here a selection, based on nothing more demanding than relevance and my own taste.

Tuesday, the 16th of January 1923
Please do not go out in the motor-car without your warmest coat.
Gloves are not enough. I heard you coughing this morning; I have
left a tincture of mint and eucalyptus in the kitchen. Helen knows
where it is, and she will heat it for you to inhale.

Wednesday, the 17th of January 1923
Harney once told me that you, O'Brien, had "a fussy side."
I'm learning what he meant. And I coughed because it was morning;
I am not tubercular, or ague-ridden, or creaking.

I read again this morning from the Browning you gave me,
I read "A Toccata of Galuppi's." Did you know that Papa and I went
to Venice once and we saw Galuppi's house? How can we live long
enough to tell you all the things I want to tell you?

Saturday, the 3rd of March 1923
The moon is full and shining through the window, and I am about
to go downstairs and dine with you. Remind me to write to Boyds
and correct the seeds order for the kitchen garden. Shall you want to
change the order of growths in the herbaceous areas? I recall you
saying last year that you felt they wanted more reds, that you had
indulged too much in your favored yellows.

Sunday, the 4th of March 1923
O'Brien! Where are you? Are you walking the herbaceous borders?
Did you see how shy Mr. Tracey (is this how he spells his name?)
became when he saw us stand together? Veterinary Surgeons have
the gentlest hearts; you should have been a Vet.

Monday, the 5th of March 1923
Beloved girl—to repeat and explain: you cannot, in my opinion,
put the beehives too close to the gardens or the herbaceous borders.
Bees need room.
 Nor should we bring an entire litter into the house. The sow
will miss them. Can you put them all back, please—except the runt,
who needs nursing. And why did you get up so early this morning?
I missed you when I awoke.

Tuesday, the 6th of March 1923
O'Brien, dearest O'Brien—you are the healer among us. Every bone
in my body has rested. Whoever our Creator is—we must declare
and acknowledge his cleverness.

Saturday, the 19th of May 1923
Beloved girl, if we suspect that this is a swine fever, we must act
immediately. I cannot think that your "pink creatures," as you call
them, must be allowed to suffer, and then infect each other. Do you
wish me to get a second opinion? Mr. Tracey is very sound, and will
come here as often as we wish.

Last night you began to talk a little of the day we met at Mr.
Wilde's. If you can bear it, tell me more, and my heart shall be easier.
That was a difficult time in my life, when I took great missteps.

And shall we again retire early?

Sunday, the 20th of May 1923
Perhaps I should earlier have raised the matter of Mr. Wilde. I think
I have been too ashamed of my later behavior to find the courage. In
those days I was frightened of everyone, and most afraid of all that
my life would be disrupted so greatly that I could not care for Papa.

Here is what I saw, followed by what I knew. Dr. Tucker—
who, even though he took a wrong view of you, had many good
qualities—sensing my fear of the world, told me once that most
people get by when they merely watch and do not act. As I had set
myself to do. In the room, I had not seen you, but I knew from Dr.
Tucker's talk that your healing matters were not going well. You were
not to know that in the view of all France's doctors (or so it seemed,
to judge from those who called upon Dr. Tucker) Mr. Wilde was
beyond assistance.

I suffered grave consternation when he told the tale of my
grandmother. For many years, we had lived under the shame of her
courtesanship, and Papa knew of many men whose acquaintance she
had made. When Mr. Wilde began to tell us of her, I thought that
I must die—even though I had begged him to. If you recollect, I sat
perfectly still. But when, after the funeral, you raised the question of
the estate, I felt the chill of fear—for Papa, for me, that our secrets
should be told. Foolish, I know, but there it was.

Monday, the 21st of May 1923
Thank you, my love. I am helped, and the years are eased by your
kind information.

　　Can you make a decision soon as to how many different root crops
you shall want for this year's kitchens? Shall you want yellow (as
distinct from little white) turnip?

Tuesday, the 22nd of May 1923
Papa worried that, in his words, I had "never been a girl"—
meaning that I was never wooed, nor did I dance where young men
danced, nor enjoy the pleasures of pursuit. He must be happy now,
wherever he is.

Wednesday, the 23rd of May 1923
If I have been the agent of your freeing from cares, I am the most
pleased man on Earth.

　　I thought that we would lose every pig, and every sow and every
litter. Mr. Tracey said as he departed, "Big heart, big care; small
heart, puny care." He was speaking of you.

Friday, the 29th of June 1923
Beloved April, why should you have to gather by yourself? Unless, of
course, you need to—but we have maids and servant-maids who can
competently take baskets and collect every petal that has blown. I am
irked that the wind so blustered the roses, but I looked again this
afternoon and saw that we have many tight buds yet to open
themselves, so fear not for your vases.

　　I never told you this: when you came to Ardobreen the first time,
my room lay near yours and I could not sleep, and so I wandered in
and then left in fear lest you wake and be distressed.

Saturday, the 30th of June 1923
It is my turn to scold. Being short of breath cannot be good. Dr.

Costigan will come tomorrow, and that's an end of it. Harney agrees with me. I wish he would stay here more often, and I fear for him. Why does he not stay here?

Saturday, the 7th of July 1923
My darling O'Brien, you are excused your last reply, and the reply to this. I trust Dr. Costigan as you trust Mr. Tracey—or would you prefer that the Vet became your physician? And why not? You have the heart of a lion and the hug of a bear—though about the care of yourself you are less sensible than my pink creatures.

    I think that Dr. Costigan spoke more plainly to me than to you. He believes that your body is trying to rest. I told him something of our last two or three years, and he professed amazement that you had not come down low before.

Thursday, the 26th of July 1923
Beloved girl, where are you? I've searched the house for you; neither are you in Major or Minor. The day being so hot, I shall lie down and rest for some time. It's four o'clock.

Friday, the 27th of July 1923
If you find this in your letters box before it is time to dine, let us walk out and look at Horace. The men placed him in the nearest pastures, and I swear that they chose the prettiest cows for him.

When I had read as far as July 1923, I myself had to take a rest. I reeled back in heated contemplation. Notwithstanding the reticence of the times, even between husband and wife, the relationship was plain.

    How often in his "History" had Charles expressed his longing for this girl? And how often had I sympathized with him? And silently agreed with those who told him that she was a losing bet?

It appears that she wasn't. Neither of them wrote for show or for other eyes. The letters are unaffected and unpretentious, the letters of two people who, although still in the early heat of marriage, are also getting on with their lives, with all the natural worries of any couple. Some are even explicit, but their privacy should be respected.

I liked how the age difference of twenty-two years came across. He is steady, almost sober, though, as ever, desperately passionate. And she is closer to skittish, livelier, though still with an ingrained sense of responsibility.

In my respite from them, I rooted around in the suitcase, and that is how I found Amelia O'Brien's journal. Odd, now, to read again her descriptions of April as "icy" and "conniving."

Perhaps Amelia, impressive and likable though she was, can't have been as wonderful at judging character as she was at running the family. After all, her own husband was for several years involved in a conspiracy that could have killed their son.

I also found an envelope in the suitcase that had sealing wax on it— and, across the sealing wax, Joe Harney's signature. The seal had not been broken, and when I drew it to Marian's attention, she told me that she knew "all about it."

"Is this to be opened?" I said.

"Not until you've read all the letters," she said. "And as you can guess, those are my father's instructions, not some rule I made up."

Laughing at this incentive, I continued reading. The mood of 1923 continued much as before, the mutual, sincere love and affection, with, in the more open expressions, strong hints at a powerful nocturnal life. Bit by bit, they record the arrival of other people in their lives. They discuss who came to dinner, and how many workmen to keep, whether the cook is getting too old, and how to drain and then refill the lake.

Throughout 1923 and early 1924, nothing unusual develops—apart from the fact that instead of waning, their passionate awareness of each other seems to intensify. In fact, in some periods of their lives, it begins to dominate their existence with the passage of time, rather than the typical converse.

The relationship begins to have almost a classical feeling to it. All passionate initiative seems to come from him, and is then matched by the force of her response. She evidently held the view that he was a man who needed to take the lead in all things, and that her place was to follow eagerly—that he might have been too delicate to accept a wife's advances.

In 1924, a change begins to appear. It happens slowly, and they refer to it over many weeks. A sense of fright enters the correspondence, and deep worry. In this, too, they match each other. It seems to be the case that they had reached such a plateau of mutual trust that neither would or could hide anxiety from the other.

Saturday, the 19th of April 1924
Dearest girl, tell me again tonight of your discovery. Shall we retire early?

Sunday, the 20th of April 1924
My love, of course we shall make all inquiries. I insist. I know little in such areas, as most of my healing did not permit of too much intimacy, owing to the fact that I am not a doctor, and the country people are reticent in the extreme, no matter what danger they feel.

Can we therefore hold back on the restocking of the styes? And let your "pink creatures" do the work for us. Yes, it will take longer, as you have already pointed out, but we perhaps need a slowing of pace.

Wednesday, the 23rd of April 1924
O'Brien—stop! Please stop now!

I too am aware that this should not be. Or certainly that things should be different. But we shall attend to it immediately. As we attended so wonderfully to the mural, the stucco, the marble, and all the other matters. Remember—we addressed what was presented to us with determination, grace, and energy.

Wednesday, the 30th of April 1924
And still, my beloved April, we go on as we are, and as we have

*been. And if, tomorrow, we are forced to alter matters—then we
shall alter them for as long as we are directed.*

That is the last of several hundred assorted letters and notes that passed
between Charles O'Brien and his younger wife, April Burke Somerville
O'Brien. From them, and from the surrounding materials, and from
what I was finally about to read, and when added to Charles's History (it
is time to drop the quotation marks and give it the full respect it de-
serves), I knew more about them than if I had lived under their magnificent roof.

The next day, I left Dublin—with the suitcase—and drove home to
Clonmel, the capital of Charles O'Brien's cherished county, Tipperary. It
took me several weeks to digest what I had learned, and to prove it true.
Not that I needed proof—the integrity of all concerned had long been to
my mind unimpeachable.

And when I had digested all, and begun my recovery, and my essential pattern of forgiveness, I found that I had acquired the courage to do
many things for which I had long wished, and at which I had always
failed.

I sold the house, discarded most of the artifacts of my parents' life, left
the little street where I had lived since infancy, and moved out here, some
miles from Clonmel, to a prettier house, from which I can look down on
the river.

My day has changed. I no longer stay in bed until the haphazard
hours of noon and later. Without fail, I cook for myself every day, and
from time to time I have company; Marian Harney spends weekends and
some of her holidays here. We never squabble; I have a sense of achievement with another human being that I never had before.

And that sense of magic I always wanted? It courses through my
imagination like molten silver. So much was damaged, so much was
shaken—and so much was recovered in such a short time. All of them are
now laid to rest in my mind.

And I have plans to write, beginning perhaps with the edition of their letters. Two weeks ago, I had a piece about Laurence Sterne, who lived in Clonmel, accepted by an English newspaper; they're showing a new version of *Tristram Shandy* on television soon. But I have greater plans than that—I am now wealthy beyond my dreams.

Yesterday, Marian Harney and I drove the twenty miles or so to walk again the ruins of Tipperary Castle. The main entrance has almost disappeared. There's a scrap of the demesne wall, and I found a rusted iron spar; I think it came from a gate pillar or something.

The place in general is like Troy, not much left but grass ramparts. Large piles of stones and rubble mark out the lines of the buildings—it was massive. All the terraces except one have long been plowed.

The bridge survives, but it is a bridge to no particular place. And the lake still has a pair of swans; I wonder if they are the descendants of the swans that Charles saw.

When I had finished reading the last letter, more baffled than ever, we broke the brown sealing wax and opened the Joseph Harney envelope. It contained a drawing of Tipperary Castle, the same that had been given to Terence Burke. And it contained a document from Joseph Harney—a letter to me, written many, many years ago.

Dear Michael,

You may never read this letter—but I have charged myself with writing it. You know who I am—although we have never met; I am the same Joe Harney who was Minister for Transport, then Minister for Health, and Minister for Industry and Commerce. You know what I did, I suppose, in the War of Independence, because there have been so many books and articles, and even a film about the battle on Northumberland Road and Boland's Mill. But you do not know about my place in your life, and in that of your parents.

To tell you the truth, I had mixed feelings about the marriage of Charles O'Brien—because I was in love with April myself. But I loved Charles more than I have ever loved any man; I loved his nobility—he had complete decency. He was the most generous, genuine man I ever met. When they married, I told myself that there was only one chance for me now to marry April—but since that would involve the death of my dearest friend through natural causes, that was no chance at all!

You realize that I'm joking—the thing I think I wanted last in life was that anything should happen to Charles O'Brien. Later, I myself married, very happily, a woman whom I adore more with each passing day.

So when they came back from their wedding, in December 1922, I bowed gently out of their lives for a time. Soon I began to visit them, and I visited often. I went there for weekends, and when the civil war ended, I took a job in Limerick, in part to be near them, and I began to take an active interest in politics.

In the spring of 1924, I received a letter from Charles, asking me quite tersely to come to Tipperary as soon as possible. April, he said, was "feeling less than well." I had a good friend in Limerick, a doctor, called Brendan Hartigan, and he had a new car, so the two of us went out together.

With Charles's permission, Brendan examined April, and he agreed with her diagnosis. "The patient always knows," he said. April, against all the odds—and, I think, due to Charles's great care of her—was expecting a child. Charles had such mixed feelings.

"How am I going to get her through it?" he asked me. I gave up my job—it wasn't a very important one, anyway—and I came out to help him. In fact, I took over the managing of the place and he devoted all his time to April—he gave her every hour of every day. Running my political life was easy enough, provided I went back into Limerick once every two weeks or so.

Charles O'Brien taught me how to love people; I never saw such devotion. His wife was going to be safe—that was what he decided. The doctors confined her to bed; they told her that if she stayed quiet, she had a very good chance of going the full term. And of course she could not get enough of Charles's company—she lit up when he came into the room, not that he was ever out of her room for long.

Against all the odds, April went the full term. A baby boy was delivered in the last week of January 1925. The mother was fine, the baby was fine, you never saw such excitement. I was there, I heard the cries; every-

thing you ever heard about the birth of an important baby—it happened
that night. And never was a baby born that was more important. Certainly you have to go back a long time for a more important birth—that
was in Bethlehem, I believe, nearly two thousand years ago! Or so I joked
to Charles and April.

After a few days, I fetched old Mrs. O'Brien and she came to see the
child, her grandson. And I agreed to stay on at the castle. The country by
and large was settling down, and who was I, anyway? I was a fellow who
carried a gun once upon a time, and those days were over. And now I was
back among people that I loved, and they had a baby. To stay on was an
easy decision.

On the night of the 15th of May 1925, a Thursday night—the baby
was about three and a half months old—there was a thunderstorm. It was
very brief, but we had lightning near the castle. It didn't trouble me; it
didn't seem to trouble anyone—the baby was already a sound sleeper,
and by now he controlled the entire place anyway.

All the next day I was uneasy. I went around in a kind of querulous
mood. You know those days when you're searching for something and
you don't know what it is you're searching for? That's what I was like. I
went to bed early, I tossed and turned, and then I went to sleep.

The next thing I knew was my door being hammered on, and Charles
shouting at me. There was smoke everywhere—and I could not make it
out. I ran out of there and saw Charles ahead of me—and there were actual flames ahead of us. They weren't so bad that we couldn't get past, and
I caught up to Charles and was beside him—and he was carrying the
baby, who was still asleep.

I took the baby from him—we had a clear path now and no smoke—
and he went back to help April. He shouted to me that she was gathering
clothes. As I finished my journey downstairs Charles reappeared, and he
skidded a suitcase down the marble steps.

I remember thinking, "This is no time to be packing a case"—but he
shouted at me to grab it. I did, and I was almost the only one up and
about. We had no bell or alarm gong or anything like that—everybody
in Tipperary knew when it was time to eat, so I had no means of warning people.

As far as I could I got away from the castle. I just kept going, the baby crooked softly in my left arm, and lugging this damn suitcase with my right hand. When I got up onto the highest part of the Long Terrace I looked back, and I never saw anything like it. There were flames everywhere in the main building. Now at last people came running out, and I wanted to shout—but I didn't want to wake the baby. So I went back down a little—but even from there I could feel the flames, so I retreated again.

I thought about putting the baby down on the grass—but I was afraid that somebody would step on him. So there I stood, helpless, hoping that someone would see me, and come and take the baby, so that I could go and help Charles and April.

We found out afterward what had happened. The previous day's lightning had hit a metal stanchion embedded in a beam that was rotten but didn't appear so from the outside; and because it looked good it had never been replaced. That beam ran right up under the bedrooms, and all that day it had smoldered. Then, when it caught fire—it went up like tinder.

In those days, we had no fire-prevention treatments for new timbers, and that corridor had all new flooring. And there were fabrics everywhere—April had some kind of tapestry hanging from every wall, and many of them were old. They all caught fire.

One of the older servant-girls came up the terrace, and she saw me and the baby, and she was so thankful. She took the baby, and I went down as fast as I could run. No sign of them—no sign anywhere, and nobody had seen them. People were moving farther and farther away; the smoke was frightful, you couldn't see a thing from the front of the building.

There was a back staircase—all those houses had staircases everywhere—and I headed for that. The servants' hall, and the rooms where we all had our offices—they weren't affected. But the main house was in an even worse conflagration. I never want to feel as frantic again in my life. I ran everywhere, I even got into the house, and then I saw that beams were coming down.

We lost twelve people in that fire. And among them we lost Charles and April. Isn't it ironic—when you think of how they had twice fought off fire? It still remains a source of awful wonder to me that the house—especially the part we had so carefully restored—was so completely burned out. As I'm recalling it now, I see that my hands are shaking.

I spent the days that followed at Ardobreen with old Mrs. O'Brien, and together we looked after the infant. Believe it or not, the old man was still alive, and still sharp. They had seen the fire; they were up all night watching it. I think she knew the worst; he didn't. What broke their heart was the fact that they were now too old to look after their one and only grandchild.

The solution came from Mrs. O'Brien. Charles had told her of one other love affair—a girl he met in Dublin, who now lived in Clonmel. Mrs. O'Brien had met her the day we opened the castle with a grand banquet. The two women had become good friends. Mrs. O'Brien was fond of anybody who was fond of Charles.

I was dispatched to find this woman—and by now you have guessed. She was Margery Nugent; her maiden name was Coleman. She had told Mrs. O'Brien how it broke her heart that she couldn't have children. And how much she had wished that she could have married Charles O'Brien. I might be wrong about this, but I think she said that she married into the county so as not to be far from Charles.

When all the papers were done, it was of course discovered that April had indeed donated the house to the nation. The idea came to her as a trick to stop the Irregulars from burning down the place—and then she and Charles followed it through and donated it formally, because at that stage they had no heir. The takeover would not be complete until they died, and in the meantime they would open it to the public on certain days a year, and get tax relief for any work they did to improve the building.

Then, the pregnancy was so all-consuming that they never got a chance to take the estate back again. They had started legal proceedings, but the lawyers hadn't even got around to making the application.

Mrs. O'Brien and I put the adoption process in motion. The papers presented no problem—Mr. and Mrs. John Joseph Nugent would be the legally adopting parents of this child, who was never to be told. I have never understood why the child was never to be told—probably because there was such a stigma attached to adoption; it usually meant illegitimacy.

Not only that, the adopting father insisted that some device be constructed whereby people would think the child was his—and to pretend that she was away in confinement at her parents' house, Margery went to stay at Ardobreen for several months. You can imagine how Mrs. O'Brien loved having her grandchild—namely you—in that house.

But I can't stand lies and deceptions, and I decided to write this letter and let the wise hand of Time take care of it.

That was the only complication. Except for one thing. The nation, after years of dithering, divided the estate lands. A family that bought Ardobreen after the O'Briens passed away got a large chunk of it. And nobody wanted what was left of the house; nobody wanted to rebuild it. So it just lay there, and people plundered the beautiful stone.

But the law specified a sum of ten thousand to the heirs of the castle, should any next of kin wish to claim it. Nobody did—because everybody knew about you and thought that one day you'd find out. The money, with interest accumulating every year, is there in the Land Commission in Dublin.

I have drawn all these facts together and left it to the discretion of my family as to whether they should ever be divulged. If they decide to tell the story to you, Michael, they'll have done so because they'll have assessed that it will do you nothing but good to be told who you are. In Ireland, that's something we don't always know.

If and when you read this, know that you were doubly fortunate. Not only were you raised by decent folk, you also came naturally of wonderful people. What man can say that he had four parents, all of them exemplary? In short, in your spirit you had a brilliant past, and in your being you had a safe existence. That's Ireland for you!

And wherever you go, you'll also have my good wishes like fair wind in your sails.

Yours sincerely,
Joseph (Joe) Harney.

It will take me years to make sense of all this—to make emotional sense, that is. I know that I'll go back over the "evidence" again and again for things that I insufficiently celebrated.

Such as the sacrifices of my adopting mother, Margery Coleman, who must have longed to tell me the story of my life. That was her main thrust—the truth of things as she saw them through her camera.

Such as the decency of my adopting father, John Joe Nugent, to behave to me so gently and amusingly and acceptingly. He taught me to sing, and he taught me the words of songs—mostly railroad songs—and how to identify a locomotive, and how his uncle helped build railroads in North America.

Such as the size of the spirit possessed by my mother, April Burke—to use the money she had been left for such a noble and brilliant enterprise, to keep beauty preserved. And to perceive the man who loved her, even if it took her a while. Or did it?

And such as my real father, Charles O'Brien, whose writings taught me that we do not have to continue as we were. Or thought we were. And that life brings out its brightest colors only when you ask.

In the Land Commission offices, I was attended to by a boy I once taught. He was a quiet fellow in school. And he became a quiet man. I had not known that I would be dealing with him.

He also knew of other papers—the inheritance from Bernard and Amelia O'Brien at Ardobreen. My adopted father would have nothing to do with it, and my mother never told me. It simply sat there and piled up, and if I never claimed it the state would have when I died. There's nothing so complicated as inheritance law.

This former student of mine had prepared all sorts of documents for me. And some of them were clearly outside his purview. I asked him why. He said that I'd told him one day that he had a mind like the poet John Keats, and that ever since then, he could always raise his spirits up on that memory.

On the street outside, I was scarcely able to walk. Or take in how much I was now worth. But I knew immediately what I was going to do.

I was going to establish—and I have—an annual award through the library for the writing of personal history. Above and beyond that, I have more than enough money to build and endow a small theater. It will have within it an exhibition space for local photographers and an annual contest for them. And if anyone wants to found a railway historical society, I will pay for that too. Thus, I shall honor all to whom I feel indebted. What man, indeed, has been fortunate enough to have four parents?

On Sundays, when the weather is fine, Marian and I drive over to the castle and trace again its outlines. And we stand on the grass-covered terraces and admire the view, the son of the owners and the daughter of their beloved friend.

FRANK DELANEY was born in Tipperary, Ireland. Before his novel *Ireland,* a bestseller and his first novel to be published in the United States, and *Simple Courage,* his American nonfiction debut, a career in broadcasting earned him fame across the United Kingdom. A judge for the Booker Prize, he has had several fiction and nonfiction bestsellers in the United Kingdom; he also writes frequently for American and British publications. He now lives with his wife, Diane Meier, in New York and Connecticut.

ABOUT THE TYPE

This book was set in Garamond, a typeface originally designed by the Parisian typecutter Claude Garamond (1480–1561). This version of Garamond was modeled on a 1592 specimen sheet from the Egenolff-Berner foundry, which was produced from types assumed to have been brought to Frankfurt by the punch-cutter Jacques Sabon.

Claude Garamond's distinguished romans and italics first appeared in *Opera Ciceronis* in 1543–44. The Garamond types are clear, open, and elegant.

From CASHELL to CALLEN

	M.	F.	M.	F.
Killenaule	8	5	8	5
Callen	10	1	18	6

Urlingford Rd.

9

Killenaule   Fethard Rd. P. 115

8

7

Graystown Cas. Ru.

6

Noan
Taylor Esqr.
Thurles Rd.   Clonmell Rd.

5

Lane Esq.

4

Thurles Rd.   Cas. Ru.
Clonmell Rd.

New Park
Pennefather Esqr.   3
Meldrum
Fetham Esqr.

Ballyshechan   2
Fetham Esqr.
Cas. Ru.   Baskghell
Ryves Es.

1

Clonmell Rd. P. 100

Dublin Rd. P. 112   Cahier Rd. P. 114

CASHELL
Ru.   Limerick Rd. P. 100

TIPPERARY

Kells Rd.

Kilkenny
Rd.   Clonmell Rd. P. 119

Callen

West Court
Galway Esq.   18

17

Enter Kilkenny Co.

Scots boro'
Scott Esq.   16   Mode shel
Chu Ru.s

Rosenaharly   Mobeher
Poe Esqr.   Scott Esqr.   Fethard Rd.
P. 194
15

14

Ch

13   Lismullin

Willford
Butler Esqr.

12   Cas. Ru.s

Lismarock
Langley Esqr.   Cas. Ru.s

11

Coolquil
Gahan Esqr.

10   Fethard Rd.

CO.

Terry sculp   Publish'd as the Act directs, 24th Sepr. 1778.